Brown Sugar Beach

TRACYMAC

First edition

Published by TRACYMAC® Publishing (Peace Place LLC)
Knightdale, North Carolina

Cover design and typography by Jessica Tilles - TWA Solutions

Interior design, copyediting, and proofreading by
Jessica Tilles of TWA Solutions

ISBN: 978-0-9891013-6-3 (paperback)
ISBN: 978-0-9891013-7-0 (eBook)

Library of Congress Control Number: 2026905029

For information about bulk purchases, special editions, or speaking engagements, visit iamtracymac.com

Printed in the United States of America

CONTENT NOTE

Brown Sugar Beach explores themes of love, family, healing, and generational legacy. Its pages reference trauma, including instances of abuse and assault, as well as emotional and psychological distress.

These elements are presented with care and intention, forming part of the characters' lived experiences and journeys toward healing.

Please read with care.

Every story has sound.
This playlist brings Brown Sugar Beach to life—one song at a time.

To listen, scan the QR code in the back of the book or visit:
https://www.iamtracymac.com/tracymac-books

She needed to feel wanted.
He needed to feel seen.
She saw him fully as he desired her completely.
And for the first time, they both felt safe.

CHAPTER 1

A Day at the Beach

Her little girl's laughter carried just above the tide, small hands scooping and patting the sand as the water whispered in and out along the shore.

Jenita watched her, something in her chest easing and aching all at once.

Bittersweet.

She wondered, not for the first time, what her daughter's life would be like without her father. Her parents used to travel with their siblings and friends, piling into cars and bringing her and her cousins to Brown Sugar Beach. It was a small stretch of Sandy Shores Beach on the North Carolina coast in the 1970s, one of the few places where Black families could gather freely. Coolers packed. Laughter rising above the waves. Children running barefoot between the water and the warm sand.

Now, nearly twenty years later, Jenita sat under an umbrella at Brown Sugar Beach, the memory of herself as a little girl never far behind, Nana Katie Mae always somewhere close in the kitchen.

When someone stopped by, quiet and heavy-hearted, Katie Mae didn't ask questions right away. "Now I know good and well you didn't come all the way over here just to stand in my doorway," she said without turning around. She slid a warm muffin onto a plate. "Baby, sit down and eat first. Trouble talks plenty loud enough on an empty stomach."

A young woman shifted nervously near the table. "Ms. Katie Mae." She sighed. "I just needed to talk."

Nana turned, wiping her hands on her apron. Her presence made people feel safe enough to tell the truth. "Well, baby." She pulled out a chair at the kitchen table. "Come sit down and tell it right. Ain't no burden too heavy to rest a minute in this house."

Katie Mae was the kind of woman people came looking for when life got heavy. She was a short, round, sturdy woman of sixty-eight. Her skin was the color of warm pecans, two deep dimples appearing whenever she smiled wide enough to reveal the gold eye tooth that sparkled when she laughed. Tiny moles peppered her face and neck, marks that had been there so long most folks barely noticed them anymore.

Yet it was her eyes people remembered most, kind eyes like Jenita's, that made folks linger at her kitchen table and tell truths they hadn't meant to share. Her soft white hair pressed and curled just right, the kind of press-and-curl that held through heat, humidity, and a good night's sleep wrapped in a scarf. Most days she moved about the house in loose muumuus, "shifts," as she called them, or flowered house dresses that swayed around her calves as she worked. Only when she went down to Brown Sugar Beach did she trade them for a denim skirt with a slip, and one of her husband's t-shirts, tying a scarf over her hair and slipping her sturdy feet into sandals that showed the thick ankles she'd had all her life.

She smelled faintly of whatever Avon perfume had most recently made its way through the catalog passed around at church, sweet and powdery, layered with flour, onions sautéed in butter, and sun-dried cotton sheets. Katie Mae believed sheets dried on a clothesline under God's sky smelled better than anything a machine could manage, and she hummed old spirituals while pinning them to the line, the breeze puffing them out like quiet white sails.

Her hands, worn from living, gardening, cooking, washing, and tending were gentle. The same hands that coaxed tomatoes and cucumbers from the backyard garden, rubbed aching temples, used salve to soothe, laid hands anointed with oil to help heal, braided children's hair, and pressed warm biscuits into waiting palms. She cooked breakfast, lunch, and dinner every day for her husband of fifty years, always making enough for whoever wandered in. In her house, nobody left hungry, and nobody left without being prayed over.

She never missed a service or prayer meeting at church, but folks knew she had another kind of knowing, too, as if God, Jesus, and the Holy Ghost lived in her and moved through her. They did.

People came quietly to her back door for herbs, prayers, or a listening ear. She was part healer, part counselor, part babysitter for half the community's children, keeping old remedies and old wisdom alive the way her mother and grandmother had before her.

Still, she was no fool about the world. Tucked safely in the house was a gun she kept for hunting or protection. She believed in praying hard but also in being prepared. Everybody knew Katie Mae, and most would tell you the same thing: if trouble found you, or if your heart was heavy, her kitchen was the first place you ought to go.

Jenita remembered asking her one day, while they sat on the shore at Brown Sugar Beach, "Nana, I love it here. I want to live here forever. Can I eat some sand?"

"Naw, baby. That sand won't be good to you."

"It won't?"

"Oh no. It's just wet dirt."

"Dirt?" She was used to seeing black soil and red clay.

"Uh-huh."

"It looks like sugar."

"Sugar? Sugar is white, baby."

"No, Nana. The kind of sugar we use when you let me help you bake cookies and muffins. Not the kind we put in cake."

"Oh, brown sugar. Yeah, it looks just like it. But it ain't it."

"Can I taste it?"

"I don't think you'll like it but go 'head taste it if you want to and see for yourself."

She took a few grains that looked just like light brown sugar, put it on the tip of her little finger, and stuck out her six-year-old tongue to taste them. "I think it tastes good, Nana!"

Nana chuckled. "You ain't taste nothin' but your own finger."

She scooped some of the wetter sand into her hand and lapped it. "Ugh! Ugh! It tastes like your cod liver oil." Having sand on both hands, the more she tried to wipe it off, the more granules she got on her tongue and lips. Her eyes watered, but before one tear could fall, Nana used her handkerchief to wipe what she could from her sweet grandbaby's tongue. Then Nana let her have what they called a "teen-nine-chee-bit" of her Pepsi to wash the few granules down.

"Don't cry, baby. Nana ain't gon' let you hurt yourself. A lil' dirt ain't never hurt nobody."

"Nana, I don't want to put this kind of brown sugar in our cookies or our muffins."

"Me neither. Just 'cause they call it Brown Sugar Beach don't mean it's sugar or always sweet. Now you know for yourself, don't ya, baby?"

"Yes, ma'am." She filled her little jaws with a big swig and swallowed with a gulp.

"Neat! You 'bout drinking all my Pepsi, ain't ya? That's way more than a "teen-nine-chee-bit." They both laughed as she kissed her sweet grandbaby's honey-brown, round face right on her little dimple.

That moment with Nana Katie Mae would be etched in her memory forever.

Jenita opened her eyes to look around at her baby playing with her girlfriends and their children and nephews who had accompanied them.

Sheila looked at her. "Lay back and relax. We ain't gon' let nothing happen to your baby."

Rhonda nodded. "She's just fine, girl. Playing with the rest of 'em. Relax."

Jenita adjusted more comfortably in her lounge chair, closing her eyes, but only to rest them because she couldn't sleep. She went right back to daydreaming about herself, little Jenita Rochelle Hall, back in 1976. She remembered playing with her yellow sand pail and matching shovel, packing the sand in the pail, using the back of the shovel to pat it down tight, flipping the pail upside down, and pounding her little fist on the bottom to make it come out easier. This would be her best one yet.

Her mom, Mable, and her aunts chatted under their breath, laughing loudly, sipping lukewarm Budweiser, and smoking Newports. She couldn't smell their cigarettes because the ocean breeze carried the smoke away. The scent of the ocean had no competition. She sat on an old quilt with Nana Katie that she'd made, long before little Jenita was born, building her idea of the best sandcastle ever.

Her dad, J.D., and his brothers managed the grill off in the distance by the picnic area. She watched them haul brown paper grocery bags and coolers filled with ice, beer, sodas, potato salad, hot dogs, homemade hamburgers, and chicken legs. No ribs this time. Her cousins and friends played in the water, hopping waves and attempting to surf using Styrofoam boogie boards. Only big kids could do that. Little kids like her had to stay near the mamas and Nana Katie. She had cousins with nicknames like Deuce, Toonsie, Junebug, Skeeter, Lil' Bit, Bolo, and Stink. Everybody had a nickname, even her: Neat. Her little cousins started helping with the sandcastle but got bored. One, a year younger, became obsessed with digging for water, but he was too far from the shore, where the sand was fine and dry, more like white sugar.

At six years old, she knew he'd be digging until dusk because the dry sand kept refilling his hole. His brother, though, was diligently trying to bury himself in the sand and everyone knew he was special, except his mama. Between stripping down butt-naked at any given moment and still putting his shoes on the wrong feet at eight years old, they all knew. He had covered himself from toes to neck with sand.

His mama kept yelling, "Do *not* put that sand on your face again! Do it again, and I'm going to make you come up here with me!"

Jenita glanced up to make sure she could still see his nostrils when his mom got caught up talking with the other ladies, but she couldn't let his shenanigans distract her from building the biggest sandcastle ever!

"Hey! Hey!" Her father's voice carried over the shoreline. "Food ready!"

She didn't answer right away. The tower needed rounding. The edges weren't even yet.

"Yes, sir. I'm coming!" she called, though she still had much to do.

He appeared behind her, shadow stretching across the sand. "Now."

She studied the castle one last time. "It's not done."

"It'll still be there, and you like hot dogs. I'm not gon' tell you again, Neat."

She quickly brushed sand from her knees and followed him back toward the pavilion, glancing over her shoulder as if the tide might take offense at her absence. Under the shelter, tinfoil crinkled, and paper plates shuffled.

"Move over." One cousin laughed. "Move your meat, lose your seat."

Her father handed her a hot dog. "Sit. Eat."

She sat. The other kids were already halfway through theirs.

One little boy, chewing loudly, looked at Jenita. "You eat too slow."

"I don't eat slow." She studied the salt on a chip or the line of ketchup before taking a measured bite. "I just taste it."

Her cousin rolled her eyes. "It's just a hot dog."

She chewed thoughtfully. Warm bread. Salty snap. Soft center. She noticed things. By the time she'd eaten half, the foil trays were being replaced.

"Here it comes!" someone shouted.

Nana Katie's pecan cookies. Sweet potato muffins with a maple and brown sugar glaze. The glaze shone in the sunlight, sugar crystals catching and holding it like tiny pieces of cracked glass.

"Ooooh!" The little kids crowded forward.

"Only if you finished your food," her aunt warned.

"I did!"

"Me, too!"

The kids waved their plates. "Look!"

Jenita looked down. A quarter of her hot dog remained.

Her hole-diggin' cousin nudged her. "Hurry up, Neat."

"I am," she said softly.

She wasn't. She took another bite. Chewed. Swallowed. Reached for her drink and sipped it. Bit a chip. Wiped her little fingers. By the time she lifted her head again, crumpled napkins and crumbs dotted the table, and the big kids were already running back toward the ocean. She blinked.

"Any more muffins?" someone asked.

"Her aunt shook the empty foil. "That was the last one."

Her cousin licked the glaze off his thumb. "Told you."

She stared at the tray. Just for a second. Her father noticed.

"You done?"

"No, sir."

Per usual, she had ended up at the far concrete picnic table under the pavilion alone daydreaming. She folded her napkin neatly and watched the older kids race past, listening to laughter rise and fall. She wasn't upset. Just...aware. Things moved loudly around her. People moved quickly around her.

She didn't. Her sandcastle would still be waiting.

At two of the other tables, the adults were setting up to play bid whist, spades, or dominoes. Leftover food covered with tinfoil, twist-tie-closed partially eaten bags of buns, bags of chips folded closed, and a half-used can of Raid that worked well enough keeping the ants away were on the other table. The melted ice in the Styrofoam coolers held just enough beer left to send her uncle on a beer run, and the other cooler had a little water left in the thoroughly washed gallon milk jug, and a few Shastas nestled underneath.

The sight of a lady playing with little children interrupted her reflections and daydreaming. She found it odd for a mother to play red light, green light with children so competitively. She seemed to have more fun than they did. Her mom and aunts might toss a ball twice, cradle a Baby Alive doll, roll a toy car, color part of a page, or brush Barbie's hair, but none of them would dare rip and run just like kids with kids. She couldn't take her eyes off the lady…this phenomenon.

She briefly forgot about her masterpiece of a sandcastle that wasn't complete, but that day was the only day she had. Although Brown Sugar Beach was the Black side of the beach, there was only one motel, and her family and friends couldn't afford to stay overnight.

She stopped watching the lady playing so happily with the children, put the rest of the hot dog in her Styrofoam cup, pretending to have eaten it, and showed her mom a clean plate. With the good desserts gone, all they had left were some raggedy Hydrox cookies that the humidity had softened until they bent before the bite. Forget it. She had to hurry because she could add at least two or three more mounds before it would be time to pack up and hit the road.

Between being sun-drained, ashy from the sand and granules everywhere, the excitement from the night before had stolen her sleep, and having successfully built her biggest sandcastle ever, she was tuckered out. Falling asleep just ten minutes into the ride home with her hand in the shell-filled front pocket of her yellow terrycloth cover-up, holding a bracelet she'd found deep in the sand, she didn't remember the four-and-a-half-hour ride home.

She awoke to Nana putting her in the tub, washing her face and her thick hair. Once dried off, with one towel wrapped around her thick, deep copper hair and another around her tiny honey-brown frame, she climbed onto Nana's high bed with its pink, fringed bedspread. To her surprise, she saw something wrapped in tinfoil. Nana had saved a sweet potato muffin just for her.

"Neat, I got the shells out your pockets, where you get this bracelet from, baby?"

"It was in the sand, Nana."

"It sure is pretty. Looks like costume jewelry. Put it in your little jewelry box."

"Yes, ma'am."

"I know it's late, but we're still going to church in the morning. I gotta sing. You can eat your muffin while I do your hair."

She loved going to church with Nana, especially on second Sundays when the good singin' choir sang. She would be sure to stand at a pew in the inner aisle to watch 'em march in! Whenever Nana led "God Is Standing By" by Walter Hawkins, everybody would be jumping and shouting, and so would she!

She loved Nana Katie dearly, and no doubt Nana Katie loved her more than anyone. She was special, but not like her little cousin who stripped at will. He even did it one time at church on a Sunday morning, swaying off beat in the Tiny Tots choir, shoes on the wrong feet, already tugging at his clip-on tie.

Not that kind of special.

A church mother tapped Nana's shoulder from the pew behind. "Sista Katie, that grandbaby of yours is some kind of special."

Jenita pouted and whispered, "Nana, I don't want to be special."

"Not like that, baby. You know you got the gift, don't you?" Nana Katie would whisper, pressing a peppermint into her palm as if it were communion.

"What gift, Nana?"

"The kind the Lord don't hand out to everybody. You see things. You feel things."

As she got older, she knew she had a sixth sense, and sometimes a third eye, which she would come to know later were spiritual gifts from God, much like Nana's.

Her other grandma spewed, "It's the pure T devil!"

When Jenita was eleven, Nana Katie passed away, too soon, and before she could help Jenita understand and develop her gifts. She wasn't the same after Nana died from complications from diabetes, but she felt Nana would always be there when she needed her.

CHAPTER 2

Love Given and Received

Fatoumata Abubakar Devereaux—Fatou—knew early on that her twin son, Ibrahima Alexander Devereaux (Zander, or Zee), had inherited his daddy's academic brilliance. By the time he was four, she'd already seen it. Blessed with intelligence, good looks, athleticism, and talent, he could sing and dance. She'd taught him.

"*Tu vois? Je te vois danser* (You see? I see you dancing)," she'd say, clapping to the rhythm as he danced effortlessly. "You feel that rhythm? That is yours. Aye!"

From the traditional Senegalese dances she'd learned as a girl in Dakar, to second-line steps she picked up the summer she met her husband, King, near the French Quarter, to whatever was on *American Bandstand*, Fatou made movement feel like freedom.

"*Un, deux*... slow down." She'd laugh, guiding King's shoulders. "You dance like you are thinking too hard."

King only smiled. "That's 'cause I'm trying to keep up with you. Or I could just take you in the bedroom."

"Yes. Tonight." She smiled and winked.

Her flawless, African blackwood skin made her straight teeth shine brighter and her almond-shaped eyes glow sharper. That smile, Lord, that smile could light a path straight out of the dark. She knew it, too, especially when she used it on her husband.

"Pourquoi tu me regardes comme ça?" she'd tease. "Why that look?"

"How else am I supposed to look at you?" he'd answer flirtatiously.

He adored her kindness, her gifts, her ancestral beauty, her small waist, and that cornbread-fed thickness she carried everywhere else like a promise. Fatou's voice carried warmth passed down from her ancestors, wrapped in a French lilt softened by years in America. When she said,"*Bonjour, mon cœur,*" (Good morning, my love)," the day felt full before it even started. When she whispered, *"Dors bien et fais de beaux rêves* (Sleep well and have sweet dreams)," dreams didn't dare misbehave.

Maybe it was because she was born into Senegalese nobility in the mid-1940s, or maybe joy just lived in her bones. She could make people feel better at funerals, and she did, especially at the repast.

"I know it's hard. Borrow my joy to ease your sorrow," she'd say, hugging someone's shoulder. "Eat. Fill your belly. That is what the living are still here to do."

Her laugh was hearty, but not too loud, and contagious. She always hummed and sang while she cooked, and two-stepped through the kitchen as if music followed her everywhere. Sometimes, she'd grab King without warning. *"Viens ici,"* she'd say, pulling him close.

"Come here? We're cooking, Fatti."

"And dancing," she'd reply, already moving.

Her hugs were legendary. Everyone got one. When she delivered baked goods with her twins in tow, even the most prejudiced white men learned quickly. "It comes with a hug," she'd say cheerfully. "Or I'll have to take it back." Before they could object, she'd already wrapped them up and moved on. Over time, they waited for it. She hugged the neighbors, the mailman, the insurance man, the fish man, and the couple who drove the horse-drawn fruit-and-vegetable wagon on Saturday mornings. "Next time, bring more peaches," she'd call out. "And don't think you're leaving without a hug." She would have hugged the ice cream man if she could have caught him.

Her home was the gathering place. Food, dancing, and love spilled out the door. She didn't have time to socialize formally, and some upper-crust Black women turned their noses up at her accent, her deep melanin, and the way she always wrapped her head.

"Let them look." She'd shrug. "God knows me."

Her hair was so short that rolling it with rice seemed necessary, and so tightly coiled that it resisted connecting. Even when brushed, each strand insisted on being alone. Between scarves, hats, *moussors* (headscarves), and intricately tied *geles* (headwraps), she kept her head covered everywhere except at home. King didn't mind. As he massaged her scalp from time to time, Fatou would exhale.

"Ahhh...*merci*, my love. That is so soothing."

She never stopped wearing her African dresses, American prints made Senegalese by the way she layered them—comfortable, regal, and quietly ancestral.

She sewed everything: her own clothes, her daughter's, dresses for her sister-in-law and best friend, and pieces fine enough to sell at the local Black-owned dress shop.

"Your hands are blessed," her sister-in-law and best friend, Tink, would tell her.

Fatou smiled. "Your hands are also blessed. God gave them to me. I just listen."

Those hands, small, smooth-palmed, worn beyond her years from hard work in Dakar and Paris, had known washboards, lye soap, boiling water, and survival. Now, in North Carolina, King did his best to give her a life fit for a queen. Considering all she had gone through, she was already living like one.

Her twins, whom only she lovingly called Ibra and Ola, found so much comfort in their mother's touch—especially her son, Ibra. Her daughter, Ola, inherited the best parts of her bubbly spirit and her cooking talent. She and her husband took good care of one another, and she felt like his queen. That's what he called her. They raised their children well, and a few others, too. Fatou took in washing from time to time, baked pies and cakes to order for Black folks and highfalutin white folks alike. She also cooked and baked on weekends for King's & Queen's.

It was a weekend-only dining and dance hall she and her husband owned, funded in part by a $100,000 inheritance from the sale of his grandfather's land, home, and shrimping company. Fatou wasn't fixated on money; she had a God-given assurance that it would always flow if they treated people well and stuck to the plan. King, though, kept count. Dreams required planning.

She remembered the very evening he burst through the door, breathless. "I got the job, Queen! We're moving to Carolina!"

She didn't hesitate. "I told you it was yours. I told you God said He would bless us."

They left New Orleans the following week.

Senior accountant at the Pine City Mobile Home Manufacturing Plant. One of the best jobs around; good benefits, solid stability, and a future that reached all the way to a piece of land in North Carolina, and someday, Brown Sugar Beach.

While King hosted, Fatou cooked. Between courses, she peeked through the accordion doors separating the dining room, dance floor, and bar, where white-linen covered tables circled a polished wood floor, the bandstand glowed beneath low amber lights, and the clink of glasses mixed with laughter and the distant hush of the ocean, watching faces light up over her Senegalese-Creole-Soul Food fusion. When the plates were cleared and the band tuned up, she stepped forward.

She closed her eyes and sang "At Last" by Etta James. The room stilled. Then swayed.

"Sing it, Queen," King called out.

On Sunday evenings, she taught the twins what she'd noticed on the floor—new steps, new dances.

"*Voilà! Vous avez compris!* Aye! That's it! You got it!" She clapped.

They learned fast. People loved watching them dance. Even when racism hovered at dance classes, their talent spoke louder. She enrolled them anyway.

As they got older, using their more American-friendly names—Zander or Zee, and Renae—they entered local dance competitions. Then state. Then national. Tap, ballet, ballroom, freestyle or anything from *Soul Train*. Trophies filled the shelves.

King shook his head one night, smiling. "All that from watching their mama."

Fatou looked at the twins, still moving even when the music stopped. "They were always meant to."

Fatou poured all that she was and all that she had into her children. Some nights, when the house was quiet and the air felt too still, she would sit at the edge of the bed, smoothing her palm over her children's backs until their breathing slowed.

"You are safe," she whispered. "*Sama xol, sa yaay mingi fi...* Your mother is here, my loves." In Wolof and in English.

Her son would stir and turn toward her voice, half-asleep. "I love you, Mama. You always say that."

Fatou smiled, though her chest tightened. "Because it is always true."

In Senegal, caste-based discrimination lingered beneath the surface of almost every Wolof community, rarely spoken aloud but strictly enforced. Fatou had been born Geer, nobility, but her status could not shield her from her father's unpaid debt, which led to their banishment from the village and forced the family to survive separately, on their own.

"Go. Take these. They were made for my mother, and do not take them off. Go now! They say it is better this way," her mother had told her, eyes lowered, voice breaking. "For everyone."

"For whom?" Fatou had asked.

Tradition required her family to be dead to her, even though she knew they lived. That knowing, without permission to grieve, hollowed her in ways no one could see.

She took what work she could find, cooking and cleaning, learning to disappear when necessary. Eventually, she became a maid and au pair for a wealthy family who saw her worth and treated her with kindness.

"You belong with us," the woman of the house once said, pressing a warm cup into Fatou's hands. "You are family here."

Fatou moved to France with them, and later to New Orleans, where her life shifted again—this time toward love instead of loss. It was there she met her husband, a man who saw her not as broken or banished, but whole and beautiful.

In 1967, when she was blessed with twins, she held them close. "I will never let you wonder," she had told them, her voice steady even as tears slipped down her face. "You will always know me."

So she loved them fiercely and deliberately, every embrace an offering of comfort, every word a promise, pouring into them, and into other children she embraced as her own, all the love and affection she had once been forced to leave behind.

King personified his name. Being Creole and Black, he could pass for white unless he let his selective Creole accent give him away. His olive complexion, slightly wavy dark hair, keen nose, deep-set eyes, strong jawline, and a football player's neck matched his blue-collar build.

Years on the shrimp boats had worked his body hard enough that he still looked like a man who never missed a day of labor. And if they didn't ask him if he was Black, he didn't say.

"Is that your real name?" folks would ask sometimes.

He'd look at them confidently. "It is."

In Carolina, he wore cheap suits during the workweek and coveralls whenever the urge struck to work with his hands. Those same coveralls doubled as after-work attire when he met his brother Louis to repair and renovate the motel.

"You ever rest?" Louis asked one evening, handing him a wrench.

"When it's done," King said, already tightening the bolt.

On Friday and Saturday nights, he was dressed to the nines as the owner and proprietor of King's & Queen's Dance and Dining Hall, and he looked the part. On Sundays, no matter how late Saturday night ran, he put on his best suit.

"I can take or leave church," he'd say, adjusting his tie, "but not God or Jesus. If we do more of the ways of Jesus, we'd be more like God than a little bit…all that jaw-jackin'."

Fatou would smile at that. She was spiritual beyond religion in ways that sometimes baffled him, but he went along anyway, trying to keep up. Besides, their twins were always singing or wrapped up in something at church that wild horses couldn't keep him from.

"They need to enjoy their gifts," Fatou once said quietly, rubbing Jergens lotion on their faces before heading out the door.

"They do," King replied. "Just don't want talent making them forget about education."

Much like their mother, the twins were naturally gifted. Still, King didn't want talent distracting them from business sense. He loved his baby girl fiercely, and he saw too much of himself, Fatou, and Louis' combined talents in his son to ignore the warning signs.

"I love you, son," he'd say, "but music will have your pockets singing the blues."

"Yes, sir."

King was stern with everyone; it didn't matter who they were. He moved in silence. He kept people guessing, and gave them hell, when necessary, especially in business.

When racist white folks refused to call him King, he corrected them calmly. "Then call me Mr. Devereaux."

They never quite figured him out.

"He hangs out with the uppity Negroes," they'd whisper. "Talks funny sometimes. What is he anyway?"

No one ever asked him directly, especially when his money was talking. King didn't care what they thought, as long as they didn't play with his family, his time, or his money. He never denied being Black or Creole. He simply let folks believe whatever suited them.

"*Mon amour*, you let people think too much," Fatou once said, helping him count receipts.

He didn't look up. "That's how they tell on themselves."

He wanted to be the best example of a man, husband, and father—in real time. He played the hand dealt to him, and when it played in his favor, he brought his family and anyone else he could help, right alongside him.

And he paid close attention. Because there was no better way to see how white folks played their hand than when they thought he was one of them.

King could build or fix just about anything and always brought their son along to learn. Leaving New Orleans had meant defying his family, who worried for him and wanted him to settle into a teaching career. But King saw beyond classrooms, beyond being told what to do or how much he could earn. He wanted more, and when he decided on something, he didn't talk about it. He moved.

Outside of his wife and children, he gave no thought to opinions that didn't align with his vision. Fatou was the center of his world mentally, spiritually, sexually, and emotionally. She steadied him when he needed grounding and soothed him in ways no one else could. He kissed her often, especially her forehead, sometimes wondering if it gave her even a fraction of the relief he felt when she kissed his cheek, rubbed his head, or eased the tension from his shoulders.

What made his heart ache was her quiet grief around the birthdays of her family still in Senegal. The sleepless nights. The soft whimpering. She didn't know he heard her. In his eyes, she was flawless—beautiful inside and out, and incapable of wrongdoing. At home, he was putty in her hands, and they both knew it. Yet she never used that power, which only deepened his love and passion for her.

His purpose was simple and unwavering: to provide so well that his family would never have to beg, borrow, or steal, and to lift someone else along the way. King wasn't a talker. But when he spoke, people listened. He reserved casual conversations for his wife and children, his brother Louis, and his sister-in-law Tink.

Louis, who was light-skinned but unapologetically Black, was, despite being married, a lady's man. His wife, Tink, was a homebody with quiet strength, grounded in spirituality and hoodoo, not voodoo. Between the two couples, four children came along, bound by plans far bigger than themselves.

They were inseparable. The bond between King and Louis was unmistakable, a kind of super glue that resisted the "don't make waves" path their parents had hoped for. Their other siblings followed that safer route without hesitation. But these two didn't flinch. They were on a generational mission.

CHAPTER 3

School Days

Fatou's little Ibra—now teenage Zander—could hardly walk through the doors of Jefferson High School without girls approaching him. He was the top jock for football and basketball, academically strong enough for both athletic and academic scholarships, a talented singer and dancer, and extraordinarily handsome. Every girl's dream and every boy's buddy. Born on December 22, 1967, to King and Fatou, who named Ibrahima Alexander Devereaux after both his grandfathers. The family had moved from New Orleans to Pine City, North Carolina, in 1970.

Pine City was a rare stretch of Carolina shoreline where the mountains leaned close enough to the Atlantic to kiss the sunlight along Brown Sugar Beach, the kind of place that felt like Malibu's beauty met Camden, Maine's small-town charm, and found itself nestled in the South.

Starting high school, he and his twin were the only students with African names in Pine City. Going by Ibrahima always required explanation. Alexander made white folks feel more comfortable, but he didn't like the way they said it.

"Ma, they can't get any of my names right. They hold on to the "r" too long, give Alexander five," holding up five fingers, "*five* syllables, not four, Ma."

"*Aye-uh-lick 'ZAN-derrr Dever'ruh'.*"

"And if they call me *Abra-HI-mer* one more time… I keep saying EE-bra-HEEMA. Ugh!"

Fatou stood on her tiptoes to kiss his forehead. "*Je comprends ce que tu ressens, mon fils.* (I understand, my son.)"

His twin, Olayemi Renae, was his spokeswoman. Talkative and bold, she was the opposite of her brother. She'd been going by Renae since third grade and, on their first day at Jefferson High, launched a two-day campaign to get everyone to drop Alexander and Ibrahima entirely. There was already an Alex. Call him Xander. Or Zee.

Hell, they couldn't get Zee wrong. It worked.

Much like his father, Zander was a man of few words, laid-back but charismatic when it mattered. His father had steered him away from relying on sports, dance, or singing as a career, while making sure he was proficient in all three to earn scholarships. That balance kept him focused on academia. But his mom made sure he and his sister had room to develop their artistic talents and enjoy them.

Genetics had been generous. Jet-black, wavy hair. A satin-warm brown complexion over every muscle. His great-grandfather's dazzling brown eyes with amber flecks. At six-foot-two, he had his dad's build, only bulkier. He didn't miss leg day or upper-body day, and he used the school's weight room religiously. He had Fatou's perfectly white teeth, her almond-shaped eyes, and eyelashes that could make any woman jealous.

He embodied her compassion and a natural tendency to give and receive affection. But in second grade, he learned quickly that he couldn't hug girls; the other boys weren't having it, and he couldn't expect hugs from his teachers either. By middle school, he'd learned how easily girls mistook his kindness for flirting and his compassion for love. They'd either decide they were his girlfriend or, among a certain few, offer themselves in the high school bathrooms.

Early on, his dad had told him he didn't have time for a girlfriend. Some girls, he warned, were shallow and cheap. But Zander accepted their invitations for oral sex in the school bathrooms, anyway, as did the other jocks those girls chose. Before practice, after games, whenever the offer came. Even when he didn't really want to, peer pressure and jock culture said yes for him. Deep down, he often wanted to say no. It was easy to go with the flow until he lay his head on his pillow at night, feeling hollow, emptied of everything except his family's hugs and warmth. Like Fatou, Zander had a compassionate heart. He'd shed a tear or two with his twin sister when she coaxed him into watching tearjerker movies. On the inside, he was the mirror image of his mother. But the world only saw a fine, educated, talented young man—dancer, singer, bulky jock—and stopped there.

Zander's confidant was his aunt Tink, who had given him his nickname as a fix for people constantly, some willfully, mispronouncing his name. He could talk to her about anything, and she never condemned him. She listened without judgment, spoke freely and softly, and taught him about God and how God lived inside him.

She prayed, performed sacred rituals, and practiced hoodoo that always seemed to help him. Tink was his vault. He could tell her things he couldn't bear telling his mother. But Tink and his mom were best friends, and in their own way, at the right moments, they hid nothing from each other, especially about their children. They were more sisters than blood.

Zander spoke candidly. "Tink, some of these white girls wanna go down on me, and the Black ones wanna hunch, like that's all they got on their minds."

Tink touched his forearm. "Zander, you just can't keep giving your body away like that, baby. It's chipping at your spirit and your soul. That ain't Godly."

"But they hound me from the time I get to school until Dad picks me up after practice. When I say no, they get bolder, grabbing at my junk, or feeling on my booty when I'm walking to class. I feel like a piece of meat. If I did that to them, I would get in trouble."

Tink looked him in the eyes and pressed a finger sharply into his broad chest. "Don't you ever do it either. Because all it takes is one time to ruin your whole life. I don't care how much these white folks say they like you. They only like you if you got their ball in your hand."

Her words sobered him. "They're still liable to string you up 'round here."

"Okay, Tink. I know. I know."

"Do you hear me, Zander?"

"Yes. Yes, ma'am. I hear you."

They sat with the gravity of that truth. Then, to shift the mood, Zander smirked. "But I ain't gon' lie; I do like getting oral sex."

"Yeah, it's good for a minute, but you're worth more than that. I see you. You got a good heart that needs to give love."

"I do." He placed his hand on his chest. "I want to love, or at least like, the girl. They don't give me time to figure out how. Like they don't care nothing about me."

Tink didn't quite know what to say, because that wasn't her world. It made her heart ache, though. She was an empath and a homebody who loved her husband, his two children, her quiet home life, supporting family in whatever way she could, hoodoo, and crafting. She hugged Zander, prayed with him, and for him daily. This time was no different.

"Wait right here. Let me go make something. Don't leave."

Using a hoodoo remedy, she'd soaked a red ribbon in Florida Water and herbs, then anointed with an oil that three generations of Holy Ghost-filled praying women had interceded over and divided among themselves, Tink had him wrap the ribbon around his dominant left hand to rebuke and ward off what she called a "whoremongering" spirit. She told him to touch it and pray over it each morning before he left the house. Miraculously, within a few days, it worked. Almost too well.

Every time he wore it, touched it, and prayed over it before leaving, it unsettled him. *Dang. I ain't getting no play.* It scared him.

Part of the problem was that his adolescent overstimulated desires created an appetite that outpaced the average young man's. He'd also heard about blue balls and wanted no part of that. So he only wore the ribbon, touched it, and prayed when he wanted to manage his urges and slow down the advances. Otherwise, he left it off.

Zander could sing—really sing. In church, whenever the Spirit moved, the congregation felt it. But at school, he held back, indifferent to the unseasoned chorus-style singing. He'd been shaped by his mama's and Uncle Louis' voices, who taught him how to "sang" gospel music by simply feeling the Holy Spirit, by listening and watching rather than following sheet music.

His academic excellence was never in question. He absorbed knowledge and applied it with ease. He hadn't had a girlfriend, but girls studied every detail of him—his chiseled frame, his dazzling eyes, his sun-kissed brown skin, his jet-black high-top fade, the shy smile, the way he licked and pressed his full, multilingual lips together, his quiet confidence. The way he dressed. The way he moved. The way his starched Levi's sat just right.

Cool. Calm. Debonair. When he ran up and down the basketball court, perfectly shaped bowlegs, one foot slightly pigeon-toed, the girls' eyes followed every step. But not one of them ever asked about him. His heart. His mind.

He desperately wanted to be seen as a person, not a persona. Not just King and Fatou's boy, not an athlete, not Jefferson High's first Black quarterback, not one of the basketball team's best guards, not the singer, the dancer, the teacher's pet, or the coaches' favorite. The weight of all those labels worn, simultaneously every day, left him mentally, emotionally, and sometimes physically exhausted. What he wanted most was what he'd watched his parents build: love with depth. Affection with meaning. A bond that saw the person underneath everything else.

CHAPTER 4

One Night

Prom night 1986 was the last hurrah of Zander's senior year. The night he would finally concede to drinking and smoking marijuana to celebrate. After he and his best friend, Frank, dismantled the dance floor, two Black girls who had been after him for sex brought him a celebratory Sun Country wine cooler and invited him to smoke weed with them. After Zander took his first deep hit, he felt some of the pressure float away—the teenage weight of athletics, emotions, sex, academics, all of it.

The alpha-male expectation of a strong and demanding sexual appetite. His father's requirements. His mother's high hopes. The heaviness of Jefferson High's hero's crown. All of it lifted from his shoulders.

Sweating and parched from dancing, he took that wine cooler bottle to the head, guzzling it faster than water.

"Ooh, this feels good. A wine cooler has never made me feel like this. What flavor is this? This feels mighty good."

At first, he felt relaxed and looked around for somewhere to sit. Then the dizziness came, and he wasn't sure his legs could hold him. The two girls walked him toward the dark side of the already dimly lit parking lot, to a limousine they'd arrived in with a group of white girls.

Zander was foggy and groggy, but lighter than he'd ever felt. One of them knocked on the darkly tinted window. The door opened.

A popular white girl, a Headen, peeked out. Her grandfather owned two car dealerships that also rented limousines, half the oceanfront property on Sandy Beach, and a quarter of Pine City. She had access to the limo, the cars, the alcohol, and all the drugs she wanted. She was what the kids called a freak, a label that followed her because she made a sport of going down on boys, chose her targets deliberately, and did not discriminate.

She had never been able to crack Zander. He vehemently turned her down, and her crew, each time. So the girls struck a deal: bring Zander to her, and they could have all the weed and liquor they wanted.

Normally quiet, composed, and attuned to his surroundings, Zander was talking loudly and stumbling. The girls worked quickly to get him into the limo.

"Hey, what's going on? I'm not ready to leave. I gotta find my girlfriend. Where's Crystal?" he slurred.

"We're not leaving, and we'll be your girlfriends tonight," one of them said tauntingly, pressing down on his shoulder to make him duck into the limo. But she didn't push him low enough, and with his balance already gone, he caught the top of the door frame with his head.

"Ouch!" He grabbed his head and saw blood on his palm—not enough to drip, but throbbing sharply.

The other girl shoved him from behind, and the Headen girl, determined to claim her catch, snatched him by the hands and pulled him in. He fell onto the seat, and before he could steady himself, the door closed and hands were already working at his belt.

One of the two Black girls had given bathroom favors to Zander and two other football players after school the year before. She reported everything back to the Headen girl, who collected boys like trophies and treated sex as conquest, willing or not. Whatever it took. There was a fourth girl somewhere in the limo, but Zander couldn't make out who she was.

Between the knot rising on his head, the disorienting loss of control, and trying to fend off eight hands pulling at his clothes, he was doing his best not to hurt them. His defensive moves weren't as strong as he thought they were. He assumed they were just going to strip him and put him out of the car naked, that kind of cruel prank had happened to a few guys the year before, probably by this same crew. He didn't care about that; he was comfortable in his body. But that wasn't their plan.

While his classmates forcibly undressed him, two of the white girls stripped quickly, leaving their expensive prom gowns twisted and stomped on the floor. One pulled his underwear and pants down to his ankles while the other worked at his shoes. Both Black girls attended his church.

The Headen girl said, "Girls, this is a big one."

"Stop. Stop! What are y'all doing? Stop!" he shouted.

They laughed.

She took him into her mouth aggressively, ignoring every refusal he'd ever given.

This time, he couldn't stop her.

There was no pleasure in it. While two of the others were arousing each other, the fourth was drunk, sitting pantyless and pressing against his outstretched forearm, no gratification in it, only deliberate humiliation. Just having her that close, he could smell her, and it turned his stomach. The stench of meaningless encounters she hadn't bothered to wash away between partners made him want to retch. He felt claustrophobic and violated. He could hardly breathe.

He wanted to cry, but he couldn't. He'd rejected them, and this was his punishment. They laughed wildly, shamelessly, and cruelly. He screamed and felt two hands clamp over his mouth.

He fought harder, pushing and twisting, but in this real-time nightmare, his body wasn't even patty-caking these rapists. He was awake but unable to move; the drugs had seen to that.

What is happening to me? How is this happening to me? Why is this happening to me? Where is Frank, Renae, Crystal—she's inside—Mama, Pops, Tink, Uncle Louis, God?

Involuntary tears ran hot down the sides of his face, pooling in his ears and rolling down the back of his neck. With his mouth covered, the laughter and movement continued. He could barely draw a breath as they were wearing down his body. Seeing one of them mounting him, he attempted to twist his hips to throw her off. She screamed out, enjoying it, reveling in his inability to fight.

He was furious and helpless.

Weed and one wine cooler don't do this. They drugged me. They had. He'd heard about boys drugging girls. It had never once occurred to him that it could go the other way. Not to him. Lying there helpless, he knew his body responded more than once, unwanted and uninvited, each time deepening the humiliation.

Bewildered. Breathless. Ashamed. Violated. Emasculated. Used. Raped. Gang raped.

His thoughts moved more slowly, foggier, yet he was fully aware of everything happening to him without his consent. He thought they would never stop or that his body could take any more.

Then the door opened.

His girlfriend stood motionless in the frame.

They didn't stop.

All Crystal saw were four naked bodies all over the boy she loved, the boy who had gotten her pregnant. No one else knew except him and Renae.

His rapists laughed when the door swung shut again. The scheme had worked perfectly: get Zander, then lure Crystal out to the car so she could see it. They hated her because she had him, and he had been faithful to her.

They finished. They dressed, stepping back into their twisted designer gowns and underwear, and walked back into the hotel ballroom as if nothing had happened, dancing on the way in, emboldened by their ratchet, wicked conquest.

He woke the next morning, naked in the limo, parked at the Headen dealership, with a splitting headache. He couldn't find his underwear. He put on his tux, shirt, and shoes and climbed out.

Old man Headen was sitting on the hood of his Cadillac. "Well, hey there, Sleeping Beauty. We been waitin' on you to wake up. Now get on home, boy."

As Zander walked away, the old man called out to Pine City's own Black Vietnam vet, an alcoholic and heroin addict. "Now, boy, you get in there and clean it up brand new. I got new passengers tonight. Do a good job, and I just might give you the rest of your go-go juice."

The man scurried.

Zander walked home.

Knowing he would never be the same…imprisoned, already, by his pain.

Zander became depressed. Sometimes, he recalled that night as abuse. Sometimes, as non-consensual. But he could only bring himself to say the word "rape" in his own mind. Who would he tell? *Men don't get gang-raped. That's called a threesome.* His understanding of manhood, the code he'd absorbed without ever being handed it directly, wouldn't allow him to feel weak, to cry, to be afraid. Even if he could get past that, how would he say it out loud? Not to Frank. Not to Renae. Not even to Tink.

His best friend, Frank, had left the prom early to go see Renae, who hadn't attended. The rest of their friend group was still inside, paired off or chasing someone or begging somebody's daughter to get what Zander could get without asking. None of them had any idea what had happened. For the rest of his senior year, Zander could barely hold his head up. He ached for it to be over so he wouldn't have to see his rapists every day. He'd get nauseous at the sight of them or the sound of their names. Seeing them everywhere made him sick—the same school, same classes. Some of them sat in the same pew at church.

Tink's God-given Holy Ghost discernment, woven through generations of hoodoo lineage and prophetic insight, was why she knew something was terribly wrong with Zander before anyone else did.

One morning, Tink stood still longer than usual in her kitchen, mumbling under her breath. "I don't like this. Something ain't right with that boy."

Zander stayed away from her, kept out of arm's reach, because he knew one touch would tell her too much. When he spotted her across the yard, he muttered under his breath, "Don't you come near me right now, Tink. Please."

Hoodoo healers were the community's doctors, midwives, counselors, and intercessors. Women like Tink, whose healing remedies combined wisdom, faith, and the science of the earth, embodied resilience: healing bodies under enslavement, soothing grief under oppression, restoring hope when systems denied them formal care or made it unreachable.

"Ain't nothing new under the sun," Tink would say. "We been mending broken bodies and spirits a long time."

But Tink understood Zander like a second mama, and she made him a mojo bag filled with roots, herbs, a black tourmaline crystal, and personal items she'd chosen carefully, and strung it on a leather cord with tiny bells for him to wear to bed.

"This gonna sit right here on your chest," she said, tying the knot. "Close enough to your heart."

She prayed the healing stripes of Jesus and protection over it, and over the mixture she blended:

Salt—purification and protection

Florida Water—cleansing and uplifting energy

Red brick dust—protection at thresholds

Bay leaves—success and divine favor

John the Conqueror root—strength, confidence, and success

Hyssop—spiritual cleansing and forgiveness, as in Psalm 51

Nine anointed oil mixtures—representing divine completeness

"That's enough," she whispered, satisfied, as the ingredients blended into a thick slurry. "Holy Ghost power doesn't have to be loud."

She made a large batch, poured it into short mason jars, and labeled them Spirit Mend & Guard Salve. She added ten jars to her apothecary cabinet. Two jars she boxed and gift-wrapped, then made a tag from the leftover wrapping paper and wrote:

Dear Zander,

I can feel you, baby. It feels horrible and heavy.

Dab this on your forehead, your hands, and feet. Pray.

God always hears and loves you, and I am always here.

I'm praying for you. You will be healed.

I love you,

Tink.

She told Fatou she had something for Zander, something to help with what they both could feel.

"I do not know what is wrong." Fatou's tears were already spilling. "But I know my Ibra is hurting."

"This ain't gonna fix everything overnight. But it'll take some of that dark off him."

Fatou was grateful to tears, knowing that even if it wasn't an overnight miracle, it might seep through the stone wall her deeply withdrawn son had built around himself. They prayed together because they knew that was the only other thing that might reach him.

"*Que Dieu vienne en aide à mon fils…*" Fatou's voice broke. "Please heal my Ibra and keep Your loving hand on his life."

"Amen." Tink nodded once. "In Jesus' name. Ancestors, you hear? So be it."

Zander had become sad, unreachable, and shadowed, yet driven by a deep need to escape. Tink placed the box on his bed, where she knew he'd find it after school.

He stood over it for a long moment. "What is this now?" he murmured, exhaustion heavy in his voice.

He bathed, put the mojo bag around his neck, dabbed the salve as instructed, and went to sleep. For the first time since the night before senior prom, he slept through most of the night without waking in a cold sweat, without the back-to-back nightmares that had stalked him every night since.

CHAPTER 5

Lead the Way

Born into a generational farming family on March 10, 1970, to Mable Lee and Johnylee Daniel "J.D." Hall, Jenita's life was never quite the same after her nana died. Nothing in the house felt the same once her paternal grandmother moved in. Love, care, and tenderness gave way to farm work and abuse.

"You better hurry up," her grandmother snapped. "That field won't work itself."

Jenita nodded. She always nodded. Anything else only made it worse.

Her mother stood at the sink, shoulders tight, eyes down, voice barely above a whisper. "She's still a child."

Her grandmother turned. "And you're still useless! All of ya. I don't know what my son saw in you."

Then she turned toward Jenita. "Anh huh, Katie Mae gone now, talmbout you special. Hmph! Well, ya ain't. That ain't nothing but the devil. And now you startin' to fill out too early, thinking you somebody. You ain't...never will be. Probably being fast already. But I know how to beat the devil and the fast right up out cha."

And sometimes she tried. Jenita felt it coming each time before it happened. The sharp grab. The unnecessary beatings. Her father stepped forward once, but too late. "That's enough, Mama."

Her grandmother laughed. "I'll take my strap to all three of you if I feel like it."

Jenita found her escape from them in the field. Quiet. She would lie on the ground with her face to the sky, praying for better, or lean against a fence post with her knees pulled in. She pulled a crumpled piece of paper from her pocket and colored slowly, carefully.

"Nana," she whispered, staring up at the sky. "Why'd you have to go?" The wind moved through the tall grass like an answer, or maybe just company. "I'm here."

She told God, "I just want to belong to a good family. I won't make no trouble. Or… somebody to hug me again."

Middle school was where something finally shifted.

Ms. Jackson, a sorority volunteer, was introducing literacy, math, and art programs to the students. She stood at the front of the classroom, smiling wide. "We're here to talk about books, create art, and tell stories. Your art. Your stories."

Jenita barely looked up.

Ms. Jackson stopped beside her desk. "You draw and paint?"

Jenita hesitated. "Sometimes."

"May I see?"

Jenita tilted the easel, heart pounding.

Ms. Jackson's eyes softened. "Baby," she said gently, "you see beyond what you see. Such detail. You're something special, and you've got talent."

Those words stuck.

At lunch, two girls plopped down beside her. "I'm Rhonda. That's Sheila. You always sit by yourself."

Jenita shrugged. "I gotta go straight home after school."

"So!" Sheila said. "We can walk that way." And just like that, the three were inseparable.

One afternoon, Ms. Jackson pulled her aside.

"Jenita, can we talk?"

"Yes, ma'am."

"I've been watching you. You work hard. You listen. You disappear sometimes."

Jenita swallowed.

"Is everything okay at home? Your parents haven't responded to any of my phone calls or letters. Do you think they want to come to the art show? We're featuring your work. I want to get you into programs that will prepare you for college."

Jenita stared at the floor. "I'm okay. They don't want me to go to college because they don't have the money."

"Do you want to?"

"Yes, ma'am. I don't want to be a farmer. I need to make it through and get to college. I promised my nana."

Ms. Jackson nodded slowly. "I hear you. If you want to go to college, then that's what you'll do. I can come to your house and talk to your parents. College may be a way out."

"My house? A way out?" Jenita asked, barely above a whisper.

"Yes. Let me talk to them. If they listen, I'll help you find it."

After Ms. Jackson paid a visit, it became clear: even as an only child, college didn't matter to Jenita's family. They wanted her on the farm. If farming was good enough for them to survive, it was supposed to be good enough for her. No need to get high and mighty. They were not supportive, but they didn't stop her either, assuming she'd fail.

She started planning. Working part-time at the local burger spot during her junior and senior years, she saved money for books and clothes. She graduated with the class of 1988.

Nana Katie Mae had planted the idea of college in her mind, and Jenita had made a promise: not only would she go, but she would also be a first-generation college graduate. The day finally came when she stood with Rhonda and Sheila, all three of them holding acceptance letters, and she smiled. She closed her eyes and pictured Nana Katie Mae just as she remembered her. For a moment, it felt like she was right there.

"Nana… I'm going to college. I kept my word."

The thought settled deep, like a promise finally fulfilled, a quiet weight lifting—one she hadn't realized how long she'd been carrying.

She decided that day she would become a teacher or find some way to help students the way Ms. Jackson had helped her. She kept working at the burger spot whenever she came home during the summers of her freshman and sophomore years at Winston-Salem State University.

Had it not been for Upward Bound, her first two years of college would have been an even steeper climb. Years of farm work before school and a job after had left gaps the program helped fill. She spent her evenings in the library instead of hanging out, tutoring between work-study shifts in the mailroom, and sought any professor willing to help. Earning barely-A averages required late nights, early mornings, diligence, and iron discipline.

When Jenita heard about the Deltas holding an interest meeting, she didn't know if she had the grades, the time, or the money, but she went. She'd been watching them on the yard, witnessing some of the student activities they led, the way they seemed to have it together in ways that made them the most compelling presence on campus. And seeing them win step shows was something else entirely.

"Ms. Jackson, I want to go to the Delta's interest meeting, but I'm scared."

"You should be, if you aren't serious about service. But what exactly are you afraid of?"

"They may not think I belong. I spend so much time in the library, studying and working, they probably don't even know I exist."

Ms. Jackson, her angel, mentor, and favorite professor, was initiated into the sorority at WSSU in 1978.

"Well, you won't know if you don't go. So I highly recommend you do."

Jenita attended the interest meeting and came away more discouraged than before. Sixteen credit hours, a work-study job, and the way she was depending on her next check to keep from turning into a Ramen Noodle, she didn't see how she could commit to the process, let alone cover the initiation fee. She shared her concerns with Ms. Jackson.

"Never count yourself out before you start."

"But people like me don't get invited to be part of anything. My daddy said I was born to keep my head down and struggle, just like him."

"If he were standing here, I'd go toe to toe with him and prove him wrong six ways to Sunday."

A few days later, Jenita burst into her office. "Ms. Jackson! I got invited! They picked me. Me!"

Jenita couldn't believe they had selected her application. She went from happy to nervous to immediate disappointment.

"Congratulations! You were selected, so why are your eyes glued to the carpet, child?"

"I don't have the money. But it's okay. I'm just glad they picked me."

"Who said you don't have the money? Let's take a ride."

They drove to the Wachovia right down the street. Ms. Jackson handed her a blank money order.

"Fill that in and get that application turned in as soon as possible. Don't let me down."

"But I can't pay you back." She sobbed.

"Baby, you've already paid enough in your young life. Just help somebody else one day when you can. You don't ever have to pay love back. I love you, Neat."

They hugged. Jenita hadn't had an adult to hold her—really hold her—in years. Ms Jackson had become family.

"I will. And I love you, too."

She'd heard a few disturbing things about initiation experiences across historically Black colleges and universities (HBCUs) and predominantly white institutions (PWIs) and didn't know what to expect. Although there were moments during her own process she wished she could forget, what stayed with her was the bond that formed, fast and unshakable, and a sense that she had stepped into something larger than herself.

Being a member made Jenita feel connected in a way she hadn't known she needed. She found her place among women who saw her, who expected something of her, and who stood for something beyond themselves. She needed that sisterhood. She needed the bond she was forming with her line sisters, those who pledged alongside her, and her Winston Salem State University chapter.

It was something she knew she'd carry for the rest of her life. On April 6, 1991, her junior year, Jenita Rochelle Hall crossed over into Delta Land, alongside her best friends since middle school, Sheila and Rhonda.

CHAPTER 6

Friends to Family

Zander and Frank had been best friends since kindergarten, and Frank had carried a crush on his sister Renae, since third grade. Frank's family was outright poor. As he got older, his natural-born hustler instincts gradually emerged. Anyone could see that poor might be what Frank's family was, but it was not what Frank was.

Renae and Frank were in the same class, and she shared her lunch and snacks with him so often that she started asking her mom to pack his lunch while she made hers and Zander's. He'd eat the free school breakfast and lunch, then save the bag lunch Renae brought him for dinner. Without her knowledge, he'd sell the chips or cookies to buy basic things others took for granted.

It wasn't just her supplying him with food. She was kind. He thought she was so pretty, and her freckles were cute. She liked to laugh, and he could make her. She was friendly to everyone, got good grades, and helped him with that part, too.

"Frank Brinkley, do your work!" she'd say, squinting her eyes at him before breaking into a smile.

She could get him to do his schoolwork when teachers couldn't. Seeing her dance blew him away. He liked to dance, too, but she and

Zander were on another level. To him, she was nothing like the other girls.

His family, if you could call it that, lived in a house propped on cinder blocks where they could see the sun through the ceiling and the ground peeked up through the floor. His father was an old sharecropper, and his mother, who was young enough to be the man's granddaughter, had Frank at fourteen and died in childbirth two years later, pregnant again by the same man who had been in his sixties when Frank was born in 1968. Her name was Vera Brinkley.

That left Frank alone with his father and two older, mean, ugly-as-cold-homemade-hamburgers half-sisters, who were both older than Vera. Their neglect and dysfunction motivated Frank to do his schoolwork when Renae wasn't there to encourage him. They were cruel and treated Frank in ways that would have given Cinderella's evil stepsisters nightmares. Their daddy knew it and did nothing.

Folks would say, "He outlived two younger women he never married and was already sniffing around after another."

Frank didn't hate them; he didn't know how, any more than he knew love. No one would ever have guessed it, though, because he always had jokes. Back in elementary school, he came in wearing dirty clothes, sometimes the same outfit all week, smelling like pee, fresh-cut collards, and kerosene. He carried on joking and laughing as if he couldn't see or smell himself.

Even as a little boy, he'd say, "I can shoot the shit with the best of 'em."

He could work a crowd anywhere: the activity bus, the classroom, the playground, the ball field, the basketball court, Sunday school class, and anywhere he could get an audience laughing. He made up words like "bone stumps" for teeth and "tiddie holsters" for bras, and he used old folks' language like hosepipe instead of water hose, spigot instead of faucet, dungarees instead of jeans, and buying something "on time" instead of layaway.

The crowd would encircle Frank and Melvin, the two best funnymen at Jefferson High. They ran the dozens on everybody else daily, but only on rare occasions would they shoot licks at each other—and when they did, it drew a bigger crowd than a fight, a rap battle, or a sheet of cardboard when some wanna be B-boys laid out for the break-dancers.

One afternoon, they'd been going back and forth for about five minutes, and the students doubled over with laughter.

Melvin started. "Frank, I don't care how much Zee's mama cleaned you up, you used to smell like hot garbage in Augu—"

Frank cut him off before he could finish. "Look at you with them crooked-ass bone stumps. Look like you been chewing firecrackers with your mouth closed and a stump is trying to get out."

Melvin had crooked bottom teeth, one chipped front tooth, and slightly bucked teeth, so when his mouth was closed his teeth poked against the middle of his bottom lip, kind of like Bucky from *Fat Albert*.

The crowd erupted and scattered in every direction, laughing.

Nobody went head-to-head with Frank after that day. That didn't stop Frank from slipping in jokes on anybody every chance he got. He could fight, too. He had a special gift for making other kids feel ridiculous for paying for breakfast or lunch when he got his free.

"Ya'll pay for this?"

One year, during Vacation Bible School, Mrs. Fatou and Mrs. Tink took on forty children, ranging from elementary to middle school, because the other mothers worked during the day. Two old church mothers would help when they could get a ride.

The prissy crowd only showed up to show off, criticize, or check a community service box. They made a point of calling her Tink—disrespectfully, they'd say—never Sister Devereaux, the way they addressed the other women. They didn't like what they called her "backwoods hoodoo," and they suspected she was working roots on their men because Tink was stunning. However, she only had eyes for Louis Devereaux, her husband, and everybody knew that, except the gossip posse.

Tink wanted to tell them so badly, "You got your eyes on the wrong one, baby. You need to be watching your back from the very ones you hangin' with." She'd seen it in the spirit long before she heard it on the street. She also knew her own husband, Louis, had wandering eyes, wandering hands, and more than a few mistresses. She knew. He knew she knew.

Mrs. Fatou knew Frank was hungry and always brought him extra. He was a growing boy playing Little League football. The church sponsored his fees and uniform. He also excelled at basketball, too, and middle school coaches were already watching him for basketball and track. She could see he was lonely; he was always alone unless he was with her children, and he lived close enough to school that he showed up to every evening event, including PTA meetings.

Frank liked to be with people and would eat if they offered. Fatou could see that Frank was just as good for her as she was for him. She felt God was giving her children to love, the way she'd had a big family back in Senegal. She wanted to help him, but she'd noticed he'd reject things if people made the charity too obvious. The exception was Renae. And he didn't mind working.

"I'll do it, but you gotta pay me half first," he'd say, delivering newspapers, cutting grass, whatever the job was, so long as he could borrow somebody else's lawnmower.

Mrs. Fatou made him a deal. "If you come to my house and help me make the bologna and cheese sandwiches and bag up the lunches, I'll make sure you take some home. Be at my house at eight a.m. sharp."

"Yes, ma'am. You ain't said nothin' but a word."

The next morning, Frank arrived two and a half hours early and was sitting on their porch when King stepped out to leave for work. He watched King pull Fatou into him, squeezing her backside that oozed between his big hands like proofed yeast dough, giving her a kiss the boy had never seen the likes of. Frank went still.

They didn't know he was there until he giggled and let out a slow, "Greeeaaaat day!"

Fatou clutched the collar of her robe up around her neck.

King turned. "Who are you?"

"I'm Frank Brinkley. Mrs. Fatou told me to come here." Frank had a way of clearing things up before you could even finish asking.

"Son, you gotta announce yourself. You can't be sneaking up on a man, especially when he's with his woman."

"I've been sitting here since five-thirty, and I know this is her porch, but y'all snuck up on me."

King and Fatou laughed harder than Frank did.

"I like this young fella," King said, getting into this car.

Fatou smiled. "I love you, King. See you tonight."

"I can't wait to come back to you, baby. I love you." He backed out of the driveway and drove off.

Fatou looked at Frank. "Why are you so early, my darling?"

"I was thinking if I came early, I could help the other lady with breakfast and work out the same deal you and me got. Do you know where she lives?" He meant Tink.

Fatou chuckled. "She lives right across the street, but your deal is with me. Come eat with us."

"Hey, is that white man a king for real, and do his wife know he be over here?"

Frank didn't realize until that morning that Zander and Renae were twins. Seeing his crush and his best friend together, plus breakfast, lunch, and dinner in the summertime, he was in heaven. He was at their house every day after that until he became family. King loved having Frank around but grew quietly furious that the boy could be gone for weeks and no one ever came looking for him.

When Frank's fifth-grade teacher berated him, calling him "a dumb, nasty nigger" in front of the whole class, Frank's response— "And that's why your breath smells like you got doodoo stuck to the roof of your mouth"—got him expelled.

Every kid in that room said, "He ain't lying."

King intervened and got the punishment reduced to a week's suspension, then took Frank to work with him every day of it.

When Fatou later learned that Frank's father had passed away, she and King became his foster parents without hesitation. He started living with them as family and they treated him no differently than Renae and Zander. When they got new clothes, Frank got new clothes. Barbershop trips included Frank until he started hustling haircuts under their carport.

King loved the hustler in him and his never-quit spirit. Eventually, he and Fatou legally adopted Frank as their son. They loved him so much that they gave him their last name. He wanted it badly. They kept Brinkley as his middle name in honor of his late mother. He legally became Frank Brinkley Devereaux in his last year of middle school. He started calling Fatou "Mama" and King "Pops" before the ink was dry. Zander loved it and didn't mind sharing his room. Frank had been his brother since day one, adoption papers or not.

Renae didn't like it. She gave Frank what she considered pure hell, though Frank had weathered worse from his half-sisters on their best days. It wasn't clear why Renae was so sharp with him when all Frank ever was with her was sweet…until sophomore year.

Students kept saying, "Your brother did this" or "Your brother did that," particularly about sports. Renae would snap back, out of character, "Zander is my twin. Frank is adopted." She'd say it with a force that sounded like malice. All to realize, deep down, she had to face the truth: Renae loved Frank. She'd been ashamed when he smelled like pee, fresh-cut collards, and kerosene, but she'd liked him even then.

In an emotional breakdown before senior prom, when everyone else had dates and she didn't, Renae cried and went to her daddy and confessed. Fatou and Tink hadn't been told until after the adoption, though they'd quietly wondered between themselves how long it would be before Renae's feelings boiled over. She was every bit a daddy's girl as Zander was a mama's boy, and King was stunned.

Olayemi Renae Devereaux came into the world second, a bouncing baby girl, the twin to her brother. She had her daddy written all over her: warm, ivory skin the color of a sugar cookie, the cutest freckles, and loose golden-brown coils, a clear nod to King's Creole roots. Her first name was a nod to his Nigerian roots. She was the younger twin by minutes, but a whole pound heavier than Zander, and from the day they started babbling, she talked enough for both of them.

"Zee. Zee. ZANDER," she'd say, tugging his sleeve.

"Mmm hmm," he'd answer, nodding like that settled it.

Much like her mother, Renae had the innate gift of being the life of the party and the energy to infuse good vibes into any room just by walking into it. She was everybody's professional auntie from the time she was five years old.

"Do it like this. Or let me help you."

"Uh-uh. You gon' fall, and then what?"

"Here. Take one. But this is the last freeze pop."

"Streetlights 'bout to come on, y'all. Let's go!"

Telling kids on the playground what to do, how not to act, and offering help and advice or whatever candy or snacks she had, Renae was jovial, a go-getter, and a go-giver. She was responsible, accountable, and friendly, all wrapped in a young body. She had her father's business sense and her mother's warmth. She had her mom's cooking skills, too, but she concentrated more on baking.

"Ma, is the oven ready yet?"

'Ola, *sois patient*… slow down."

"I am patient, Mama."

When everyone else was chasing boys, Renae was baking or practicing for dance contests she and Zander entered together.

"Which song you wanna use?" she'd ask.

He'd shrug.

"Come on, Zee, you gotta feel it."

"Mmm hmm."

He didn't say much, but once the music started, his body spoke for him, cool and effortless, every step sure, every turn smooth, moving in sync with Renae like they'd been born to dance together. They had a good run, but danced less as they got older, with Zander pulling more toward football and basketball, while every girl in school was pulling toward him. Renae was so sick of girls always asking her about her brother.

"Zee got a girlfriend? Is Zander talking to anybody?"

She'd exhale hard. "Girl, go get your lesson or some business."

She thought they were immature. Baking, dancing, and sewing became her companions. As puberty settled in, some folks couldn't tell her and her mother apart from behind. She was proud of her Senegalese heritage and would interchange traditional Senegalese attire and Black American girl fashion like breathing, sometimes crossing them up so thoroughly it looked like she couldn't make up her mind, and maybe she didn't have to.

"*Tu es magnifique!* I like your outfit, baby girl," Fatou would say.

"You always do, Mama." She'd smile.

"Because it is you."

Looking like a kaleidoscope with curves, embracing it with contagious confidence. If authentic joy and ease and good energy were a person, it would be Renae. She was the more potent version of what her mother might have been if she wasn't carrying the weight of her Senegalese family left behind, the grief carried quietly in Fatou's heart and mind. Renae felt none of that heaviness. She moved freely.

She loved her mama.

"That's my girl," Fatou would whisper, brushing past her.

Zander was her best friend. "You good?" she'd ask.

"I'm a'ight."

King made her work hard in school and after, but she had him wrapped around her finger, and she knew it. She also knew she could get anything she wanted from him, but as an extension of her mother, she never had to ask. Sometimes all she had to do was look at him, and he'd already be reaching for his wallet or his keys. "I got it."

She could talk to Zander about anything because he wasn't much of a talker but a great listener and observer. Without his occasional "mmm hmm" and slow nod just like their Pops. Anyone watching would think she was talking to herself. Animated hands, expressive eyes, not brassy but never mysterious: you always knew exactly where Renae stood.

She first noticed Frank because he wore the same green, blue, and white striped shirt and cut-off black shorts all week long.

"He ain't got no other clothes?" she whispered.

Zander shrugged. "Ask him."

His hair was always uneven, as if he'd cut it with dull scissors because he did, at school. He smelled. Sometimes she'd hold her breath.

"Lord," she'd mutter, wondering why.

But there was something about his sense of humor, his gift of gab, his fierce protectiveness of everything he was learning to love, and he had the hustle in him that made her like him.

"Don't mess with her," Frank snapped at a bigger kid one day.

Renae raised an eyebrow. "I ain't ask you to."

He grinned. "I know."

He acted just like Pops. And he was cute.

She didn't like that he and Zander had gotten so close, worried Frank would start seeing her as a sister. She hated that with a passion.

As time went on and he came to live with them, he bathed daily, bulked up, smelled good, and dressed to impress. That only made her like him more. Frank got fine.

When she found out her parents were officially his foster parents, she turned to baking to soothe her teenage heartache. She baked and ate, and it showed. But she didn't lose an ounce of confidence. Once the adoption was final and Fatou and King had given him the last name, she felt confused and displaced, carrying feelings for someone who was now, on paper, her brother.

Frank started cutting hair under their carport for pocket change that he always saved. Saturday mornings, boys lined up in their driveway on their bikes, waiting. He could cut the latest fades, high-top fades, Gumbys, and whatever parts and styles young boys wanted. The local barbers didn't offer those looks and quietly lost their younger clientele to Frank. He was better and cheaper.

Renae got her hair cut in layers, stacked and tapered in the back, with Frank keeping her neckline faded. She talked him into letting her offer low-budget facials to his clients—warm, wet washcloths laid over faces, loose hairs brushed off with a soft new paintbrush, finished with Pond's cream and a splash of Brute aftershave. She charged a dollar. Or for the same dollar, two big cookies or a thick slice of cake.

She and Frank had the creativity, grit, and energy to always find a way to make money. She'd get jealous and wander outside whenever another girl came to get her neck done. She offered them the same facials but upgraded—a Noxzema cleanse for an extra fifty cents, then the Pond's finished with a splash of Exclamation perfume while Renae herself wore Gloria Vanderbilt. She'd make small talk just long enough to be nosy, while doing her best to ignore or redirect any fast-tailed girls who'd come along asking about Zander.

Frank would cut Zander's hair in the bathroom upstairs, sitting in a chair they'd move into the tub. He was particular about his hair, but he'd come outside afterward to listen to Frank's "crazyment." His laugh was quiet and easy, but it came with tears when something really got him. He'd occasionally slip in a smooth joke on Frank or anyone who deserved it.

But when fast-tailed girls showed up, especially the ones known for going down on boys, he'd hightail it into the house or head across the street to Tink's until he started dating Crystal. After that, he was either in the house or out with her. Theirs was a puppy love that made the happy happier and the jealous more jealous. Zander wasn't confrontational unless seriously provoked, which made Renae and Frank feel naturally protective of him. They took the job seriously and carried it out with ease.

But every time Renae sat in Frank's chair, his heart would pound and his hands would shake. He had to concentrate to keep the clippers steady. Zander noticed and kept it to himself. Frank loved Renae, but he was too grateful for being a Devereaux, a son, a brother, a nephew to let his love for her move out of pocket. He allowed himself to love her the only way available: like a sister. Not Renae. Her father's go-getter drive wouldn't let her romantic feelings bow to an adoption paper. Her heart wouldn't allow it. So, when she went to Pops and confessed her love for Frank, the one thing she asked for was permission not to be forced to love Frank as her brother, even if she couldn't act on it.

Fatou and Pops tried to console her, but when prom came, she knew it would feel wrong to go with Frank, so she didn't go at all. Frank went alone. He arrived late, money to make, prom attendees' hair to cut, walked in dressed to impress, laughing and joking and turning out the dance floor with Zander, the two of them running through every move that had a name. But when Zander headed out early with plans to meet Crystal at a hotel outside of town, Frank made his way home.

He stopped at the store on the way and picked up Renae's favorite candies. When he got home, she was sitting on the front porch alone, looking like she'd lost her best companions: her baking, her dancing, her sewing, and Frank. She'd been crying earlier, and Tink had done what she could to console her in ways her parents couldn't reach. Frank walked up the steps, moved past her, and sat down beside her on the swing.

"What's wrong, Renae?"

She said nothing.

He waited patiently, then opened the small, brown paper bag and dumped it onto her lap so fast she had to press her thighs together fast to catch the smaller pieces.

"Dang, Renae! Your thighs gettin' so big they chew candy, too?"

Her big, pillowy, sugar-cookie thighs didn't let a single piece slip. He noticed. He liked what he saw.

"Shut up, Frank. You so stupid."

"So stupid, I bought you some candy." He reached down, pretending to take a piece back.

Renae smacked his hand with all the frustration and candy-protection she could muster—harder than she meant to. No boy's hand had ever gotten that close to her thighs.

"Stop, boy!"

"Ouch! Why you hit me so hard?" He frowned, pulling his hand up to his mouth to soothe it. Frowning was rare for Frank, and it showed, not just that it hurt, but that it hurt his feelings more. He would never try to touch Renae inappropriately, never try to hurt her, or hurt her feelings. She knew that.

Realizing that the smack was too hard, she laughed and mimicked her mama's Senegalese accent. "Dis big bwoy gon' cry? Aye!" She rolled her eyes, sucked her teeth, and turned her head just right.

She had the accent, the movements, and the sound perfected. Picking up each piece of candy—thighs still clasped—she looked at Frank for silent confirmation, then took the paper bag from his hand and began putting everything back: Chico Sticks, grape Now and Later, a box of Lemonheads, a Snickers bar, a pack of Hubba Bubba, a double pack of Wrigley's Doublemint gum, and a pack of Nutter Butter cookies.

Frank returned from his micro moment of ego shock. "Them peanut butter cookies ain't yours!"

He held his hand out. He would have snatched the whole bag back from any other girl, but not her. She placed the Nutter Butters in it, dropped her head, and went right back to her sadness. He grew quiet, which was rare for Frank, because he was afraid to say the next thing. He knew that if he tried to comfort her, the truth of how he felt would fall right out of his mouth. Frank didn't have a lie button.

He was truthful to a fault. And with Renae, Mama, and Aunt Tink being the only women he'd ever loved, his mother having died when he was three, he revered them all. The two of them sat in silence, which was uncomfortable for two people who never stopped talking. But their mutual love was saying more than either could, louder than the cookie and candy wrappers they were pretending to be busy with.

They both reached for a Chico Stick at the same time. Though they'd touched each other before, something was different this time. Both drew their hands back as if they'd been shocked. Then they reached for it again. Their eyes met. Frank had the bigger half. He yielded.

He looked directly into her tear-tinted, lovable eyes. "You can have it, Renae."

"No, you take it. I'll eat the Snickers."

Silence settled between them again. The TV from inside, random cars passing, the hum of the streetlights was all there was. Frank cleared his throat a few times, eating his Chico Stick faster than most people could manage without choking, half-convinced she could hear his heartbeat.

"Frank, I don't like you being my adopted brother. You should have just told them to let you stay as Frank Brinkley and live here regular."

"Why not?"

"Just because."

"Because why?"

"Because I don't," she said, chewing through the Snickers caramel.

"You don't have to be mean about it. I didn't ask to be your brother. I ain't even want to be your brother. I wanted to be Zander's brother."

"Well, Sherlock, how you gon' be Zander's brother and not mine when we're twins?"

"You just had to come with the family package, huh?"

"Whatchu talking 'bout?"

"You heard me."

"Well, why didn't you wanna be my brother?"

Frank looked straight ahead and put a whole cookie in his mouth. Renae studied his profile. His fair skin, his athletic frame in his tux, the streetlight catching the side of his face, he was more attractive than she wanted to admit.

She listened to him crunching. "And why are you eatin' those pitiful store-bought cookies? If you wanted peanut butter cookies, I could have made you some."

"You don't want me to be your brother, but you'd make me cookies?" His mouth was still full, eyes still forward.

Renae didn't answer right away. He swallowed the cookies and the words together.

"Huh?" She turned just as he turned toward her.

"You gon' make me some cookies?"

"No. Not now."

"Tomorrow?"

"No. Unless you're paying."

"How much?"

"Five dollars a dozen."

"A dozen?" Frank exclaimed. "Sheeeeeet, that's robbery!"

Renae laughed out loud. "Yep. And I know you got money."

"You got money, too. Probably more than me if that's what you charge for some damn cookies." They both laughed.

"What's so special about your cookies that you're charging five dollars?"

"Because it's me making them. That's why."

Frank reached into his front pocket the way he'd watched the Devereaux men do, pulled out a wad of folded bills, and drew one from the middle. He held out a twenty.

"Money don't impress me. I got money, and my daddy's got money."

"I wasn't trying to impress you, Renae. But if you're making cookies for me, they'll be worth twenty dollars because you're making them."

It was what he said, and how he said it, and the way he looked at her when he said it, like he could feel her heart through her eyes. It told her everything. His reason for not wanting to be her brother was the same as her reason for not wanting to be his sister. The unspoken had finally started speaking.

They were slowly leaning toward each other when the headlights of Uncle Louis' car came down the street, fresh off pretending to be a prom chaperone.

Renae snatched the twenty from Frank's hand. "I'll have your dozen tomorrow."

Frank dropped his head so she wouldn't see him blush. She opened the screen door as it closed behind her with a loud, metallic clap against the door frame.

Once he heard her slippers sliding across the hardwood floors inside, he whispered to himself, "They ain't the only cookies I want. I love you, Renae."

Frank knew his heart belonged to Renae. Zander knew it. Fatou and Tink knew it.

CHAPTER 7

Names Change

Zander could croon gospel tunes and R&B as if he'd lived through every note or break into an old Senegalese song in ways the ancestors would be proud of. But none of that had a place in Jefferson High's chorus class in 1985. There, he kept it to Sammy Davis Jr. or Nat King Cole to appease white folks. Walking in one day, he spotted a girl. She seemed to know a few of the other students, but he didn't recognize her right away. Their eyes met. He looked away fast, because he had his ribbon on, the last thing he needed was another wannabe huncher getting the wrong idea.

But when it was time for class to begin, their teacher wasn't there, which meant unruly behavior and hell for a substitute. Some boys went straight for the timpani drums, gongs, and cymbals in the shared band room. Some girls joined in on the percussion. A few planted themselves on the black piano bench and started plunking away. The substitute never had a chance.

Then in walked his uncle Louis.

Zander blinked rapidly, lashes working like they were trying to put out a fire, making absolutely sure he was seeing what he thought he was seeing.

Uncle Louis looked directly at him. One look said everything: "You BED-NOT say a word." No words needed when the eyes have it.

Louis was two years younger than King and shorter, slimmer. They didn't look alike, but they shared the same stately presence that ran in the family—perfect posture, a debonair and quietly intimidating presence that commanded any room they entered. Zander carried a younger version of it.

He could run up and down a football field or a basketball court like a champion, but right now his legs were failing him entirely. He wanted to move. He was stuck. The only things working were the fear spreading through his chest and the air drying out his wide-open mouth.

"Problem, young man?" Uncle Louis slammed the door behind him so hard that several students squealed out loud. "I said—do you have a problem, young man?"

"Nn… nn… no, sir," Zander stuttered, licking his lips to get some moisture back so he could swallow.

Thunderously, as if it were God himself speaking: "Well sit down! Find a seat and sit down now!" The same fear that had rooted Zander to the spot helped him find his legs to do exactly that.

"And I want everyone else seated before I reach my chair." Every student scrambled. Some didn't make it to an actual seat and dropped wherever they were, whether on the floor or against the wall. No one dared part their lips to ask a neighbor who this man was.

"I am Mr. James. Louis James. And I am your new chorus teacher."

His legal last name was Devereaux. But King and Louis had a long-standing agreement: when it served them, Louis, Tink, and their children used King's and Louis' middle names as a last name, a deliberate, strategic camouflage for paperwork involving property, contract bids, or anything else that required keeping nosy people out of their business.

King and Fatou owned King's & Queen's and the Brown Sugar Beach Motel, and King specialized in carpentry. Louis and Tink owned a subcontracting business, and Louis was a licensed electrician, a license the local, oppressive power structure was doing its best to undermine. And now, a schoolteacher. King and his bachelor's degrees were from Southern University, an HBCU—King's in business administration and his in music—and he used it as something to fall back on rather than a ceiling. Louis played piano at King's & Queen's, welcoming Black and white folks and anyone in between. He could "sang." Or he could keep it "What's Going On" smooth, that slow Marvin Gaye groove, and have the whole crowd swaying without trying.

Louis loved money and music, though he had a habit of calling on either when it suited him, much like he did with gorgeous women, a trait people noticed but rarely held against him. He did not discriminate: Black, white, Creole, African, French, Hispanic, mixed race. One of his children's mothers was Italian. If the women were beautiful, he couldn't resist, and they generally couldn't either. Tink took his breath away. Just not enough to curb his appetite for other beautiful women.

She knew exactly who and what Louis was before they married. Nothing changed after. Tink never conceived children of her own, but she kept his as her own and was largely unbothered by Louis's escapades, because she could intervene whenever she chose, and he knew it.

As Louis made his way to his seat, he made eye contact with each student as he passed. "I know I walked into the band room. But this is not band class. No one is to ever touch an instrument during this period unless I hand it to you—even if you're in the band, even if you play." It was a new day.

Zander hadn't noticed until now that he'd ended up sitting beside the girl he'd spotted earlier. He recognized her now, she came to North Carolina some summers from New York City to stay with her aunt in the neighborhood. While Mr. James established order with the precision of a drill instructor, no one in the room seemed to breathe without permission.

"Everyone, turn to the last piece you've been working on for the Christmas concert."

"Ah. I see." He sat and plunked out the first few notes slowly, as if searching for them—then swept his hand up and down the keys in a blended medley of classical, jazz, and gospel that silenced any remaining doubt about who he was. Impressive. Zander chuckled to himself. "Get it, Uncle Lou." He played at church, too, and directed the choir. The man lived inside music, even when he pretended otherwise.

Once they began to sing, the mood lightened just enough for the girl beside him to whisper, "Don't act like you don't know me, Ibra."

"Shh. "Don't nobody call me that. It's Zander. Or Zee."

She whispered, "Well, don't act like you don't know me, Zander or Zee." "I know you, Crystal."

CHAPTER 8

Rewind, 1985–1988

Crystal hadn't been back to North Carolina to visit her aunt since middle school, back when she breathed hard through her mouth, had bad acne, and what some boys cruelly called a chicken head. Short hair, slightly bucked teeth, but a nice smile.

"Leave her alone," Zander had said back then, tossing a towel over his shoulder. "She's cool."

Now, the new and improved Crystal barely recognized that girl herself. She was beautiful, shaped like a BET video girl, even if she didn't quite know how to work it yet. Her deep mocha skin was flawless, her black Jheri curl silky, her smile Kodak-ready thanks to braces that had done their job.

When Zander finally worked up the nerve to see if he could get his "mack" on, Crystal tilted her head and asked, "Why is that red ribbon on your arm?"

He hesitated. "Just... something my auntie gave me."

"Aunt Tink?"

"Yeah."

A few years earlier, Zander and his friends had treated Crystal like their little homey—the one who held towels at Brown Sugar Beach or sat on the sidelines while they played ball. They talked about girls they liked right in front of her, comfortably, as if she didn't count.

Somewhere along the way, that changed.

Crystal didn't realize how much she'd changed, only that the same boys who once benched her in the friend zone were suddenly paying attention. On sight.

Case in point: Zander.

After weeks of drill-sergeant-style instruction, Uncle Louis, known as Mr. James at school, had the chorus sounding polished.

"Again," he'd bark. "From the top. And mean it."

Zander hadn't known that winter slowed motel business or that Uncle Louis had taken the teaching job to make up the difference. He didn't know about the conversations Louis had been having with teachers and coaches, either.

"Your boys have potential," one coach said.

"They need scholarships," Louis replied flatly.

Solo selection came, and everyone assumed Zander would get one. He always did.

Mr. James never called his name.

Zander stayed after class. "Uncle Louis—Mr. James—I just wanted to—"

"No." He didn't look up.

Zander tried again later, outside of school. "Why?"

Uncle Louis sighed. "Your daddy already told you. Music will have your pockets singing the blues. No, Zander. No."

That one hurt.

Losing always cut him deeper than he let on—a missed solo, a lost game, a test that didn't go the way he'd planned. When things pressed in ways that Mama, Daddy, Renae, Tink, or even Frank couldn't fix, he stopped wearing Tink's ribbon.

"I'm good," he said whenever someone noticed.

The one thing that shifted him was Crystal. Everybody was talking to her now, but she only had eyes for him. She didn't chase him. They were friends first. That made people jealous.

"You're always with her," somebody said.

"So?" Zander shrugged.

Crystal had heard about his reputation and wanted no part of it. "I'm not that girl," she told Renae once.

"Good," Renae said. "Zee better stop trying to be that boy."

Zander was tired—tired of the bad crowd, tired of pretending. His parents' love stood in sharp contrast to everything he saw everywhere else.

"Man," somebody at the barbershop laughed, "hit all you can while you can." Even some men from church nodded along.

His coach thumped him on the shoulder one afternoon. "A good blow job can clear your mind after practice or after a game. You'll play better."

But afterward, alone, Zander felt something chip away at him each time. *This ain't it*, he thought.

It had started at thirteen, and by seventeen, the summer before senior year, he already felt worn down. He wanted something more. And the only person he wanted that with was Crystal.

"She's a virgin," Frank said quietly one day.

Zander shrugged. "I know."

He knew Crystal's story: Brooklyn, a brother with AIDS, crack in the household, family sending her south to live with Aunt Cheryl.

"Better in Carolina," her parents had decided.

Aunt Cheryl's grown kids were college graduates. Cheryl had lived alone. At first.

"You good here?" Zander asked Crystal once.

"Yeah. Most days I miss my mama and daddy."

Crystal dressed cute but modest. Kmart clothes, no labels. She still turned heads.

"She looks way better than half these fast-tailed girls," Renae said.

At Christmas, Mr. James gave Crystal a solo. When she finished singing, there wasn't a body in a seat.

"Encore!" someone shouted.

Only Zander knew she was singing from pain. When he asked her to be his girlfriend that summer, she said yes.

"I liked you forever," she admitted later.

The first day they became official, he'd begged her to wear his letterman jacket. When she walked in wearing his letterman jacket, if looks could kill, she would've died nine times over. But she wasn't bragging; she was just wearing his jacket.

Fast girls hovered.

"She's with me," Zander said, firm.

They walked everywhere together. Ate lunch together. His friends called him lame.

"Whatever," he said.

He waited patiently.

Crystal worked alongside him, Renae, and Frank. Aunt Cheryl had suddenly told her she needed a job.

"For what?" Crystal asked, confused.

Money had gotten funny. Pops noticed. So did Fatou. She and Tink saw Cheryl's brand new 1986 Cutlass Supreme, but only her crack-dealing boyfriend drove it. She showed all the signs of being a functioning addict.

"She may stay with us," Fatou said finally.

King paid her to work. "Work alongside Renae and the boys, that's your job now."

Crystal smiled for the first time in weeks. "Thank you."

Thanksgiving was major for Fatou and Tink. They went all out for the customers at King's & Queen's, their employees, for church members, for anyone in need, and over the top for their own families, stretching the celebration from November first to December 22, the twins' birthday. It was better than Christmas. But their busyness kept them away from the house for long stretches, and Zander and Crystal saw their moment.

His room was the perfect spot, positioned over the carport, with a sightline to the driveway so they could see and hear anyone coming. Zander already had the condoms. They had the location and the privacy because Frank and Renae were gone, quietly working out their own situation. Everything was in place.

Crystal was tense because he would be her first. Zander was on edge for the opposite reason: for the first time, he was supposed to guide. Every encounter he'd had before, some girl had taken the wheel. He was quietly most preoccupied with the bra—his friends had bragged about unhooking one single-handed while kissing and touching at the same time. He'd shared only extended kisses with Crystal. That, at least, they were good at. It was the one thing that steadied both of them.

They kissed softly at first, small, tentative pecks, then deeper, as if stopping might break the spell of how comfortable this felt. She was used to her body responding to him; he was used to taking care of himself after she left. But this time, they could keep going, and they did.

He took his time with her, touching gently and following her cues. When he struggled with the clasp of her bra, she laughed and freed it herself. The sight of her made him pause. He had never moved this slowly before, never been the one guiding the moment. He wanted to be careful with her.

When he lowered his head, he tried to please her the way he had heard other men describe. She wasn't sure what she was supposed to feel yet. It was warm and unfamiliar, and she felt too shy to fully relax, but he seemed eager to learn her body, so she let him continue.

When he sensed she wasn't enjoying it as much as he hoped, he shifted. Slowly, he used his fingers the way he had once before. This time she responded immediately, her hips moving against his hand without thinking. He paused, checking in with her as he attempted to move inside her.

"Does this hurt?"

"A little," she said softly. "But keep trying. I want this."

She pressed her hips forward to receive more of him. He felt pleasure while she worked through the discomfort. Still aroused from what came before, he barely lasted a minute. She was quietly relieved to have reached this milestone with the only boy she'd ever loved.

Crystal's home situation grew rougher. King and Fatou didn't know she and Zander were sexually active under their roof; they simply wanted to take her in the way they'd taken in Frank. But Aunt Cheryl wouldn't allow a formal arrangement, even as she stopped caring about what Crystal actually did.

On Valentine's Day, the school buzzed with love-grams and gift exchanges. Zander and Crystal were one of the expected couples. He had gotten her pregnant. They'd been careful, but one time led to a second, and they forgot protection. After he'd learned to control his body's response and she'd finally understood what all the fuss about sex was, she wanted to try again. When Aunt Cheryl found out she was pregnant, she threw a fit and threatened to send Crystal back to Brooklyn. But her parents wouldn't take her back home pregnant. Fatou stepped in without hesitation, taking Crystal and the baby in so she could finish high school. Zander and Frank moved across the street to Louis and Tink's—convenient and proper. King and Fatou didn't think it right, customary, or Christian-like for Zander and Crystal to live under the same roof unmarried.

King and his Queen were not about to let a teenage pregnancy derail Zander's future. They wanted the same for Crystal, but she was determined not to leave her child. Fatou understood completely. She and Tink folded Crystal in and took her under their wings, while Zander, Renae, and Frank headed off to college.

Zander didn't tell Renae or Frank what happened on prom night until they were away at college. Even then, he spared them the details he didn't have the stomach to repeat. He named names. He shared the facts. That was all.

Frank's silent rage was immediate and unmistakable. Equally silent tears. A festering, unfamiliar desire to do violence that reminded him of his own childhood traumas, the ones only Fatou and Tink knew about. He had no jokes. No smile. No words. Nothing to add, nothing to deflect with. Just the weight of it. He blamed himself. *My brother and his family saved my life, and I wasn't there to protect him. For damn sure, that will never happen again.*

Feeling sympathetic trauma, Renae was in tears of disbelief! She believed every word, as her brother had never lied to her about anything, and this wasn't something you invented. Zander made them both promise, and he made it a demand: never tell a soul.

In the fall of 1986, the three of them settled into college. Zander and Frank enrolled at Tubman State University, a private HBCU in Jaxton, North Carolina. Renae went to Piedmont Culinary School, specializing in baking and pastry arts. They assumed they'd drift into their own separate college lives and barely see each other. Instead, Zander and Frank were inseparable, and they drove to see Renae on weekends when they didn't have games.

Zander earned both academic and football scholarships. Frank earned a full ride playing basketball. And just like in high school, the same kind of groupie girls who were attracted to Zander in high school found Zander at TSU. No love, no real intimacy, barely kissing, just receiving oral sex he wanted and didn't want, facilitated by athletic peer pressure, he still hadn't figured out how to refuse.

Frank had his share of girls, too, checking off his peer pressure boxes with the fellas and teammates. But his heart stayed with Renae. And Frank wasn't her only one, either. Now that they were apart, they mailed love letters. Frank pumped ten dollars in quarters at a time into payphones to call her. Renae shook her head at her long-distance phone bill every month. "Shoot, gas is cheaper."

Knowing the family would be together for Sunday dinner, Zander called home religiously. He didn't hang out with his teammates as much as they would've liked, which gave him grace to focus on football. He wasn't in love with the game—maybe he never had been. What he cared about was what Pops and Uncle Louis were building: business, making money, and real estate. He disciplined his mind to stay there, because too much empty space let in the things he didn't want to think about.

Frank, now six-foot-three, was the leading scorer on the basketball team. Between being the life of every party and running an unofficial barbershop out of his dorm room, he had also claimed the payphone on his side of the hall. Nobody challenged him on it. When it rang for someone else, the whole floor would holler, "Aye, man, you got a call on Frank's phone."

He was lovable, popular, a natural jokester, and one of the best barbers around. But everyone also understood not to test him, especially where his brother, Zander, was concerned. Zee, as all his teammates called him. That nickname had followed Zander from home and caught on fast once he became popular on the yard, as his football highlights started showing up on local TV and his stats ran in the papers. Nobody could mispronounce Zee. Yes, it mattered more than people realized. It stuck. And somewhere in the sticking, it felt like he'd quietly left the wounded version of himself—Zander, the victim—a little further behind.

Frank and Renae were seeing each other in secret. What had started as a timid kiss on the cheek, then extended hugs, then a peck, had become something entirely adult, grown folks love, a few times over, sealing what they'd felt for each other regardless of what any adoption papers said. They were so committed that they'd quietly given each other a shared pet name: "Snucks."

"Don't call me that out loud," Renae warned him once, laughing.

"Too late, Snucks," Frank said, grinning. "It fits just like we do."

It would have been easier to keep carrying on at a distance, but Renae completed her culinary certification with honors and awards and returned home to work in the dining hall and at the motel. The semester was nearly over. Zee and Frank would be heading back soon.

Zee was eager to be present for his child, even though Crystal was no longer interested in him as a boyfriend or future husband. She didn't hate him; she was done with the romantic part and committed to co-parenting, full stop.

The trio's plan had always been to return home and fold their education into the motel and the family's expanding businesses. That plan still held. But it wouldn't come without risk, tragedy, and hardship, none of them had seen coming.

Renae turned the question over in her mind: how were she and Snucks going to manage their relationship once they were all back under the same roof, working together? It had been manageable when she came home alone. With Frank and Zee returning, she felt the tangle of it tightening. She and Frank had started sleeping together regularly and were, plainly, addicted to each other. Frank loved every inch of her—her skin, her five-foot frame, her size, down to the bone.

"Plus size is fun size," he'd say.

Renae would slip away to see him when she was off; he'd book the hotel rooms. She didn't think her parents and aunt and uncle knew. They did. They remembered their own "sneakery" well enough. "Chips off the old block don't fly far."

Though Renae and Frank shared no blood, the adoption papers made it feel complicated, like something wrong that felt exactly right. But after the terrible accident, none of that seemed to matter the way it once did. They needed each other to grieve. They went to the justice of the peace and got married. To them, the marriage rendered the adoption beside the point. Pops didn't argue.

CHAPTER 9

As Fate Would Have It

Aunt Tink—Ann Marie Oxendine Devereaux—was a gorgeous woman who made women straighten their backs and men clear their throats. *Cosmopolitan* cover-worthy without trying. But if anyone had ever suggested such a thing, she would have smiled politely and said she belonged on the cover of *Jet* or *Ebony* instead.

Beauty, however, was the least remarkable thing about her. What set her apart was older than mirrors. She carried hoodoo the way other women carried Scripture—memorized, internalized, lived. She did, too.

"Ann Marie," her father would call from the yard in Charleston, watching her crouched over some half-finished creation. "What you tinkerin' with now?"

She barely looked up. "Fixin' it."

He'd laugh. "That's all you ever do. Tinkerin' and prayin'. Tink. That's what I'm gon' call you." And the name stayed.

Her hands could make earrings, bracelets, crocheted blankets, hats, scarves, baskets, and pottery. But it was what they did unseen that marked her. Her mother was the first to correct people about what that was. It happened on a humid afternoon when a woman from down the road lingered too long on their porch, eyes drifting over the drying herbs in the window.

"I heard y'all do that voodoo," the woman said carefully.

Tink's mother didn't flinch. "Hoodoo. And it is not the same."

The woman crossed her arms. "It's all spirits and spells."

"No," her mother said calmly. "Vodou is a religion. It comes from the Fon and Ewe people of West Africa. Enslaved Africans carried those traditions to Haiti, where they blended with Catholicism and became Haitian Vodou. That's a faith, rooted in ancestors and community. Those dolls people talk about? That's mostly white folks made-up storytelling and misunderstanding, not the religion itself. That's what I know about that."

She stepped aside so the woman could see the jars lining the shelves. "What we do is hoodoo. Folk healing. Prayer over remedy. It developed here, in the South. On plantations. In kitchens. In backyards. That's why some say 'workin' roots', because some of the teas and healing herbs are roots from the ground. And they ain't never supposed to be used to harm nobody."

She picked up a jar of salve. "When doctors wouldn't treat us, this did. It healed us up good. When the law wouldn't protect us, this shielded us. Kept us alive. When babies burned with fever, this drew it out."

She held the woman's gaze. "Church walls ain't the only place God moves."

The woman had nothing else to say.

Inside that house in South Carolina, spirituality was not elective. It was breath.

Tink's father was half-Lumbee Indian and half-Black. Her mother was half-white and half-Black. Charleston blood braided with ancestral memory. They didn't pass superstition; it was spiritual survival.

"Education is fine," her mother would say while grinding herbs. "But knowing how to keep yourself and your people alive and well? That's sacred."

Each of the four children carried a gift: protection, healing, prosperity work, justice petitions, ancestral veneration, discernment.

Tink carried all of them. She was prophetic in a way that unsettled people. She would say things softly that later unfolded loudly.

When her father moved the family to New Orleans for opportunity, his own shrimping boat and his own crew, her mother had her own reasons for agreeing.

"Maybe down there," she told her husband quietly, "our babies won't face so much color foolishness. Creoles understand mixed blood. Light skin. And they understand spirit."

New Orleans understood spirit. But it misunderstood her. It didn't take long before whispers followed her white-clad figure through the market.

"She do voodoo."

Tink stopped correcting everyone. But when someone asked her directly, she answered. One afternoon, a young mother brought her coughing child.

"You ain't gon' stick pins or needles in nothing, are you?" the woman asked nervously.

Tink's brow lifted. "Pins are for my sewing. The only needles I have are for my sewing, crocheting, and knitting. If you see something you like, you can buy it after I tend to this child." Her voice stayed steady. She had learned people feared what they didn't understand.

She warmed mint salve between her palms and began rubbing it onto the boy's chest, behind his ears, and along the soles of his feet.

"Wrap him tight in that towel. Let him sweat."

The woman hesitated. "This ain't...witchcraft?"

Tink tied the cloth gently around the boy's neck. "If you ever had castor oil for your stomach," she said calmly, "or Epsom salt in your bath...if your grandmother ever bound cabbage leaves to your mama's breasts to dry her milk after weaning a baby...placed a small piece of folded brown paper bag between the upper lip and gum (the frenulum) to turn off a nosebleed...if somebody gave you a hot toddy to break a fever...sweetgum tea to quiet a cough or soothe a sore throat...used rags dipped in turpentine oil to bring down the swellin' or draw out the pain you've already met hoodoo."

She began whispering Isaiah 53:5 and praying Psalm 91 and 23 under her breath.

"It's prayer married to what the earth provides."

The boy's breathing eased before they left her porch.

Hoodoo was not a spectacle. It was a sacred, earth-rooted system that drew from West African folk wisdom and native herbal knowledge. Not a religion, but a collection of practices—healing, protection, prosperity, justice work—woven through Scripture and ancestral memory. It defied professional medicine not because it despised doctors, but because doctors often despised the people who needed it most. It kept enslaved bodies whole. It soothed the poor. It mended skin and bone. It restored dignity.

Someone once compared it to Jesus spitting in dirt and making mud to heal a blind man. He could have simply spoken healing or touched him. But He didn't. Tink never argued that comparison.

Backyard neighbors whispered while hanging clothes on the clothesline.

"She say she talk to dead people."

Tink walked over to the chain-link fence that separated the backyards.

"That whispering ain't quiet enough. I don't set-roun' chantin', trying to bring nobody back or worship nobody but God. All I do is respect the lives of people who have gone on. 'Cause ain't a soul ever been born whose spirit ain't still alive. I just let the good ones teach what they learned and show me what I can't see for myself. When they wanna talk, I quiet my mind enough to listen and preshate 'em for letting us put our feet on their shoulders. And if you ever laid a wreath, put flowers on a grave, talked to a headstone or their picture, come together to remember 'em after they long gone—you do it too. I'm just better at it."

She dressed in all white, matronly skirts, pressed blouses, headwrap wound carefully at the crown. Her two jet-black braids hung down her back like punctuation marks. The simplicity toned down her beauty. The white made her look pristine. Holy.

Feared by those who didn't understand her. Protected by those who did. By twenty-two, unmarried and luminous, she had become a subject of suspicion.

"A woman that pretty and ain't got no husband?" someone muttered in the grocer's line. "Something's wrong with her. Must be spoiled."

Tink simply lifted her chin. There was nothing barren about a woman saturated in spiritual inheritance. Her predestination had been whispered over her before she had language for it. And whether people named it properly or not, the same God they prayed to, the same Holy Ghost that moved them to shout in church, moved through her hands and gave her prophetic sight.

King and Louis operated like one well-oiled machine, as if the hand of God guided every idea and move. They kept a low profile, stacking every hard-earned penny—all of it legitimate. Managing their businesses, working full-time jobs, and accumulating enough to buy land and property. In 1972, they purchased eight acres up the hill, in an undeveloped wooded area on the opposite side of the highway from the beach.

The hill wasn't quite as high as the more mountainous elevations behind it, an enormous, spotty, uneven mound thick with pine trees. About 150 acres total, with only around 50 of them developed with houses. The rest was dense forest. The landowners had contracted with a paper factory to harvest trees every twenty years. The owners posted intimidating PRIVATE PROPERTY—KEEP OUT signs along the hunting grounds. The tenants went in anyway. They needed to.

The two-lane highway divided and simultaneously redlined the landscape, the Black side from the white side. White property owners held the lion's share of privately owned beachfront land. Black families had once owned a significant portion of that, too, but secretly redrawn property lines, illegal land grabs, intimidation, scams targeting the illiterate and the vulnerable, dating back to 1880 had stripped that away. The hill still had nearly 200 old, dilapidated houses, and the authorities should have demolished most of them. That was where Black folks lived.

Headen-Jefferson Construction Company had deliberately pushed them against the tree line, driving them up and away from Brown Sugar Beach, a pattern established generations earlier by their predecessors and carried out without question. The hill was the one place they were allowed to settle with some degree of peace, and even there, Headen-Jefferson built their rental houses poorly, using subpar materials, while underpaying the Black construction workers who worked for them. By 1972, years of coastal weather and neglect, worsened by each passing hurricane, had worn the structures down until many looked more like shacks.

The families up there lived on micro lots in shotgun houses, some built so close together that a man with an average wingspan could touch two neighboring homes at once. The roads were unpaved. Driving up or down was risky on a dry day and treacherous in the rain. The narrow path allowed only one car at a time, and a good rain would wash out the tire-worn track entirely, leaving cars mired in mud and requiring neighbors to push them out together.

Most families up the hill didn't have cars, anyway. There was a well-worn walking path. There was also a more convenient tunnel, but they weren't allowed to use it. With no public transportation, most residents either walked down the hill to do domestic or blue-collar work for white families or took a bus to neighboring towns to work in tobacco or cotton fields. Their rent payments were so inflated that the arrangement was barely distinguishable from sharecropping. Two of the three grocery stores and the pharmacy ran tabs with predatory interest rates. And if the Headen, Pettigrew, or Jefferson families didn't own a thing outright, they influenced it.

This was the only life they knew. But they also knew that despite their living conditions and the gravity of their economic cycle, they understood community. What it meant to be neighborly. What it meant to pull together as a village: bartering, watching each other's children when working opposite shifts, celebrating holidays together, laughing, dancing, grieving, fighting, and making up. Together. Not always because they wanted to. Because they had to.

"Man, you see that sign?" Louis pointed. "Huge FOR SALE—150 acres, residential, will subdivide. Write that phone number down."

The sign was white with red letters, posted up the hill behind the houses. What they didn't know was that loggers had harvested the pine trees just a year or so prior. The undeveloped acreage looked like pure opportunity. The Headen, Jefferson, and Pettigrew families owned the land, and, to King's and Louis's surprise, the Headens sold them eight acres without a fight.

But once the ink dried, a few weeks later, the Pettigrews produced a soil scientist and their good-old-boy director of the county health department, who co-signed an official report declaring that the land wouldn't perc.

For land to perc—percolate—meant it could absorb water at the rate needed to support a septic tank. If the land failed, the county health department could declare it unbuildable. No septic system. No home.

"Can't build nothin' on land that won't perc," they said with a smile. "But we'll be happy to take it off your hands and buy it back."

Among themselves, they gloated. "We got a good two years before the trees get too tall. Plenty of time to reel in as many suckers as we can."

They had run this scheme many times. Black or white, it didn't matter, any unsuspecting buyer who saw the FOR SALE sign and the phone number. Those devil's best servants dealt mercilessly with their victims, leaving them hopeless and, most times, penniless. The families would sell the land back for pennies on the dollar, still obligated to high-interest loan balances, and find themselves back to renting shotgun houses on the hill, waiting on a Section 8 list, or leaving altogether.

The only eight acres up the hill that didn't get sold back were King's and Louis's. They were furious, hotter than two erupting volcanoes, but they didn't sell. Because Tink told them to hold on. She'd seen something. She and Fatou had been right too many times before for King and Louis not to listen.

When the other victims found out the Devereaux brothers had held on, some thought they were out of their minds. At least the others had gotten something back. But that something didn't begin to cover the loan balances they were still obligated to pay.

The Devereaux families, who had arrived in 1972, spent five years living in their Brown Sugar Beach Motel before moving into a mostly white neighborhood ten minutes away in Pine City, near King's & Queen's.

"You sure about this place, King?" Fatou asked, standing in the doorway, one child on her hip.

King held the other. "It's temporary."

She raised an eyebrow.

"Everything is temporary," he added. "Even this."

In 1977, their brand-new homes were ready, three bedrooms, two and a half baths, two stories, partial brick and wood, quarter-acre lots. They were ideal. One for each family of four, directly across the street from each other.

"Across the street? Oui! Oui!" Fatou laughed and clapped.

"So, when I need you, I just holler," Tink said.

"You already do," Fatou shot back. They hugged and laughed.

"Ohhh," King said, standing in the driveway, hands on his hips. "Look at us."

Fatou shook her head, smiling. "God's blessings, *mon amour*."

Oh! The looks King got once neighbors figured out that the woman they assumed was his maid was in fact his wife.

"Excuse me," a neighbor said once, lowering her sunglasses. "Is she—"

"My wife," King answered flatly, pulling Fatou closer. "And you may call her Mrs. Devereaux."

Fatou smiled sweetly. "Good morning."

The two couples popped champagne on the driveway to celebrate.

"To us," King said, lifting his glass.

"To love and our children's futures," Fatou added.

Louis and Tink clinked theirs. Louis smiled. "And to never letting nobody tell us what we can't have."

That accomplishment alone fueled them with such excitement. They pressed on.

It took years and a truckload of patience, but everything within a hundred miles was beginning to boom. A new four-lane highway was finally coming through, bringing good jobs, opportunities, and easier access to both the beach and their acreage up the hill. Horizontal construction was underway on the main road. Vertical construction was spreading through Pine City one business at a time. And just as things were building momentum, another level of racism and white narcissism stepped into the frame.

Local white preachers, the mayor, town council members, business owners, the sheriff, and the former property owners—already multi-millionaires who controlled the private waterfront—confirmed what some had suspected: King was Black. They moved to rescind his real estate dealings—the homes, the eight lots, the motel, the dance hall. All of it. They knew what the new roads meant. Tourism. Money. Growth. Pine City and Sandy Shores had always hosted mostly in-state seasonal visitors. There was one large franchised beachfront hotel, two locally owned sizable motels, and about twenty-five beach rental houses, all of them unwelcoming to Black people.

The only option for Black beachgoers was the much smaller, twenty-room Brown Sugar Beach Motel, squeezed to the edge of the property with only distant street-side metered parking. But what it lacked in size, it made up for in spirit. The modest two-story motor-court motel, built in the early fifties and painted in cheerful beach colors, had metal railings and doors that opened onto a breezy walkway facing the ocean. Inside, the rooms were simple but lovingly kept, with polished wood dressers, chenille bedspreads, cool tile bathrooms, and jalousie windows that welcomed the steady whisper of salt air. For many families, it wasn't just a place to stay; it was the one place at the beach where they knew they belonged.

The devil's relatives—the Pettigrew, Headen, and Jefferson families—knew the new highway's route. They knew Brown Sugar Beach Motel was about to become prime real estate, the hub of it all. They wanted it. All of it. Badly.

They also knew that restaurants like King's & Queen's and new tourist attractions would transform this segregated stretch of coast into a lucrative vacation destination, and the thought of King and Louis at the center of that infuriated them. The Devereaux brothers wouldn't sell. Not one property.

King and Louis also knew exactly where that highway was heading and had positioned themselves accordingly. When the racist opposition turned legal, King fought them in court. And won. Discrimination, obstruction, bad-faith dealing—he went up against all of it. The Devereaux vision, education, determination, relationships, and relentless work ethic had paid off. They were winning. And in winning, they were beginning to influence and empower Black families, poor families, and worn-out white families who had been working for the wrong people their whole lives.

CHAPTER 10

Never Saw It Coming, 1978–1988

That enraged the white supremacists in and around Pine City, threatening what many feared would become an all-out race war. As usual, hate-filled white folks played offense when no one was bothering them, which forced Black families and the few other families of color to play defense, simply trying to survive and live in peace.

After several fires consumed Black homes, after vandalism scarred the Devereaux businesses yet again, Pine City stopped breathing at night.

"Be home before dark," mothers warned.

"Don't answer no knock you ain't expectin'," fathers added.

Even laughter quieted. The shattered motel windows, twice that month. The dance hall doors splintered. Spray paint screamed slurs across brick walls that had taken years to build. King stood in the motel parking lot one evening, staring at the damage.

Louis joined him. "They want you tired."

King's jaw tightened. "I don't tire easy."

"They want you scared."

King looked up the hill toward the homes of his employees. "Then we'll give our people something else to see."

That night he gathered the men.

"We not hunting nobody," King said evenly. "But we not hiding either."

Joe Lester Pringle shifted his weight on his injured leg, rifle resting against his shoulder.

"We walk in shifts," King continued. "From dusk to dawn. No foolishness. Just presence."

Joe Lester nodded. "They bold in the dark. Let 'em see we ain't scared of it."

Zee swallowed hard. "Pops, you think they'll shoot?"

Joe Lester answered before King could. "They've already shot, son. You and Frank head back to the house and look after the family. I don't want y'all in this."

Silence followed that. Joe Lester knew something about bullets. Someone had shot him in the prohibited wooded area while trying to feed his family, leaving him to bleed long enough to limp for the rest of his life. No doctor. No apology.

He often said, "God kept me. Tink saved what was left."

Tink had cleaned the wound when infection threatened to take his leg. Prayer. Persistence. Poultices. When King later hired him as head custodian, Joe Lester stood straighter than he had in years.

"I won't let nothin' happen to you, your family, Tink, or this place," Joe Lester whispered. "Not while I'm breathin'."

King clasped his shoulder. "That's why you are here, my brother."

One Black man had suffered a beating, and worse, a young Black boy lost his life. The Sunday of the funeral, the air was thick with mourning.

Inside the church, the boy's mother wailed, "My baby didn't deserve this."

"No, ma'am," the pastor said, voice breaking. "He did not."

King and Louis stood in the back, hats in hand.

Louis leaned slightly toward him. "This ain't just vandalism anymore."

King nodded once. "No."

Then someone slipped into the church whispering urgently, and heads turned.

"They done set the motel on fire."

The words didn't register at first.

"What?" King asked sharply.

"Half of its gone."

Louis closed his eyes briefly. "On a Sunday."

"At a child's funeral," someone muttered bitterly.

King inhaled slowly. "Let's go."

The motel still smoked when they arrived. Flames had eaten through half the rooms, blackening what the fire didn't destroy. Joe Lester stood near the edge of the lot, ash on his jacket.

"They waited 'til we were gone," he said.

King stared at the damage.

"They want us to sell," Louis said quietly.

King's voice was low, controlled. "We are not selling!"

The tension lingered for months. No arrests. No explanations. No justice.

But as winter pressed in, something shifted. White shop owners who also suffered vandalism began showing up.

One older white man removed his cap awkwardly. "This ain't right," he said to King. "We don't all stand with that mess."

King studied him. "Then stand with us."

And they did. Black folks gathered first.

"We will rebuild!" Fatou declared. "Tink, we will cook for the workers."

Joe Lester tapped his rifle against the porch post. "We still patrol."

Louis addressed the growing crowd one evening. "They burned wood," he said steadily. "They didn't burn will."

Murmurs of agreement rose.

King stepped forward. "This place ain't just rooms. It's jobs. It's dignity. It's proof we can."

"We with you!" someone called from the back.

Another voice followed. "All the way!"

And they were. Fear had tried to isolate them. Loss had nearly gutted them. But hope—sparked by leadership steady enough not to panic—bound them. Black folks banded together like never before. Those who were not against them, they welcomed in. The motel would rise again. Not because hate cooled, but because the community refused to quit.

Fatou and Tink had started preparing for their much-anticipated 1988 Thanksgiving marathon, but neither of them drove. So, when Louis got off from school, he offered to take Fatou to the store while King was at work. Tink felt to stay home. She also knew Louis was keeping up an after-school affair and didn't have the energy to watch him come home shapeshifting. She saw a few customers, had too many pecans to shell and too many greens to clean and parboil, and she used those as her excuse.

Fatou invited Crystal to come along because none of them had been out much lately.

"Crys, would you and the baby like to ride?"

"Oh! Yes, ma'am!" Crystal said, enthusiastic.

Fatou chuckled. "Dress him warmly and come along. I have his hat."

"Yes, ma'am."

"Lou will be here soon. Make sure you dress warmly too."

"Yes, ma'am."

It had worked out for Crystal to live with King and Fatou, even after she and Zee decided they didn't need to marry to co-parent their son. Crystal was done with Zee as a partner, what she'd witnessed on prom night had horrified her, and if that weren't enough, a quiet rumor circulated that there were pictures. She'd come to realize she had been more in love with the idea of him, the boy she'd fantasized over, the one who made her body feel alive for the first time—than with the real Zander. The one she'd caught in that limo. And after she caught him, she felt like he'd changed, gone cynical and unreachable. But she couldn't deny his efforts as a young father. He was loving, attentive, and present with their son in the same way King had always been with him. Her baby was well loved. So was she.

Louis pulled up and blew the horn. Crystal got in first. Fatou handed her the baby and pulled herself up into the truck. The three of them sat snug while the baby slept, wrapped in a blanket, resting on Fatou's lap. That grandbaby gave her a joy and a hope for the future she couldn't put into words.

"He will be great one day!" she'd say to God, as if God had no choice but to accommodate it, and everyone around her had no choice but to believe it.

"Ladies, before we head to the store, I need to check on the stakes up the hill. Word got back to me that the Headens have been moving them inward again before the state surveyors get there. Joe Lester and his crew crouched and watched it happen."

Fatou reached across Crystal to touch his arm. "Lou, I do not want any trouble." Louis could be a hothead when provoked.

"I know, sis. I won't cause any trouble, especially with y'all in my truck. But I've got my piece and my peace with me. Now that we know our land really does perc, I only want to check on the stakes."

"Okay. But hurry, now, I have much to do."

"Won't take long, sis. Sit tight."

Crystal adjusted the radio. "Good, because I ain't never been that far up the hill before."

Louis took the rugged path between sparse undergrowth, the crunch of the tires beginning to smooth a trail for later trips. As soon as they approached their land, he could see that someone had moved the stakes at least a hundred feet inward.

He hit his palm on the steering wheel. "Well, I'll be damned!"

Fatou rolled down her window and saw the same, shaking her head. It was plain as day. Louis went quiet, and quiet from Louis meant trouble. His heart sank and his blood boiled at the same time. They all felt it. The thick silence sat longer than Fatou felt comfortable.

To lift it, Fatou said, "Let us go, Lou. Something does not feel good to me."

Louis didn't move.

"Let us go! I told King last night, God has already worked it all out. Do not worry, *mon frère*! That is our land, bought and paid for properly. I can see you and me looking down on everything from this hill! I heard God tell me great things are coming for our family and this land. Tink saw it and said it too. That is confirmation—*Dieu a parlé*. God said it."

Louis didn't flinch. He stared straight ahead. Then, sadly, he turned the truck around and headed back down, driving much slower for safety and for thought time.

Fatou pressed on. "Do you not hear me, Lou? God told me. God talked to me. Aye! It was as clear as noon daylight." Tears in her eyes, patting her grandson's back as he slept peacefully on her lap. "God will take care of our family. I heard it deep in my soul—but as loud as a great cathedral bell. Do you hear me, Lou?"

Louis looked at her and raised one corner of his mouth—a small, effortful smile, borrowing her faith like a man who needed it badly.

"Yeah, Fatti, I hear y—"

Out of nowhere, a white work truck rammed the back left side of Louis's truck, lurching it forward, spinning the back wheels in a slow, sickening donut. The driver reversed about three hundred feet, floored the gas, ramming into them again, smashing halfway inward the left side of the truck bed, forcing the truck forward, sliding. Fatou and Crystal screamed. Fatou grabbed the baby and pulled him against her chest.

Louis pumped the brakes. Nothing.

A second truck crashed into the driver's side door, tipping the truck, sending it rolling—slowly at first, then faster with each turn, over and over and over down the hill. The screams from Fatou, Crystal, and Louis came loud at first, then faded with each rotation, swallowed by the loud, overlapping "Woo Hoo's!" and "Hot dayyums!" of both drivers and their evil, cheering passengers, who got out to watch the truck come to rest at the bottom, upside down, wheels slowly spinning.

No sign of life. They cheered again, climbed back into their trucks, and sped off into the cleared pine tree area, the fastest route back down the far side of the hill, away from the scene.

Within twenty minutes, sirens filled the air from miles around. Every police car, sheriff's cruiser, state trooper, fire truck from local townships within forty miles, and county hospital ambulances converged on the scene. After the truck finally reached the bottom of the hill, road construction workers were caught up in the aftermath, and several other vehicles were involved. By the time King got word, traffic was backed up for miles on the two-lane road, with construction already shutting down one lane.

Realizing he couldn't get through to the scene, he headed straight to the hospital. Staff told him the ambulances hadn't arrived yet. There were fatalities, but some survivors.

King had never been so unhinged in his life. Praying, pacing, waiting. Nothing felt real. Everything moved in slow motion. He thought about how pretty his Queen had looked in her lavender muumuu that morning, the one she'd slipped on after making his breakfast and his lunch and after making sweet love to him, the way they often did. She made him feel like he could do anything, and he would do anything for her. He remembered her saying that God would take care of their family.

He'd replied, "Queen, as much as God is in you, if He said it, I believe it." He'd kissed her lips, then her forehead, the way he did every morning before he walked out the door. She'd stood at the screen door the way she always did. He'd touched the car door handle and, for some reason, doubled back for more. He kissed her so good it made her blush and giggle. Now that was all he could see.

The sound of the ambulances blaring broke through the fog.

His Queen, his brother Louis, and Crystal were all pronounced dead at the scene.

King had the sole responsibility of notifying their children, Tink, and Crystal's Aunt Cheryl. Each call layered a new numbness over his heart, changing its rhythm in ways he knew would be permanent. Having to identify the bodies turned his silent rage into something without a name. He had no strength to scream.

It wasn't until hours later, sitting in the ER waiting for Tink and Cheryl to make it through the traffic that he realized—in the depths of his shock—he had forgotten about the baby.

He stood straight up so fast his steel-toed boots nearly left the floor. "Waa— waa— wait." He took off in what felt like every direction at once. "Wh—where's the baby? Where is my grandson?" He was turning in circles, eyes searching every face. "Where the hell is my grandson?" His boots seemed to hover over the square tiles as he ran to the front desk and grabbed the attendant's arm.

She snatched it back, wide-eyed. "Sir! Do not touch me!"

"Where is my grandson?"

"You don't have to yell!"

Lowering his voice, his tone was still fierce. "Where is my grandson?"

"Who is your grandson? Last name?"

"Devereaux."

She scanned the patient list, sliding her pen down and back up the first sheet, then flipping to the next. He whispered frantically, "Where is he?"

"I don't have a baby or little boy, Devereaux, and I haven't seen a boy come in here. Did he come in by ambulance?" She called the ambulance bay. "Do you have a baby Devereaux back there?"

"No," the nurse replied. "But we do have a John Doe."

"Description?"

"White male. We also have two white males around twenty to thirty, three Black adults—all involved in the accident and all with ID."

"No, that's not who we're looking for. When did the patient come in? We haven't had anyone arrive by ambulance since the three DOAs, who've all been sent to the morgue, and these men. More are on the way. I'll let you know if they bring in any children."

She turned back to King. "Sir, we don't have anyone in the ambulance bay who could be your grandson."

"But where is he? He was in the car with my wife, my brother, and Crystal. They were brought in from the accident."

The attendant, now piecing together that King was the grief-stricken family member of the victims from that catastrophic accident they'd all been crying about in the break room, was confused. Reports stated that the victims were Black, and he didn't look like a relative.

"Hold on, sir. Let me get my supervisor."

Just then, Tink and Cheryl came rushing through the ER doors. Cheryl ran straight toward King. As he opened his arms, she began beating his chest with her fists.

"You and Louis killed my baby! You killed my baby!"

King's numbness returned. He didn't stop her rapid blows. He couldn't feel them. When his eyes found Tink's, the pain between them was palpable, thicker than cinder block, louder in silence than Cheryl's guilt-ridden, half-high tantrum. Time stood still between them.

Tink stood motionless, dressed in all white except for the black house shoes she hadn't thought to change. No words. No sound. Even the spiritual world that always whispered to her had gone mute. Nothing. King's eyes were flooded for the first time. He had nothing.

All the way to the hospital, riding wildly in Cheryl's boyfriend's back seat, Tink had hoped it was a dream. It had to be. Because God, her ancestors, and her prophetic gifts had not warned her. Not this time.

But seeing King's red-faced grief left no doubt. Under the weight of it, she couldn't stand.

Tink collapsed. King pushed Cheryl aside and left her wallowing on the floor, "Let me see Crystal! Let me see my baby girl!" Two nurses helped Cheryl up while they pieced together what they could from her words, barely decipherable between crying, drunk, and high. They got her onto a bed and calmed her enough to eventually take her to the morgue to identify Crystal's body as next of kin. Cheryl's boyfriend never got out of her car.

King scooped Tink up as a nurse led him to an empty bed across from Cheryl's. Two starkly different kinds of grief in the same room. Cheryl was loud, cussing, and fussing at the nurses, getting louder every time she saw King. Tink was unconscious, and a nurse called for support.

"Ma'am! Ma'am! Can you hear me?" The nurse rubbed Tink's chest.

King clasped his fingers behind his head, knowing that if anything else happened, he'd go down too. He wanted to wake up. Right then. Right there.

The front desk attendant came trotting over, pulling a police officer by the hand, almost dragging him. "Here he is! "Sir," she tapped King gently on the back. "Here's one of the officers from the scene."

"Where is my grandson? The baby—where's the baby?"

The officer said, "There won't no baby."

"Yes. My wife told me she and Crystal were getting a ride from Louis."

"I said there won't no baby."

King's eyes widened, shifting frantically from side to side. "Well, where is he?" He ran to the front desk. "Can I use the phone?"

He dialed using the black rotary phone, and a nurse said, "You're gonna have to use the pay phone," a nurse started to say. But the attendant cut in. "No. He can use this one. Dial nine first."

King picked up the receiver and went completely blank. He could not recall a single number he'd memorized. He slammed it down and fumbled through every pocket on his work coveralls, searching for his small phone book. He passed it twice in his haste. Finally found it. Opened it. Drew another blank on who to call first. He steadied himself, dialed Renae. Busy signal. He pressed the lever, waited for a dial tone, and tried again. It just rang.

"Damn," he said through his teeth. "She must be on her way."

Zee and Frank were en route from TSU. Louis's kids were on their way too. King flipped through the phone book, hoping a neighbor's name would jump out. Joe Lester. Joe Lester Pringle was working at the motel. He answered on the first ring.

King explained everything so fast that Joe Lester felt like he was in a movie. The only words that grabbed him were: "I know it sounds crazy, but I'm losing my mind more every second. I can't half think straight, and I'm desperate as hell. Go see if my grandson is at my house."

Joe Lester moved fast. The traffic going in his direction wasn't as backed up. King told him the key was taped under the porch swing. Joe Lester felt for it, ignoring the splinters from rubbing so hard. Got the key. Fumbled it into the lock—upside down, then right side up, neither worked, then back again. "Damn, I had it right the first time." The door opened. He could still smell the hint of bacon from breakfast Fatou had fried that morning. He searched every room, looked in places a baby would never be, just to be thorough.

He called King back, which was a long-distance call from their house, at the number the attendant had given him. "I need to speak to King Devereaux," he said, already knowing what he had to say.

By the time Renae arrived at the hospital, she and King were standing around Tink's bed. Renae was trying to hold herself together with the force of her personality, in full denial.

"I know somebody better find my nephew before I knock every last one of y'all motherf—" She caught herself. "Don't tell me to calm down, lady. I'll knock you and them down, one by one. And let me catch Cheryl cussing my daddy one more time. She didn't care about

Crystal when she was alive and refused to even meet her son. I'll shoot her simple, crackhead ass, too."

King would normally calm her down, but he didn't have the strength, plus he felt the same way in silence. He went to take Joe Lester's call.

"King… your grandbaby ain't here."

"Well, where—"

"I don't know. Where else you want me to look, boss?"

King hung his head, resting his elbow on the desk, using the palm of his hand to prop his head up. Silence. Joe Lester waited in awkward silence for his next order. He could only hear King's breathing.

"King? You there?"

"Yeah."

Joe Lester wanted to give hope, "I'll find him, King. I will find your grandbaby."

King hung up with absolutely no hope in those words. Not even enough curiosity left to wonder where the baby might be. He went back to tell Renae and Tink. That became Renae's mission. Joe Lester, meanwhile, returned to the motel after talking with Renae and gathered his work crew, the same men who patrolled for security. No questions asked. They rolled five deep, armed.

Traffic was still backed up toward the accident. They could see the blue-light reflections from police cars directing traffic and working the scene. Joe Lester and his crew had spent most of their lives hunting in those woods, and now that the forest had been cleared, they knew the back way up, too. As they slowed to a crawl around a steep bend on the narrow one-car road, they saw them: seven men, two white commercial trucks. One with dented bull bars and one with a damaged front end, both bearing the overused Headen logo plastered on the sides. And old man Headen's Cadillac.

They were standing around the trucks, smoking and drinking. Old man Headen, two of his sons, his grandson Andy Headen, two of Pettigrew's, and one of the Jefferson clans. Joe Lester took his foot off the accelerator just enough to let his truck coast slowly. Old man Headen stepped forward. "What you doing back here, boy?"

"Just riding up the hill, sir."

"Y'all niggers don't own no land back here. Private property."

Joe Lester, knowing the Devereaux's still held their eight acres, said, "King Devereaux sent us up here to check on something for 'em." His upbringing in Pine City wouldn't let him stand on his own name.

"He ain't no damn king. What are you checking on this time of night?"

"Just something he asked me to do for 'em."

"What you checking on dirt for, boy? Ain't nothing else up there yet but dirt." The white men laughed. The joke wasn't funny. It certainly wasn't that funny.

"Y'all hear about the accident?" Joe Lester asked.

"I asked you a question, boy." The laughter stopped.

At that moment, Joe Lester saw a Pettigrew inching toward the back of one of Headen's trucks, easing toward the gun rack. He wasn't the only one who noticed. All four men in his truck responded accordingly.

Andy Headen smirked. "What accident?" The others snickered.

That was enough. Joe Lester and his crew knew something was terribly wrong.

"It was a bad one down the hill. They say it was a truck."

"We don't know nothing about that." More snickering, some covering their mouths like schoolboys.

"Oh. Okay." Joe Lester kept his voice flat. "Well, sir, let me get by so I can check on what I need to and get out of your way."

"Naw, nigger."

Hours had passed, and Louis's truck still lay mangled at the bottom of the hill. Joe Lester didn't want trouble. But the Devereaux family had been good to him and every man in his truck—given them family, safety, hope, the best-paying jobs, and the fairest employers they'd ever known.

"Well, if you won't let my truck through, we'll just get out."

His crew was ready. Two rifles clicked inside the cab with precision. Three men jumped from the truck bed simultaneously, as if choreographed. The Headen crew, the most malicious of them all, had been celebrating, relaxing, and drinking heavily, leaving them no time to draw their weapons.

Joe Lester's front passenger, Sylvester, a Vietnam vet, short, frail, shell-shocked, big-hearted, came around the front and pressed his gun to Andy Headen's temple. Old man Headen had worked this man mercilessly for years, paid him in heroin and moonshine. The Black community had taken him in. Cheap liquor still had a hold, but the heroin had let go. He slept wherever he needed to when he needed to sleep it off, and somebody on the hill always fed him.

"Now y'all put your hands up, let Joe Lester through, and there won't be no trouble."

Old man Headen said, "That's my grandboy, nigger. You're in real trouble now. Y'all just pulled guns on some of the richest white men in the state."

Steady, gun pressed to Andy's temple, finger sliding from safety to trigger: "And I'll shoot at least one of ya smack dab in the forehead tonight. If one of y'all move, he's dead and I'll die happy. We'll meet in hell so I can do it again. Heh, heh, heh." He smiled at them.

Joe Lester eased back into the truck, eyes never leaving the white men. The vet and two others held them at gunpoint while Joe Lester and his remaining passenger drove slowly forward and headed up the back side of the hill.

When they crested, they could see spotlights and police lights spread across the scene. Joe Lester paused for half a second, struck by how stunning both sides of the beach looked from up here, an elevation the people living on this hill had never been allowed to fully enjoy.

A Black state detective stepped forward. "Hold it right there. Don't pull up any further. This is an active accident scene."

Joe Lester stopped immediately. He told them about the men being held at gunpoint down the back side of the hill and about the baby who had been in the car and was now unaccounted for. State troopers and State Bureau Investigators took off to make arrests. A few deputies, along with Joe Lester and his passenger, began searching.

Word spread fast. Every neighbor on the hill who was home came out with flashlights, combing the dense area.

Emotionally, King was hollowed out. Steeped in sorrow, the weight of grief was palpable across Pine City and Brown Sugar Beach. Numb and emptied, King could hold only one thought: *Where is the baby?*

Zee was shattered when his family was killed in that racially motivated attack. He hadn't dealt with the prom night assault, and by the time he turned twenty-two in 1990, his body felt run through and depleted from years of masking pain the same way he'd been violated. Girls going down on him multiple times a week in a blur. He was using it to self-medicate, trying to convert what had hurt him into something that could soothe him. Some of the women treated him the same way those girls had, like a conquest. As Tink had told him years ago, he could feel his soul being chipped away. Too much pain. Too many voids. He was numb.

Receiving oral sex often, having sex rarely, made him feel something. *Hell, I ain't even asking. Are they using me for something, too?*

The accident happened in November of his junior year, 1988. He was too distraught to return to school. Pops needed help running the businesses and navigating the criminal and civil lawsuits. Renae, Frank, and Tink needed each other as anchors to help make sense of the remnants of their lives. Renae had become a new mother, and the grief of losing her family and her best girlfriend was almost unbearable. What kept her from crumbling was Frank, her twinship with Zee, helping Tink and Pops, and the new baby, her and Frank's son, Quincy.

Frank swung between depression and isolation one day, frantic workouts the next. He didn't go back to TSU either. He, Pops, and

Zee entered an unspoken workaholic contest. Pops still reported to the accounting job at the plant, unnecessarily, and went straight to the motel or the dining hall, now a full restaurant, when he clocked out. No dancing. No singing. Zee followed the same pattern. He picked up every side hustle he could find: personal trainer, security guard, certified masseuse, and coaching little league teams that his family members played on.

On rare occasions, he partnered with Renae to teach hand-dancing, the Shag, salsa, or classes to prep couples for their wedding first dance. Anything to keep moving. Anything not to be still at home, where his mother's spirit lived in the walls, the furniture, the curtains. Her presence was a comfort when he needed to feel Fatou's warmth. It was unbearable when he ached for her physically.

He enrolled in accounting classes and got his residential and commercial real estate licenses. Frank got his barber's license and rented a chair at a local shop, but the owner kept poaching his clients or skimming from every cut Frank did. Frank wanted his own shop and couldn't wait for slow money to get him there.

Renae graduated from Piedmont Culinary School, stepped into her mother's place cooking at the restaurant, and started taking cake orders on the side.

Frank decided to join the military. The Devereaux legal battles were dragging on, and money wasn't coming in fast enough to take care of their now two children. Pops was spending every dime between the criminal and civil cases attorneys, employee payroll, and construction costs, trying to expand all the businesses at breakneck speed.

He would hire anybody who needed a job, and as he would say, "Had a heart and mind to work."

And now, as a husband and father of two, Frank refused to keep depending on Pops to carry him. A smooth-talking recruiter made the math sound irresistible, steady paychecks, promised bonuses, benefits. Frank enlisted in the United States Marine Corps.

In a move equal parts grief-escape and loyalty, Zee enlisted alongside him through the buddy system in 1989.

They deployed. Their unit was among the first on the ground during the war in the Persian Gulf War in Iraq.

"Man, these are bombs bursting in air for real," Frank yelled out to Zee.

They served in the same unit, on the tip of the spear, during the most violent stretch of the conflict. Riding in a tightly moving convoy, a mortar hit the Humvee ahead of their five-ton truck, which was carrying ten Marines. Frank, in the back, sustained an injury that mangled his left leg. It had to be amputated above the knee. Zee, seated directly behind the driver, suffered massive third-degree burns covering the left half of his abdomen and wrapping around the middle of his back, sustained while climbing out of the burning vehicle. Four of their fellow Marines died in the blast. Frank, Zee, and the remaining four were all honorably discharged as disabled veterans with medals earned in the fire.

One of the surviving four was a woman Marine named Cora, their staff sergeant. She was fourteen years into her service, an intelligent Black woman, 12-years older, and a little rough around the edges. Not the most conventionally striking woman, but formidable. She was married and rarely spoke about her husband, even as her troops overshared freely about their families. The two Devereaux Corporals were the exception. They overshared about nothing.

What had started as a leadership relationship, Cora saw real potential in both young men, shifted when she began reading Zee's eagerness to learn as a romantic interest. Within a short time, they began a secret affair. Neither called it love. Knowing his own history but not hers, and she not knowing about his assault, it was plain that they were both starving for comfort and found it in each other.

Zee's reserve gave her the freedom to trust the silence would hold, unless he told Frank, which she suspected was always possible given how little those two kept from each other. She thought their bond was admirable. Cora brought her experience and patience to Zee whenever they had sex. No woman before her had ever taken time with his body, offered genuine intimacy, holistic pleasure, certainly not all at once. He brought his young man's curiosity, stroke, and a confidence that surprised her when he handled her, along with an older man's steadiness, though he remained reluctant about performing oral sex. He didn't seem to know how. She taught. He learned well. They both enjoyed it.

The one consistent disruption: whenever Cora's lips moved toward his genitals, he would pull away, sometimes nauseated. It unsettled her. She knew something had happened. She never asked. He never told. She didn't press. She simply stopped and backed away, and they'd hold each other instead, not for love, but to temporarily quiet the noise of their separate traumas. After the accident, there was no formal goodbye. No need. They both knew what it had been.

CHAPTER 11

Life Comes at You Fast

Finally, Jenita's senior year, WSSU class of '92. Her course load was lighter because Ms. Jackson had advised her well.

"Neat, take the harder classes early. Your senior year, you'll need room to focus on work and internships."

"Yes, ma'am."

The lighter load gave her more time for sorority and student activities. She'd been helping with the Senior Activities Committee, posting flyers about senior pictures in the student union, the caff, the girls' dorms, and stapling them to trees. She'd reminded people verbally, too. Yearbook pictures were at noon in the auditorium. A Greek yard party was happening that night, Jenita's first. As a senior and a Delta, she was finally going. The giddiness on the yard was thick enough to taste.

Whenever something big was happening on campus, like a game, a party or picture day, the electricity in all the dorms would flicker or cut out completely, overloaded by clothes dryers, illegal microwaves, hotplates, blow dryers, and curling irons all running at once.

She'd learned to get up early because her thick, bra-length, deep copper hair took hours. On its own, the waves were there but subtle. But with Luster's pink curl activator, they deepened and defined, usually into a coiled ponytail or braids she did herself. She'd play bootleg braider for extra money when her work-study check came up short, and the beauty shop wasn't in the budget. But today was picture day, which called for the blow dryer and curling iron.

Doing her hair with the band practicing "Don't Stop 'Til You Get Enough" floating up from outside—she and her roommates doing the Reebok, the Prep, and two-stepping around the room. Flutes fluttering, woodwinds winding, brass on blast, percussion locked in the pocket.

The excitement about graduation and the yard party made her forget, for a moment, what she was hiding. She'd told Rhonda and Sheila because the three of them kept nothing from each other. She knew more of their secrets than they knew of hers, because until recently, she'd barely had any. Except for her spiritual gifts. And the terrible beatings from her grandmother. But they'd known about those since middle school.

She couldn't dwell on any of it. She had a to-do list. Starting with submitting her graduation application, which always came with a long line and someone liable to get something wrong at the table.

"Jenita Rochelle Hall? Who is Jenita Rochelle Hall?" the senior class coordinator called out.

"Me. I'm Jenita Rochelle Hall."

"Oh. I thought your name was Neak. Short for Reneka."

"No. It's Neat. Short for Jenita Rochelle Hall. Neat is a nickname for friends and family."

"Let me fix it on my roster. Do you have your application fee?"

"No. I have a waiver because of my financial aid."

"Last name Hale?"

"Hall. H-a-l-l. Jenita Rochelle Hall."

The coordinator peered over her glasses. "Oh. I see. Report to the auditorium at noon for pictures."

Jenita already felt irritated. Exams. Fees. Worrying about Warren, his job, and his mean-ass parents.

She thought, *As bad as we all want to get out of here. What senior doesn't know today is picture day? But, dang! This is almost over—parties, games, homecoming, the band, activities with my sorority sisters and frat brothers. Almost done.*

Freshman year and living in Atkins Hall felt like a lifetime ago. Senior year was here, and they were all ready to leave, but no one was talking about how afraid they were to go.

I wonder what's next. We'll be adults. Jobs to get. Checks to earn. Apartments to rent. Bigger bills to pay. But no more exams! And then a sadness pulled at her. No more HBCU life. No more hanging out on the plot or the yard, late-night foolery, eating with friends in the caff. No more…

Thinking about the future made her circle back to how her secret had come to be. Jenita was easy to talk to, comical and spiritual, but not in an overly churched, sanctimonious way. She could see things. She could feel them. She felt Warren, whether he admitted it or not.

She was gorgeous, fascinating, and unlike any girl he'd met. Since puberty, she was grown-woman thick in all the right places. Honey brown complexion. Full, wavy, deep copper hair in a mid-back ponytail. The dimple on her right cheek could almost pool water. Jenita had Nana Katie Mae's eyes, wide and doe-shaped, soft with the same kindness that seemed to understand more than most, as if she could see the spirit behind things other people only looked at. A button nose, pretty heart-shaped lips that revealed genetically straight teeth, and an infectious smile.

She didn't have many clothes to choose from, so she dressed modestly chic, not trying to attract attention. Nothing too tight unless her behind was covered, though she didn't mind showing off her big, tenderoni thighs from time to time. Her wardrobe leaned plain, saved by bright colors and her own unique flavor. She wore light fragrances like accessories. Eclectic, thrifted pieces that looked like they might have come from countries she hadn't visited.

Not the trending campus look—no Coca-Cola shirts, Sassoon, Gloria Vanderbilt, or Jordache. "Girl, they cut those too narrow for my hips, anyway." At five-foot-seven and about 170 pounds, her style was as if she worked as an artist who could swap out two pieces and be ready for a business meeting.

Rhonda and Sheila frequently told her, "Neat, you better be glad you're cute with that hourglass shape, because you dress five minutes from homely." Then borrowed her accessories to wear with their own more on-trend outfits.

Jenita looked down at her engagement ring and remembered how prized Warren had made her feel when he proposed, right in the middle of campus, in front of a crowd gathered near the Greek plots on the yard. Maybe not the ideal proposal for older people. But for two HBCU students, that was as romantic as it got.

The ring was a simple sterling silver band with a half-karat diamond, the four prongs holding it made the stone look bigger than it was. Warren had quit school in the first semester of his junior year to work, and it had infuriated his parents. They hated Jenita.

His father, Warren Sr., was a dentist. His mother was a realtor from a long and rare line of Black commercial real estate agents. Wealthy, polished, the kind of family that looked like a church fan portrait. Warren Jr. was their youngest and only son, born after three daughters. Their golden boy. The next Ingram doctor, lawyer, or local politician.

He had a Malcolm X quality: dark-framed glasses, strong jawline, features that worked better together than they did individually. Smart, soft-spoken, masculine. About five-foot-ten, medium build, always dressed in whatever trend was current: Pumas, FUBU, Karl Kani, Kangol hats, Nike, Starter jackets, Fendi, MCM, pro athletic jerseys. Name brands didn't impress Jenita much. She barely registered the hype, and when she did, she ignored it. He was also a musician—playing piano since he was four, classically trained, with a natural ear for gospel and jazz. She loved listening to him play when they stole moments in the chorus room.

Warren was simply good-looking and so shy that it took him three weeks of pretending to need the library just to work up to speaking to her. He finally got his roommate to ask her name.

"Who wants to know?"

His roommate pointed at Warren. "I'm asking for my friend."

"Him? Are y'all freshmen?"

"No. Sophomores. Are you?"

"No. I'm a junior, class of '92. And I don't want to waste your time. I don't have time for nobody, especially no sophomore."

"So, I can't get your name?"

"Why?"

"For my roommate."

"If your roommate wants my name so bad, why can't he ask me himself?"

"He's a little scared."

Warren spoke up. "I'm not scared. Shy, maybe. Not scared."

"Well. Thanks for coming off mute, sir."

He chuckled. "You're welcome, ma'am."

"What's your name?"

"Warren. Warren Ingram."

"Oh."

"And yours?"

"Jenita Rochelle Hall."

"Jenita, which dorm are you in?"

"Okay. Now that's one too many questions. I ask the questions."

"I'm in—"

"I didn't ask." She extended her hand to shake theirs. "Well, young men, have a good evening. It's a little too cold in here for me."

He nearly came apart when she touched him. He didn't notice his mouth had opened. He held that moment in slow motion. Unforgettable. He didn't realize he was still holding her hand.

"You okay?"

"Yea… yeah."

"May I have my hand back?"

"Yes." He recovered. "I was warming it up for you."

"It ain't that cold. Boy, bye."

"Bye, Ms. Jenita Rochelle Hall."

"Hmm. The young one has manners."

She walked away pretending to be unfazed. She'd have to be blind not to notice how good-looking he was. She noticed. She let the attraction fade long before she got back to her dorm.

For weeks, they ran into each other at the library every day, ending up at the same table, sneaking in french fries from the student union, talking about everybody and everything.

Jenita and Warren were each other's firsts, not first kiss, but firsts. That meant something to both of them. Once they started dating, they weren't a flashy campus couple. Their love was mature, quiet, almost like two settled old souls in young bodies. No second-guessing, no games, no cheating. When they said they loved each other, they meant it like forever.

They both wanted their first time to be memorable. Heavy petting could only satisfy their urges for so long. Getting worked up in the dorm had gotten old. Between roommates, loud music vibrating through the walls, people hollering in the hallway, and surprise knocks on the door, they decided on a hotel room.

She didn't have a car. His parents had taken his car when they found out he was dating her, as punishment. They hated her. So, they took the bus to the Holiday Inn. He'd reserved the room by phone using the credit card his father gave him for emergencies. He'd never done it before.

He walked hesitantly to the front desk while Jenita sat in the lobby pretending not to know him, reading a book.

"Warren Ingram." The desk clerk looked up. "Let me see. Hmm. Do you have a driver's license?"

"Yes."

"Nineteen? Almost twenty. Is this your credit card?"

"Yes."

"Let me look up the number… 948…9…4…8… I don't see—"

He could feel sweat working its way down the sides of his temples. He was praying his deodorant held. Stress-fear could make him musty before he knew it.

"Oh, I think I have it right here. Let me call… One night?"

"Yes, ma'am."

"Good manners. Will you be alone?"

He stuttered. "Ye— yea— yes. I'll be alone."

Jenita's eyes went wide as she attempted to read the same line of her book for the seventy-sixth time. *Alone? How am I getting in the room?* She made eye contact with him and gave a small, firm shake of her head.

"Uh. I mean— no. I'm not alone."

"How many? And because you're under twenty-one, I'll need to hold your card."

"Just two."

"Two more people?"

"No—no, ma'am. Just me and one other person."

"Is that your little girlfriend over there who keeps looking up from that book?"

"Yes, ma'am."

"Well, I need to see her ID, too."

Jenita hopped up, shoved the book into her backpack, and had her wallet out before she even reached the desk.

"You're twenty-one?"

"Yes, I am."

"Well, since y'all look so cute, I won't hold the card. No luggage?"

"Just these bags."

Silence.

"Okay. Room 344. No smoking. No loud music."

"Yes, ma'am."

The walk to the elevator might as well have been in cement shoes on wet tar in the middle of a summer heat wave.

CHAPTER 12

Their Way or No Way

Young love is powerful, and it can get you pregnant. Jenita and Warren loved each other as deeply as young love has the capacity to, and they had become best friends. They hung out, enjoyed each other's company, and had woven their way into each other's friend circles.

Her sisters and close friends liked him well enough. His gospel music crowd liked her, introducing her to Commissioned, John P. Kee, and The Winans, artists she genuinely vibed with, especially "Choose Ye." She couldn't sing or play a note, but her love for good music was equal to theirs.

Physically, their relationship was a lot of hugging, kissing, and heavy petting, but penetration was quick. Warren hadn't learned to manage his climax, and because Jenita had nothing to compare it to, she didn't know there was more to expect, or that she was entitled to her own. What she didn't know didn't stop his soldiers from marching into her uterus just months after they started having sex. Pulling out was not an effective form of contraception.

She was a senior. He was a junior. By the time she took a pregnancy test, she was three months along, which meant she would walk across the stage at graduation with her baby inside her.

Warren was scared, but he was also genuinely excited about becoming a father. He quit school immediately and got a job. His parents were furious. They wanted Jenita to have an abortion and didn't care what happened to her. They literally had Warren's life all planned out from birth: what he would be, where he would live, and who he would marry.

"You don't have to marry that foul whore," Mrs. Ingram shouted at Warren. "And you don't have to become a father. It's probably not even yours. Either make her get an abortion or let her raise that country bastard alone."

"Your mother's right, son. She trapped you. She did this to you."

Warren was mild-mannered but tried to stand his ground. He couldn't out-argue or outthink them; they bombarded him from every angle, in every conversation, the moment he told them. By the time he did, he had already been working full-time at RJ Reynolds for months in a warehouse. He'd signed a lease on an apartment, bought an engagement ring, a used car, a couch, and a mattress—all on the bank account they'd provided before they cut him off completely.

Their hatred for Jenita and their unborn grandchild upset their whole lives. Jenita, meanwhile, was finishing her degree in Elementary Education with a minor in Sociology and had begun a paid internship at a franchise Kids Playhouse Center—daycare, after-school care, and tutoring. She worked mornings as an administrative assistant and picked up additional paid hours afterward.

One evening, Mr. and Mrs. Ingram were waiting outside when she got off work. She was driving Warren's car, it was convenient, since he worked swing shifts and double shifts whenever he could get them.

Mrs. Ingram came at her, yelling. "Why are you ruining my son's life and our family?" Startled, Jenita went wide-eyed and silent. "You heard me, Ja-NEETA! Why did you trap my son when there were plenty of those ghetto country boys you could've done this with? You nasty whore!"

"I didn't trap Warren. I lo—"

"Shut up! Your stupid ass doesn't know a damn thing about love!"

"Yes, I do."

"I said shut up!"

The much taller Mrs. Ingram backhanded her across the face so hard that it knocked her to the ground. Jenita had been hit with a switch and beaten with a belt by her daddy and whipped by his mother, but she had never been struck in the face. The pain and throbbing on the left side of her face were excruciating. She cupped it in her hand. She could feel warm blood running down her wrist and forearm, Mrs. Ingram's enormous diamond ring had cut her.

Before she could process what was happening, she felt kicks, repeated, aimed at her stomach. She curled into a tight fetal position, protecting her belly.

Another tutor walked out. "Hey! Stop! What's going on? Jenita, are you okay?"

Jenita stayed balled up as tight as she could. Ms. Ingram didn't stop.

Her co-worker yelled. "I'm calling the police!"

She tried to help Jenita up. She got kicked, too. She ran back inside to call the police.

ꕥ

Dr. Ingram grabbed his wife by both shoulders. "Come on, honey."

Two co-workers came out and helped Jenita up. Once they convinced her it was safe to unfurl, she got to her feet.

Dr. Ingram, without a trace of shame, shouted at her. "How much will it cost for you to leave my son and get an abortion?"

Her co-workers had no idea she was pregnant.

"I called the police," one of them said.

He ignored her, pulling a leather checkbook from his inside jacket pocket. "How much, dammit? I can write a check right now. Fifty thousand. Is that enough? Is it?"

Jenita cried, navigating toward Warren's car by looking through her fingers, eyes toward the ground, never uncovering her bleeding, swelling face.

"The police are coming!" her co-worker called out.

Dr. Ingram didn't flinch. "Is $100,000 enough?" He reached the car and smashed the checkbook against the window. She didn't look at it. She started the car and sped off.

When Warren got home that night, he showered and climbed into bed the way he always did, thinking she was asleep. When he leaned in to kiss her, he saw the compress on her swollen, bloody cheek.

"Neat?" he whispered. "Jenita? What happened?"

She cried all over again, telling him everything.

He barreled out of bed and dressed in a hurry, hands moving faster than his thoughts. She begged him not to go. She had never seen him so enraged. She chased him down the stairs but wasn't fast enough, and she wasn't dressed enough to follow him into the parking lot. He sped away.

She paced, then called her sisters, Sheila and Rhonda. They arrived faster than the police ever could. Jenita had always shown up for them with no questions asked, her own struggles set aside, so showing up for her was never a debate.

Everything in Sheila and Rhonda wanted to cuss, fight, and shoot. Shoot? Sheila would destroy. They tended to her wounds but knew she needed the hospital, for her face and for the baby. She was certain Mrs. Ingram's kicks hadn't reached her belly; she'd been too tightly curled. She had bruises on her back, thighs, calves, and arms. They convinced her to go and to press charges. Sheila stayed at the apartment to intercept Warren. Rhonda drove her to the hospital.

The baby was fine. Jenita needed eighteen stitches on the left side of her face and Tylenol for the pain spreading through her body. Nurses photographed the injuries. She pressed charges. Her co-workers came to the hospital and gave police statements.

Warren came home walking slowly up the sidewalk, so sunken that his shoulders seemed to be trying to touch. He'd already lost visible weight, and whatever his parents had said to him was written on his face. As he got closer, Sheila opened the door. All three of them were stunned to see that Warren, too, had been beaten.

Sheila asked for his parents' address.

After that, they felt the need to anchor themselves. Three weeks later, they married at the Forsyth County courthouse. Sheila and Rhonda stood as witnesses, holding Jenita's hands tightly afterward.

"You okay?" Sheila whispered.

Jenita nodded. "I am now."

Nothing came of the charges she'd pressed. Warren persuaded her not to show up to court in exchange for his parents agreeing to leave her alone.

"They'll stop," he said, weary but hopeful. "I promise."

They didn't. She kept the restraining order in place. The Ingrams stayed away physically, but never stopped calling, never stopped pouring venom into their home through the phone.

One night, Warren rubbed his face, voice flat with exhaustion. "I'm so tired, Neat. They've turned most of my friends against me, and nobody in my family will talk to me."

She reached for his hand. "I know."

He still played his keyboard more than he watched television. Sometimes she sat on the floor beside him, just listening.

"Play that one again," she'd say softly.

He would. But every song sounded sad, even when it wasn't meant to be. She brought in the two friends his parents hadn't managed to reach, let them come over for a jam session, and talk music with him.

"You still got it, man," one of them said.

Warren smiled faintly. "I just ain't feeling it."

She never stopped encouraging him. The talent was still there, still soothing, even as the light in his eyes slowly dimmed. He worked every hour the job offered.

"I'll take the shift," he said more than once.

Almost six months later, graduation day arrived. Jenita stood in front of the mirror, tugging at her gown.

"Jesus be a zipper. Please zip," she muttered.

It barely closed over her eight-month belly. She laughed at herself. "I'm about as wide as I am tall. And all this hind part."

She wasn't ashamed, though shame came at her from every direction. People talking. A classmate or two who looked away. Whispers. Her father told her she couldn't come home unless she confessed her sin in front of the whole church.

"Now that I'm a deacon at church, you have brought shame on us."

Her mother said nothing. That silence hurt worse than anger.

Her DST line sisters and Ms. Jackson were her family and her refuge.

Ms. Jackson pressed her hand to Jenita's back. "You are not doing this alone."

Ms. Jackson bought the baby a crib and diapers, paid for Jenita's hair, and bought her a maternity dress. She quietly collected donations from her 1978 DST line sisters and family.

"Thank you so much," Jenita said, choking up. "I wouldn't be here without you. I wouldn't have made it."

Ms. Jackson pulled her close. "I will always be proud of you, Neat. I love you like the child I never had." She was the only elder who told her "I love you" since Nana.

When the announcer finally reached the H's, Jenita slid to the edge of her chair.

"Please don't miss it," she whispered, eyes closed.

"Jenita Rochelle Hall."

As soon as she heard the "Juh," she pulled herself up by the chair in front of her and made her way out of the row. A hush moved gradually through the auditorium—classmates, family, faculty—as she waddled across the stage.

There had been talk about whether she should be allowed to walk. Ms. Jackson had shut that down fast. "And who is going to stop her? She earned her degree. With honors. Didn't she?"

Warren stood and yelled at the top of his lungs. "That's my wife!"

When Jenita saw him standing, clapping and smiling, beside Ms. Jackson, her sister Sylvia, and her sisters and some of her sorority sisters, tears poured down her round, puffy maternity cheeks.

"Thank you, God," she whispered. "I did it, Nana. Winston-Salem State University, class of 1992."

Two weeks later, Harmony Joy Ingram was born, weighing seven pounds, eight ounces of joy.

"She's perfect," Warren whispered, holding her, glowing with his new father's light.

Life was moving fast. Jenita landed a full-time position at Kids Playhouse Center, managing two locations. She enrolled Harmony there after maternity leave.

"This couldn't have come sooner. Benefits too!"

Especially since Warren had been fired from RJ Reynolds, no reason given.

"Again?" Jenita asked quietly.

He nodded. "Mama's and Daddy's work."

Blackballed everywhere. Sadder by the day. His keyboard gathered dust. Four months later, his phone rang.

"I got a job," he said when he came through the door. "Guess who got a job today?"

Jenita clapped and jumped. "Who, baby, who?! Congratulations!"

The twelve-hour shifts and the long commute wore them out. No arguments. No name-calling. No cheating. Just silence. Ships passing in the night. Sometimes she wished for a disagreement just to feel a pulse in their marriage, their friendship.

On their second anniversary, he had to work.

"I can't afford to miss the overtime," he said apologetically.

"I understand. I know you'd be here if you could."

That morning, he got up extra early and surprised her with breakfast in bed. It made her so happy that she kissed him with everything she had. He hadn't welcomed her affection in over two months. She held him as close as she could, desperately missing him. She felt him receive it like something he'd been needing, too.

One thing led to another. He still hadn't mastered control and finished quickly, as always. Jenita was satisfied with the closeness, skin to skin, just being near him. She desperately needed that. He seemed lighter afterward, too.

"Happy anniversary, hubby. I love you so much."

"I love you. Happy anniversary, wifey." He smiled at the door, brighter than he had in months.

She spent their anniversary cooking, cleaning, washing clothes, and caring for their two-year-old, whom she adored. She was excited about being pregnant again and hadn't told him yet. She was waiting for the right moment. She moved through the apartment, listening to "I Am Here" by Commissioned, a song she'd put on repeat as she often did when something spoke to her. After more than an hour, she turned it down because she felt the presence of God in the room.

She'd experienced this before, hearing and feeling God speaking to her and remembered Nana Katie telling her it was a privilege to carry on a whole conversation with God, inside or out loud. "That's the relationship, Neat. No church, no preacher, no altar needed for that. Knowing Jesus for yourself will help you be more like Him and help you do what He did." She knew she couldn't use Nana as a veil between herself and God anymore. This was different: an intimate relationship with God for herself. This time, she felt the presence of God as if God were right here in the room. She felt an assurance from that day forward that God would never leave her. She knew it was God.

"I feel You," she said aloud. "I know You'll never leave me."

Then the sirens grew louder as she drove toward the hospital.

"What happened?" she asked breathlessly.

"There was an accident," they said.

Sheila and Rhonda were already there. After being fired again, Warren walked out quietly and jumped from the warehouse roof.

Warren D. Ingram Jr.
1971–1994

His parents blamed her for his death. They made his funeral a torment and threatened to take Harmony. They had her served with custody papers just weeks after his burial.

She thanked God for protection, always present, and for Ms. Jackson, who guided and shielded her when she couldn't shield herself. She thanked God for her sisters, who had become her refuge and her family.

But grief is not undone by gratitude. With her husband gone, his family's resentment closing in, and an uncertain future suddenly hers to carry alone, she faced a choice shaped more by survival than her religious upbringing or desire. She did not believe she could mother two children by herself.

CHAPTER 13

Adulting Ain't Easy

In 1997, Jenita earned her master's in sociology from North Carolina A&T State University. Her education, strategic experience, and record of excellence earned her a permanent full-time position at Winston-Salem State University, where she taught Sociology from 1997 to 2002. That was thanks in no small part to Ms. Jackson and several influential board members who did the right thing when the Ingrams threatened to rescind their endowment over Jenita's hire.

In 2002, she piloted a new position at WSSU for juniors and seniors, helping them refine their degree focus and tap into creative talents that could complement their professional fields. The program sparked collaborations with the North Carolina School of the Arts, North Carolina A&T State University, Bennett College, Tubman State University, launching arts-centered initiatives and morale-building activities in partnership with student services and alumni mentoring. It worked exceptionally well. She networked broadly and traveled to other HBCUs and universities, advocating for student and alumni collaboration opportunities across institutions.

Out of that work, she built her own consulting company, Neat Harmony, LLC—training faculty in higher education on how to implement these programs, helping students find genuine joy in their professions, and creating alumni bridges back to their institutions that benefited future employers by reducing rapid turnover.

At the start of each year, when she welcomed new students and faculty, she used what she called her Debbie Allen, "Fame" voice:

"Everything you see is art, design, and sound. Look around... It's all art. The way you dress, decorate your home, the style of your car. Everything. Your smile. From the intricacy of a one-of-a-kind snowflake to something as common as writing or typing a single letter in any language or font—it's all designed. And when it comes to sound, be it noise or notes, your laugh or music, design exists even in each rest.

"What an artist does is birth something from spirit to existence—invisible to visible, inaudible to audible. When they are restricted from creating, they feel constipated, can't breathe, suffocated. Now, while I can't help you with constipation, you've been accepted into this program with a mission that encourages you to breathe freely and design creatively.

"I am Jenita Rochelle Hall, owner of Neat Harmony, LLC, and adjunct professor at the HBCU, Winston-Salem State University. Welcome to your creativity."

She stayed employed by WSSU for the benefits and took full advantage of their brand, student pool, and supportive faculty network.

Jenita was far from broke. She had done well enough for herself and Harmony, now a college freshman, considering where her journey as a widow and single parent had started. She credited it to the tried-and-true wisdom that it's not about what you go through but how you get through it. And practically speaking, catching a sale, going to the back of the store, knowing when double coupon day was, Groupon. She thrifted and shopped consignment. She didn't advertise it, and no one was the wiser, because she knew how to make it her own.

Curious by nature, but cautious enough not to let curiosity run away with her. Adventurous, spontaneous, sensitive, affectionate, and playful. While she wasn't the life of the party, she could work a room when she needed to. An avid lover of the arts, she attended every free concert, festival, museum, craft show, and recital she could find, with Harmony on her hip or by her side. She didn't fully realize how much that love would shape her profession and her business. She created weekend writing rooms at local libraries, for music writing, non-technical writing, and poetry.

In 2003, she started microlocs purely for convenience in her thick, naturally deep copper hair, now just above waist length. Her round face, smooth skin, and dimple gave away nothing about her age. Plain but polished. She rarely wore makeup, not even to cover her scar.

After Warren's death, she struggled mentally, emotionally, and financially. She took side jobs, sold homemade soaps, lotions, and quality beaded bracelets at craft shows, baked cookies and muffins from Nana Katie's unwritten recipes that she tweaked for collegiate fundraisers. Kindhearted but firm.

She paid off her thirty-year mortgage in fifteen years, knowing she might not be able to carry both a mortgage and Harmony's college tuition at the same time. Her home was her refuge. It was her safe place to retreat from the world, from harm, from noise and proof that she wasn't just born to struggle. Still, inside the home she had fought to keep, peace lived. Her sacred haven.

Soft lamplight warmed the rooms; vanilla and peach candles flickered on polished tables, and the art-rich walls displayed a few of her paintings, bright colors and wide skies that made the place feel bigger than it was. Painting and music had been her sisters long before Rhonda and Sheila.

The taupe sofa was deep and inviting, layered with velvet and woven pillows in warm peach, cream, and cocoa tones, their rich textures giving the room a quiet elegance, and a quilt Nana Katie once stitched. Harmony's drawings were stuck proudly to the refrigerator with bright alphabet magnets; small bursts of crayon color that made the house feel even more alive. The rooms carried a warmth that felt almost like being held. Burning scented candles was a daily practice, especially the ones she and Harmony, her mini-me in every way, made together.

She did bootleg braids for Rhonda's sister at the salon when she had the time. She was frugal because she had to be, and creative because she learned how. She saved for two years to take Harmony to London as a graduation gift. She attended conferences and conventions that allowed her to travel several times a year. In addition, she took trips to Thailand and the Caribbean.

Once, she went with a group of her unmarried collegiate girlfriends, all of them looking for love. But she felt like it was a waste because none of them were Stella, and nobody got their groove back except Sheila. Then again, that was normal.

One of Sheila's favorite sayings: "Whoever sticks can stay, but if they fall, bring 'em all."

They went on a cruise she genuinely enjoyed and planned to go again, but schedules conflicted. She didn't want to travel abroad alone, so she made a point of researching and taking mini trips out of state that felt safe for her and Harmony. When Harmony was small, she took her to Brown Sugar Beach as often as she could, because she and Harmony loved the ocean, and outside of gas and the drive, the beach was free. Both her cars were paid off and in good shape, and she rented when it made financial sense. Harmony took one to college.

Anyone who knew her, sisters, close collegiate friends, coworkers, students, would say she was tremendously resourceful, had a third eye, was a joy to be around, an advocate for creativity, and would give the shirt off her back—and had. They would also say that from day one, Jenita showed up for her sisters, for Ms. Jackson, and for anyone she grew to love, as if her life depended on it.

But she believed her greatest qualities were her spiritual gifts and her intuition. God had welcomed her into a quiet, sacred, linguistic, spiritual expanse that guided her through the natural world she lived in. Simple. Quiet. Sure.

Since becoming Harmony Joy Hall's mother, she lost a few pounds every January and gained them back by Christmas.

"Mama, you doing that diet again?" Harmony would ask every New Year's Day, watching her sip lemon water.

"Yes, ma'am," Jenita would reply, laughing. "2012 is my year."

Harmony would squint. "You said that last year."

"And I meant it last year, too." They both laughed.

Now at forty-two, her weight had peaked at 225 pounds at five-foot-seven. And she still dressed, as Rhonda and Sheila had teased since college, "…five minutes from homely."

"Mama, you are not homely," Harmony said from the doorway while Jenita tried on a flowing pants set. "You're so pretty, and I look just like you!"

"Yep. And if I'm pretty, that means you're prettier. As for homely, baby, your Aunt Rhonda and Aunt Sheila have been saying that since 1989, and they stay borrowing something. I don't mind, though."

Harmony tilted her head. "Well, they're wrong."

Without her hourglass shape, her hint of style, and the occasional flash of her big, tenderoni thighs, they might have had a point. But her flowing pants sets and dresses, oversized knee-length tops with leggings or fitted jeans, colorful dusters, and pops of African print made her bohemian chic when it mattered—and when it didn't, her soft fragrances stole the show.

"You always smell good, Mama," Harmony would say, burying her face in her shoulder.

"If I don't get the clothes right, at least I'll be clean and smell good. Like my nana taught me. Quality only."

Her style helped camouflage her large breasts, full hips, thighs, and the rolls she could hide if she remembered to suck in.

"Mama, why are you holding your breath?" Harmony asked once.

"I better stop before I pass out," Jenita said, exhaling and laughing.

"If you gon' pass out, at least do it while I'm here."

Jenita laughed. Harmony's wit was as sharp as hers.

Her midsection and breasts had softened with time, but she was comfortable in her honey-colored skin and her "insulation," as she called it.

"That's not fat," she'd say, patting her stomach. "That's insulation. Family. Keeps me warm in winter."

Harmony would nod seriously. "Good. I don't want you cold."

She exercised sometimes—walking, light weights, dancing in the kitchen—trying to outrun the diseases that ran in her family.

"Come walk with me," she'd say.

Harmony would groan. "Can we walk to the ice cream place?"

"You can walk it off, but it will never leave or forsake me."

Even with her midlife muffin top, she remained voluptuous—a shape women admired, and men liked to see coming and going. A body her father had scolded her for, and that her paternal grandmother had tried to discipline out of her after Nana Katie Mae passed.

"You looking too fast and grown. Probably using it to catch some boy," that woman used to say. As if Jenita could help genetics.

Now, whenever old insecurities crept in, Harmony would interrupt them without even knowing it.

"Mama, you are such a good person."

Jenita would pause. "Thank you, baby. You, too. But why do you say that?"

"Because you are!"

Somehow, that always settled something deep.

Every few years, the Ingrams reopened a legal case trying to take Harmony Joy Hall. No. Never. Jenita had legally changed both of their names to Hall. She adored that girl. Harmony was her pride, her joy, her priority. The only time she turned her cuss button to full blast was when they came circling back.

"Ain't no damn way. Ah, hell naw."

They had driven their son to his death. There was no scenario in which she would ever allow them anywhere near her daughter.

Sometimes she'd cry whenever guilt would visit her about the abortion she'd had weeks after Warren's funeral, a panic-driven decision made after being served with the Ingrams' custody papers. But Kirk Franklin's "Imagine Me" ministered to her deeply, speaking to her childhood, her grief, and her own choices, and slowly transformed that guilt into tears of genuine gratitude.

Once, after a court notice arrived, Harmony saw her mother go tense. Harmony knew who the Ingrams were. After she turned eighteen, she wanted nothing to do with them. Jenita never had to say a negative word. Harmony had witnessed the harassment firsthand.

"Thank you for taking such good care of me, Mama."

"As long as I'm breathing, baby."

Jenita rarely dated and didn't have time and had no interest in raising somebody's grown son. She didn't want a revolving door of men in her daughter's life. Her most serious relationship lasted about a year and was, if she was honest, more about having a reliable plus-one than genuine love. He had two children with two different women. Drama followed accordingly.

Most of their relationship was spent either debating his situation or debating his suggestion that she sell her three-bedroom, two-and-a-half-bath home. He wanted to sell his two-bedroom, one-bathroom townhouse so they could buy something together, unmarried. She wasn't entertaining that. When he proposed just moving in, she wasn't hearing that either. It wasn't all his fault. She cared for him as a person. She just didn't love him as the man she needed or deserved. They ended it in 2000.

She felt that marriage would constrain her, and as a single parent, she didn't trust anyone else to have that level of influence over Harmony's life. She needed her space. She knew she couldn't have the best of both worlds, and she'd made her choice.

When it came to sex, she found it overrated. It took her years after Warren's death before she had it again. She found the rare occasions when she took care of herself more satisfying, but always felt guilty afterward.

Sheila weighed in regularly. "Jenita. Neat. Girl, that's what's wrong with you. You work too hard, and you need to stop acting like a nun and get you some hard happiness."

For her thirtieth birthday, Sheila knew a vibrator would be too forward for her, so she gifted her a stimulator. "If you're not going to have sex, you cannot be on manual for the rest of your life. Girl. Here's some help."

Rhonda added, "And I bought two packs of batteries and a Visa gift card for when you need more." They all laughed.

It took Jenita months to get up the nerve to use it. She'd been raised to believe sexual pleasure outside of a relationship was sinful. But she used it, and she had orgasms. She was saddened to realize she'd never had one with a man. In her life, she had been with her husband Warren, her ex-boyfriend, whom they called Mr. House Hunters, and one deeply regrettable fling.

The fling: she'd listened to Sheila and agreed to "live a little." Sheila set her up with a friend's cousin. He was attractive. That was all. Dinner was dry and awkward. She had sex with him twice the same night, the second time giving him the chance he'd asked for to do better than the first. It was worse. He was aggressive and forceful, with no tenderness. Just momentum, as if he were chasing a record. Never again. And for the rare moments she could delay guilt long enough and was in the mood, she put in fresh batteries.

Her coworkers pushed online dating. They even built a profile for her. Their own frustrating experiences convinced her to steer clear. Whenever anyone suggested a man, her standard reply became: "No ham, no spam, no thank you, ma'am."

After her breakup, Jenita redirected her energy fully, raising Harmony, supporting her students, building her business, and paying off her home. In that order. She loved her students deeply, and they returned it tenfold. Ms. Hall was the campus auntie. Caring for them beyond what was required came naturally to her. She felt the privilege and the responsibility of becoming what Ms. Jackson had been for her.

Her friends, sorority sisters, and coworkers said she cared too much, gave too much—even for them. She invested particular energy in students whose degrees weren't in the arts, but who used creativity as an outlet or a potentially profitable hobby. Some students, like Warren, had been forbidden by their parents from majoring or minoring in music or art despite real talent. Her program gave them a legitimate path. Elective credits, work-study opportunities through their skills, paid services for alumni events, or simply space to create, breathe, and decompress.

She seemed to have one student each year who became a favorite. Mike was hers from 2005 to 2009. He was a business management major, a freshman, and not technically eligible for her program until the Dean recommended him. Brilliant academically, a gifted musician with an extraordinary voice. A textbook introvert struggling to adjust to college life. Jenita accepted him anyway. Because he was two years younger than his peers and more withdrawn, she took him under her wing. She cooked for him and a few other students every Friday, and they could count on Ms. Hall to have something good. On birthdays, she'd host small groups of four to six at her home for dinner, a privilege students bragged about openly.

She had a gift for loving and caring in ways that were never misconstrued. Some faculty members complained she was doing too much, and that was generally as far as it went. But there was something about Mike. She loved him like a son. Because he was a freshman, she was careful to call his family and secure permission before any off-campus engagement.

They were hesitant at first and asked to come to the school to meet her. She arranged it. They hit it off immediately.

"Miss Hall, you're all right with me. I feel like I've known you at least half my life."

Jenita laughed and touched her arm. "Me too. Thank you for trusting me with Mike outside of school. I'll keep you posted, and I promise to report. Call me any time."

"Any time?"

"Any time."

"Okay. I'ma hold you to that. Might even surprise you."

"Feel free, here's. Here's my number and my home address." "Sure thing. We're going to have to do lunch again. I love good company and I love to eat."

"Me too. Can't you tell?"

"Aww, shucks, girl. I know those thick thighs have saved lives and that cushion is for good pushin'."

"But if you ain't got nobody pushin', it's just cushion."

They laughed all the way to their cars.

With the family's permission and the school's approval, Mike and three other students began spending weekends at Jenita's home when it was easier for her to transport them to school events. Mike came most often, and his family knew about every visit. They knew Ms. Hall was good for him. He blossomed. His grades held strong, and though his family never fully embraced his instrumental or vocal gifts, they were grateful he was genuinely happier.

Jenita's spiritual senses never gave her a moment's pause about Mike being around Harmony. She prayed over him and with him the way she did her own child. He became Harmony's big brother, sometimes teaching her chords on Warren's old keyboard and sometimes tutoring her in math, which was not Harmony's strength and Mike's gift. He arrived shy and guarded, and by his junior year he was still an introvert but with far more courage to step into extrovert spaces. He started a band with eight students, including his freshman cousin and his girlfriend Tiffany, whom Ms. Hall had introduced them, convinced they'd be a good match. She was right.

She invited Mike's family to their first performance, a paid alumni event, and they were blown away. His aunt was generous with compliments. His uncle kept watching Jenita sideways, as if searching for a disqualifying flaw. *Hmph. If he finds something on me, I'll be just as surprised.* He'd told his wife afterward, "Ain't nobody that nice 'cept you and Mama. Something's got to be off somewhere."

Miracle Mike was what they called him for years, and he was relieved when it finally stopped. He understood it, though. He had been thrown from a car window, snatched by force from his grandmother's arms. Fatou had rolled her window down to get a closer look at the stakes Louis was pointing out, and before she could get it back up, the truck hit. It could have been worse, possibly fatal, had Crystal not listened when Fatou told her to dress him warmly. He wasn't just layered, he was in a onesie coat, swaddled in a wool blanket, with a toboggan and hooded layer drawn snugly around him.

After two and a half hours of searching, cold and unconscious in the dark, Joe Lester Pringle found the almost two-year-old. When King got word that his grandson was alive, he felt as though he exhaled for the first time since he'd left for work that morning.

Michael Alexander Devereaux — his maternal grandfather's first name as his own, and Zee's middle name after that. Zee's son had survived.

Mike was hospitalized for months with a concussion, a broken leg, and internal injuries. He was raised with deep love by his father Zee, Aunt Renae, Uncle Frank, Great-Aunt Tink, and Pops, alongside his cousins, the oldest among them Quincy Brinkley Devereaux, Frank and Renae's firstborn. When Zee and Frank joined the military, Mike spent weekdays with Renae and weekends with Tink while Renae worked at King's & Queen's and built her wedding cake business on the side.

Mike was so thoroughly loved that he didn't know to grieve his mother or his grandmother. Renae and Tink covered all the motherly ground. When Zee came home in 1991, badly burned and carrying PTSD, fathering his kindergarten-age son became the priority. His own physical and mental health care went to the back burner. He loved his son dearly. Between Mike's homework, basketball workouts, academic activities, and part-time work alongside Zee, Frank, or Pops, Mike had little downtime outside of Sunday dinners and holidays.

Sunday dinners were where the family gathered to do business, eat, and pray. Tink kept them Christ-conscious and grounded in Jesus, handling prayer and spiritual practice that went beyond church. She didn't have the patience for the pastor's jealous wife or her circle, and she'd long since stopped apologizing for her hoodoo. She kept Fatou's Senegalese traditions alive as best she could, alongside their Creole heritage. She hadn't taken a client since Louis was murdered, but the family and close friends were the beneficiaries of her anointing, wisdom, ancestral veneration, and prophetic sight. She had stopped wearing all white after the accident—all black for a full year afterward. Under Renae's steady encouragement, color crept back in slowly.

Renae managed the food and fellowship. She stayed her father's girl because that's what King needed more than she needed anything from him. Pops mentored, updated everyone on the lawsuits, and outlined the plans. Zee, Renae, Frank, and Tink managed the business side. Sunday dinners were also when Pops formalized what became the family vault—a monthly contribution system for family members and close friends who were of age and not in school. Each month, a vote determined who received the pooled funds: someone starting a business, covering a major purchase, contributing to the King's & Queen's scholarship fund, or learning a trade. "Sweets by Renae" was the first third-generation LLC to come out of it. Mike watched that system from childhood until the day it was his turn to decide: college or trade.

He chose WSSU, on mathematics and basketball scholarships.

CHAPTER 14

Grounds & Maintenance

Jenita got a last-minute call from Sheila: she'd been invited on the 2012 Tom Joyner cruise by a friend and wouldn't be able to make the wedding. Again, Sheila was being pulled toward someone, man or woman, and again, she wouldn't be Jenita's plus-one. Jenita decided to go alone. She had to. She'd been asked to speak and bless the couple at their rehearsal dinner. There was no backing out, and nothing in her wanted to.

This young man felt like a son to her. She had introduced him to his bride-to-be when they were both her students back in 2005, and now, seven years later, they were tying the knot. She'd had a vision of them getting married from the moment she made that introduction, but she'd only told her sisters and Ms. Sylvia. She had to be there. The family had covered her stay at the new five-star hotel in Pine City, the only one in the area and in eastern North Carolina.

It had been over ten years since she'd been to Brown Sugar Beach, a place she'd visited since childhood. She was disappointed about Sheila, but not offended. She'd already spent too much on her rehearsal dinner dress and the wedding dress not to wear them. She packed: dresses in the garment bag, overpacking everything else in her big suitcase, all her necessities, shoes, and too many just-in-case outfits — plus her toiletry bag.

She cleaned the house, did laundry, shampooed her locs, and prepared the gifts for the ladies' luncheon. She put the cash in the card for the couple, signed it, called Harmony and Rhonda to let them know she'd be leaving in the morning without Sheila, and went to bed.

She was fast asleep when a gentle whisper woke her. Get up. Leave.

"Now."

"God, now?! It's ten o'clock. You know I don't like to drive at night, especially not this time of night. It'll be after two in the morning by the time I get there."

She argued with herself out loud, knowing full well she was going to obey. That inner voice, God. It never led her wrong. She fussed while getting dressed: travel sweats, a ballcap, walking sneakers, earrings and her heart charm necklace. She packed her suitcase and the gifts into the trunk, put the card in her purse, and did her usual security check of the house.

Then she stopped. The same voice told her to call the hotel and confirm she could check in after two in the morning, a day early, at her own expense. She told them she was part of the wedding party, gave her confirmation number and, to her surprise, they told her to come on.

By the time she was ready it was nearly eleven. She didn't want to wake Harmony, who was away at college, or Rhonda, who was out of the country, or Sheila, who was probably with whoever she'd stood her up for. She knew all of them would try to talk her out of it. But for safety, she needed someone to know. She knew Ms. Sylvia would be up, either closing up her restaurant, Sylvia's Seafood and Soul, or prepping for the next day.

Ms. Sylvia had become her auntie after her sister Ms. Jackson passed away from heart issues she'd carried since childhood.

"You getting on the road this time of night?" Ms. Sylvia asked.

"Yes, ma'am."

"I know I can't talk you out of it when the Holy Ghost gets you up out of bed. So, I can't talk you out of it. I won't try. I'll just talk you all the way in. You filled up yet?"

"Yes, ma'am. But I rented a car. I'm leaving as soon as I print out the directions from MapQuest."

"Why don't you just buy a map?"

"Because I don't know how to read a map. This gives me turn-by-turn."

She picked up the rental at the airport and got on the road, continuing her conversation with Ms. Sylvia.

"Neat, you need directions to Brown Sugar Beach? I thought it was a straight shot, the way I remember."

"The way I remember too. But they say it's built up so much down there that everything's changed. I haven't been since Harmony was little. I don't need directions to get there, I need them for when I arrive."

"Oh, I see. Well, be careful. And I prayed over you. Those white folks down there can be something."

"Thank you. It's a Black folks' wedding at a big-time white folks' hotel. My former students, getting married. I feel like a mama, an auntie, and a matchmaker all at once."

Thank God she'd printed the directions. Pine City had exploded. It was not asleep at two-thirty in the morning. Barely anything looked familiar except the ocean. There was a new Brown Sugar Beach billboard—huge, well-lit, and sleek. Where was the old Sandy Shores sign that used to be first? She thought she passed the hill with the black folks' shotgun homes but couldn't be sure. She had to hang up with Ms. Sylvia just to concentrate on the turns.

When she finally turned onto the street leading to the hotel, a sign read: Private Road — Hotel Guests Only. She was a guest. She proceeded, came upon an unguarded security shack and the rolling gate was wide open.

She rolled down her window. "Hello?" She tried again. "Helloooo?" Nothing.

ꕥ

Jenita drove past the security gate and found no one. But she knew she'd come to the right place. She could already see the upper floors and the lit sign of the hundred-room hotel rising ahead of her. She followed a winding road lined with palmetto trees, the green palms swaying and bouncing in the cool May breeze, visible even in the dark.

The landscape was immaculate, the lighting elegant all the way to the covered entrance, something like she'd seen at exclusive Caribbean resorts. Exquisite. She arrived at the front doors genuinely awestruck that something this magnificent existed only three and a half hours from home. An oasis. Nothing was where she remembered it, and nothing was what she remembered it being.

She parked beside two hotel shuttle vans near the entrance. No valet in sight. The branded podium was upscale and empty. She scanned the area.

Out of the corner of her eye she spotted a man, back turned, emptying a bag of mulch into one of several large planter pots, smoothing and pressing it with gloved hands. He was working fast. Seven other pots perfectly placed around the front and side entrances had already been filled.

She got out, locked up, put her purse on her shoulder, and trotted toward him before he could move on. "Excuse me, sir. Sir?"

He didn't stop. His headphones were deep into "Better Days Ahead" by Norman Brown.

"Excuse me, sir!" She waved. "I'm sorry to bother you."

He looked up, blinking as if he wasn't sure what he was seeing. He set the half-empty mulch bag down, pulled off his gloves, and tucked them into his back pocket.

He removed his headphones. "May I help you?"

"Yes. May I leave my car here while I go check in? I didn't see a valet."

He glanced at his watch. 2:38 a.m. *I guess I'm the valet tonight.* "Do you have a reservation?"

"Yes. Not until tomorrow, technically, but I called earlier and they said I could come tonight."

He looked puzzled but walked with her toward the entrance. As he got closer, Jenita, making herself comfortable the only way she knew how, extended her hand like she was opening a boardroom meeting.

"Hi. I'm Jenita Hall."

"Hi, Ms. Hall." He shook it with equal professionalism.

"And you are…" She was already reading the embroidered lettering under the hotel logo on his polo shirt. The letters read: GM.

"Oh—GM." She said it with full confidence. "Does that stand for Grounds and Maintenance?"

"You could say that. That's a lovely fragrance you're wearing."

"Thank you. And you are worth your weight in gold, sir. You've done amazing work. I hope they pay you well. Because the landscape is just breathtaking, at night no less. I can't imagine what it looks like in daylight."

"You think so?"

"Absolutely."

Mr. Grounds & Maintenance held the front door open for her. "Let's get you to the front desk." The moment she crossed the threshold, she felt like she'd stepped into another world entirely. The interior was even more luxurious than the outside had suggested. She felt like a tourist in New York City, stopped moving almost immediately, looking up, then left, then right, then up again, trying to take everything in.

He walked ahead and slipped behind the reception desk, found the mouse, and looked up to get started on her check-in. She had made it approximately four feet inside the door. She was captivated looking up, down, left, right and repeating the same panoramic pattern.

His attention shifted from looking for her to watching her. He had never seen an adult react to the lobby that way, that pure, unguarded rapture was something he'd only seen in children and the elderly. She was neither. Something about it caught him immediately as he became intrigued by her shameless, innocent awe.

Mr. Grounds & Maintenance was supposed to be watching the guests' services desk while the two, night managing employees were on their break. Two employees returning from their break snapped her out of it.

"I'm sorry." She was still looking up at the ceiling as she made her way toward the guest services desk, which seemed a mile away through too many beautiful things. She wasn't someone who hadn't traveled. This was different. A five-star hotel with museum-worthy art and a stained-glass cathedral ceiling at the beach. She felt emotion rising before she could stop it.

She was sensitive, empathic, and observant by nature and always quick to cry good tears at the drop of a hat. Love, babies, old couples, celebrations, goals met, hers and others, weddings, great testimonies: any of them could do it. This was all of them at once. One tear slid down one cheek. The other eye cupped its own. She probably looked sad.

He came back around the desk quickly. "Ms. Hall, are you all right?"

"Oh, yes. Don't mind me."

"What's wrong?"

"Nothing." She wiped her face quickly. "I'm just a softie and a wuss for nature, art, and beauty. This is just my wussing." She opened her purse for a tissue she didn't have. He reached into his pocket and produced a clean, pressed, neatly folded handkerchief and held it out between two fingers.

She took it slowly. *I haven't seen a man carry a handkerchief in years.*

"Thank you, sir."

"You're welcome, ma'am."

He noticed the scar on her cheek. He was relieved, quietly, that these weren't sad tears.

She looked up again. "This stained glass is a thing of beauty. But at the beach? One good hurricane and it's gone. It's so fragile. I could lie on this floor and stare up at all the nautical themed glass all day — it's like being underwater."

He smiled. "Feel free. I have. I'm glad someone else appreciates it."

"Appreciates it? Who wouldn't? Wait. You actually laid on this floor to look at it?"

"Many times. And since you like it that much, I'll tell you a secret. But you can't tell anyone."

"You don't know me well enough to trust me with a secret."

"I'm a pretty good judge of character. The way you noticed the grounds outside and now your appreciation for design, the way you're responding to all of this, I can already tell that I can trust you with this one."
"Okay."

"All right. But for the record, I am a very trustworthy person. Your judgment is correct."

"I can tell." He held her gaze a beat too long and caught himself. She was still looking up and didn't notice.

"What's the secret?" she asked, curious as a child.

"You ready?"

"Yes!"

"It's not actually stained glass."

She looked up again. "I'm looking right at it."

"But it's not."

"What is it, then?"

"Lights and paint."

"Lights and paint?"

"Yes, ma'am."

She was even more intrigued, stared upward as if widening her eyes might change the answer.

"Think about it," he said. "It's nearly three in the morning. So why does the lobby look like it's daytime? He pointed upward. "Back lighting behind the ceiling—a hard, dome-shaped clear material painted with gradient colors and textures. Then varying intensities of uplighting and side lighting along the perimeter, with a few hidden at floor level behind the planters and some of the art pieces." He walked her eyes to each one.

"Oh my…" She started seeing it—how paint and light, in the hands of brilliant artisans, had turned a ceiling into a nautical world that had fooled her completely. "This is extraordinary."

"I agree wholeheartedly. They did remarkable work."

"Who are the artists?"

"The Black Artists Guild from France."

The nautical theme ended at the ceiling. The rest of the lobby. The fabric walls and artwork were a unique blend, something Jenita couldn't quite name. It was a blend she'd never seen assembled so well. Bohemian, African, Native American, East Indian, and Asian influences coexisting in a palette of vivid blues, greens, yellows, and pinks that somehow read exciting without ever becoming busy. Tasteful. She loved all of it. Just when she thought she'd absorbed everything, something else caught her eye. A grand bubbling fountain occupied the center of the marble floor, which was broken up by four circular inlays in different mosaic patterns. In certain spots, the white marble reflected the ceiling above, making the room feel infinite.

While they finished up her VIP check-in, the real valet had returned with both pieces of her luggage on a cart. As he got closer, she looked past him.

"Did you get my garment bag from the back seat?"

"I looked, Ms. Hall. There was no garment bag."

The bliss drained out of her instantly. In her haste to obey that voice and get on the road, she had left it lying across the back of her couch at home. Both dresses. The rehearsal dinner dress and the wedding dress, hanging there in Jaxton.

"Oh, my goodness." She pressed her hand to her forehead. "I forgot my outfits."

The woman attendant felt her disappointment. "Oh no."

There was absolutely no way Jenita was driving three and a half hours back home.

The attendant's voice was warm and steady. "Ms. Hall, I'm so sorry. But one of our world-class concierges has been assigned to you and will be more than happy to assist you with wedding attire or anything else you need."

That sentence sounded very expensive. She'd already spent beyond her norm on the dresses she'd left behind. The word "concierge" made it sound like more.

"Is there a mall?"

"Yes. About ten minutes away in Pine City. But it would be our pleasure to assist you in-house. Even if you need apparel outside our boutique, we can arrange to have it brought to you."

CHAPTER 15

It's Always Something

Mike followed in several of Zee's footsteps. A sought-after, first-string athlete in high school, though he leaned toward basketball over football. Academically gifted, well-liked, handsome, musically talented, and his dad's little man. When Zee left college after losing his mother, he poured every ounce of love, life, and affection he had into his son. It still never felt like enough.

He'd been blessed to experience his mother's overwhelmingly good love and affection. The short-lived love he had with Crystal left him with guilt, knowing Mike would never experience either of them the way he deserved. He felt guilty for being alive sometimes. It took years of consistent, concentrated and extensive therapy, his family's support, and doing the work to move slowly through that. His focus and purpose became clear: raise his son, take care of his family, and help people of color build real wealth through local and international real estate and the stock market.

He took good care of Mike the best he knew how and leaned on Renae, Tink, Frank, and Pops to fill any gaps. Mike lived with Zee in the completely renovated home his grandparents had originally bought until Zee had a new house built later. Heartbroken in ways that never fully healed, Pops never slept in the family home again after the accident. He took a permanent room at the motel. Tink never returned to her home either and moved into one of the rental properties she and Louis had owned. Louis's children left shortly after his death to live with their mothers—a layered, exponential loss for Tink that she carried quietly. It opened the way for Renae and Frank to move into Tink and Louis's house, right across the street from Zee and Mike.

Whenever Zee traveled for business, establishing professional relationships and partnerships, growing the family enterprises and his own company nationally and internationally, Mike stayed with Renae and Frank.

After the military, one of Zee's business partnerships led to an engagement. A wealthy Black French family wanted to strengthen their business foothold in the United States, and Zee wanted to expand his international real estate brokerage into France. Fatou had raised her twins with Wolof as their first language and taught them French as well. They took French in high school, and Zee continued in college. Easy A's. He spoke it fluently when he traveled.

In 2005, he moved quickly into an engagement with a woman he did not love. They liked each other well enough, and they both understood the business value well enough to broker a marriage. Zee had long since stopped believing true love was in the cards for him.

Chantel was uppity, status-obsessed, and spent extravagantly, which was consistent with how she and her siblings had been raised. But she considered Zee her very own top-shelf specimen, arm candy she could use to make others envious. That was her nature: shallow, selfish, a daddy's girl whose ambitions began and ended with luxury and minimal effort. Her family's mission was to add money and children to their assets. Zee's genes combined with hers, in her estimation, would produce a cute baby — another thing to make people jealous.

He knew Mike would never fit into her world, and between Pops, Renae, Frank, and Tink, no one was going to allow it. Chantel only ever intended to visit America on her own terms. She had no interest in living there. Zee had no intention of living in France. They kept their expectations open, except that Zee kept his plan for full custody to himself.

They didn't have sex often. When they did, for him it was baby-making-sex, get to the end and skimp on the means. What mattered to him was ensuring she delivered on American soil so he would easily get custody. He didn't care who her family was or what they thought. There was no version of his life in which he was not raising his child.

Then, the second time they had sex, when she saw him without his shirt. She stared at his injury with disgust.

Zee's body was beautiful, a well-balanced combination of tone, muscle, and maturity in all the right places, but she couldn't move past the skin grafts that covered his left side and wrapped around to half his back. The grafted skin was leathery, patchy, with different textures and colors from the rest of his smooth brown skin. He noticed that look.

Before sex, she said, "Those mismatched patches stick out like they don't belong. *Mets une chemise, maintenant.* (Put a shirt on, now). Ugh—it's a big turnoff." She rolled her eyes.

That cut him profoundly.

How could she be so heartless and cold, knowing full well how it happened?

He felt that way when he looked at himself in the mirror sometimes. He had just never imagined hearing someone else say it boldly and with that kind of indifference. He was already a quiet man. After that, he said less to her, and he never let her see his torso again—not even during sex. And in his competitive business nature: as much as he enjoyed giving oral sex, she would not be getting that from him.

Even when she asked for it, even when she begged, all he could hear was: Put a shirt on. Ugh.

About six months into the engagement, she still wasn't pregnant. Sex had become a tolerable, moderately purposeful task, something he did for the business arrangement and to maintain appearances for her family. They saw each other twice a month, neither using birth control.

Chantel went to see a doctor. There needed to be a pregnancy and a wedding to formalize the business deal, in that order. She asked Zee to be examined as well. He went, reluctantly, to his primary care physician, a Black woman he trusted, who referred him to a fertility specialist. After several tests, the results came back: extremely low to no sperm count.

He hadn't known. Most men don't. Military service exposes soldiers to heavy metals, chemicals, and radiation, particularly during wartime, any of which can suppress sperm production, lower count, or impair function. He was deflated. Emasculated all over again.

He had accepted that he might never truly love or be loved by a woman. But he had wanted another child. Tink had told him once he'd have a daughter.

When Chantel and her family found out, they called off the engagement. The Devereaux family could not have been more relieved. Zee returned to what he knew—work. He drowned himself in it. Insomnia was brutal on his body and extraordinarily profitable for business.

And then, as if things hadn't already been heavy enough, he and Frank became heroes. Unintentionally.

Renae had opened the second location of Sweets by Renae in the eight-store strip mall Pops had developed. A convenient spot where customers didn't have to fight beach traffic for a cupcake, cookie, or donut. It also gave Renae a sense of being out on her own, which she was. She paid rent to D.E. like every other tenant.

Frank did the same for his barbershop, Frank's Place. Decked out with billiards tables, flat-screen TVs, arcade games, and a cigar room. A proper men's haven.

Beyond wedding cakes, Renae had kept her custom orders small, but once she hired help, she expanded. She'd say with a wide smile, "If Mama, Uncle Louis, and Crystal could see me now."

Then came her first major commercial order. The local branch of United Bank was celebrating its centennial anniversary. The Devereaux family had banked with United for years, and when it came time to celebrate, Sweets by Renae was their go-to. They ordered a grand themed cake and a hundred cupcakes. For heavy, high-stakes deliveries, Renae trusted no one except Quincy, Mike, Frank, and Zee.

That day, Frank drove Renae's delivery van with her, Zee, a towering money-themed cake with elaborate decorations, and a hundred gold-coin cupcakes. Security routed them around back and down to the basement. Frank and Zee knew the drill: obey Renae's every instruction or there would be verbal hell to pay. How to lift the cake. Where to place their hands. How fast or slow to move on stairs. Once the cake was set in the conference room and felt like they could take a breather from drill sergeant Renae, they all heard a sharp, unmistakable pop.

Frank and Zee recognized it instantly.

Shrieks and screams erupted from the lobby. Frank shoved Renae to the floor and crouched. Zee went flat. The two combat veterans locked eyes, made a split-second decision: get Renae out, then move toward the threat. The back door was close enough for her to slip through. They moved her to it.

Frank carried a weapon in a chest holster. Zee kept one at his back, and a second holstered on his leg. This was still Pine City, and the Devereaux family's success had made them hated by every racist and supremacist in the county. Their combat readiness surfaced without thinking.

They moved toward the sounds—whimpering, and a voice shouting words they couldn't yet make out. Frank's prosthesis didn't allow him to crawl or move as fast as Zee. They moved forward, Zee stayed low and Frank stayed high. After several tense minutes, their hearts were beating fast and Frank could feel sweat stinging his hairline after he had given himself a fresh edge-up that morning.

They had been perched and crouched near a cracked door watching this bank robbery play out like a bad B-movie.

The gunman had a teller pressed against him as a shield, forcing her to rake money into a bag while two other tellers, hands shaking, fed bills into more bags. Everyone in the lobby was face down on the floor, their belongings scattered. He waved his weapon and berated them for not moving fast enough, slurring his words and full of slobbery rage. He was shouting that the bank and niggers had stolen all his family's money and he was there to get it back.

People were whimpering, fearing for their lives and it was obvious the gunman was drunk, high or both.

"Shut up before I shoot you!" he snapped at a woman leaning against the wall.

The teller he was using as a shield said softly, "Please don't shoot anybody. We're getting your money."

"Shut up!"

"Okay. But please—don't hurt me."

"I said shut the hell up!"

Zee looked up at Frank. Frank already had his weapon raised and aimed. Zee touched Frank' shoe. No response—prosthesis side. He touched the other shoe. Frank flinched and shot him a look. What you touch me for?

Zee mouthed, "That's Andy Headen."

Frank didn't catch it.

"That's Andy."

Andy heard him. "Who's back there?" Silence. "Who's back there?"

Zee pressed himself flat against the wall. Andy fired at the door, shattering the glass insert. Screams rang out through the lobby.

"Shut up!" Andy bellowed.

His grip on the teller tightened. She dropped the bag. Bills fell like fall leaves.

"Look what you did! Who is back there?"

Frank pushed the door open slowly. Zee slid out beside him. Both weapons drawn, fingers on the triggers.

"Put the gun down," Frank said. "Put it down!"

Andy blinked, still having the gun pressed on the woman's head. "Is that… Frank? Zander?"

"Yeah, man. Put the gun down."

"You can't tell me what to do. This is y'all Devereaux's niggers' fault anyway."

Zee kept his weapon steady. "Andy. Put the got-damn gun down. Now!"

Andy Headen. The prom night girl's brother. One of evil's notorious playmates, right along with the Headen-Pettigrew-Jefferson crew, kept it busy. He had been the youngest of the five men charged with premeditated murder and aggravated assault in connection with the deaths of Fatou, Louis, and Crystal, and the attempted murder of Mike. The four older men had gone to prison. Old man Headen died in custody. One of his sons was murdered inside. Another received life. The two truck drivers got the death penalty. The conspirators were sentenced to twenty-five years per fatality and ten years for what they did to Mike.

Andy, barely twenty at the time of sentencing, had received twenty-five years. Somehow, he'd gotten out on parole for good behavior.

And here he stood—robbing the bank that had once held his family's slave money, scam money, tobacco and cotton investments, and the blood-soaked returns on decades of predatory business. The Devereaux family's civil cases had allowed them to become the legal instrument through which every recoverable dollar was reclaimed. Pops and Tink used that money to buy nearly every piece of land that they had once owned. Some they bought at auction through tax liens; some they bought for pennies on the dollar. Sound familiar?

CHAPTER 16

Help Is on the Way

Andy hated Zee for earning the coveted quarterback position at JHS—the one Andy had long considered his birthright—and pushing him to second string. He and his sister had been part of the miscreant posse from the beginning. He was a convicted felon, an alcoholic, a drug addict. A bad seed, plain and simple. And now here they were, fifteen years later, staring down each other's gun barrels.

"Shut the hell up, Zander. You ruined my life."

He started crying drunk tears, not realizing he was tightening his arm around the teller's neck.

"Come on, man," Zee said, weapon still aimed at Andy's shoulder.

"I ain't doing nothing no Black monkey-ass say."

"Then can you at least let her go?"

"Her? You worried about her?" The teller began to cry out loud.

"Shut up bitch!"

Just as Andy moved to pull the trigger, Zee fired — hitting him in the shoulder of his gun arm. Frank's bullet hit his hand. They had both rightfully earned their USMC Expert Marksmanship Medals.

Andy went down. The teller ran, screaming.

Andy died later from toxic levels of alcohol and narcotics in his system, compounded with his wounds and prevented any meaningful healing from the gunshots, neither of which would have been fatal on their own.

To Pine City and eastern North Carolina—to everyone who knew the calculated evil the Headens, and their associates had done over the years—Zee and Frank were heroes. People exhaled. There were still racist relatives and those they'd managed to recruit, but something had shifted.

Frank and Zee were celebrated. Hometown athletic champions. Decorated war veterans. Successful Black businessmen—and now heroes. It couldn't get more legendary than that. Could it?

But they didn't feel like heroes. People admired the wins. Very few stopped to consider the gravity of the fight, the cost, or the pain underneath it.

Frank handled it the way he handled most things: he went back to weekly therapy fast and did the work to ease the fact that they were in direct connection with a man's death, outside of war. He was coping well. And in true Frank fashion, he found a way to joke his way through it, calling himself the new sheriff in town. Somewhere in him, he felt a quiet, complicated relief—Andy and the devil's volunteers had been the ones who snatched away his first encounter with love and a real mother: Fatou. The family was grateful both he and Zee were alive and that Renae had gotten out.

Zee didn't think he could take another thing.

Zee often felt God was angry with him. Had to be. Why else would this much keep happening? He was breaking down. He could travel anywhere in the world, but he couldn't outrun himself anymore. He couldn't run from the pain, the grief, the trauma, the violation, or the lives that left him conflicted—both those taken in war and the one lost in that bank. Couldn't run from his own relentless, sharp-edged Blackness in the business world.

He found himself wondering: if I hadn't left for college, I could have driven Mama to the store that day.

He blamed himself for the suffocating weight of it all sometimes. Because he had witnessed it once and heard about other times: a group of his fellow athletes, high school boys and young men from surrounding schools doing the same thing to unsuspecting girls that had been done to him on prom night. He had never said a word. He carried it like a moral injury, convincing himself his pain was justifiable punishment for his silence.

The bank incident broke him further down. He never considered suicide, but he didn't want to engage with anything. He hadn't smoked or drunk since prom night. He'd grown so accustomed to women's bodies in a beach town—where they were everywhere, sometimes aggressively on display—that he'd stopped registering them entirely.

Talking with Frank one afternoon, he said, "I don't even think I have a type. What's wrong with me, bruh?

Frank didn't miss a beat. "Man, it's them got-damn C names. Crystal, God rest her soul. Cora, you ain't have no business layin' up with her old ass. Chantel, I told you 'bout her musty ass before you started messing with her. You mess with another woman named 'C' and I'll shoot your smokey ass myself. You see what I did to that white boy."

Frank's shot had gone clean through Andy's hand. That alone hadn't killed him—it was the illegal narcotics and alcohol running neck and neck with his blood that did it.

"Yep. Boo yow! Fool with another 'C' and it's gon' be me and you, high noon, at the O.K. Corral."

Zee leaned forward and laughed. Anyone else would have called it a chuckle. Those who knew him knew that was his hearty laugh. Frank laughed loud enough for both of them anyway.

"Hold still before your head gets skint up with these clippers."

Frank despised seeing his brother disappear into himself.

He often thought, *What if I hadn't left the prom early that night?*

A good laugh couldn't fix Zee's gloom. He felt like Schleprock—the Flintstones character from Pebbles and Bamm-Bamm—walking around under his own personal storm cloud, with the luck to match. He spiraled deeper. Few could tell, because his depression was masked with work, relentless workouts, stomach trouble, and insomnia. Quietly, desperately, he wanted to disappear.

But he thought about Mike. He thought about Pops.

So instead of disappearing, he ran toward help.

Between Tink's prayers, Pops's steadiness, Renae's nagging, and Frank's pleading, he ran to get qualified care. As God and the prayers of his mother, Tink, Renae, and his own would have it, he ran exactly where he needed to go. Intensive mental health therapy. A genuine, personal relationship with God. And in 2007, he willingly chose celibacy and entered it with intention.

He finally took his primary care physician's referral seriously. He'd watched it work for Frank. At Renae's constant and loving insistence, he checked himself into an outstanding holistic wellness center.

Becoming vulnerable took time. He had never established the kind of trust outside of family and wartime Marine Corps brothers that vulnerability required. And he was so overloaded — pain, grief, suppressed emotion stacked on top of more of the same—that he didn't know where to start. He also knew, with absolute certainty, that after his family had been murdered in a premeditated act by seven white supremacists he, for damn sure, wasn't going to be vulnerable with anyone white.

It was a white-owned wellness center. His Black therapists were superheroes. Not all heroes wear capes.

CHAPTER 17

What Happened Was

When people accused him of being a perfectionist, Mr. Grounds & Maintenance brushed it off as simply liking things done well. His accusers never complained when that standard applied to them. He found a particular tranquility, some called it Zen, in staying locked in on whatever task was in front of him. Take this wedding, for instance. He'd walked the grounds after the landscape crew knocked off for the day. Unsatisfied with what they'd left, he decided to redo it himself, the way he wanted it—even if it took until two-thirty in the morning. Had it not been for Ms. Hall, he'd probably still be outside piddling.

He found himself turning her over in his mind. Something in her handshake. The intrigue hadn't settled; if anything, it had peaked when she stood in that lobby, fascinated by the art.

She cried. And she mentioned wanting to lie on the floor. He'd told her he had done exactly that, many times, and he'd meant it, particularly at this hour of the morning. Ms. Hall was exceptional. She had asked him question after question about the lobby: the décor, the art, what music was playing. He'd enjoyed every answer, and he'd loved the way she listened to each one with her whole attention.

He drifted from the front desk to let the clerks do their job. But before he went, he looked at her again. He noticed how attractive she looked, just off the road at 3:00 a.m., and looked once more.

Naturally pretty face, that dimple, a sweet-smelling presence that filled his lungs and made him exhale fully. Did she look familiar, or was it just something about her that felt familiar? He couldn't decide, and he wasn't going to get caught staring. He felt something in each glance he stole while the staff worked through her preferences.

VIP check-in at this hotel was thorough: food allergies, other allergies, preferred mealtimes, room service versus dining room, turndown service, wake-up calls, favorite scents and colors, brand preferences for toiletries and hair care, beach versus pool versus cabana, excursions, need for a driver, business or pleasure, maid or butler service, drawn bath or shower. If Ms. Hall had filled out the questionnaire that came with the wedding invitation or called ahead, which was an option, her check-in would have been considerably faster. She hadn't known it would be this involved.

He listened to her responses as he drifted away. In the luxury hotel world, guests tended to want more and grow more demanding the moment they felt entitled. Her simplicity made him want to know more about her. He slipped away undetected and kept working through his list.

The hotel was hosting the wedding guests and rehearsal dinner, while the wedding and reception would mark the inaugural event at its off-site events center. The groom's family was pulling out every stop, and the hotel was positioned to make this the event that put them on the luxury map—measured against any five-star venue of comparable size.

He had a long list and plenty still to inspect. Including the boutique, where he'd just noticed the mannequin's display dress had not been changed. He shook his head and headed that way.

During check-in, Jenita couldn't quite decide whether to be impressed or intimidated. She was leaning toward being intimidated, until the valet came back without her garment bag. Mr. Grounds & Maintenance overheard what had happened as he was coming back through the glass door. He caught her disappointment from across the lobby but trusted that the concierge team would handle it.

As she and the bellman were making their way past the boutique toward the elevators, they saw him reach up to bring a mannequin down from the display rack. Jenita slowed.

"Oh, my goodness—that's a beautiful dress."

He turned it toward her. "You think so?"

"Yes. I do."

"Lorraine only makes a hundred of these signature dresses. This may be the last one."

"That's exclusive!" She had stopped walking, drawn closer to get a better look.

"Ten each in women's sizes medium through 2X."

"It's beautiful. And I need a dress. This is prettier than both of the ones I left at home."

"Would you like this one?"

"Is it for sale?"

"Everything we have is for sale at the right price." He smiled.

"What size is it? It looks too small."

He worked the dress off the now half-naked, upside-down mannequin. "Let me see… they have clips cinching the waist. It's… an XL."

"An XL? Hold it out."

He held the dress up against his own body to spread it wide.

She sized it up with her eyes, "…Hmm. I might be able to wear that."

"I think it'll fit you." He couldn't be certain—her oversized T-shirt gave nothing away about her shape.

"May I touch it?"

"Of course." He stepped toward her; she moved further through the boutique door toward him. She reached for the fabric. As he drew his hand away to give her room, their hands brushed.

She touched the dress softly. "Ooh—the fabric feels as luxurious as the print."

Mr. Grounds & Maintenance felt a small jolt that startled him. He pulled his hand back.

"I'm sorry. Did I shock you?"

"No." He looked at his hand. "Well… a little."

"I'm sorry."

"Not your fault, Ms. Hall. Probably static from the dress."

"How much is it?"

"I'm not sure. The display pieces don't have price tags, but I can find out."

"Oh, please don't go through the trouble at this time of morning."
"No trouble at all."

"I can come back in the morning."

"How about you take it with you tonight? That way you can try it on."

This five-star service is no joke. He placed the dress on a satin hanger, slipped it into a boutique garment bag, and held it out. She reached for it.

"No, ma'am. Our VIP guests don't carry their own bags while they're at home with us." He handed it to the bellman to hang on the cart, then watched as she followed the bellman toward the elevator.

King had never shed a tear and expected the same from Zee. Renae, Frank, and Tink—in that order—cried enough for all of them. What kept King from turning his horrendous pain and justifiable rage into retaliation was the same thing that had always anchored him: his love for his Queen and his family was far greater than his anger. He was driven by an insatiable need to carry their legacy forward. But he moved through life with muted emotions, his grief sealed beneath the surface.

He channeled his brute anger into pursuit—criminal justice, civil justice—relentless and uncompromising. He was bold, brazen, and fierce. He left the family home in Pine City because he couldn't live in it without Fatou. He took a permanent room at the motel and spent every available hour filing cases and staying on top of the criminal and civil lawsuits against the Headen, Pettigrew, Jefferson clans, the county and the city itself.

He had to do some of the legwork himself, knowing local law enforcement might favor the clans and that state and federal officials moved too slowly. He used his savings and $50,000 from the life insurance policies he and Tink held on Fatou and Louis to retain top attorneys and hire private investigators.

He didn't realize until the day after the murders that the brake line on his own car had been cut. It was later discovered that the brake line on Louis's truck had been cut too. Investigators and—surprisingly—local police, city officials, and the sheriff's department didn't behave as expected. The new regime fully cooperated. Much of the old regime was indicted, implicated in a web of crimes, charged, and sentenced. State law enforcement, the FBI, the highway patrol, out-of-state private investigators, and the high-powered legal team King assembled uncovered a treasure trove of evidence.

The accident opened a wound in Pine City's history that had been festering for six decades. Once the perpetrators were in custody, the full scope of their crimes came spilling out. They were found guilty of three counts of vehicular manslaughter and, in the judge's words, "negligence, recklessness, gross indifference to human life, and tampering with vehicles." That was only the tip of the iceberg. Their sentences were fitting, if never fair in proportion to the pain and suffering they had caused.

The evil ran deep and wide, tangled across generations, city officials, and others. What began as the biggest legal news Pine City had ever seen became a saga that stretched from 1988 to 1998: arson, murder, rape, statutory rape, conspiracy, money laundering, kidnapping, sex trafficking, drug trafficking, child labor, assault, real estate fraud, unlicensed liquor manufacturing. The full alphabet of crimes. They served evil faithfully and made it proud—until the courts buried them beneath it.

After winning the criminal cases, King filed and won record-breaking civil judgments. Victims' groups followed with class action suits: employees, renters, contractors, rape survivors, and more. The courts ran every one of them into the ground.

Mr. King Alexander Devereaux and Ms. Ann Marie Devereaux were each awarded $7.4 million. Cheryl and Crystal's parents stayed at odds with the Devereaux family—blaming Louis for Crystal's death and resenting Zee for winning custody of Mike—hired a slip-shod TV lawyer and were awarded $500,000 for Crystal. Mike was awarded $1 million.

Law enforcement found millions in cash stashed throughout the defendants' properties and accounts. Beyond that, they held vast assets: businesses, land, property, stocks, and bonds. King and his brilliant attorneys went for the estates. Because of new roads and the anticipated surge in tourism, land values in the area had skyrocketed by the time the civil awards were settled. Imagine that. As King would say with vehement boldness, "I want every blade of grass they ever owned."

During the proceedings and long after, King refused to allow anyone white— including his own attorneys— to call him Pops the way his family and their village did. He required King or Mr. Devereaux. He extended that expectation to his family, including the more than twenty relatives who had relocated from New Orleans. He was the man. He had a dream to fulfill.

Tink held on to what God had spoken to her years earlier: the evildoers had been getting by with it—but they would no longer get away with it." What the Devereaux family didn't recover, other victims won.

Devereaux Enterprises now proudly held land that the enslaved had been abused on. Property that sharecroppers had been scammed out of. Land falsely declared unfit for development when it was prime real estate. Slumlord housing. Property stolen by those who built their wealth on injustice across generations. Farmland. Three miles of private beachfront that had been forcibly taken from Black families, leaving only a sliver, just enough for the Brown Sugar Beach motel, which had been overcharged to King in the first place. They cleaned house. With interest.

He had been a tall, strapping man before the tragedy. By the time the legal battles were over, he had shrunk in stature and aged badly. He was so thin his pants pockets nearly met in the back. He hadn't changed his pants size, so the waistband buckled and he'd punched extra holes in his belt; his daily black suspenders were the only thing holding his pants up. He looked much older than he was.

He wore the grief and the weight of his family's plight and the Black community's plight on his back, evident on his drawn face. Fighting and winning had cost him, and it showed. His lack of melanin didn't help; it made him look more like a gaunt, big-eared old white man. But his commanding presence remained, mostly wordless.

He hadn't glanced at another woman, taken time for leisure, or done much laughing. All business. Even after the decade-long legal battle wound down, he stayed locked in. There were dreams to build, visions to execute, people to hire, a legacy to establish and expand. It wasn't until he finally allowed Zee, who was always willing, always ready, to serve as his right hand that they knew to surround themselves with trusted, capable people.

Renae, Frank, Tink, Joe Lester, and Reggie were all carrying triple their weight. They began to recruit strategically. Family members and friends who already had businesses were an easy lift. They scouted collaborators and investors who would be a genuine fit for Devereaux Enterprises—as partners, not passengers. Some partnerships were obvious from the start.

The foundation they were building would rival anything on the East Coast. They knew it would take time, hard work, talent, and uncompromising excellence. But if D.E. was going to become a true hospitality phenomenon, it would need world-class services built in-house.

That meant thinking down to the finest detail, including a tailor and a seamstress. They already had Sweets by Renae's first location, The Tinkery card and gift shop featuring Tink's work alongside local and international artisans, a world-class spa, and a small nightery called Zydeco. Now they needed Lorraine.

Everyone in Pine City—Black and white—knew Lorraine was the best. She had trained both her nieces in dressmaking and tailoring. She was celebrated for making custom wedding gowns and formal attire. Her nieces designed daywear and beachwear and had shown at New York Fashion Week. Lorraine had to be part of what they were building.

Fatou had once sewn for her boutique, and King had kept that friendship cordial over the years. He was the best one to bring Lorraine to the table, so he began meeting with her. At first, it was purely business. She was a spinster, the late bishop's daughter. She had found King attractive years ago but had never entertained a thought beyond that. As their business conversations deepened, and as Zee, Frank, Renae, and their circle demonstrated that D.E. was being handled capably, almost to his satisfaction, King allowed himself to notice the signals

Lorraine was sending. It had been twenty years since his Queen Fatou was taken from him.

Lorraine agreed to partner with the Devereaux family, along with both her nieces. And somewhere in those meetings, she and King began to date. Eventually, they started living together. They were older, and they didn't talk about marriage. But they didn't let their age stop whatever this was—companionship, comfort, and a quiet and steady warmth. They both understood she could never replace his Queen. But she could meet him where he was, and they could walk beside each other for whatever time remained.

CHAPTER 18

Who Wudda Thunk?

Mr. Grounds & Maintenance was trying to stay on task with his usual precision. He checked a few things off the list, but not without distraction. He went to the wine cellar to pull inventory for the rehearsal dinner and kept losing count. He got a ladder to take it to the rooftop, where the decorators would need it in place. And then he just...stood there. Arms crossed, staring out at the ocean. The rooftop view was extraordinary at this hour, and it was not what had stopped him.

He couldn't stop thinking about Jenita Hall. *Who is she?* He stood there breathing in and out the way he had on many nights and mornings, except this time, something was different. He felt something. *What is this?* He had been on the rooftop for twenty minutes. It should have been a one-minute drop-off.

Grounds & Maintenance had nothing to do with the guest lists for the rehearsal dinner, the wedding, or the reception. But while he searched his thoughts, and reminisced about Jenita Hall's voice, her scent, he wondered how she got the scar on her face, her smile, that dimple, her wonder at the lobby, her candor, her simplicity, her authenticity, and that brush of her hand, something came to him. He moved fast toward the elevator.

Good. Light under the door in the events planning office. He knocked.

"Come in."

"I see I'm not the only one burning the midnight oil."

"No, sir. But you're always working."

"True. I need to see the guest lists for tomorrow."

"Which one?"

"All of them."

She handed him three manila folders: Rehearsal Dinner, Wedding, Reception. He sat in the corner chair, ankle resting on his knee.

"Are you looking for something in particular?"

"Yes."

"Tell me what and I'll help. I practically have them memorized."

He opened the first folder and ran his finger down to the H's. "Hall. Jenita Hall."

"Yes, she's on the list."

"Any other Halls?"

"Yes. A brother and sister, Larry and Beulah Hall."

"Are they here for the whole weekend?"

"Yes."

"Okay." He looked relieved. He straightened the lists, slid them back in the folders, and handed them over. "What time are you leaving?"

"In a few minutes. I need at least a few hours of sleep. Marathon weekend ahead. I know you're excited."

"I am. This is the hotel's first of many firsts."

"What time are you coming back in the morning?"

"It is the morning."

"I mean, when are you coming back?"

"I'm here. I may catch a few winks in the staff hospitality suite."

"I don't know how you do it."

"I just get it done."

By the time he finished the bulk of his checklist, he swung through the kitchen during a shift change, making sure the new buffet cooling station was set up and tested before breakfast service. The dining room looked exceptional: black tablecloths, white runners, centerpieces that were works of art, plush black armchairs, padded booths, and terrazzo flooring. He crossed to the warm station side to check the steaming on the chafing dishes.

When he looked up, he saw Ms. Hall walking toward the boardwalk.

What is she doing? It's four-thirty in the morning.

She was still wearing the same tracksuit, oversized T-shirt, and ballcap. He noticed her full hips and thighs and was both attracted and quietly amused that she thought she was hiding all that curviness. He watched her until she disappeared from view.

When Jenita reached her room, she stopped in the doorway. It was magnificent. The fragrance, the décor, the full marble bathroom, herringbone light oak floors, down bedding, artwork, thread-count sheets, a stocked minibar, mirrors, thoughtful lighting, and high-end furniture. She'd received a double since Sheila was supposed to be her plus-one. Now she had all this plush to herself.

The assistant assigned to her was waiting at the door when she and the bellman arrived. She walked Jenita through every amenity, offered to unpack, draw a bath, turn down the bed, or take a food and beverage order. Happily overwhelmed, Jenita thanked her for the tour and for the instructions for all the gadgets and confirmed she could manage on her own. When she tried to tip her, like the bellman, the assistant declined. The wedding guests had already been taken care of.

She slipped the twenty back in her wallet.

Her room had oceanfront views on two sides. "I got a corner lot. Sheila is going to hate that she missed this."

She felt like Ms. Celie the day that woman handed her the keys to her mama's house and her stepfather's store.

She opened the balcony door. The ocean smell and the breeze met her like open arms. She inhaled as deeply as she could through her nose and let it out slowly through pursed lips. The outdoor furniture looked better than most people's indoor furniture.

She walked over to the sliding glass door on the side view and repeated the ritual, then noticed a pier.

"Hold up. When did they get a big pier?"

There had always been a wooden pier further down the beach, on the white side, where Black people weren't welcome. This was something else: 820 feet of concrete, wide, well-lit, with benches, the same ecru color as the boardwalk. She had to see it up close. She was too excited to sleep, and if she moved now, she could catch the sunrise from the pier.

Brown Sugar Beach had transformed beyond recognition. The boardwalk, lined with surf shops, restaurants, gift shops, an ice cream parlor, and a candy store, Pine City hadn't just come up; it had boomed.

The pier was perfect. The sun wasn't up yet, so she breathed, prayed, listened, and meditated on the beauty, then let herself be still. Then she put her headphones on and played "Until Sunrise" by George Duke on repeat.

A few other people were out: a couple, some runners, fishermen, walkers, and a handful of people like her, just gazing. She glanced toward the boardwalk, and there was Mr. Grounds & Maintenance, rolling along in a golf cart. She watched him. He didn't see her. She didn't try to get his attention.

The sunrise was perfect, as it always was. She headed back in. She was getting tired and had forgotten to call Ms. Sylvia. She pulled out her phone. Two missed calls.

"Ms. Sylvia, I'm so sorry."

"Neat, I was 'bout to send the cavalry if you hadn't called me back."

"I'm sorry. I got distracted. Ms. Sylvia, you should see this place. Pine City looks like somebody lifted it out of a dream and set it right here at Brown Sugar Beach…"

She called Harmony next. By the time both conversations were done, she had already walked back to the hotel. She didn't normally eat this early, but she was a little hungry. She wanted to shower and get into those high-dollar sheets. The next day was free before the pre-wedding brunch on Friday, and she was so excited about seeing them. She had seen Mike several times since his undergrad days. Harmony invited him to her sweet sixteen birthday party. He came to a ceremony at WSSU when Jenita received an award. She talked to his family from time to time, mainly check-ins about Mike. But she hadn't seen them in person since his grad school graduation.

She didn't want room service and was looking for something grab-and-go, knowing she was dressed too casually for the dining room and really just wanted oatmeal, and she'd settle for the kind she could pop in the microwave. As she was heading toward the guest services desk, there he was again.

"Good morning, Ms. Hall. Out and about already?"

"Wanted to catch the sunrise. Went for a walk."

"Are you a sunrise person?"

"Yep. Sunsets, too. You?"

"Every chance I get."

"I don't get to see it like this."

"Then you'll have to come back more often. It puts on a show twice a day."

She noticed his voice sounded smoother than it had a few hours ago, or maybe she just hadn't been paying attention then. How had she not noticed? She felt slightly self-conscious because he was looking at her. Not staring, not gawking, but focused and steady.

"Do you all have oatmeal?" she said, turning toward the dining room.

He chuckled. "Oatmeal?"

"Yes. Oatmeal." She put her hand on her hip.

"We can get you whatever you like."

Hmm. I wonder what he'd say if I asked for fatback, biscuits, and molasses.

"Will you be dining in the dining room?"

"Don't be funny, sir."

"What?"

"In this?" She touched the bill of her cap and tugged at her shirt.

"You look fine to me." His gaze didn't shift, but there was a glimmer in his eye, as if more of her was being revealed to him than she intended.

Nice eyes. "Mm-hmm. No, sir." She looked away quickly.

"Shall I have the kitchen send something to your room?"

"I thought you were Grounds & Maintenance, which looks sensational this morning, may I add."

"Yes, you may. Thank you." The way he said it was different from a few hours ago. Warmer. More deliberate.

"Do you work in the dining room too?"

He smiled and dropped his gaze. "We all pitch in wherever we're needed."

"That's commendable. Now, about my oatmeal. If it's on the menu, can I add my own toppings?"

"Whatever you like. But oatmeal? That's all you want?"

"Yes. It's cool outside and a good bowl of oatmeal with raisins, walnuts, brown sugar, cinnamon, nutmeg, vanilla, and a pat of butter—that's a good, warm breakfast."

"Now that… that does sound good."

"It's a good rib-sticker."

"I'll bet it is. Would you like it in your room?"

"Yes. Please."

"Consider it done."

"Thank you."

"More than welcome, Ms. Hall."

What was that? She moved toward the elevator, wanting to shower before room service arrived.

A knock came about twenty minutes later. She peeked through the peephole, saw the same assistant from earlier, and opened the door in her robe. The assistant wheeled in a cart with a white tablecloth draped over what appeared to be considerably more than a bowl of oatmeal.

"I think you may have the wrong room."

"Did you request oatmeal, Ms. Hall?"

"Yes."

"This is your oatmeal."

The assistant lifted the silver domes one by one. Plain oatmeal with a hint of vanilla. A white porcelain platter arranged with every topping she'd mentioned—butter balls, raisins, walnuts, brown sugar, cinnamon, nutmeg—each in its own little dish with its own tiny spoon. A beautiful fruit and nut arrangement. And beneath the final dome was every breakfast beverage imaginable. In little bottles set in ice were orange, apple, cranberry, grape, and tomato juices, vanilla chai, milk, and Fiji water.

She didn't want to seem ignorant or country. She could hear Nana Katie's voice. "Close your mouth, baby."

"That'll be all. Thank you so much."

She stared at the cart after the assistant left. This place is unbelievable.

Across the hotel, he was already smiling to himself. *Oatmeal. All the food in this kitchen and she wanted oatmeal.* He let himself linger on the images he'd collected of her again: her kind eyes, her nose, her teeth, that scar, the deep dimple, her smile, her hair, the way her lips moved when she talked, her alluring shape. All of it in full color. *Ms. Hall is something special.* He shook himself and headed back to the rooftop lights that still needed stringing.

The next morning, Jenita meditated on the beach, walked to the pier for the sunrise, swam in the hotel's indoor pool, ordered a Southwest omelet with toast that tasted as good as it looked, did a little shopping along the boardwalk and in The Tinkery gift shop, settled into a lounge chair under an umbrella pitched by a beach attendant, read, and napped. That evening she watched a local band do covers and stayed for the sunset. What a marvelous day.

Mr. Grounds & Maintenance observed most of it from a distance, everything except the pool. It took every bit of discipline and patience he had not to step into any of her scenes.

Her alarm went off at nine Friday morning for brunch at eleven. She was glad she'd taken Sheila and Rhonda's advice and leveled up her brunch outfit. She tried on the boutique dress. She looked in the mirror and fell in love. It lay perfectly, and the sash would let her cinch the waist with her good girdle. Ooh, this is beautiful. She still needed a wedding dress. She'd ask the ladies where to shop.

She got downstairs at ten-fifty with gifts in tow. She stood in the dining room doorway behind a couple speaking to the maître d', scanning the room. The moment she spotted her, the maître d' turned.

"Ms. Hall?"

"Yes. Right there. I see her!"

"Right this way."

When Renae saw Jenita, she got up from the booth, and they trotted toward each other like schoolgirls, hugging and swaying.

"Ooh, girl! You look beautiful, and you smell good as always. You haven't changed a bit."

"Yes, I have. I'm no taller, but there's more of me."

"You are not alone in that. But you look good! I'm so glad you came. Where's your friend?"

"Last-minute trip."

Renae tilted her head. "Last minute. Okay. Well, you're here, and that's what matters."

"Yes. And you didn't tell me how absolutely beautiful this hotel is."

"We're very proud of it."

"We?"

"Yes. We."

"We who?"

"My family."

"Your family?"

Renae laughed big and loud. "Yes, girl."

"Whaaaat?"

Renae took her arm as they walked to the booth. "Welcome to The Reaux, Jenita."

Jenita went stiff. "You didn't know?" Renae asked.

"No." She sat slowly, looking around, taking in the richness, still processing.

"We completed it two years ago, in 2010. Honey, you won't believe what it took to get here. Maybe one day I'll tell you. I could write a whole volume of books." Jenita watched the waiter slowly pour water into her glass. She put her straw in and sipped. She swallowed harder than the amount of water she'd taken in.

"I'm so sorry. I had no idea your family owned this gorgeous hotel."

"How not? Devereaux… 'The Reaux.' Get it?"

"Who is Devereaux?"

"That's our last name."

"I thought your last name was Alexander." Renae let out an even louder laugh and covered her mouth while Jenita's eyes swept left and right.

"No, baby. It's Devereaux."

"Oh, I'm sorry. I have you saved in my phone as Renae Alexander. Mike's last name is Alexander. I'm so sorry I assumed."
"Jenita, girl, you got it all wrong. Mike's last name is Devereaux, too."

Jenita's head went sideways. *You mean to tell me I had this young man in my life, in my home, around my child, loved him like a son, and he loved me back, and I didn't know his last name?*

Renae read her face. "When we enrolled him at WSSU, he decided to use his middle name as his last name. He didn't want anyone to know he was a Devereaux; wanted some anonymity, wanted to stand on his own. I'm so proud that he did. But girl, Mike is a Devereaux through and through."

Just then, Tiffany and LaKisha arrived. "Hey, Ms. Hall!" Hugs all around.

"Hey, pretty bride-to-be! Congratulations!"

"Thank you! If it weren't for you, I never would have met Mike."

Jenita asked point-blank, laughing at herself, "Did you know his last name is Devereaux? Because I certainly did not. I wrote 'Mr. & Mrs. Alexander' on your card." They all laughed as Renae introduced her youngest daughter, LaKisha, who had cute freckles just like her mama.

Jenita kept the thought to herself: *If Renae's last name is Devereaux and Mike is her brother's son, did she keep her maiden name for business? Well. Being this wealthy, it would make sense.*

Renae had pre-ordered their food to save time and wanted Jenita to have the absolute best. The food never seemed to stop coming, everything from classic breakfast items to crab legs, lobster, shrimp prepared more ways than Bubba Gump ever named, gumbo, boudin balls, okra soup, their twist on Dibi, Jollof rice, beignets, and more. Every dish looked almost too beautiful to eat.

She and Renae talked the oxygen out of the room and laughed like they'd known each other since childhood, while Tiff and LaKisha scrolled on their phones and contributed in and out of the conversation. Millionaires, but they don't act like it. Regular people. Good people. Fun people. Genuinely kind. Had Renae not told her, she never would have guessed.

Ooh, wait until I tell Harmony, the girls, and Ms. Sylvia.

They scheduled brunch for ninety minutes. When Jenita checked her watch, they had about fifteen minutes left. She reached for the emerald-green gift bags she'd brought, with metallic gold tissue and full curly ribbons, each name written in calligraphy by one of her students.

"Ooohhh, you didn't have to! Thank you, Jaa-nee-taaah!" Renae was thrilled before she'd even opened hers.

For a split second, Jenita second-guessed herself. They have everything. They may not want little trinkets from me. But they can't buy these, because I made them.

Renae opened hers first. She covered her mouth. "How did you know?"

"Oh my God, Ms. Hall, it's perfect!" Tiff held hers up.

LaKisha turned hers slowly between her fingers. "Mama. I'm wearing this one."

Jenita had made each of them a quality beaded bracelet in different textures and shades of green, mostly emerald, with a few authentic jade beads and Baht gold accents she'd bought in Thailand a few years back. She'd made one for herself, too, with the leftover supplies.

"How did you know?" Renae asked again, admiring it on her wrist.

"Know what?"

"We ordered jade bracelets that weren't going to arrive in time. Just a little something to officially welcome Tiff into the family."

"I had no idea. I didn't know."

"Honey, you know something or somebody. Because these are first-class and perfect."

LaKisha said, "They look way better than the ones we ordered. I didn't even like 'em. But this?" She admired it on her wrist.

Tiff said, "Ms. Hall, you are the best. I'm wearing this down the aisle. I love it! You always know how to make somebody feel loved."

Hugs. Air kisses. Jenita knew God had given her the nudge to buy those beads long before she knew what they were for. She knew the wedding colors from the invitation. That was all she'd needed.

"Y'all are so welcome," Jenita said, hand over her heart, blowing each of them a kiss. "Now, I don't want y'all to be late. It's almost twelve-thirty."

"We actually have more time now," Renae said. "We were going to run to the jewelry store for matching bracelets, but you saved us the trip."

"Where's the mall?" Jenita asked.

"Near my bakery. What do you need?"

"I made the mistake of leaving both my dresses at home." She explained how it happened.

"Oh no!" Renae was genuinely sympathetic.

"I have a replacement for the rehearsal dinner. The staff let me try on a dress I spotted on a mannequin in the boutique."

"You mean Ms. Lorraine's?" Tiff asked.

"Yes."

"She made my wedding dress. I love it."

"I can't wait to see you in it. The dress I got last night is stunning. I tried it on this morning, and it put the one I left at home to shame. But I still need something for the wedding."

"What size do you wear?" Renae asked.

"Depends."

"I know that's right." Renae patted her own hips and belly in solidarity. "Usually what, though?"

"Usually a fourteen/sixteen or an XL."

"I may have some new things you can choose from. They're 18s and 2Xs, but you can get them tailored."

"Really?"

"Yes, ma'am. They're right over at Ms. Lorraine's. I ordered several dresses for the wedding and had them shipped directly to the tailor's. I always have to get things hemmed anyway. I've got eighteens and 2Xs. We can get them tailored. Let's go shopping!"

"But did you enjoy your food?" Renae asked. "Because you didn't finish anything."

Jenita had loved every single bite. She just couldn't eat fast enough before the next dish appeared, while her brunch companions kept a perfect pace. She was used to being the slow one. They used lemon-scented water in crystal finger bowls and linen napkins for the crab legs, but nothing beats soap and warm water, so they took turns slipping to the restroom. She was sitting with Black millionaires, and her thoughts still hadn't fully settled.

Jenita went last. While she was in the restroom, Renae and the girls talked about how wonderful and down-to-earth she was, how thoughtful the bracelets were, how comical and warm she'd been, and how glad they were she'd accepted the invitation. The restroom, of course, looked like something from Lifestyles of the Rich and Famous, attendant included.

Mr. Grounds & Maintenance approached the table. "Well, hello. What are you all doing in here?"

"Having brunch, sir." Renae looked up.

"Do you have time to be at brunch? Tiff, don't you have a rehearsal dinner tonight, a bachelorette party, and a wedding on Saturday?"

"Yes, yes, and yes, sir." Tiff smiled the smile of a happy bride.

Renae asked, "How long have you been here?"

"Since yesterday." Without waiting for an invitation, he sat down hard and exhaled.

"When are you going to get some rest?"

"I was on my way to grab a nap in the staff suite when I spotted you."

"You're the only one who ever uses that room."

He ignored that. "Don't y'all have a lot to do today?"

"We have time. I wanted to give Ms. Hall a warm welcome."

"Ms. Hall?"

"Yes. Ms. Hall. The one who was so good to Mike. His third mama. The one he talked about all the time. The one you never wanted to meet."

"She's here?"

"Yes. Just went to the restroom. Get up before she comes back."

"Is she coming?"

"Not yet. Oh, there she is. That's Mike's, Ms. Hall."

"My Ms. Hall, too," said Tiff.

He couldn't take his eyes off her as she walked toward them, capturing all his attention without asking for a bit of it. He was just as caught off guard as Jenita was when she put together that the Devereaux family owned The Reaux.

Mr. Grounds & Maintenance was baffled. "I thought Ms. Hall was an old woman." He blinked. "That's Jenita Hall? Mike's Ms. Hall? His WSSU Ms. Hall?"

"Yep. Got here this morning."

"I know. I was outside when she pulled up."

"And you didn't introduce yourself?"

"I didn't know *that* was Ms. Hall. There's another Hall on the guest list. I thought that was her. I had no idea."

He stood abruptly as Renae tapped his thigh. Jenita was almost back at the table.

Jenita smiled. *Dang. Mr. Grounds & Maintenance is everywhere.*

He stepped aside to give her room to pass, then lightly took her hand to help her into the booth.

"Jenita, do you know who this is?" Renae asked.

"Yes. I don't know his name, but I know he's over grounds and maintenance."

Renae, Tiffany, and LaKisha all laughed. Mr. Grounds & Maintenance smiled with his mouth closed. Jenita looked between them, trying to figure out if they were laughing at him or her.

"Ladies, stop laughing at Ms. Hall, or I'll have to ask you to leave."

"They're laughing at me? I thought they were laughing at you. Uh oh. What's so funny?"

Renae could barely get it out. "Jenita, where did you get grounds and maintenance from?"

Jenita pointed at the embroidered letters under the hotel logo on his polo. GM.

"Girl. GM stands for General Manager." More laughter from Tiff and LaKisha.

"Oh, my Lord. The general manager of the hotel?"

"Well… yes and no. The general manager of D.E., Devereaux Enterprises. All our family's businesses."

Jenita placed her elbows on the table, clasped her hands, and let her forehead rest on her thumbs. "Are you serious?"

"Dead serious." Renae was still tickled but trying to wind it down.

Jenita had never once asked this man his name. She had given him a nickname and a job title in her own head, and there was nothing wrong with that, not a single thing. She'd meant it as a compliment; she thought he was excellent and diligent and looked mighty good doing it. But now she was frantically trying to remember whether she'd actually said "Mr. Grounds & Maintenance" out loud, or worse, to his face. She wasn't sure and was so embarrassed. All she could do was slowly shake her head, stare at the floor, and hope it would open, giving her a much-needed exit.

And then, because the universe apparently wasn't done, Renae said, "That's Mike's daddy. And my twin brother, Zee."

Mike's daddy. Twins.

Zee extended his arm and offered her his hand exactly the way she had offered him hers when they first met—a formal, boardroom shake. She didn't look up right away. She couldn't.

"You're going to leave me hanging?"

"You're Mike's dad?" She looked up at him.

The innocence in her doe-shaped eyes made him melt. A warmth moved through him that was so soothing he felt himself soften and bend his elbow. Cupid had emptied his quiver, every arrow, all at once, straight through. Man down. Mayday. Code Blue and Code Red simultaneously. As she raised her hand to accept the shake, he took it gently and covered it with his other hand. He couldn't have jerked away this time if he'd tried. He didn't want to.

"Yes, I am. Hello, Ms. Jenita Hall. I'm Alexander Devereaux."

Jenita was glad she was already seated. His touch, the way he looked into her eyes, his voice, her name in his mouth, the slight tilt of his head as he spoke.

Did it sound like this when I checked in? "Hi, Mr. Alexander Devereaux. Nice to meet you." She smiled bashfully.

"Nice to meet you, too. Again. I like the way you say my name."

His full smile, white teeth against deep brown skin, made him look devastatingly handsome. He lifted her hand, moved his top hand just enough to expose the back of hers, and pressed his lips to it softly, still looking into her eyes.

"The pleasure is all mine."

Floor, never mind. Please disregard my earlier request. Do NOT open. She Bambi-blinked, trying not to get hypnotized by his eyes. Her eyes inadvertently hypnotized him right back.

She'd missed all of this earlier. Because he was that fine, she had automatically neutered him and filed him under "friend zone." A man who looked like that probably assumed everyone wanted him. She wasn't about to embarrass herself. She had mentally run through the standard checklist: player, married, on the down-low, a ho, a pimp, broke, a dud, an addict, a mama's boy, at least three or four dramatic baby mamas, or some combination. She and her girlfriends all had Walgreens-length receipts on men that were fine, and considerably less fine. And now he was a millionaire on top of it. Shoot. He probably had somebody in every area code, national and international.

She cleared her throat, unnecessarily, consciously engaged her diaphragm for a more composed tone, stood up straight, fixed her eyes on the middle of his forehead, and said in her most professional voice:

"My sincerest apologies for never asking your name, sir."

He smiled. "No apology necessary. I knew yours. I just didn't know who you were. But I know now."

"Me, too." She slipped her hand from his.

"I'm honored." No blinks. No smile. "Wow."

The joke, and the shock, landed squarely on Renae. Her silent gasp said everything. She had never, in her entire life, seen Zee behave that way with a woman. Not ever. Especially not someone he'd just met. Certainly not in public. The way he stared. The smile. He kissed her hand.

What in the world? The thought lingered.

Tiff and LaKisha were equally floored. LaKisha had never known her Uncle Zee to date or show interest in anyone since Chantel, and she'd met this woman for the first time alongside him. Tiff had been with Mike since undergrad and had never once seen his father show romantic interest in anyone, not a single sign of it. He worked, and he'd always said his family was all he needed. He had consistently proven it. Their laughter had stopped completely.

Zee broke the silence, still not looking away from Jenita. "I won't hold you ladies up. We all have a full weekend ahead. Please let me know if you need anything at all, Ms. Jenita Hall. I will personally see to it myself. I'll leave a word at guest services."

CHAPTER 19

Carrying It All

Renae had three good, hardworking men in her life, and the only woman she had to share them with was Tink. Most people would consider that a tremendous blessing, and it was, though it also had the potential to make a woman spoiled. Renae wasn't. She fully appreciated being loved so thoroughly. Looking so much like a lighter-skinned Fatou didn't help matters. But not having to share also meant carrying the weight of their emotional safety, their need for tenderness and feminine energy. That was a different kind of load.

She didn't want Pops or Zee to be as lonely as she knew they were. Both of them fed their loneliness with work—mental and physical labor, protecting, earning, solving, creating, designing, planning, building, perfecting.

She managed the bakeries and the restaurant. Frank's barbershop had become a community cornerstone for Black men, whether they needed a cut or just somewhere to be. Frank also helped with beautification, landscaping, and janitorial services when his shop was closed—all things Zee managed and worked alongside him. But after things fell apart with Chantel and the situation with Andy, Zee realized he needed help. He checked himself into a spiritually grounded, spa-style holistic wellness center, and his mental health journey took a sharp turn for the better. His transformation was remarkable.

He had always been reserved. Now he meditated and prayed daily. He stopped eating meat and tried a raw vegan phase for a while.

Frank had thoughts about that immediately.

"Man, your first name is already Ibrahima. You wear tailored suits and bow ties all the time. Somebody is going to ask you for a bean pie. What are you gon' give 'em? Lettuce? Hummus?"

Zee laughed.

Frank pressed on. He cut a bite-sized piece of his lamb chop, dripping with thick brown gravy, flecked with pepper and sliced onions, scooped up some rice, and held the fork out. "Now you ain't eating meat? Mama taught Snucks how to make the best smothered lamb chops known to man. She is turning in her grave. Take a bite, bruh. Please take a bite so Mama can stop turning."

Zee's laugh had changed since his healing. Fuller. Louder. He laughed and laughed at Frank the way he always had. "She dizzy, man. Please. Just one bite."

"You ain't right," Zee said, still laughing. "Never have been. I'll get my own."

Zee took care of himself with intentional discipline, following every practice and regimen, engaging with music therapy, exercising, and allowing himself to feel things even when it made him vulnerable and others uncomfortable. He learned that his tears and his capacity for compassion weren't signs of weakness but of cleansing, and that sometimes it was the more masculine thing to feel. Now don't get it twisted: his Black man's code only granted access to a select few family members when it came to that vulnerability. His business and boardroom presence was brick.

He spent so much time at the spa during that season that he came to genuinely understand the value of holistic wellness, and that understanding was instrumental in making sure The Reaux's spa was built to a world-class standard. But the most consequential decision he made in his healing, the one that did the most to address his sexual trauma, was choosing celibacy.

Frank, of course, had something to say.

"Man, you can't just stop. You're going to get backed up so bad that Roto-Rooter won't be able to fix it. It's going to come out your eyes. You'll sneeze, and that won't be snot."

Zee loved his ridiculous brother. Frank and Renae were both extroverts; Zee was an introvert away from the boardroom. They were draped in jewelry; Zee wore a watch and one gold "Z" pinky ring, a gift from his nieces and nephews. Renae and Frank hosted every cookout, holiday party, and impromptu gathering that came along. He showed up, stayed a while, and went home to quiet. He was lonely.

They had five children and the kind of marriage and sex life that generated them joyfully, at times in impressively creative locations. He had one child and was eight years into celibacy. Renae and Frank rarely traveled because of the kids, Pops, Tink, the restaurant, and the bakeries. Their combined energy would have incinerated the average person; they fed off each other like fuel. Zee, meanwhile, was the family jetsetter, acquiring investors, brokering notable real estate deals, and building partnerships nationally and internationally. He had even made trips to Senegal, following leads while researching his mother's family.

He and Pops both needed physical labor to think, decompress, and release whatever was building up inside. Manual work, carpentry, landscaping, repairs, and beautification were how they processed. Renae understood her men. But their loneliness weighed on her. She knew no other woman could replace Pops' Queen or Zee's mother, but she was beginning to feel the strain of being every woman for both of them, on top of everything else. She had enough love, joy, drive, strength, and energy for Frank, her children, and her businesses because she knew how to let those things work with her rather than against her. But Pops' grief and Zee's grief were heavy in a way that was different from her own. She used her grief as a foundation to stand on, not a hole to stand in. So, when Pops and Ms. Lorraine found each other, she felt the kind of relief that releases a breath you've been holding for years. She loved Ms. Lorraine. And she remembered how much her mama had loved her, too.

Learning about Zee's prom night broke her heart. So did his war injury, the Chantel situation, and finding out he was infertile. She loved her twin dearly. He had worked so hard on himself and turned his mental and spiritual health around completely.

She wondered sometimes: was he at peace with celibacy because of infertility? Was that how he'd made his peace with it?

She wanted her brother to know love. She had tried, more times than she could count, to introduce him to women worth knowing. Nobody got to second base with Zee. And every time it didn't work out, she lost a potential friend in the process. As the family's prosperity grew, she also had to be honest with herself about motives. Were these women trying to be her friend, or did they want Zee? As wealthy and as eligible as he was, it was usually the latter. She watched him show up for their kids, coach and cheer for family friends' children at sports events, look after Tink, and take her as his plus-one sometimes when he attended business-related social events or traveled. They loved having him as their third wheel. But she wanted so much more for him. He deserved it. And if it couldn't look like what she and Frank had, fine, she'd accept that, but she couldn't stand the idea of him being lonely for the rest of his life.

She had been praying the same prayer for decades: "God, please give Zee somebody to love. He has so much love to give. And let somebody give him all the love he deserves." Sometimes she'd cry. "Mama, please help me. Help Zee. Help him find love." The tears were always mixed, some for her brother, some because aching for him always brought her back to missing her mother.

She also prayed with a laugh: "And please, God, keep Uncle Louis's ways far away. I don't want Zee like that."

She meant every word of it, simple and blunt as it was. The things that kept her from being swallowed by it all: her prayer life, Frank's love, laughter and comfort, time with Tink, baking, good food, a day at the spa, or a fresh hairdo.

Watching Zee with Jenita, Renae felt something she didn't expect—jealousy. She genuinely liked Jenita and had wanted her as a friend. That kind of genuine friendship didn't come easily for her.

For one, some people had always felt she and Frank never should have married. Two, some had looked down on her for getting pregnant before their wedding. Beyond that, some Black folks in their world kept a careful distance from the Devereaux family because of the legal battles Pops had waged and won, battles that had required the family to build, hire, and maintain their own security. And on top of all that, she had Frank, five beautiful babies, twin grandbabies, Mike to love and help raise, extended family to support, businesses to run, Pops to look after—until Ms. Lorraine—Tink to check on, Zee to check in with, and somewhere at the bottom of that list, herself. *Can it be my turn?* Jenita felt like she could be the real thing. Her first genuine friend since Crystal.

But now, seeing Zee openly awestruck and unashamed from the first moment? That was new. That was unsettling.

For the first time she could remember, she felt threatened by another woman, and by her own brother. She wanted to protect him from going head over heels for someone he'd just met, and possibly making a fool of himself, or worse, getting hurt again. She didn't know if she could carry another heartbreak for him. And yet, she was also quietly thrilled about the friendship she'd been wanting for herself. She needed it. Her children were older now. The businesses were well-staffed and well-run and didn't require as much of her time. She had time and money and nobody to share either with.

As they walked toward Lorraine's Boutique, she prayed they had something Jenita would love. And she knew she needed to do some praying of a different kind altogether. Still a daddy's girl at heart, she wanted to talk to Pops. She wanted to talk to her mama because she knew Fatoumata Abubakar Devereaux was watching and had come through in a pinch more times than Renae could count. And she was going to talk to Tink. Tink could speak truth in love in a way that had a person completely exposed before they realized she'd been working on them. She had a way of making the skeletons in a closet start talking and dancing on their own. And they always left with something—a download of God-given clarity, words that settled their mind, a salve, a piece of jewelry, a scarf, or a plate of food. Sometimes all of the above.

CHAPTER 20

Past, Present, and Future

Zee pulled Frank aside. "Have you seen her?"

"Who?"

"You know who I'm talking about. Jenita."

"I can't see nobody I'm not looking for. Man, why are you trippin' about her? This ain't you, Zee."

"I don't know. I just can't help it."

"You need to get a grip. You just met her for the first time." "Why didn't you or Renae ever tell me about her?"

"You weren't interested in nothing back then. I mean, she was cool and good for the kids, and Snucks liked her. I just didn't think she was anything special. As a matter of fact, you didn't even want to meet the woman because you said she was gon' get Mike messed up in music. I remember one day I had to get you to pipe down because you wanted to cuss her out when she got them those paid gigs. That's the same Jenita. Go 'head and cuss her out now. Hell, I'll watch." Frank rested his elbow on the table and sipped his Monnet. "You need some of this yak man. Hit this one time, you'll be fine."

"You know better and the last thing I want right now is to not feel every moment of this. I wonder where she is."

"It's only six thirty-five. It doesn't kick off until seven. You trippin' for real." Zee sipped his water. "Damn. Look at Matilda with her old, pompous ass. I still can't stand her or her janky-ass dentist husband."

"Probably can't stand herself. How you a dentist with a raggedy mouth…punk ass mother…"

"She's hateful and arrogant. They weren't even invited; she used her brother's invitation. You know Pops is cool with him because he's the agent who schooled Pops on his first big commercial real estate deal. He owns that new real estate magazine now."

"I got some magazines for their triflin' asses."

Zee scanned the rooftop—new faces, old faces. His eyes settled on a female classmate who had experienced the same thing he had on prom night. He was glad she appeared to be doing well. She looked well, married, and had children. He hadn't known about her assault when it happened. Now, on this side of his own healing, the empathy was deep. It brought back the disgust he had always felt for the posse of Black and white boys and girls who moved through their county like small-town villains. They were few in number, but the damage they left behind was far too many people. Thinking back on what they'd done to him, and feeling the difference between then and now, he realized how much he'd healed.

❧

Zee and Frank stood by the bar near the elevator, their default position, unofficial security as always. Frank couldn't move as quickly with his prosthesis, but he was a fast draw when he needed to be. No matter how much they had built or how well they had done, the enemies hadn't all gone away. White people who wanted to take them out, and a handful of envious Black folks who wanted to bring them down.

Ding.

The elevator doors opened. And like a scene from a film, there stood Jenita—alone.

Frank was still cataloguing Matilda's offenses into Zee's ear, but Zee had gone somewhere else entirely. He was locked in on her.

She was enchanting. She took a few steps and paused, scanning the rooftop for a familiar face. She caught Zee in her periphery and looked deliberately in the other direction, still slightly embarrassed by everything she'd learned at brunch, still quietly enraptured by him kissing her hand. She scanned slowly, unhurried, looking for anyone else she might know or who looked friendly enough to approach.

She caught several people's attention. Smooth, honey brown skin. Locs pulled up in the front and draped down her back like a copper waterfall. Light makeup that accented her eyes, lips lined and glossed. She was gorgeous and carried herself with an ethereal quality she didn't seem to be aware of. Her off-white chiffon duster caught the gentle breeze, covering a form-fitting green maxi dress with peace lily flowers, a sash-cinched waist, and a V-neck that revealed just enough cleavage. Her gold African-inspired statement necklace and coordinating earrings made her look regal and soft at the same time. Gold ankle-strap stilettos. Small gold purse on a chain at her shoulder. Intriguing but approachable.

Before she could feel out of place, Renae appeared out of nowhere. "Ooh! Girl! You are drop-dead gorgeous!" She went in for a hug and whispered in her ear, "That mannequin was not doing that outfit justice. You look fabulous, friend."

"Thank you, friend. You look so pretty." Renae was in a multi-colored green and gold African dress with a matching shoulder scarf and emerald pumps, beautifully set against her fair skin and golden-brown loose coils that bounced with the slightest movement. She locked arms with Jenita and commenced a full circuit of introductions.

Several family members greeted her with some version of, "Oh, this is Mike's Ms. Hall."

And then there was Mike. Her baby boy is about to be somebody's husband. The moment he spotted her, he ran, scooping her up off the ground as they hugged. Everyone noticed.

Zee, barely whispering with excitement, "Luh...luh...luh...look! There she is, man. Mm hmm! She is fine as hell. I could tell she had a booty, but I had no idea she was built like that under all those loose clothes. Lord, have mercy." He was pretending to sip his water, looking over the rim of the glass.

Frank said with exaggerated aggravation, "I see her, man. Damn. I told you I seen her before. She cute. Fat ass. I mean, she a'ight. But I don't see what you're losing your mind about. You seen ass before. You don't even want none. You, Renae, and Mike trippin'. Even LaKisha came home talmbout her." He paused. "Her middle name probably starts with a 'C' anyway."

It took Zee a second. Then he chuckled. "Shut up, man. You. You're already crippled, walking around on one leg. Crazy as always. Don't go blind. She is lovely. There is something different about her."

Security had vetted each weekend guest. But after Renae told Frank how out of character Zee had acted, Frank had Joe Lester and Reggie run a deeper check on Jenita. D.E.'s security team was first-rate, led by Joe Lester Pringle, aging right alongside Pops, and by Zee and Frank's Marine Corps GySgt Reggie Smith, a former street soldier who now ran the team with the same discipline he'd given his troops. They turned up an old assault report she'd filed, charges later dropped, the assailant's name redacted. Several restraining orders, as well as the most recent of which expired over two years prior, were redacted.

They talked it over and guessed at the assault. Maybe domestic violence. Maybe her deceased husband caused the scar. But who had she needed multiple restraining orders against? They weren't sure.

Frank was disappointed. They hadn't found any real dirt; nothing worse than a speeding ticket from 2005. He didn't want Zee to get hurt. To him, nobody could be this clean. And why had she acted like she didn't know who the Devereaux family was?

"She probably looked us up online and came in here playing dumb. We may be new money, but we're one of the wealthiest Black families in the state. There's old and new money and media on this rooftop tonight."

He couldn't bear watching Zee get hurt again. And quietly, he felt that he and Zee had been enough for Renae all this time.

"How is this heffa gone come and have everybody's nose open but mine? Sheeeet. Somebody has to have some sense." He mumbled it mostly to himself.

Zee set his glass down.

"Man, I'm going to go speak to her." He walked away immediately.

Frank put his own glass down, got that leg lined up, and followed. "You going to cuss her out?"

Mike saw them coming. "Ms. Hall, this is my dad."

"Hey, son." Zee hugged Mike and kissed his cheek. Everything they were to each other was in that embrace.

"I had the pleasure of meeting Ms. Hall this morning."

"Yes, we did," Jenita said, voice measured, professional. "You may call me Jenita, Alexander. And again, my sincerest apologies for not knowing who you were."

"No apology necessary. You can call me Zee, Zander, or Alexander." He took his time looking at her, head to toe and back up. The chemistry he felt for her radiated without his permission. "We know each other now, and I hope we get to know one another better."

She felt it. *Stay strong, girl. Whew.*

"Well, Alexander, I'm sure there are plenty of other guests here you'd like to get to know."

"Not half as much as I want to get to know you."

He was still beholding Jenita but pulled back the intensity slightly; he didn't want to make her uncomfortable. But he didn't look away.

The wedding planner appeared and pulled Mike, Tiff, and Jenita aside for a last-minute run-through with the musicians.

The string quartet played beautifully. Tink led a prayer and a moment of meditation. Jenita spoke about the art of love in companionship for about fifteen minutes. Zee stood in the back and couldn't have been more deeply moved. Then she and Tink anointed Mike and Tiff with oil as the couple knelt. Tink used a white ribbon to loosely bind their wrists together. She read a prayer in Wolof to honor Fatou, then spoke blessings in Creole to honor the Abubakar and Devereaux ancestors. Tiffany's family was Baptist and had wanted someone Baptist-approved. Though Jenita wasn't ordained in the Baptist denomination, Tiffany's positive testimony and Jenita's Baptist upbringing gave them the comfort they needed. They wanted the blessing delivered in Black folks' Baptist Jesus and in English. The combination made for a deeply spiritual moment that honored every room it was drawing from.

When the music changed to smooth jazz, the whole mood followed. The gathering became something closer to a professional mixer; many of the hundred guests who weren't family or hotel staff were there to network. During that shift, Jenita slipped away to go back to her room to change her shoes. She had been in four-inch strappy stilettos for nearly two hours.

Zee lost sight of her and couldn't make his search obvious. Tink solved it for him.

"Zander, what is going on with you about this woman?"

"I don't know, Tink. When I went to lie down today, you know how I am with sleep, this wasn't that. I could not stop thinking about her. I kept replaying every word we said, the two times we touched, her voice, her face, her pretty eyes."

He was half in a daze, watching it replay like a film, himself completely out of character, but without one ounce of regret.

"I may need you to help me get this off me."

Tink rubbed his arm slowly. "Nah. Ain't nothing on you. That might just be your heart trying to talk to you. I felt something when we held hands and prayed over Mike and Tiff."

He exhaled. "I don't know."

"You don't know, Zander?"

"No. I just met her. That's what's so crazy. She's got me all turned around, Tink."

"You heard if she's a mystic? An empath? A seer? You know, like me?"

"I don't know. But if she keeps making me feel like this… she's going to be Zee'er."

CHAPTER 21

Open to Change

Coming off the elevator, Jenita scanned the rooftop for familiar faces again. Then she saw them. She turned immediately and reached for the elevator button, but the doors had already closed. She held the button, pressing it again and again, willing the doors to open. The car was already gone.

Renae, Frank, Tiff, and her parents were all working the room; social butterflies making sure glasses were full, bellies were full, and everything was on time, and introductions had been made. This event was personal and intentionally professional, and they were running it that way.

Renae appeared with a couple beside her. "Jenita, I was going to introduce you, but they said they already know you. Do you know Matilda and Dr. Warren Ingram?"

Zee followed her out onto the boardwalk. He didn't ask about the Ingrams. Their appearance alone had ambushed her—another round of the blame, bullying, and verbal assault she'd endured for twenty years—and it had sent her into a tailspin. She never ate. She apologized to both families for leaving before the dinner ended.

Zee and Mike offered to walk her to her room. She accepted. On the way down, she pressed "L" instead of "7."

"I'm going to the lobby."

He and Mike looked at each other.

"Y'all go back and enjoy your family and your guests. I just need to clear my head."

When the elevator opened in the lobby, both men were greeted on all sides with "Good evening, Mr. Devereaux" from employees and guests alike. Jenita noticed. Her state didn't allow her to be impressed.

She wasn't really going to lie on the floor; she just wanted to sit in a chair and stare at that ceiling. But the lobby was bustling.

"Where are you going, Ms. Hall?" Mike asked.

"I think I'll go for a walk. Get back to your beautiful bride-to-be. I'll be fine."

"You sure?"

"Yes."

Zee said, "May I walk with you?"

"I want to be by myself."

"Okay."

Mike hugged her. She kissed his cheek. "I'll see you Saturday, baby."

"Yes, ma'am. Thank you again for blessing me and Tiff. You have no idea what it means to have you here." He hugged her once more and walked away.

Zee gave Mike a quiet nod: I got this. Mike smiled at his father.

"I'm fine walking alone. You can go back, too."

"Okay."

She walked through the sliding glass doors, through the crowded hotel terrace, and onto the boardwalk. Then she glanced back. Zee was about fifty feet behind her.

"You don't listen."

"Yes, I do. You said you wanted to walk alone."

"Yet here you are."

"But I'm not walking with you."

"Ugh."

"You've got your purse and that gift bag. May I carry the bag for you?"

"I got it, sir. Thank you. Just go away." She huffed and kept walking, wishing she could just cry. Not with him back there.

As she neared the pier, she looked back again. He wasn't following anymore. He was sitting on a bench, facing the ocean, staring out at it as if he'd never seen it before.

She felt bad for snapping at him. She also realized she had walked much farther from The Reaux than she'd intended, and she was getting cold. The ocean air had been perfectly brisk earlier. Now it was too much for her thin dress. Her pride wouldn't let her turn around with him sitting right there. And he showed no sign of moving.

She got cold enough that her nose started to run. She hadn't packed tissues in her party purse.

She saw him stand and look in her direction. She hoped he'd walk back toward the hotel. Instead, he walked quickly toward the pier. She knew he was coming and tried to put on an I'm not cold face. Her duster was blowing. She pulled it closed and sat down fast.

"Jenita. I know you're cold." He was already taking off his blazer.

She was prideful. She was not a fool. She took it, looking at him with genuine gratitude.

"Thank you."

She stood to put it on. He helped her, taking her purse and the gift bag from around her wrist. He draped his blazer over her shoulders, but she was so cold that she put her arms in, pulling it all the way on. She felt toasty from his body heat in the blazer and from the fabric. She was immediately warm.

He noticed the tip of her nose. "There's a handkerchief in the inside chest pocket."

She reached for it quickly, a little embarrassed. She wiped her nose and noticed how good his blazer smelled.

She felt things from too many directions at once. Him. His perfectly timed kindness. His attentiveness. The big, loving heart she could see every time she looked at him. His warm blazer. His cologne. Him.

And underneath all of that: twenty years of legal torment and the Ingrams' bullying, tangled up with the joy of celebrating Mike and Tiffany. She hadn't had a moment to sit with how beautiful the dinner had been, how generous the Devereaux family had been to their guests, to her, except for Frank. He hadn't been unkind, but she could feel he wasn't warming to her.

She was forgetting the majesty and sweet nostalgia of being present at Brown Sugar Beach, the place she'd loved since childhood. Where were Rhonda, Sheila, Ms. Sylvia, and Harmony? She thought about calling. But she didn't want to talk. They cared, but caring sometimes kept them from just listening.

That mixed bag of emotions made her cry.

Zee sat beside her on the bench and placed his arm around her shoulder—easy, friendly, not presumptuous. She sobbed. He didn't know the specific pain, but he knew what it felt like for pain to raise its head unannounced. Even healed pain can show up unexpectedly and pull a few sad tears as it passes by.

"I know you don't know me. But do you want to talk about it? I'm a good listener. I don't have to say a word."

Before either of them knew it, the sun was coming up.

They talked. Her curiosity, spontaneity, and open-mindedness intrigued him thoroughly. She admired the way he stayed patient with her questions and wasn't visibly annoyed when she was slower to open up than he was with some of her answers. The way she asked questions pulled things out of him: youthful memories, creative impulses, a playfulness that building multimillion-dollar businesses and professional stoicism tends to bury. She made it feel mature and wise to be adventurous—to play.

Oh, how she made him laugh.

Any other time after seeing the Ingrams, she would have gone straight home out of fear. Their presence was triggering in a way she couldn't always predict. But with him, she felt protected in a way she never had been. They lost track of time entirely, talking and laughing and even crying together from nine in the evening until five in the morning. He carried her gift bag as he walked her back to the hotel and to her room.

"Good night, Alexander."

"Good night and good morning, Jenita. I'll see you at the wedding."

Zee walked into his house to find Mike still up.

"Dad. Where have you been? You've been out all night. Were you working?"

"If you're still dressed, you haven't been here long either."

"Bachelor party."

"How was it?"

"You know my frats. They turned it up and out. Wild."

"Not too wild."

"Not me. Them." He shook his head. "But Dad, this ain't about me. Where were you? You have to stop working like this. Why do you hire people for an event and then do their job yourself? I tried to call you, Uncle Frank tried, Aunt Renae tried. Were you out fishing? No, you still have your suit on from last night. Uncle Frank said you were probably working to decompress the way you do when you're stressed. Are you stressed about me? I'm going to be alright. I just hate that you'll be alone here. When are you going to get somebody?"

"Whoa. I walk in and get the third degree, and my own son has a full interrogation ready, with the answers, too?" Zee laughed. "But I bet you don't have this." He held out a set of keys.

"This house is my wedding gift to you, for you to give to your bride. No mortgage. No rent. And there's a $100,000 renovation budget so your wife can make it exactly what she wants." Twenty-five hundred square feet, brick, two stories, four bedrooms, three and a half baths, a deck, and a pool.

"Dad. Man. Are you serious? Man. For real?" Mike pulled his father into a tight hug. Zee held on until Mike let go first. *My baby boy is going to be a husband*, he thought.

"Where are you going to live?"

"Don't worry about me. I'll have everything moved out while y'all are honeymooning. And I'm seriously considering resuming construction on the house."

"That house?"

"That house. We can talk about it over breakfast. I can't let you be hungry on your wedding day. Plus, I need some intel."

"Intel?"

"Tell me everything you know about Jenita."

"Ms. Hall?" Mike's smile went wider than it had when he got the keys. "Dad. You trying to get with Ms. Hall? Whaaat! I don't know, man. Neither one of y'all wants to be with anybody."

"I'm not above change, son. Maybe she isn't either. Sometimes it only takes one person to change everything."

"Ms. Hall, Dad. I mean… she's real artsy, spiritual, kind of like Tink, funny, chill, spontaneous, she likes people, but not too many people. And you…you—"

"I'm what?"

"Ha. Not."

"What am I, then?"

"You're always working. You only hang out with family or with leads, and that's still work. You appreciate art and music, but you don't do art or music. You're spiritual, and you're laid back and quiet. She's…" he shrugged "just different."

"I hear you." *All I know is that woman is truly something special,* he thought.

"Lord, don't let me tear up this rental car." Jenita prayed it out loud.

Queen's Hill was *Architectural Digest*-worthy. The drive up from The Reaux to the Louis James Convention Hall, the new multipurpose extension of the hotel, was steep and winding in a way that was beautiful and slightly terrifying for visitors. She was tired, excited, and a little tense. Not just from the road, but from not knowing what else she'd see or say to the Ingrams. Or to Zee.

She wondered if she'd talked too much, shared too much. After all, he was a stranger. But then, he'd talked just as much and opened up with equal vulnerability. And the longer he talked, the more familiar his voice felt, as if she'd known him for a lifetime, or two, or three.

When she'd laughingly told him that his looks had automatically filed him under "player" in her mental filing system, he'd found it amusing and then talked about it honestly, how he'd never had a type, how years of working at Brown Sugar Beach had desensitized him to what used to turn heads. He mentioned Crystal and Cora. His injury. Chantel, though only the engagement part. He talked about how celibacy had become less of a sacrifice once he grew disgusted by the idea of being touched without love. And since he'd long since decided that loving and being loved romantically wasn't something he deserved, he'd let that desire go quietly and poured everything he had into Mike, Pops, Tink, Renae, Frank, family, and work. They were his fuel, every business, every stock trade, every deal, every flight and meeting. He and Pops had even built a pipeline to bring relatives from New Orleans into D.E., including Louis's children and some of Tink's nieces and nephews. And he'd spent real time trying to trace Fatou's family in Senegal, to fulfill something Pops had always wanted.

She'd given him the cliff notes on Warren's suicide, his parents' violence, the assault that left the scar, and the Ingrams' ongoing harassment was still circling after all these years, angry about Harmony's last name, still angling for access they'd never earned.

He'd told her, without being specific, that Matilda was known in their shared circle of Black commercial real estate for business bullying and always up to some trickery and back-channel maneuvering. She'd been trying for years to get a foot into his international market. He'd never opened the door.

She talked about how disconnected her biological family was and how much she admired what she'd seen so far in his. He asked about her work, her passions, her dislikes, and her dreams.

Through all of it, he was absorbing every vibe she gave off—unguarded and enamored by her honesty and humor. He looked at her in ways he had never looked at a woman, taking in all of her at once: physically, mentally, spiritually, emotionally, sensually, even what he could only call futuristically. Every time she caught him, he didn't look away. He leaned in closer.

It made her shy.

"Why are you looking at me like that?"

"Like what?"

"Like you're looking right now."

"How can you tell when you keep looking away and closing your pretty eyes? I'm trying to see something."

"I'm not." She laughed, looking away.

"Look at me, and I'll tell you. You should be used to this."

"Used to what?"

"Being admired."

"No."

"Nobody has ever looked at you like this?"

"No. You're just tripping. It's the ocean, the stars, the whole ambiance of this place." She looked around. "That's all this is." She laughed.

He laughed, too, then stopped. He looked at her locs, her eyes, her smile.

"They should have. You're exquisite." His gaze didn't waver. The weight of his full attention was something she could physically feel. Her heart picked up. The butterflies came. She held back her blush by folding her lips together and turning her head to look anywhere but at him. "Why won't you look at me?"

She threw her head back laughing, hand over her mouth. "As Fred G. Sanford would say, 'I cain't!'"

He could imagine Fred perfectly. They both laughed until the laughter faded into the quiet of the night, and they walked under the moonlight back to the hotel.

"Thank you for tonight."

"Thank you. The pleasure was mine."

"And thank you for helping me get away from the Ingrams. I owe you one." "It was two of them. So that's two."

"Two? Not one?" She considered it. "Fair. They do make two."

"So, you're good for two?"

"I'm good. And speaking of good, good night, Alexander."

"Good night, Jenita."

CHAPTER 22

Plus One

Tink asked, "Who's your people, baby?" Jenita named the relatives she could.

"Uhh huh... but not them, baby. The ones that's gone on that God let 'em talk to your spirit."

Jenita had just parked beside her at the Louis James Convention Hall. She answered with a small smile, not quite taking the question seriously. "I talk and listen to God and my Nana Katie Mae all the time. Most times I do what they say."

"Ain't nothing funny about that, baby. You have the gift. I can feel it. It's all on ya." Tink slipped her arm under Jenita's as her escort.

It was a short walk, slightly uphill to the entrance, and Tink was leaning on her a little as they went. Jenita didn't know quite how to respond. She didn't know Tink well yet, and after what Zee had told her last night that Tink was deeply spiritual and practiced hoodoo, the question sat with her differently. It made her think of Nana.

Guests were arriving by covered golf cart or Reaux-branded shuttle van. "Well, this is fancy," she said to Tink. "I saw some of these people last night. Where are they all coming from?"

"The hotel. You didn't want to use the transportation?"

"No. When it's time for me to leave, I'd rather not have to wait."

"Me, too, baby. They get mad at me now because I still drive myself. But they don't fuss too much since I live up here on Queen's Hill."

"You live up here?"

"Yes. Most of the family does. That's my house up, over there."

"Oh, my goodness." The homes were magazine-worthy. Gorgeous, sprawling, tasteful. The landscaping was as lush, colorful and beautiful as The Reaux itself.

"Yeah, King and Zander got a company to design the whole thing—the houses, this place here." She gestured at the building. "Named after my late husband. Louis James."

Zee appeared. "Zander, go grab my gift out of the car."

"Yes, ma'am. Good morning, Tink. You look as pretty as ever." He kissed her cheek.

She kissed his and patted his face gently. "Morning, baby."

Then he turned that bright, beautiful smile on Jenita. Seeing him for the first time in full daylight, he looked fine as hell. She had to compose herself.

Those eyes. That smile. His salt-and-pepper mustache and tapered beard, immaculately groomed. A fresh fade with just enough deep salt-and-pepper waves on top. The light against his sun-kissed, decadent brown skin. White open-collar shirt. Paisley pine-green vest with a matching ascot. Emerald cufflinks. Polished black loafers. His perfectly fitted black tuxedo pants and his blazer hooked over one finger, carrying the faintest trace of his cologne.

My, my, my. He is so fine.

He leaned in and lightly kissed her cheek. Her hand yesterday, her cheek today. *This man*, she thought. *This man right here. Lord, if he ever kisses me on the lips, I won't be no more good.*

"Good morning, Jenita. You are beautiful. That dress, your fragrance." He smiled. "Altogether lovely."

"Good morning. You look very handsome, Alexander." Without his blazer on, she could see his broad physique clearly. And the weapon in his holster.

"Alexander?" Tink said. "Y'all don't have to be formal in front of me. Renae told me y'all were out at all times of night."

They glanced at each other. Jenita was surprised, but Zee had told Frank and Renae it was the best night of his life. He knew exactly how fast family news traveled.

"We just walked on the boardwalk and sat on the pier talking."

Tink winked. "Must've been some good talking, 'Alexander.'"

"Yes, indeedy. It was."

Tink looked at Jenita, then back at him. "Zander, don't talk to nobody like that." She patted Jenita's hand. "Now go get my gift and let this young lady take me inside. Put it on the table for me."

"Yes, ma'am. I have to stop by my office first."

The wedding décor was amazing. Sheer emerald and gold fabric draped the walls. Flowers everywhere, from the ceiling to the floor and everything in between. Metallic gold chairs. The backdrop for the wedding party was like an enchanted forest: a waterfall, saplings with spring-green leaves placed with deliberate care. A brass archway wound with bountiful ivy. A candelabra for the unity candle lighting. A green padded kneeling bench. The string quartet was tuning up in the corner.

"Oh, my goodness. They really did this up, didn't they?"

"Yes, ma'am. I have never seen anything like this for a wedding. I thought the hotel was beautiful. This is something else entirely."

An usher came to escort Tink to her seat. As another approached Jenita, she spotted the card box on the table and remembered hers was locked in her glove compartment. She slipped back outside.

She saw that Sheila had returned her call. She hadn't been available for the three-way when Rhonda filled Sheila in on the Ingrams. Sheila was pissed. Cussing and furious, fussing at herself for having gone on that cruise. Jenita was still on the phone when she reached the entrance and Zee came through the doors looking around, about to ask the valet if he'd seen her before spotting her.

"I was wondering where you went."

"I had to run to my car. Look, I wrote 'Mr. and Mrs. Alexander.' I'm sorry."

"That's not your fault. I'm sure they'll love it because it's from you."

"You think so?"

"I know so." He looked at her. "You are so beautiful, Jenita."

She wore one of the dresses Renae had ordered—a brocade emerald off-the-shoulder mermaid gown with metallic gold piping around the belled sleeves. Ms. Lorraine's niece had tailored it perfectly. Jenita wasn't quite as comfortable in it; it wasn't her usual style. But she hadn't wanted to refuse such a generous gift from her new friend, and when she'd seen herself in the mirror that morning, she felt genuinely pretty.

Her brunch mates and the boutique staff hadn't held back. They hyped her the way her softened-but-still-brick-house body deserved. Shimmering gold peep-toe stiletto mules. A gold metallic wristlet from the boutique. Her locs in a high bun with a few spiraled in the front, making her look like a goddess. The dress brought out a confidence that surprised even her.

When he opened the door for her, he couldn't help but let her walk a few steps ahead. *Mm. Mm. Mm.* It moved through him, unspoken.

"May I escort you in?" He held out his arm.

"Yes, you may." She slipped her arm under his and he placed his hand over hers. They looked at each other. She looked away. He didn't.

"I couldn't stop thinking about you. Now I can't take my eyes off you." *Très belle femme.* The words settled quietly in his mind.

Inside, the usher looked up. "Your name, ma'am?"

"Jenita Hall."

"Good afternoon, Ms. Hall." He checked the seating chart and held out his arm.

Zee said, "Ms. Hall, would you mind if I escort you to your seat?"

"I'd like that."

As they walked down the aisle together, every eye in the room followed them. People who didn't know her whispered. People who did know Zee wondered why the father of the groom and best man was playing usher. She was the last honored guest to be seated, second row. She wasn't used to this much attention. Once she sat down, she looked straight ahead and pulled her posture up tall. The mermaid cut wouldn't allow her to cross her legs. She couldn't see where the Ingrams were sitting, and the not-knowing chipped away at her fresh confidence.

She heard someone whisper, "Ms. Hall." She ignored it. Then a hand touched her shoulder. She turned to find one of her former students, one who had struggled in college, who reminded her of her cousin Deuce, whom her grandmother had treated cruelly. He was one she'd favored, and she hadn't seen him in years. He stood up, left his row, and walked boldly over to hug her.

All eyes swung to them. Then he pointed to an entire row of her former students—Mike and Tiff's classmates. They were all about to get up and come to her at once when the wedding planner called the room to attention. The ceremony was beginning. But it settled something in her, knowing they remembered her, knowing there were now other faces from her past in this room besides the Ingrams.

The groomsmen entered. And there was her baby, Mike, standing tall, out of his shell, radiant. His best man was his fine daddy. Mike looked over at Renae and Tink, who were already in tears. Tink remembered sitting her tiny great-nephew on phone books at the table and feeding him his favorite—rice and butter, as much as he wanted. Renae was seeing the son she didn't give birth to and thinking about his grandmother and his mother and how much they would have loved to witness this moment. Pops cried.

Jenita reached into her purse for a tissue. She was watching the once-timid Mike standing at the front of a room, about to marry the young woman she had introduced him to. She remembered her vision. She cried, too.

Quincy and three of Mike's Alpha Phi Alpha Fraternity, Inc. brothers rounded out the groomsmen. She recognized two of them, and they recognized her. They nodded, and she waved back quietly. Then she swept the lineup and found Zee looking directly at her. She wanted to hold his gaze so badly. She couldn't. If she did, he'd see that everything she'd learned about him so far was exactly what she'd always wanted. And he was too good to be true.

This is just for a weekend. The words brushed through her mind.

She was not going to let those eyes take her over. She noticed Tink and Renae follow his gaze across the room. When they found her, they smiled and waved. And she caught Zee giving her a slow, reassuring wink, as if he could hear her thoughts. He didn't care who was watching.

"Ms. Hall! Ms. Jenita Hall!" The photographer's assistant waved her forward. "The bride and groom would like you to join them for pictures." Mike and Tiff pulled her into a hug as the assistant positioned her between them, then brought in Renae and Tiff's mom, then Zee, Tiff's father, and Frank.

When the group shots were done, Zee turned to her. "May I get a picture of just the two of us?"

She smiled and said yes. He pulled out his phone and LaKisha stepped up. "I'll take it, Uncle Zee, but you never use your Facebook."

"Maybe I will." She took several shots, and Jenita asked her to take one on her phone, too.

Jenita slipped away while the wedding party continued, and her former students pulled her over to catch up. They started taking selfies with her, marveling at how nice she looked.

"Dang, Ms. Hall!" She laughed, obliged, and took a few of her own. She didn't post often, only for something special, but she was all dressed up, and this was one of those days. She looked so beautiful, in fact, that

Renae and Frank's chubby seven-year-old grandson Alex sent his twin sister Dria over to ask her to be his girlfriend. Zee said no.

The wedding planner called her name. "Ms. Jenita Hall!"

"Right here."

"I'm sorry to interrupt. We're creating some additional seating and I noticed your plus-one wasn't accounted for. Are they here?"

"No. My apologies, she couldn't come." Out of the corner of her eye, she saw the Ingrams lurking, waiting for an opportunity to pounce privately.

From across the room, Zee's voice rang out clearly: "I'm her plus one."

He'd spotted them lurking. He'd watched her go from festive to withdrawn the second she registered their presence. Everyone in that room knew perfectly well that Zee's seat, as father of the groom and best man, was with the wedding party. He crossed to her quickly and said it again, calm and certain:

"I'm Ms. Hall's plus one."

The wedding planner, who was his cousin, Uncle Louis's daughter, looked at him sideways. The way he looked back at her was enough. She didn't question it.

"Yes, sir, Mr. Devereaux."

Jenita took his arm. "I owe you three or four now?"

"No." His voice was firm. "That one's on the house."

The photo session stretched on, and Jenita was fading, tired from staying out all night, though with no regrets. She yawned.

"I know you're tired."

"I am. You should be, too."

"I am. And this is taking too long. They still have a second site for the shoot down on Brown Sugar."

"While y'all are doing all that, I'm going to take a nap in my car. I need to change my shoes anyway."

"Nap in your car? No. Please don't do that."

"It's either that or I skip the reception. I need at least thirty minutes to push through."

"I have to drive a cart down with the wedding party, but there's a chaise lounge and a couch in my office."

"A chaise lounge and a couch? You be working or sleeping in there?"

He laughed. "More working than sleeping. But they're both brand new. I haven't used either one yet. They're yours. It'll be at least another thirty to forty-five minutes."

"I may take you up on that, but I still need to get to my car first."

"I'll walk you."

"You don't have to. People are already talking."

"So. I'm used to it."

"I'm not."

"You may have to get used to it. Ready?"

She changed her shoes. He took a call: the wedding party was loaded and waiting. He stepped away briefly. "Aye man, take my cart to get them down the hill. I'll drive my truck. Thanks."

She asked, "The golf carts are a nice touch. Why use them instead of just the vans?"

"We're using both. The carts are quicker because we avoid traffic lights and come through the tunnel."

"Tunnel?"

"There's a tunnel that runs from Brown Sugar Beach up to Queen's Hill. It's been here for decades, but Black people weren't allowed to use it. We widened it so vehicles can pass through, mainly for events and residents." It was well lit, a gradual incline leading to the gated residential area of Queen's Hill.

"Wow. I'm at the top. I am just in awe of all of this."

"You're not the only one in awe, Ms. Jenita Hall."

She started toward the main entrance. He steered her gently in the other direction. "Back way. If I go through the front, I'll get a dozen 'Mr. Devereaux's' before I get ten feet, and I'll never make it down to the beach. I can't do Mike like that."

"I don't want to make you late."

"I won't be late if we go around."

When he unlocked his office, the décor was the epitome of him, masculine, warm, inviting, sleek, sexy. Black leather couch and chaise lounge. White leather armchairs. An African blackwood desk with matching bookcases. A credenza lined with framed photos. Coffee table, end tables. A white, black, and gold Venetian-print area rug that gave the whole space warmth and an opulent ease.

"Your office is very well put together, Mr. Alexander Devereaux."

"Thank you. You know you can call me Zee. Restroom's right there. Everything you need to freshen up is in the cabinets. Snacks, drinks, and water are in the refrigerator. Help yourself to all of it. I'll be back after the shoot. Please wait for me here."

"Okay. Thank you, Zee. I'll wait."

He smiled and left. She stood in the middle of the room feeling like she was living a dream with her eyes half open. She tried all the chairs, bouncing each one to test the quality. Top of the line. The bathroom was black marble with white and gray veining. The cabinets held white-and-gold washcloths, hand towels, bath towels, disposable toothbrushes coated in peppermint toothpaste, mouthwash, colognes, lotion, soap. A narrow closet held two black suits, four white shirts, and several bowties.

The thought came soft and sure. *Wow. This man is a dream.*

She was still looking for a red flag. She hadn't found one yet. *Maybe because I'm stressed, overstimulated, hungry, and sleepy.*

She settled onto the chaise lounge, wiggled herself as comfortable as a mermaid gown would allow, and pulled the tan-and-black Hermès throw off the back. Forty minutes later, Zee returned. He knocked softly and opened the door slowly.

She was fast asleep.

He stood for a moment, just looking at her, hating that he had to wake her up. He was so glad she had said yes and felt safe enough to rest.

"Ms. Hall…" he whispered. "Jenita…"

Zee escorted her to her seat, pulled her chair out, and the wedding planner left the one beside her open.

"I'll be right back."

He knew only rumors about the Ingrams, no direct knowledge. But after everything Jenita had shared with him on the pier, he had quietly made sure they would have to go through him to reach her. The image of her being struck and kicked while pregnant made his jaw tighten.

He found the security detail. "Keep watch. I'll have them walking backwards down the hill if I need to." Then he located the Ingrams and told them simply, "Give me a reason." He had the nerve to wink as he walked away.

Back at her seat, Jenita took in the table. She'd been seated with the parents and grandparents of the bride and groom and the other honored guests. She would have wondered about the white man at the table if Zee hadn't already told her about Pops. Frank and Renae were there, too, because in every way that counted, they were Mike's parents.

Renae glided over. "Girl. You looked like a goddess coming down that aisle."

"All thanks to you. You have no idea how grateful I am. And you look amazing."

"Baby, that dress should be thanking you."

The food was exceptional. The reception décor matched the ceremony. The deejay hit every generation. Renae danced with Mike as the mother of the groom. Then Mike asked Jenita to dance. She wasn't a dancer, but she could hold her own on a two-step, and she knew her line dances: the Electric Slide to "Before I Let Go" by Maze featuring Frankie Beverly, and the new one called the Wobble that her students had taught her. When those came on, she was ready.

Renae kept begging Zee to dance with her. He finally gave in. Anyone who had ever wondered why they used to win couples dancing contests, it was obvious. It had been years since they'd danced together in public. He was so smooth; Chicago Style Stepping with full ease, dipping and swinging Renae's little round body around like it was nothing. All Jenita could do was watch and marvel.

He brought two slices of cake and sat back down beside her. "Will you dance with me after we eat?"

"Oh, no. Lord no. And Jesus knows, too."

"Why not?"

"I can't dance like that. You didn't tell me how well you danced."

"I told you my mom had me and Renae all over the place."

"I thought that meant little-kid dancing." He laughed.

"Nah, baby. She had us competing against grown folks. We used to knock 'em down."

"I can see that."

"But I haven't danced like that in years."

"You could've fooled me."

"Dance with me. Please."

"No, sir."

"You owe me one."

"When I said I owed you one, I didn't mean dancing."

"Please."

The way he said it weakened her. She pressed her lips together.

"Please."

"Okay. But I am only two-stepping."

"You won't even have to do that."

"What, then?"

"I want to slow dance with you."

She knew it was over. Her resistance had left the building. "Okay. One song. And that counts as one I owe you."

"Deal."

"Let me go outside to take care of something."

One of the guys from the security team materialized quietly behind her as he left. She noticed, but it no longer startled her. She also noticed the Ingrams glancing over periodically, and for the first time, she simply "nothinged" them. She bobbed her head to the music. She fetched Mr. King and Ms. Lorraine each another slice of cake when they asked. Ms. Lorraine admired her dress and her perfume. Tink just smiled that particular smile, the one that circled back to what she'd said outside.

About ten minutes later, the deejay dropped one of her that's my jam songs: "All I Need Is Love" by Tim Bowman, led by Stokley. She wasn't about to go to the dance floor alone, but she heard God whisper, "Enjoy yourself. Dance."

She slipped behind a roll-away divider that was hiding stacked chairs and danced by herself. When security indicated to Zee where she'd gone, he could see her gold flats moving at the bottom and the hem of her dress swaying with the music. She was singing along, word for word, beautifully off key. He caught Renae's eye and Frank's, pressed a finger to his lips at Frank, and the three of them crept closer for a look. The music was loud enough that she never heard them. Renae watched her new, fun, free friend two-stepping and twirling and felt pure joy. Frank watched and felt something crack open in his wall of skepticism.

Zee fell in love.

When the song ended, Renae clapped. Zee smiled. Jenita spun around, startled and mortified. Then Frank said, "You call that singing? It sounded painful. And that was dancing?"

"I haven't seen you dance."

"I'd do better than that with one leg." He lifted his pant leg to show his prosthesis.

She hadn't known. "I'd put you to the test, but I don't want you to hurt yourself."

"Hurt myself? You ain't shit, back here dancing behind a wall. Who are your partners, chairs?"

Zee and Renae braced themselves. They knew Frank's mouth, but before either could step in, Jenita said, "At least my partners have four legs."

They all fell out laughing.

"I think you met your match, bruh," Zee said.

Frank was still laughing. He could dish it and he could take it. He cut his eyes at Jenita. "You might be all right. Don't get too comfortable."

Back at the table, Zee asked, "Didn't you say you couldn't dance?"

"I can't."

"Yes, you can."

"Not like you and Renae."

Frank butted in, "And me."

"Pfft."

The deejay put on "You Are My Lady" by Freddie Jackson and Frank automatically took Renae to the dance floor before the first verse ended.

Zee said, "I'd like to wait for the right song, if you don't mind."

"I don't mind. What's the right song?"

"I'll know it when I hear it." They talked and laughed through two slow songs.

Then Zee said, "This one."

Luther Vandross. "If Only for One Night."

He stood, came around behind her chair to slide it back, and held out his hand. She held it all the way to the dance floor. She felt like a princess in a fairytale. She placed one palm on his shoulder, her forearm against his chest—the safety position, close enough, control intact. He held their joined hands against his chest and placed his other hand at the small of her back. He felt soothing to her. She felt perfect in his arms.

Two minutes in, she laid her head on his chest and let the music and the lyrics wash over her. It was a dream she had been too afraid to let herself have. He had heard this song a hundred times and never had someone to give it to.

Tonight, it was his prayer.

He knew, standing there, that he wanted far more than one night. He had concluded: he would do whatever it took to make her his. For the first time in his life, he was holding a woman with his whole heart.

She let go of everything and slid her arms up around his neck. He understood. He held her closer. He whispered against her ear, "You are truly special to me, Jenita." She wanted to answer. She didn't. The deejay moved seamlessly into "Beauty" by Dru Hill, then "Love Ballad" by L.T.D. They danced without stopping until he led her off the floor.

It was nearly six o'clock. Jenita was relaxed, raptured, quietly aroused, and bone tired.

He walked her toward her car, and she found it blocked in.

"Let me take you back in the cart. You can see the tunnel, and I'll have the valet bring your car down."

Nothing about it gave her pause. God and Nana had not flagged this man.

"Okay."

He helped her into the cart and draped his tuxedo blazer around her. She saw his weapon tucked at the back of his waistband and noticed, as he'd said, that the tunnel route down Queen's Hill back to The Reaux was considerably faster. As they neared the hotel she asked, "Do all the men in your family carry?"

"Yes."

"Why?"

"Well, not everyone likes me the way you do." He smiled and winked.

"Who said I like you?"

"That dance gave me a clue or two."

"Stay focused. Why do you all carry?"

"Some of the same reasons I told you about last night. Not everyone appreciates what we've built or what we continue to do."

"White folks?"

"A few Black folks and others, too."

"Have you ever had to use it?"

"I have. A few times."

"Did you kill somebody?"

He gave her the short version: military combat before his injury, the bank robbery, Andy dying later from the toxic mix already in his system. He also told her the adult women in the family were trained and carried as well, that there had been robberies and break-ins at the businesses over the years, but never the homes, and that he and Frank had received threats in the years after Andy, though not recently. Carrying was a precaution they'd never seen a reason to stop.

He answered every question she asked, openly, because he wanted to, and because something in him believed she'd know if he didn't. He lifted his pant leg to show the ankle holster, and he thanked her. Her questions had reminded him to confirm the new drivers with Reggie. She wasn't afraid of guns; her nana, grandfather, father, uncles, and cousins all hunted, and she'd fired both shotguns and handguns before. But she wasn't used to seeing civilians carry so openly, even legally.

"I thought about getting one for protection, but I never felt safe with Harmony in the house and students coming over. I haven't had students stay overnight since Mike, though. Now that I live alone and people are unpredictable, I've been thinking about it again."

"I understand that."

"I'd need to take classes first. Learn to shoot properly."

"I can teach you."

"Maybe you can."

"Did I ever thank you for everything you did for my son?"

"Yes. This is the fourteen billionth, eight hundred millionth time since last night."

He laughed. "I wish I hadn't been so hard on him about the music. We talked all the time, but he never told me any of that. And the times he mentioned going to stay at Ms. Hall's, eating sweet potato muffins, rutabagas, chicken pot pie, liver and onions with gravy, mac and cheese, pecan cookies, I pictured an old church mother or an old dorm matron. You know the kind that started kicking you out of the women's dorm fifteen minutes before curfew."

"Okay! First of all, is that how he described me? An old dorm matron? Wait until I see Mike."

"No. He never described you. I wish he had." He slowed the cart slightly and looked at her, from her lap to her face and back down.

"Second of all, don't look at me like that. And third, what do you know about getting kicked out of women's dorms?"

"A little. Most times they came to mine."

"Okay playa." He shook his head and they both laughed.

He parked in his GM space and took the VIP entrance, avoiding the lobby. He had her party favor bag and her heels in one hand when an employee passed and did a barely concealed double-take.

"Good evening, Mr. Devereaux." A nod at Jenita. "Ma'am."

They walked toward her room, talking about the beauty of the wedding, the pleasure of each other's company, and the dancing. She thanked him for his attentiveness, for the nap in his office, and told him she was looking forward to being friends.

"You're welcome. May I cash in my second I.O.U. and get a goodnight hug?"

"Sure. I told you I was good for it."

She turned to offer him a church hug. He explained gently that he'd rather not have his business visible on the security cameras in the hallway and asked if he could step just inside her room. He promised to remain respectful.

"Promise?"

"I promise, Ms. Hall."

No red flags. "Okay."

The door closed. He set her shoes on the floor and her gift bag on the chair. She slipped off his blazer and handed it back. He laid it over the chair. Then he stepped toward her, just inches apart, and they both could feel one another's body heat and sensual energy. He looked down at her. She looked up. Just for a moment, she answered his eyes directly. He had been wanting that.

He wanted to kiss her so badly. He had only asked for a hug. She wanted him to kiss her. She thought he would. She was ready. He wrapped his arms around her waist, resting them just above the small of her back. She put her arms around his neck. No space between them. He let out a slow, deep breath that felt like it had been held for years.

That sound again, low from somewhere in his chest. "Mm Mm Mmm." A vibration she could feel. He rubbed her back slowly, with intention. Her body started to go soft in his arms, and it frightened her a little.

She began to ease her arms back and he said, "Please don't let me go. Not yet. A little longer. A little tighter, please."

She held on tighter.

"Mmhmm. Can you feel that, Jenita?" She was aware of his body responding, but she understood that wasn't what he meant. She stopped thinking and just felt.

He asked again. "Do you feel that?"

She did. A presence. Something warm and particular. A closeness that had no name. Full-body tingles. That's what he meant.

"Yes," she whispered, breathing shallowly. "I feel it."

They held each other for a few minutes, and when he felt himself getting too aroused, he quietly dropped his arms out of respect. He had never felt so calm and so turned on at the same time, from a hug.

She slid her hands down to his chest. Looking him in the eyes, she asked, "May I kiss you?"

"Please," he whispered. "Please."

She tilted her head back and studied his face, unhurried, taking each feature in turn: his hairline, eyebrows, his eyes, the bridge of his nose, his cheekbones, his lips, his mustache and beard. She kissed his top lip, then his bottom lip. His right cheek, then his left, then the tip of his nose. She placed her hands on the sides of his face and kissed him in the same pattern again. Then she kissed his lips with her mouth slightly open.

Zee didn't know what it was to be kissed that tenderly, nor be tended to that intimately. Not once in his life.

It filled him. He felt safe and certain. She let the tip of her tongue meet his lips and then kissed him openly, warmly, and unhurriedly. His control weakened. He kissed her back in a way meant to take in everything she was giving. The passion, care and intimacy between them was unlike anything either had given or received, in a hug or a kiss. He knew he had to stop before he was going to lay her down, but he wanted to honor her and honor the celibacy he'd held for eight years. She had arrived unannounced, and he and his celibacy had not yet had a conversation.

As if she sensed it, she began ending the kiss in reverse, the same gentle way it had begun.

They both exhaled. Hands dropped.

"Thank you for the kiss, Zee."

"I have never been kissed like that…so damn good, Jenita. Never in my life." He placed his hand along the side of her face and delicately moved his thumb slowly across her scar. "You are so tender. So pretty." He paused. "May I ask you something?"

"Yes, Zee."

"You said you could see us being friends, right?"

"Yes. Of course."

"When you hug your friends, do you feel what you felt just now when you hugged me?"

"No."

"Okay. Do you kiss your friends the way you just kissed me?"

She dropped her head and blushed. "Never. No, I do not."

He lifted her chin gently. "I see."

"You see what?"

"Jenita, I don't want to be your friend."

He kissed her forehead, picked up his blazer to cover himself and walked out the door.

As it clicked shut, Jenita slid down the wall.

He walked back to his golf cart, the cool air settling him down. He pulled out his phone. "What do you have Monday morning around nine?… Good. Meet me at my other property on Queen's."

Back at the reception, most of the guests had gone but his family was still there. Frank was outside smoking cigars with a few men and spotted the cart pulling in. He walked over. "Man. I know you been accelerate, but did you hit it that quick?"

"You know it's celibate, not accelerate, crazy." Zee laughed and shook his head. "And no, I didn't. But she for damn sure has my heart, mind, nose, eyes, and ears wide open. I'm gone, man. So gone."

"Gone? You? You ain't never been gone."

"Gone."

He greeted the other men as he passed and pulled Reggie aside to confirm everyone needed to be packing at all times and that the new drivers would start Monday. Frank crushed out his cigar and followed him inside.

The deejay had brought the volume down but was still playing good music. Pops and Ms. Lorraine were just leaving the dance floor. Tink was there with Mr. Horace, who had been sweet on her for some time. They all settled at a table together and Zee got a pitcher of water and filled everyone's glass, then pulled up a chair, turned it around, and sat facing the back of it.

Pops looked at him. "You all right, son?"

"Yes, sir. And no, sir." He knew exactly why Pops was asking. He just wanted to hear him say it, and he was bracing for the barrage of questions and jokes he knew were coming about the way he'd been behaving with Jenita all weekend. They didn't disappoint.

"You got something going with this woman?"

"Not like I want to. Not yet."

"We can tell. I know when I see it. A man knows when he knows. You know." Ms. Lorraine said Jenita looked stunning in that dress and what a genuinely lovely person she seemed to be.

Renae leaned forward. "I can see you like Jenita in a way I've never seen you be about nobody and it scares me a little. She's also my friend, and I don't want that to get complicated."

Frank said, "She checked out on paper. I'm still running my own test in person. I have a built-in lie detector."

"And? Did it detect any lies?"

"One."

"What?"

"When she said I couldn't dance." Everyone laughed. "But I'm not the one dancing behind a wall with chairs."

"She needed to get away from your crazy self," Zee said, still laughing.

Tink said, "Zander, you told on yourself on that dance floor. My goodness."

Mr. Horace, holding Tink's hand: "Don't I hold you like that, Tink?"

"Not here. But I may let you later." Everyone laughed.

Zee let the laughter settle, then spoke. "Listen, y'all, and hear me good, all of you. Pops, I'll be careful, but I cannot let her get away from me. And yes, I know. I agree with you, Ms. Lorraine. Tink, I don't have the words for what it felt like to hold her and be held by her. Frank, I think she scared you because you may have just met your match. Renae, sis, I promise I won't mess it up, and I won't come between your friendship. If anything, you may get a sister-in-law." He let that land. "Because I am going to do everything I know how to do to marry that woman and take care of her. For the first time in my life, as a full-grown man, I am in love. I love Jenita Rochelle Hall."

The table went quiet.

Everyone was stunned.

Except Tink.

CHAPTER 23

Questions and Answers

She was still replaying the kiss and wondering about what he'd said about not wanting to be her friend.

Around ten o'clock, a text came in. "Jenita, I truly enjoyed being in your presence. I hope you're getting some much-needed rest and that you won't see this until tomorrow morning. I won't be able to sleep at all, with you, your hug, and your kiss heavy on my mind. You are truly something special. Please call me when you're awake. Zee."

Reading it made her heart and her body smile, inside and out. She wanted to text him right back. She didn't. She couldn't sleep either. She tried, tossed and turned until she'd twisted all the sheets into a pile, and finally gave up and got out of bed. She put on the hotel robe, wrapped herself in the comforter, and stepped out onto her oceanfront balcony. She stood there taking long, slow inhales of the crisp ocean air, then settled onto the cushioned lounger and watched one or two figures walking the boardwalk below.

It made her think warmly about how she and Zee had been those people just last night and earlier. Now, well past three in the morning, she was watching someone else.

He held me so tight. Kissed me so good. Here I am, over forty years old, and I have never been held or kissed that passionately. And what was that…that warm, slow zing between us when we held each other? I've never asked a man for a kiss before, and when I kissed him, without my usual hesitation, it felt like we belonged. But he said he didn't want to be my friend. I think I know what he meant. I just don't want to read too much into it too fast. I just met the man two days ago. Well. Three now.

She looked down at the pier. There he was, jogging on the beach, heading back toward the boardwalk. He had told her he ran three to five miles, four to five days a week. She stood up to see him better. Watching him slow to a brisk walk and disappear through the hotel doors made her want to call his name. She didn't.

She texted: "Good morning, Zee. I enjoyed our time together as well. I appreciate your hospitality and your attentiveness. I just watched you finish your run. I can't sleep either."

He replied immediately. "Why can't you sleep?"

"I blame you."

"Why?"

"You. That dance. That hug. That kiss."

"I'll gladly take the blame. Would you like to talk?"

"It's almost three in the morning."

"Seems like our sweet hour. Lol."

"Lol. I guess so."

"It is." Two minutes passed. "Good night, Jenita."

Dang it. I missed my chance playing hard to get.

Before she could type good night back, another message arrived: "Unless you'd rather talk." She held her breath for half a second and texted without hesitating: "Yes. Please give me a call."

"Hello, Jenita." His voice on the phone felt like a velvet blanket fresh out of a warm dryer, wrapped around her on a cold night.

"Hi, Zee."

"You're beautiful even when I can't see you."

"Thank you."

"Are you always up at this time of morning?"

"No. Not unless I'm prepping for a presentation. You?"

"More or less, yes. I've been working around the clock since the hotel opened. I took it down a notch for a while, but then the wedding took me over and I missed my run yesterday. I'm hoping to get back to something resembling a schedule once things settle. When Mike's back and in the groove, we'll return to the succession plan."

"If you don't mind my asking, what does that look like?"

"Not at all. Pops will be retiring as President and CEO, and I'll step into that role, which is more of an oversight position. Then I'll gradually shift the GM responsibilities to Mike and Quincy as they grow into it. We need both of them because of how much we've expanded. Quincy has Renae's and Frank's energy. He loves to travel and network. Mike is more focused, more of a paperwork guy, laid back like me."

"He sure is."

"They'll both be mentored by me, Pops, and our senior leadership and board members through the transition. Everyone who's been with Pops and Tink from the beginning will be staggering their retirements and grooming whoever comes after them. They've all more than earned the right to rest and enjoy their golden years."

"That's lovely, keeping it in the family." She was trying not to sound too impressed. "Thank you for sharing that."

"I'll tell you anything you want to know."

"Anything?"

"Yes."

"Hmm."

He laughed. "Anything. Go ahead."

"Okay. Why did you say you don't want to be my friend?"

"Before I answer that, when are you leaving?"

"Are you trying to put me out?"

"Oh, no. I don't want you to leave at all."

"Sure." She cleared her throat. "Anyway, I was going to leave tomorrow, but I need some actual sleep before I drive. I haven't slept here at all for two nights. I need to speak to guest services. Or maybe I should take that up with the GM, since somebody had me out all night."

"I'll see what the GM can do. I don't want you to leave. All night still wasn't long enough. You are an incredible woman, Jenita. A beautiful surprise. I mean that. I genuinely wish you didn't have to go."

"I'll leave Monday morning."

"One more day. I won't bother you. You need rest."

"Thank you. You do, too."

"So, to answer your question: that's why I don't want to be your friend. You are absolutely remarkable to me. I don't want to start out as friends and end up in your permanent friendzone."

"But you just met me."

"I'm telling you, I feel like I've known you my whole life. I'm only just now meeting you in person."

She loved the sound of it. The words. His sincerity. He was bold and certain. They both went quiet for a moment, and in the silence, something was happening, a kind of connected stillness, a synergy speaking for itself.

"I've never kissed a woman the way I kissed you. Never hugged anyone like that. And never been kissed or held the way you kissed and held me."

"Now, if I was born at night, it sure wasn't last night. Please."

"I haven't. Not ever. Not once in my life."

"Mm-hm."

"I'm telling you the truth. Have you ever felt anything like that before? It was more than the hug and the kiss. It was something else entirely. Indescribable to me. And you?"

"Ahem. It's getting late. I mean early."

He smiled through the phone. "Well, I appreciate you replying to my texts and letting me call to hear your sweet voice, Ms. Jenita Rochelle Hall."

"My whole name?"

"Yes. I like it." He thought, *I'd love Devereaux after it.* "Before you go, may I ask you something else?"

"Yes."

"I know you said you 'cain't,' but for real, why won't you look at me?"

"I do. I did."

"Blinks don't count." He chuckled.

"I just cain't." She laughed and fell back onto the bed, covering her eyes as if he could see her.

"Why not?"

"Can I keep it real?"

"The realer the better, beautiful."

"I know you've heard people tell you how mesmerizing your eyes are."

"Yes, but it doesn't stop them from looking." He laughed. "You give me two, maybe three seconds, if that."

"Because I see more than just looking at you."

"Hmm. What do you see?"

"I see you. Your compassionate heart. I see someone who has longed his whole life to be seen and loved for who he is, not for what he looks like or what he has. I see that clearly. And I don't want to see anything you don't want me to know yet."

"Wow." He paused. "Wow. You do see me. Feel free to look at me, or in me. I don't want to hide anything from you."

"And when you look back at me the way you do, your eyes look like Superman's laser-beam, panty-dropping eyes. And I will not be a casualty."

They laughed until they were out of breath and stayed on the phone until eight in the morning, when a knock came at her door. He had sent room service with the full oatmeal spread from the first morning, identical in every detail, plus another Southwest omelet with potatoes, toast, and everything that came with it.

"Aww. You are so thoughtful. I can't eat all of this. Two carts, Zee?"

"I would have brought them myself, if you weren't my sweet kryptonite."

"Wait. Kryptonite was poison to Superman."

"A good kind, then. Weakening, but in every good way. I felt it before we danced, before the hug, before the kiss. You soften the rough parts of me without even trying, Jenita. I can be myself with you and let my guard down and feel safe doing it. I want to do the same for you. I would love to explore what's beyond a friendship with you. That's why I don't want to be your friend. Does that answer your question?"

"Yes." She was completely undone by him, his authenticity and straightforwardness.

"Anything else?"

"No. I cain't."

She needed to feel wanted. He needed to feel seen. She could see him the way no one else had. He embodied everything she'd quietly wanted. For the first time, they both felt safe.

That afternoon, Zee said, "Renae, I'll back off and be patient since you can't. I don't want Jenita to feel like I'm using you to get to her."

"Zee, you're just wide open, and out of the blue. Like Frank was saying, you acted like women, as love interests, were no longer and had been off the table for you entirely. And now you tell the whole family you want to marry her? She is a wonderful person, and she and I are becoming genuine friends. But real relationships take time. Any kind."

"But didn't you know, when you were in high school, that you loved Frank? Even after he had legally become our brother? You were seventeen, Renae. I know what I know, and I am a grown-ass man who has been through hell and back. I can't control when love walks into my life. It surprised me, too. I thought of all people you would understand. Don't you think I can recognize the love of my life? If I didn't know better, I'd think you don't want another woman loving me besides you, Tink, and family."

Renae started crying. "No. No, Zee. How could you think that? You deserve to be loved and happy. It's just…I cannot bear watching you get hurt again. I don't know if you could survive another pain like that. It would halfway destroy me to watch you hurt again and have to find your way back out of darkness again, or worse. You have done so much work on yourself, and I am so proud of you. We love you. The whole family adores you. Every one of those kids looks up to Uncle Zee. You have given so much of yourself, and we cannot stand the thought of you being hurt."

"But what about me, Renae? What if it's my turn? I've watched everybody have love but me."

"We love you."

"I know that. But not that kind of love. Someone to love me for me. I have so much love to give that woman that; I thought that part of me had died. But when I saw Jenita, it all bubbled up, and I felt alive. Celibacy, not having romantic love, was manageable. It was as though my love waited to meet her before it would come back."

"And family love, all your success, that hasn't made you feel alive?"

"Yes. But not like this. I didn't realize until now how long I'd been everybody's third wheel. Yours and Frank's, everybody's, Uncle Zee, showing up for everyone's everything. I don't regret it and I'll keep on. But it wasn't until I was out on that dance floor, not watching from the sideline, that I understood what I'd been missing. I had someone, not just anyone, but her. And she has no idea how completely she has me."

"You could have anyone. Women have been chasing you for years. There has never been a shortage. You shut them all down without giving any of them half a chance."

"Which is exactly why she is so precious to me. She didn't know who I was or what I had. She treated me with genuine respect. Her curiosity. Her simplicity. The way she cared about how hard I was working and actually acknowledged the work itself. She didn't chase. She isn't about money. She was just being herself with me. I don't get that from women."

"But just because she was that way doesn't mean you have to marry her."

"It's more than that. Everything in me wanted to know more about her the first night. Then when I saw y'all at brunch, I felt drawn to her. And when she came off that elevator at the rehearsal dinner, I knew I wanted to be with her. And then, Renae, I have never talked all night with anyone in my life. Not even you or Frank. Not since Mama." His voice broke a little.

"I haven't felt that safe and secure since then. We told each other things that strangers don't share. And when we danced, when she let me hold her and the way she kissed me, I knew I wanted her to be my wife."

Renae was crying again. "Wife, Zee? I just...does she feel the same way? What if she doesn't? That's what I'm afraid of."

"That's a risk I'm willing to take with her. I love that woman. And if she doesn't love me that way yet, I have enough love for both of us, and I have patience. I have so much to give her. I can give her the world." He paused. "I went back and listened to the song we caught her dancing to by herself. She told me it's one of her favorites. I've had it on repeat."

"What was it?"

"'All I Need Is Love', Tim Bowman and Stokley. I can give her that. And I know in my heart she can give me that. That's what I need. She's who I need. I don't know how I know, but I do. I just know. And I don't want to argue with you, Renae. I appreciate you and Frank wanting to protect me. I won't mess up your friendship with Jenita. But don't try to stop me from pursuing something I know we both need and want. Let me love somebody, too."

Renae hugged him tightly. "Okay. I hear you. I won't stop you. And I am so sorry for not thinking about how you feel. Forgive me for being selfish."

"I forgive you. But when you talk to her, please don't talk about me. I'll do the same. I don't want to crowd her or make her feel like I need you running interference for me."

"I won't. Maybe I need to ease back on the friendship."

"I'm not asking you to do that. You were treating her like something we used to argue over as kids. This ain't that. We're all adults."

"You're right. I'm sorry." She half-laughed. "Maybe I need to listen to that song. And I definitely need to pray, talk to God, talk to Mama, talk to Tink."

Frank, who had been sitting there the whole time, said, "Y'all arguing over a chick who probably ain't shit."

In unison, without hesitation, they said, "Shut up, Frank."

Frank laughed. He held Renae, kissed her, and wiped her tears. Then he came up behind Zee and wrapped him in a bear hug, pinning his arms to his sides.

"Go 'head, man. Get off me." Zee tried not to laugh.

Frank held tighter. "Daayum! You ain't never said that many words in a row, as you did just now, in your entire life. Don't pass out. Breathe. And stop tusslin' before I tell her you blocked her car in so you could drive her back to the hotel." Both of them were cracking up. "You finally realize you need some pussy. Thank God! I was worried. Though with all this crying you were looking like a lil bald head pussy! How long do it take for your junk to grow back, though? I'd hate for you to show up too soon and disappoint the woman."

Laughing as he broke free, Zee said, "For your information, she already proved it came back. Better."

"Hey, Zee, you asked me to call before I checked out. I was just about to call the bellman."

"Let me have my assistant handle that and your car. May I?"

"Yes."

"May I come see you once the bellman's gone? I won't take too long. I know you need to get on the road."

"Yes." She had been hoping she'd get to see him before she left. She'd tried to sleep but spent the day restless, lounging, and quietly daydreaming.

The bellman arrived. "Ms. Hall, the concierge asked me to let you know you don't need to stop by the front desk. Your attendant has your complimentary parting gifts, and I'll place the bag in your car. Please leave your key card in the room. We hope you've enjoyed your stay at The Reaux."

"I have. It's been outstanding. Thank you." She reached for her wallet.

"All gratuities for the wedding party's guests have already been taken care of. Thank you, ma'am."

She put the twenty back in her wallet.

When he left, she did a quick check in the mirror. Her heart was already picking up speed.

The knock came. She knew it was him.

"Hello, Jenita. You are so beautiful."

"Hi, Zee. Thank you."

"May I come in?"

"Yes." He stepped inside and let the door close softly behind him.

"You look so good every time I see you."

"It's sweats, a T-shirt, and a cap."

"Still beautiful. And you smell wonderful."

"You look handsome, General Manager." She pointed at the embroidered GM on his blazer.

He wrapped his fingers around her pointing finger. "I'll be whatever you say."

Their eyes met. She immediately shut hers and covered her face like a child playing peekaboo.

"See? See? Superman's laser-beam-heat-seeking, panty-dropping eyes."

"Wait." He laughed. "You didn't say 'heat-seeking' before."

"We were on the phone. Now I can actually see 'em."

"How can you see anything with your pretty eyes closed?"

"I don't have to see what I can feel."

"Do you feel me, Jenita? You haven't felt anything yet." He lowered her hands and put his arms around her waist. He waited for her to resist. She didn't have a drop of resistance left. He drew her toward him until his breath was lightly brushing her face. She knew that looking up now would lead to the kiss she wanted.

He lifted her chin with one finger. "Look at me. Please."

She opened her eyes slowly, dreamy, taking her time, traveling from his neck to his chin, his lips, the sides of his face, and finally his eyes. He held her and looked steadily into her, and she felt as though he could see all the way through her. She couldn't look away.

He leaned in. "May I kiss you?"

"Yes, please."

He kissed her as if he were trying to tell her everything he felt—past, present, and future—all in one. She felt lost and found. Beautiful and adored. Secure. He felt seen and safe, whole. Weak and strong. Loved. Their kiss became a long, unhurried, deeply passionate embrace. Both of them warm and wanting.

"What can I do to get you to stay?"

"Aww. I wouldn't mind a few more days. But I have to go home."

"When can I see you again?"

"I don't know."

"May I call you?"

"Yes. But I have a busy week ahead."

"I'm a patient man. Just please don't put me in the friendzone. I'll give you some time."

"I appreciate that."

"You're welcome, Jenita Rochelle Hall."

"Thank you, Ibrahima Alexander Devereaux."

"I love the way you say my name. Perfectly."

He escorted her to the VIP exit, gave his assistant a quiet nod that meant you can go, and they stood together beside her car.

"You feel so good."

"You, too."

"You are a wonderful woman. I don't want to let you go."

"I have to."

He closed her door. She rolled the window down.

"If you want company on your way home, I'd love to talk."

"Okay. We'll see."

"If not, will you call or text me when you get home?"

"Yes."

She didn't call. She couldn't. All she could do was think about him the whole way, listening to "Beautiful Surprise" by India.Arie on repeat. Her three-and-a-half-hour drive home felt like minutes. She texted when she pulled into her garage: *I made it home. Thank you for a wonderful weekend. I had an amazing time and enjoyed every moment of our time together.*

His reply was immediate: *I'm so glad you made it safely. I dozed off and woke up thinking of you. I can still smell your fragrance on my blazer. You're all I can think about, Jenita. I can hardly wait to hear your voice again.*

CHAPTER 24

Google and Facebook

"Neat, you didn't Google the man?" Rhonda asked.

"No! I didn't even know he existed. I knew Mike had a father, but Googling wasn't something I did back then. We're talking 2003, '04, '05? I didn't have time. I was raising my child, working, fighting the Ingrams in court over custody and visitation, playing Ms. Fix-It for Deuce, or at least Ms. Duct Tape or Ms. Don't Make It Worse. I was trying not to fail my students while the program was being challenged, running youth programs with my chapter, moonlighting to pay attorney fees, student loans, mortgage, and life in general. Chile, please. Googling a man or his daddy was not on my list."

"But I always told you, when you travel, Google the location, the hotel, the restaurants, everything."

"I do. And I did," she said. "But I have never in my life Googled who owns a hotel. Have you?"

Rhonda said, "Not normally. But we just looked up The Reaux, and the owner listed is an old white man. Then we Googled the whole family. Girl, we need to meet. Now."

"I still have to return this rental car and I am exhausted."

"I already called Sheila. She's picking up food from Sylvia's."

"I said I'm exhausted."

"We won't stay long."

Jenita knew that was impossible. She also knew that even if she told them not to come, they weren't going to let her rest anyway. And she had so much she wanted to share, though she was already wrestling with how much she should keep to herself. When Sheila texted that Ms. Sylvia had offered to drop the food off, Jenita knew that meant Ms. Sylvia would be staying, too.

She called Harmony to let her know she was home safe. After they hung up, she got a text from Renae checking on her. She replied, thanked her for the extraordinary weekend and her abundant generosity.

Renae responded, "You're truly welcome. Let's talk next week. I sent you a friend request on Facebook."

Jenita wasn't really on social media. Harmony had set up her account years ago, and she checked it infrequently at best. The last things she'd posted were Harmony's high school graduation and a scholarship ceremony from about a year back. She unpacked, hung up the garment bag she left, made a dry-cleaning pile, showered, and put on a cup of tea to brace herself for the incoming barrage.

She accepted Renae's friend request and found several others waiting: Zee, LaKisha, Tiff, Mike, and four requests from former students. Renae's page was as bright and busy as she was—full of her and Frank, her children and grandchildren, the bakery, the hotel, the dance classes she taught, and everything else she loved. She had posted a few photos from the wedding with the caption: "Congratulations to my nephew-baby and my new niece-baby. I am one happy auntie-mama! More pics to come."

She went to Zee's page. He had posted wedding pictures, too, and to her surprise, including the ones he'd taken with just the two of them. His caption: "Today I watched my son become a husband. Wishing you both a lifetime of love and God's favor."

She stared at those photos. Zoomed in on the pictures of just the two of them. What a man.

She scrolled through his other posts. He'd been on Facebook since 2008 but had only ever posted about Mike. His most recent post before this one was from 2009, a photo of the family at the ribbon-cutting ceremony in front of The Reaux, with the caption: "Dreams do come true. This is for you, Mama. Queen Fatoumata Abubakar Devereaux. Rest in love."

And now, years later, it was Mike's wedding. Out of everything photographed over the whole weekend, he had posted seven pictures. Two of them were just the two of them. He had comments turned off. No replies under anything, just hundreds of likes per post and 4,999 friends. She had 253.

She closed her eyes and let herself go back through everything they'd talked about, all the things neither of them would have shared with someone they'd just met. The sound of his voice. His tenderness. The way his laugh made his eyes water when something was really funny. How masculine and vulnerable he was at the same time. The depth of his knowledge, the ease of his humility. The way he protected and paid attention. The dancing. The hugs. The kisses.

Oh. My. Gawd. The way he kissed me. She had never kissed any man so willfully. But it had felt like more than desire, something natural, something that fit. And she loved the way he received her.

She prayed immediately. "God, please don't let him play with me. Don't let me play with my own mind either. Don't even let me dream, Jesus, if this isn't real." Is he for me? Could this be?

The doorbell rang. All three women came in at once, washing their hands, pulling plates and glasses from the cabinet, setting up the kitchen island like they owned the place.

Ms. Sylvia said, "We know you tired, so we'll get everything together. Just sit. Now Neat, you mean as curious as you are about everything, you really didn't know anything about them "big time" Devereauxs?"

"No, ma'am. And remember, I thought Mike's last name was Alexander. Same with his aunt Renae."

Sheila set her folder on the counter. "Well. I've got the 411."

They ate and drank wine, and whatever Zee hadn't shared on the pier or on their moonlit walk, they filled in. Sheila and Rhonda had done their good research and printed out articles and photos that didn't turn up on Facebook. Ms. Sylvia, with that elephant memory of hers, recalled the murders and all the news coverage from the time and added what she'd gotten from her old-lady network, the things that never made the papers.

The Devereaux family was wealthy. Zee's estimated net worth alone was over eight million. They hadn't talked about money or material things when it was just the two of them. During Mike's college years and after, Zee had used that time to build aggressively, traveling constantly, cultivating investment opportunities for Devereaux Enterprises and for his own company.

His company, sometimes high-risk, but consistently high-return, dealt in international commercial and residential real estate. Alal International (*alal* meaning wealth and prosperity in Wolof) was essentially a Sotheby's built for Black people, people of color, and real estate investors and developers of all backgrounds. They couldn't find a valuation for it anywhere.

Between the internet searches and Ms. Sylvia's connections, what had felt minutes ago like hopeful, fulfilled joy now felt like a twilight zone. Jenita tuned out. She loved them without question, but this was too much, too many unknowns landing at once, too many things she had never known or thought about or been prepared for. They sipped and talked among themselves and offered her a stream of should-haves and what-ifs that quietly shut her down. It took them a good thirty minutes to notice that although she was sitting right there, her mind had left the room. Once they noticed, they cleaned up. She fell asleep on the couch before they could finish. They covered their dear sister, locked up, and left. She woke in the middle of the night, sent a PTO request to work for one more day, and went to bed.

For a whole week she wondered if it had all been a dream. She looked at the pictures on her phone to confirm they were real. She thought about what it would feel like to lie on that lobby floor and stare up at that ceiling right now. She missed him. He hadn't called or texted. He had, however, gone to her profile and loved her profile pictures and each of Harmony's graduation photos. She'd liked his wedding post in return but hadn't responded to the individual pictures. She wasn't about to look thirsty. But she hadn't heard anything else from him. She heard from Renae often.

Eight days after leaving Brown Sugar Beach, her phone rang.

"Hello."

"Hello, Jenita. This is Zee."

"Hey, Zee. It's good to hear from you."

"It's good to hear your voice. How have you been?"

"Busy, but that's a good thing."

"Did I catch you at a good time?"

"Yes. I was just packing."

"Where to, if you don't mind my asking?"

"Atlanta. I'm pitching my program at a collegiate conference."

"I hope it all goes well."

"Thank you."

"How long will you be gone?"

"I leave tomorrow, back on Sunday. Then a girls' weekend trip to Virginia."

"I was hoping to see you."

"Maybe when I get back."

"I could come have lunch or dinner with you in Atlanta. I know exactly where it is."

They both laughed. He wasn't joking.

"I bet you do."

"I could come to wherever you're staying or take you to one of the restaurants I know well there."

"So, you frequent Atlanta."

"Yes. All business."

"I'm sure you've had a date or two."

"I haven't been on a date in years. Definitely not in the ATL. I have business colleagues there in the hospitality industry with some very good spots, but no dates."

"I see."

"Do you?"

"Do I what?"

"Do you see how much I'm into you? I'd love to spend more time with you."

"I don't know… I guess."

"Would you let me take you out, so you don't have to guess?"

"I think we can do that."

That next weekend, she and her girls went to the Salamander Resort in Middleburg, Virginia for a spa retreat. Jenita had invited Renae. They were immediately on board, and Renae fit right in, a balanced blend of the three of them, filling a space in their circle they hadn't realized was empty. They had a blast. Rhonda fell in completely. Sheila liked Renae but, not unlike Frank, was keeping her own quiet eye out. Renae invited them all to The Reaux, and the only obstacle was syncing their calendars, which was always the real challenge.

Sheila, a traveling IBM'er who had intentionally built a life without a husband or a wife, children, or anyone else's schedule to answer to, also co-owned an adult club called Decadence. She was in the process of expanding, invested in several businesses including her sister's beauty shop, and supported her nieces and nephews. Rhonda had her physician husband, three children, two grandchildren, her tenured professorship, her church, her chapter leadership responsibilities, a quiet consideration of running for public office, and an extended family that kept her on wheels. Her life wasn't picture-perfect, but it was as close as it could get, even behind closed doors.

❧

At the spa, Jenita mentioned to Renae that she'd been wanting to attend the Brown Sugar Beach Jazz Festival on Juneteenth for years. Her girls always had family commitments that weekend, so back in January, she'd decided that even if she had to go alone, she was going—bought her ticket and booked a room at the Marriott, long before she ever received the wedding invitation.

Renae lit up, as if the conversation struck her best, good nerve.

"Ooh. That is our biggest give-back event and our busiest weekend of the year. We celebrate ancestral history, promote Black businesses, select awardees for year-long entrepreneurship and mentorship programs, African and African American fusion culture and education, our King's & Queen's Scholarship Awards for trades, raise awareness about hate crimes and civil suits, voter education, and the music and the dancing! You cannot stay at the Marriott. Please stay with us."

"Girl, that is a lot of everything!"

"It's what we do. It's our family's why. Please say yes."

"Maybe another time. It's so sweet of you to offer. I'll be fine at the Marriott."

Jenita didn't say what she was actually thinking: that The Reaux was too rich for her blood. She had already contacted guest services because she'd never received an invoice for her early arrival, room service, parking, the dress, or the other gifts she bought. She knew the total would be significant and intended to pay it before she went back. She'd also checked and knew The Reaux was fully booked for the Juneteenth weekend. She didn't want to bring any of that up with Renae. This was pleasure, not work. Her new friend, not a concierge. And she would never be anyone's moocher. Never that.

Renae pressed on. "That's also Snucks' birthday weekend. We're doing a family barbecue at our house that Sunday after the finale church service, for the first time in over twenty years, now that we finally have the staff to give us the weekend. I'd love for you to stay with us. And if you'd be more comfortable, I can easily comp you a room at The Reaux."

"That is so kind of you, Renae. But I've already paid for my room and I'll be just fine."

"Will you at least come to Snucks' party? It's going to be so good!"

"Can I think about it?" There was no real reason to say no, except that neither of them had mentioned Zee, and she was afraid to ask.

Zee sat in one of Frank's empty barber chairs, scrolling through her pictures on his phone—her profile, Facebook, and the one he'd posted of the two of them together.

"Bruh. She is so fine to me. I just…"

"Man, I know you ain't on Facebook. I hate that shit. The kids made me a page I won't never use it."

"I haven't been on it in years. But when I heard her students asking for her page at the wedding, I asked, too. Her daughter looks just like her. Same cute dimple."

"Yeah, I remember Snucks telling me that she had a daughter. You know she went road trippin' with Jenita and her girls to some spa in Virginia. I told her she should've just invited them all to The Reaux. But she said she wanted some time away. My sweet Snucks needs some female friends."

"She does."

"I actually talked to Jenita the other day. She was on the phone with Snucks and got passed to me."

Zee looked up. "You did? What did you say?"

"I was just talking shit."

"Running that mouth."

"Anything I run, I can back up."

"You better not have said anything out of pocket."

"Me? She's crazier than I am."

"How? Ain't nobody crazier than your black ass."

"Sheeeet. She was throwing jokes right back, joke for joke. She's stealth with it. She ain't good as I am, but she's quicker than most and she can hold her own with the best of them."

"Don't be messing with my woman."

"Oh. Your woman?"

"Yes."

"Does she know that yet?"

"Not officially. But I know she's feeling me, too. Don't no woman hug and kiss a man like that, with that much tenderness, if she ain't feeling him. The way she looks at me…" He shook his head. "Whew."

"So, when are you going to ask her?"

"I wanted to ask her the night we kissed. I'm being patient. It's getting harder, though."

"Have you even talked to her?"

"I texted a few times. I wanted to give her space. She said she had a busy week, and I knew Renae was going to Virginia with her. After that whole argument with Renae, I didn't want to step on that either."

CHAPTER 25

Drums or Flats

For their first date, Zee went back and forth on whether to go all out, the way he wanted to cater to her, or keep it simple, which was more her style. He didn't want to overdo it. But he also wanted her to know he had put real time and thought into it. He didn't want to ask Renae the way he had in times past.

He prayed: "God, lead and guide me. Mama, show me." He started looking up places in Jaxton so she wouldn't have to drive to the beach. He also knew they wouldn't have the privacy he wanted in his neck of the woods. Without too many options to choose from, he decided on a picnic lunch; rent a pavilion and decorate it himself.

Her curiosity got the better of her. She kept asking where they were going because she knew after Tubman State University closed, Jaxton returned to a quaint small-town pit stop on I-85 with five stoplights, three blinking, a farming community with a sleepy downtown and roadside stands selling boiled peanuts, tomatoes, and cucumbers—not the kind of place he was used to.

She pulled into Jaxton City Park and there he was, standing under the pavilion. Handsome as ever. White button-down shirt. Khaki pants. A white fedora tilted just right. Brand-new white Jordans.

He opened her car door and held her hand to help her out. She'd brought a chilled bottle of sparkling cider. He took it from her, kissed her hand and her cheek, then closed the door and held her hand as they walked carefully over the gravel in her flat, strappy khaki sandals.

She had on a loose tan knee-length polo dress and a white summer brim. Hair pulled back in a low ponytail. Large hoops. The heart charm necklace she wore all the time, and lip gloss. He told her how pretty she looked, how good she smelled, and how much he liked her dimple, especially in the sunlight.

The pavilion looked summer-pretty. He had covered the table in a white and red floral linen tablecloth and used push rods to hang white weighted sheers all around, swaying in the breeze, with tiny white LED lights strung through them. The tablescape: white china with a red border, wine glasses, water glasses, red linen napkins, two dozen red roses in a glass vase.

"Oh, my goodness!" Her hands went to her cheeks.

"Yes."

"Are you serious?"

"Yes. About you. Red and white, your sorority colors."

Then she noticed that the sheers were moving because of two oscillating fans he had positioned at either end. He'd placed citronella candles around the perimeter.

"Aww, Zee."

"Yes."

"You didn't have to do all of this."

"Yes, I did. Please, sit." He turned on smooth jazz and poured ice water from a crystal pitcher. Then he brought out fried party wings, seafood pasta salad, lettuce wedges with diced tomatoes, chopped bacon, and dressing, watermelon balls, and lemon cupcakes. It was the most refined yet simple thing anyone had ever done for her.

"This is lovely."

"Thank you. Flats or drums?"

"Flats."

"What?!"

"Never mind. Drums."

"No, no. I said that because I prefer drums, so this works out perfectly."

"Oh. Then I'll take flats." He fixed their plates.

She complimented the food and the presentation. He watched her eat.

"Jenita, you sure you like the food?"

"Yes, it's delicious. All of it."

"You're eating slowly."

"I always do."

"Mmhmm. Are you going to finish your chicken?"

"I did."

"You left all that meat on the bone. May I?" He pulled the wings from her plate, eating the rest of the meat and the gristle.

"Lord. Why do some Black folks feel like they have to eat a wing down to a fossil?"

He laughed. "Y'all are wasting food. You can't stop yourself when it's seasoned down to the bone." They fed each other watermelon balls on toothpicks and shared the cupcakes.

What started as a noon date continued until the moon peeked out. But his foresight with the sheers, the string lights, the candles, and the fans made the evening just as romantic as the afternoon. He had been sitting across from her, but when he shared pictures of the house he was building, he moved to her side of the table and stayed. Then he straddled the bench to face her and wrapped both arms around her shoulders. She leaned into him as he rested his forehead against her temple, then kissed the scar on her cheek and held his lips there, holding her closer.

"I don't want to keep you out too late. But Lord knows I want to keep you, Jenita." She laid her head on his shoulder, felt his pulse, and closed her eyes.

She prayed to herself. *God, let him be for me. Please.* It surprised her because she hadn't been looking for a man or for love. She hadn't known a man like this existed, not for her. If not for the ten o'clock park curfew, they would have stayed there all night, the way they had at the pier.

As he began putting things away, not letting her do anything except blow out the candles, she said, "I was running my mouth and didn't even think about you having to drive back."

"First of all, I've been talking just as much. And second, I'm not driving back tonight. I have a room because I hoped we'd enjoy the day into the evening, and I knew I wouldn't want to drive back late."

"Where?"

"The Hilton in Greensboro."

"Hmm. Not quite the digs at The Reaux."

"Right?" He laughed.

When he reached up to take down one of the push rods, his shirt lifted just enough. She'd known about his injury; he'd told her.

"Zee, does that hurt?"

"What?"

"The burn. I mean your grafts."

He pulled at his shirt. "No." For the first time, something in him retreated.

"I'm sorry if I offended you."

"You didn't offend me. I just didn't realize you could see it."

"I only saw a little."

He reached up for the next rod. She was standing directly behind him.

"You can say no. But you said I could ask you anything."

"You can."

"May I see it?"

"My grafts?"

"Yes."

"Why?"

"I felt moved to ask. You don't have to."

He turned around slowly, as if he didn't have a choice, and began unbuttoning the bottom of his shirt. There was nothing sexual about the moment, only fear alongside the relief of something that had felt inevitable. He watched her face as she looked at his hands on the buttons. He turned more toward the moonlight and held his shirt open, never taking his eyes off her.

She gently slid his tank shirt up and leaned in for a closer look. "Oh my. It does go halfway around." She looked up into his eyes. He looked scared. "I'm so sorry you went through that kind of pain. You've taken such good care of it. May I touch it?"

He swallowed. "You want to touch it?" He still hadn't told her about what Chantel had said.

"Yes. But not if you don't want me to."

I'm standing here with my shirt up, he thought, *outside, at night, and this woman wants to touch what only doctors, medical massage therapists, and Tink have ever touched—to apply medication and salves when it was fresh. I might as well be standing naked in the middle of a busy street.* He exhaled slowly.

She looked up at him. "Please."

He closed his eyes to brace for whatever was coming. He flinched at the first light touch of her fingertip.

"I'm sorry. Did that hurt?"

"No. I just wasn't expecting it."

She added another finger, then another, until all her fingertips were moving slowly across the layered colors and textures of his skin. She slid his shirt higher, touching the grafted area with her hand, then both hands, covering his torso in a long, unhurried pass.

He opened his eyes to watch her. Her eyes followed her hands. She touched him with such deliberate, affectionate care, not the way someone applies medication, not the way someone stares at a wound. She touched what had been the worst physical pain of his life as if she understood how much it had hurt and was trying to heal it from the inside out, holistically, without wishing it away. He had never approached it, never touched it himself with anything close to that kind of compassion.

"Where is your harvest site?"

"My thigh. Have you ever touched a skin graft before?"

"Yes. One of my students had a graft on her leg. I used to help apply oil for her. But when I saw yours, I felt like I was supposed to touch you." She looked at it the way someone looks at something rare. "Even with all it went through, you're beautiful, Zee."

To her, it looked like ultra-rare bronze marble.

He couldn't hold it back. He let his shirt fall and dropped his head. She kissed his silent tears and never stopped touching him. This wasn't sexual. There was no arousal. This was spiritual. This was healing.

They held each other. She kissed his lips, then his cheeks, and gently lowered his shirt. He buttoned it back up and finished taking down the curtains and lights while she, without any argument from him this time, folded the linens and curtains and placed them in the bins.

He made a few trips to load everything into his truck while she waited under the pavilion.

"Let me get you to your car before these mosquitoes carry you off." They hugged briefly and kissed quickly.

"Zee, did I offend you?"

"No, sweetheart. You fascinate me. You talk about my eyes, but you're the one who mesmerizes me."

Zee planned their next two dates with long drives built in with intentional stretches of uninterrupted road time for conversation and sharing music. Zee picked her up for all of them.

The second date: a private fundraiser in Durham featuring a Ledisi concert and dinner, where she performed one of Jenita's favorites, "Alright." The third was to museums and historical sites in downtown Raleigh, a walk through the farmers market that reminded her of growing up on a farm, and dinner at NC Seafood Restaurant just steps away. The fourth was a spontaneous day trip to Busch Gardens in Williamsburg, Virginia. He drove. Her treat. A couple of times when he dropped her off, after their old-school front-porch goodnight kisses, he left and came back for one more. The fifth date: they met halfway at a pottery-and-paint studio and ate burgers at a drive-in for dinner.

Jenita hadn't told Zee she was going to the Brown Sugar Beach Jazz Festival on Juneteenth. She and Renae talked often, but neither of them brought Zee up, and he didn't bring Renae up with Jenita either. She had held off telling him because she didn't want him pushing her to stay at The Reaux. She also knew he had no real privacy there, and she wanted to be able to kiss and hold him, and if she was being honest with herself, her daydreams had been going further than that. She finally brought up the festival over dinner.

"Oh no, Jenita."

"What?"

"I just committed to Puerto Rico to acquire a property, and then I'm hosting a brokerage group in the Bahamas to finalize a major sale. I wish I'd known."

"When do you leave?"

"June twelfth. Back on the seventeenth."

"That's the whole weekend."

He pulled out his phone as if he could add days to his calendar. "Damn. Damn. Damn."

"Okay, Florida Evans." She smiled. He didn't.

"This is the first one I'll miss, and I didn't want to. And now knowing you'll be there, I really hate it. At least let me cover your room."

"No. I've had a room booked at the Marriott since January."

"You don't want to stay at The Reaux?"

"I called after the wedding. It was fully booked."

"Jenita. I would clean house for you."

"No. Like I told Renae—"

"Renae knew?"

"I mentioned it to her..."

"When?"

"At the Salamander. In Virginia."

He went quiet. She could feel him working through it.

She touched his arm. "I didn't say anything because I didn't want you arranging a room for me. And by the way, I never received an invoice from my stay after the wedding."

He looked at her and shook his head slowly.

"I didn't want to book a room again without having paid for the first one."

"Jenita, none of the wedding guests paid for their rooms."

"But I wasn't just a wedding guest. I had an early arrival, room service, and the dress, and my gift shop and bakery purchases. The invitation said I'd receive an invoice."

"And you never will."

"Zee, I can pay my own way."

"I know. And this is exactly the conversation I hoped we'd have."

"About money?"

"About this. Because I see you, too, Jenita. I see your hard work. I can imagine what it took to get where you are, raising Harmony, buying your home, paying tuition, building everything you've built. And I notice that it's hard for you to let me do things for you. You insisted on paying for lunch on our second date. You bought the tickets on our fourth. You won't let me give or do without a negotiation."

"Right. I won't."

"Why not?"

"Because I can pay my own way."

"But you don't have to. Not with me."

"I'm not a moocher, Zee."

"I know that. You don't have a mooching bone in your body."

"Exactly. So, I don't need you or Renae covering my room."

He smiled a little. "Sweetheart, I know I can't make you do anything you've made up your mind about, and I'm not going to try. But sooner or later, I hope you'll let me take care of you the way I want to." He put his hand over hers where it rested on his forearm. "Next time, please tell me. If you don't want a room, that's okay. I just wish I'd known you'd be at the festival, because I would not be flying out that weekend. I want to be with you every chance I get."

She had been bracing for an argument. He'd completely disarmed her. All she could say was, "I'm sorry for not telling you. And I'm going to miss you."

"I'm going to miss you, too, Jenita. I hate it." He turned her hand over and raised it to his lips. "I truly hate that I'm going to miss you."

CHAPTER 26

Back to the Beach

Jenita double-checked that her garment bags were in the car, put together a birthday gift for Frank, and grabbed her umbrella; the weather was calling for rain. Renae called to ask if she was coming in early enough to beat traffic and have lunch with her and Frank at one of their spots. She loved Renae and Frank. He was genuinely hilarious; someone she could laugh with and at in equal measure. Since she couldn't check in at the Marriott until three, Renae offered to give her directions to their home on Queen's Hill. Jenita wanted to satisfy her curiosity. The farthest she'd seen up close was the convention hall. She was also hoping to catch Mike and Tiffany, who were back from their honeymoon.

Renae's instructions: "When you get to the foot of the tunnel, tell the security guard to call me so you don't have to drive up the steep side of the hill."

The drive felt quicker this time. She was excited, even knowing she wouldn't see Zee. At least she'd see the places where she'd spent time with him, places she hoped she'd never forget.

Renae and Frank's home was immense. A six-thousand-five-hundred-square-foot, two-story red brick with white trim, black shutters, white columns, and a red front door. Three-car garage and a golf-cart garage. Manicured lawn, evergreens and flowering bushes, a water fountain, circular driveway, outdoor pool, jacuzzi, and a one-thousand-two-hundred-square-foot guesthouse. Renae came running out to greet her, wearing an apron.

"Girl, come on in here, I'm putting the finishing touches on a cake. I should have had them do it at the shop, but they're swamped with festival orders. I'll just do it myself."

"Your home is beautiful."

"Thank you. Make yourself right at home. You want something to drink?"

"No, I just finished my water. But I do need the bathroom."

"Second door on the right."

Inside looked just like Renae—eclectic, quality but comfortable, pops of color where they might not belong in any other house, and yet somehow it all worked, making every room feel fun and inviting. She could see Frank's imprint, too: big furniture, and one chair in the living room that was unmistakably his. An oversized recliner with a Dallas Cowboys throw and matching pillow. That was another running joke between her and Frank. She did not like Dallas. Anybody but Dallas.

"Renae, this is so beautiful."

"Chile, I'm glad you like it. I don't get visitors outside of family, so I am tickled to have you here! I wish you'd just stay with us. I promise we'd treat you way better than the Marriott and leave you alone when you need peace and quiet. Well, I would, I can't make any promises for Snucks. You two get going and I just laugh and bow out. He likes you. He really does. And that's not something I can say about many people, even among those of us closest to Zee."

"Renae, how come we never talk about Zee?"

"It's just better that way. You and I have our friendship, and you and Zee seem to be getting along nicely."

"We are. I really like him. I'll honor whatever's best."

"It ain't because I don't want you to know. But I was being selfish for a while, honestly. But I had a dream. Girl, I cannot wait for Zee to get back so I can tell him. I can't wait! You want a cupcake?"

"Sure."

"They're lemon. You like lemon?"

"I love lemon."

"Help yourself to whatever's on that tray. Eat the whole thing if you want."

Her phone rang. "Hey, Snucks. Yes, she's here. Hush before I tell her. Okay." She hung up. "Snucks will be here in about twenty minutes to pick us up."

"Okay. Let me let my people know I'm here. She called and texted everyone and saw a message from Zee asking if she'd made it. She texted back.

"Yes, been here about twenty minutes. How was Puerto Rico?"

"Beautiful. Would've looked even better if you were there."

She let that one go. "How's the other deal coming?"

"Close."

"I'm praying it settles in your favor."

"Thank you, Jenita."

"You're welcome."

"Y'all still going to lunch?"

"Yes. Frank's on his way now."

Frank walked in. "Snucks, you just let anybody in here."

Jenita opened her arms. "Hey, Frank."

"Don't be trying to hug me when you're staying at the damn Marriott. We have plenty of bedrooms and a whole guesthouse. You too good to stay with us?"

"I'm not too good to stay with Renae. But since you live here, I'm way too good."

"You ain't shit."

"So!"

"Snucks, leave her alone. That's probably exactly why she doesn't want to stay here. You won't give her any peace."

"You're damn straight… the Marriott. Hmph!"

"You're talking all that yang, and I brought you a birthday gift. Isn't today your birthday?"

"That's what they tell me."

"How old are you?"

"Forty-damn-four. How old are you?"

"Forty-two."

"Well, you look—"

Renae cut in fast. "Snucks!"

"She started it. Where's my gift?"

"I ought not give you anything." She went out to her car. Renae called after her that he could wait. Jenita came back in and handed Frank a custom gift basket.

"Is this for me?" He looked genuinely surprised.

"Yes. I thought about the sick and the shut-in. You, sick in the mind, and need to shut up."

He laughed hard. "And I'ma keep talking… the Marriott. Hmph!"

Renae came out of the kitchen. "What did you get? Oh, my goodness…that is so thoughtful. Where did you find all of this? It's beautiful!"

"All this is for me? Do you want me to open it now?"

"Yes, because we don't know how much time you have left with us."

"More time than the Marriott." He began to pull at the cellophane. "Damn, you got this thing wrapped up like Alcatraz."

"I knew it would bring back memories."

Inside: a Dallas Cowboys caddy, four Havana Cellar cigars, a torch lighter, cutter, holder, ashtray, and humidifier. Chic-O-Sticks, because she remembered him saying he hadn't had any in years. Her homemade men's soap and lotion. And a can of WD-40.

"What's the WD-40 for?"

"So you can lotion both legs."

Frank and Renae went weak. They were already laughing and that finished them both off, doubled over and trotting away cackling. "Renae, I made you a basket, too, because you have to live with him." Knowing Renae loved lavender, she had put together an everything-lavender basket bigger than Frank's. Lavender candles, her homemade lotion and soap, body spray, room spray, her favorite grape-flavored Now and Later, and lavender chocolate. Renae's big laugh turned immediately into equally big tears.

"Jenita, you are so sweet. Nobody outside my family has ever done something like this just because. You didn't have to. I love you! I love this!" They hugged.

Frank was still going. "I got your WD-40. Always grinning, flashing those bone stumps…I know your brain meat is soggy as hell now. I got ya damn WD-40."

Little did she know Frank would tell everybody, and WD-40 would become the joke of the summer.

They pulled up to Cooper's Surf and Turf. Renae said, "I hope you like the food here."

"She better," Frank said, holding the door open, "because we ain't going anywhere else."

"Whatever." Jenita rolled her eyes. Cooper's was one of those places where everybody knew everybody; nothing fancy, but the line wrapped around the to-go window, and the crowd inside told you everything you needed to know about the food.

Jenita and Renae talked while Frank texted, spreading the WD-40 story and checking his security cameras from his phone.

Renae's phone rang. "Hello. Yes. Oh no. Everything? Well, Uhh huh…well you know what's best. Well, we can still do the cookout Sunday at our house, but that means I've gotta get that pig before he leaves. We're at Cooper's right now. Okay, Snucks is with me, so we'll head over there in about an hour. Alright." She hung up. "Y'all. The promoters are canceling the concert because of the rain. That was Pops. He and Tink decided to move all the activities and award ceremonies inside the school, but the school isn't available Sunday, so we have to fit everything into tomorrow. And Joe Lester needs us to pick up the pig because he's going out of town for a funeral. Lord, if it ain't one thing, it's another."

"Well, Snucks, we just gotta roll with the punches, baby. What do you need me to do?"

"We'll go to Joe Lester's farm and get the pig when we leave here. Need to get there by two o'clock. It's about twenty minutes away."

"No worries. We'll eat and head over and take WD-40 with us."

"Thanks, Snucks. Leave my sissy alone."

Renae's phone rang again. "Excuse me. Hello. Where are you? What? For real? Lord, you are… I don't know what to say." She switched into French.

Frank smiled. "Must be Zee. That's the only one she does that shit with."

"Can you speak French, Frank?"

"Do I look like I talk in cursive, or French?"

"No. But you do look—ha!"

"Aht! Aht! Don't say another damn word. I still got to get you before I let you get me again." They both laughed.

Renae hung up. "Jenita. I just need you to know I had absolutely no idea."

"No idea about what?"

"Zee."

"Zee what?"

Frank said, "He's here ain't he."

"Yes. Two days early. Took private planes to get back."

"Where is he?" Jenita asked.

"Pulling into the parking lot. I'm sorry, I had no idea."

"Why are you sorry? I'm pleasantly surprised."

Frank pointed at himself. "My brother is coming to get yo ass for that WD-40 shit you pulled."

ꕥ

She saw Zee moving past the windows like a man on a mission, and she couldn't help but blush. He looked so fine she could practically smell him through the glass. Their food was arriving just as he got caught up talking to Coop and another man near the entrance.

Frank picked up his fork. "I'm eating. I don't eat cold food unless it's supposed to be cold."

Zee finally made it to the table, kissed Renae on the cheek, dapped Frank up. When he came around to Jenita he opened his arms. "I hate to interrupt your meal. May I please have a hug?"

She was so glad he asked, because she had wanted to run outside the moment she saw him through the window.

"Mm Mm Mm." He held on.

"I thought you were still in the Bahamas."

"I was. This morning. Two planes later, here I am."

"I'm happy to see you."

He looked her over like a favorite meal. "I'm happy to see you, too."

"Zee, you hungry?" Renae waved the waiter over.

Still looking at Jenita: "Yes. For more things than one. But I'll settle for cooked food right now."

Jenita blushed and sat back down. The waiter greeted him. "Hello, Mr. Devereaux."

"Hey, man. I'll take—hold on. Jenita, where's the rest of your food?"

"That's it."

"I know you ain't get all that junk in your trunk eating that little bit."

"Hush, Frank."

"Is that all you ordered?" Zee asked. "Did you already eat something?"

"No. I ordered a half portion because—" All three of them leaned in. "I eat slowly. When I'm with a group, and there's a time crunch, I order half, so I finish when everyone else does."

Frank laughed. "If that ain't the stupidest thing I ever heard." Jenita laughed most. "Hush, Squeak."

"What's the time crunch?" Zee asked.

Renae filled him in—outdoor activities canceled, Joe Lester's, the pig.

"Y'all go ahead to Joe Lester's." He turned to the waiter. "I'll have the grilled salmon, and fried shrimp, slaw, baked potato, and sweet tea. What did you order, sweetheart?"

"Shrimp and scallops."

"Can you bring the lady a full portion, please?"

"I'm fine, I don't want to hold them up."

"Take your time, sweetheart. I'm going to sit right here with you. There's nowhere else I'd rather be."

Frank and Renae finished up and left for Joe Lester's.

"Thank you for waiting with me. I get grief about this sometimes."

"I thought you were trying to be dainty when you were with me."

"No, I've just always been a slow eater."

"Well, from now on, you don't have to order half of anything. I'll sit with you. Feed you if you want me to."

"You are so kind. I'm really glad to see you."

"I'm glad you are. There was no way I was going to know you were here and not come. Did you decide where you're staying?"

"It's too late to cancel without losing my deposit, and I don't want to impose on the Snucks."

"I can call and get your deposit back. I wish my house were finished; you could have stayed there. But we do have two oceanfront rentals vacant this weekend. And I'd still love to have you at The Reaux, if you'd consider it."

Zee took Jenita on a slow drive through it all: the rental homes, apartments, and commercial properties D.E. owned, the ones he owned personally, through Pine City and Brown Sugar Beach. He shared a little history about each one. She listened, and he kept catching himself saying, "I don't usually talk this much." But she loved the sound of his voice, and having grown up without family closeness after Nana died, just seeing the empire they'd built together, out of so much tragedy, was awe-inspiring.

As he turned toward the tunnel, he said, "May I show you my house? In person?"

"Yes. I've wondered where you actually live. You're always at the hotel."

It really bothered her. The way he poured himself into everything—his body, his time, constant work, protecting everyone—and then went back to a hotel room alone every night, tired and restless. Lonely. It made her heart ache for him, even if it had long since become just his life.

"I do still keep a room there. And I move around to some of the rental properties sometimes when I need quiet or have repairs to do."

"These homes are extraordinary. This is a whole family compound."

"I like to think of it as our village." He pointed out Pop's house, Tink's, the Snucks', Mike's, relatives', friends like Joe Lester's and Reggie's. Then, tucked into a cul-de-sac, was one that stood apart from all the others.

The only tan-and-black-speckled brick on the hill. A wraparound front porch with an ocean view in the front and mountains at the back. Black metal roof, black shutters, four-car garage, and a golf-cart garage. Unlike every other home on the street, there was no centered fountain.

It appeared smaller than the others until they got closer and it revealed itself: a sprawling split-level with a finished basement, five thousand square feet, a heated lap pool with a retractable roof, and basketball and tennis courts. The exterior looked mostly finished, but judging by the construction vehicles, stacked materials, and empty pool made clear the work wasn't done.

"This is beautiful." A dream home.

"I'm glad you think so." They hadn't gotten out of the truck because of the rain. "I resumed construction about seven weeks ago. They're not working today because of the festival. Would you like to see inside?"

"Yes."

He pulled into the garage and warned her they'd be walking into what looked like organized chaos compared to the outside. "I had it half-finished and then decided to gut the kitchen and take off the second-story rooms. I want more of a rambling ranch feel, and I brought in a consultant for new plans and designs."

"This is enormous." She looked around.

"It only looks that way because there are no walls yet. It'll be an open floor plan though."

"With or without walls, five thousand square feet is enormous." She thought briefly of her own one-thousand-seven-hundred-square-foot house, the joy and the stress of buying it, maintaining it, every renovation she'd tackled herself. "I can already tell it's going to be gorgeous."

"How can you tell?"

"Because I've been through renovations. All I can say is time, patience, and thank God you don't have to live in it while it's happening. And if you had any hand in designing The Reaux and the homes up here, this is going to be something."

"I made some suggestions for a few things. I won't take all the credit."

"I'm sure your suggestions will make this look just as amazing." She looked around.

"Do you have any ideas for this space?"

Jenita took the Snucks up on their invitation and decided to stay in the guesthouse for the weekend. When she and Zee drove up, Renae came bolting out of the house with a level of glee that exceeded even her usual. She was normally warm and bubbly, but this was over the top.

"I am so glad you decided to stay, sissy!" She hugged her tight and rocked. Then she turned and hugged Zee the same way. The two of them looked at each other wide-eyed over Renae's shoulder. "Zee, get her bags and y'all come on out of this rain. I need to talk to you right quick. But y'all come in first. Where have y'all been anyway?" She was already moving. "Jenita, I'm gonna need some help in the kitchen. LaKisha is here, but my other girls are helping Tink, and the boys went with Pops to help set up the school for the presentations and awards. It's an all-hands-on-deck Devereaux weekend, and I absolutely love it."

LaKisha led her to the guesthouse while Renae snatched Zee off into an office and closed the door. Jenita could hear her talking going fast. "*Ma mère m'est app*—!"

LaKisha paused in the hallway to listen. "It must be something Mama doesn't want anyone to catch because she's talking fast in French. I can understand it when she slows down, but she's excited about something."

Jenita smiled to herself and followed LaKisha across the backyard, past the pool and the gazebo, to the cutest little cottage she'd ever seen. LaKisha showed her around, gave her the key, and left. Just like the main house, it was unmistakably Renae—comfortable, colorful, and busy in the best way. She settled in, made her "I'm okay" calls", shared the address and brief updates, sent a few texts, looked around with her full nosy attention, and headed back to the house.

Renae ran down the list like a short-order cook calling tickets. "Deviled eggs, meatballs, well, the sauce, Rotel dip, pasta salad. Can you handle all that? Tink and the girls are preparing chicken wings, veggie and fruit trays and beignet dough they'll fry on the spot later. They have to come straight out the grease!"

Jenita knew she could handle all of it. She just hadn't expected to be doing it this weekend. Renae explained that tonight was a last-minute get-together, since the concert was canceled and the hotel dining room was fully booked, and tomorrow was Frank's birthday party, which had been moved inside because of the rain.

Once she understood the assignment, she got settled. She could make this stuff in her sleep.

Renae worked on potato salad, cleaned greens, and had multiple crockpots going with string beans, succotash, and gumbo. All for Frank's birthday. Zee, Pops, and Mr. Horace were pitching a tent and preparing to roast a whole hog underground, taking shifts through the night. To Jenita, it felt hectic. To this family, the frenzy was festive. She had never been in the middle of something like this outside of helping Ms. Sylvia cater, and she found herself adjusting her pace to match theirs.

Renae's chef's kitchen had everything: double ovens, three sinks, a butler's pantry, an eight-burner gas stove, a four-burner electric, and more counter space than she knew what to do with. Jenita rolled up her sleeves. There wasn't a single thing she needed that Renae didn't have. This was light work with pressure behind it.

They talked and laughed and sipped wine like they'd known each other for years. Jenita kept noticing that Renae kept calling her "sissy."

Frank came back sweaty, wet, and muddy. Zee followed behind him in fresh clothes, wiping his face with a hand towel.

"Snucks is the only one who looks like he's been digging for that pig," Renae said.

Frank kissed her cheek and gave her backside a flirtatious squeeze. "You know it, Snucks."

"But those boots stay in the garage. I don't want that mud in my kitchen."

"You let her in here, and she's cooking? Oh Lord! Her cooking will probably have my stomach sounding like boots in a dryer."

"Leave Jenita alone," Zee said.

"I ain't paying him no mind," Jenita said, wiping down the island.

Frank left the kitchen holding on to a private thought: deep down, he really did like Jenita for Zee. He had the same fears Renae had, and he'd be the one holding things together if they fell apart, that much he knew. Zee was gone for this woman. But Frank couldn't deny that he might have also just met the sister he'd never had. He couldn't tell her that yet. He just felt it, and felt they might be moving too fast, and felt a kinship he hadn't asked for.

Zee always kept a change of clothes in the car. He never knew when he'd need to shift from executive to manual labor.

"Renae, you got her working?"

"She's not treating it like work. She cooked everything faster than I would have, and it all tastes good. Try one of those deviled eggs before she puts them away."

Jenita had a few extras on a side plate. Zee leaned in. "Can you put it in my mouth? I haven't washed my hands yet." She moved to let him take a bite. "The whole thing. I want to taste all of it."

She could feel every layer of what he meant. Earlier at his house, they had already kissed at length and fondled, still clothed.

"You are a beautiful woman, inside and out. I have never met anyone like you."

"Thank you. You're not so bad yourself."

"Did you wear that dress and that perfume for me?"

"No. I had no idea I'd even see you. So…"

"It's for me. Because of how much I love seeing you in it." He moved behind her, held her close, and kissed her neck, then up to just behind her ear. "You smell intoxicating."

"Stay sober."

"One day. One day. Mm Mm Mmm." He pulled back to look at her and waited to see if she'd turn around and meet his gaze.

She did. "I'm looking. What's that expression about?"

He licked his lips slowly. "Using my imagination. Wondering what it will be like to…"

"Well." She held his gaze. "Stop wondering." She puckered playfully and gave him a small peck.

"Did you just kiss me like you think I'm playing?"

She laughed and covered her mouth. He moved her hand and placed it around his neck.

"Kiss me again like you mean it. Let me taste your sweet mouth."

The way she tasted, the softness and the quiet confidence with which she studied his face each time, weakened his walls, acknowledged his healed pain, calmed what remained of his fear, and brought his whole body awake. Neither of them looked away when they both noticed the evidence through his tracksuit.

"I want you so bad." Shallow breaths, soft kisses between words. "You drive me crazy, Jenita."

"You drive me crazy, too, Zee."

The way she looked at him, the way she guided his hands to her cheeks and pressed into his touch as they kissed, every signal was green. The only thing keeping them from taking it further was the dust-filled, half-finished construction site around them.

"Our first time will be somewhere special, at the right time, with this incredible woman, after I ask you to be my lady and you say yes. Hopefully. I can hope you say yes, can't I?"

"You can hope all you want."

"What if I asked you right now? Would you?"

"I don't answer questions unless I'm actually being asked."

"This isn't where I planned to do this, or how I wanted it to go down. But I can't help myself." He held both her hands. "Jenita, will you be my lady? My girlfriend?"

"Zee, it's only been five weeks since we met."

"Six. Almost seven. Is that a no?"

Everything she knew about him so far was more than she'd ever wanted in a man. She wanted to say yes. Yes. Take me. Yes. She swallowed it.

"I'm flattered. But it's too soon."

"Too soon for what?"

"That kind of commitment."

"But we're already doing it. I'm not seeing anyone else. I haven't in years. You're not seeing anyone else. We're already exclusive."

"I don't know you well enough yet."

"Can you commit to what you do know? Anything you don't know yet that you don't like, you don't have to commit to that. I came back here for you. Just you. When I walked into Cooper's and saw you, when I hugged you, I felt such relief just having the chance to ask you this. I was going to wait until after the festival. But you, here, now… Jenita, I am in love with you."

CHAPTER 27

A Family Affair

Back in the Snucks' kitchen, they both knew exactly what he'd meant about wanting to taste all of it. "Mm. This is so good," he said, licking the tip of her finger.

Renae grabbed a deviled egg off the plate and put the whole thing in her mouth. "I tried to tell her. I asked for the secret, she won't give it up."

"Don't tell her," Zee said. "That way, I have a reason to keep coming to you whenever you make 'em."

"It's my Nana Katie Mae's little twist."

Renae chewed, covering her mouth. "Keep on twistin', sissy, because you may need to make some more. They're going to love these and everything else."

Zee could tell that "sissy" landed a little strangely for Jenita. It would have for him, too, if Renae hadn't already told him why she was using it.

Renae slid a bag of sweet potatoes toward him. "All hands-on deck, start peeling." Renae was surprised when Zee picked up the peeler without a word, though he kept his eyes on Jenita the whole time. When Renae stepped out for a moment, Jenita said, "You are going to have to stop staring at me."

"I can't help it. You're standing right in front of me looking that good."

"Yes, you can."

"Like you always say, 'I cain't. I just cain't.'" He laughed and shook his head.

"Then go over to the other side and turn your face to the wall." She said it jokingly. He did it immediately.

Frank burst through the door. "Zee, why in the hell are you standing in the corner peeling potatoes?"

"Jenita told me to." He laughed.

"Ahh shit. See what not getting pussy will do? Got you in the henhouse, getting your punk ass pecked. And you haven't even pecked her yet."

All three of them laughed. Then, in unison, "Shut up, Frank."

Renae came back fanning herself. "Whew! I had to turn that AC down. These hot flashes won't leave me alone! They are relentless. Everyone should be here around seven. If you want to go to the guesthouse and freshen up for a couple of hours, please do."

The house filled up steadily with laughter, music, overlapping conversations, children running, dancing, and playing.

When Pops came in with Ms. Lorraine, he called out, "Where's my Ola, my Ibra, and my Franka?" He loved those three with everything he had. They all came to meet him. "Look at Queen's babies."

He made his way into the kitchen and looked at Jenita warmly. "Good to see you again." He kissed her cheek. "You're who all the fuss is about."

"Hello, Mr. Devereaux. It's wonderful to see you, sir. I wasn't aware of any fuss."

Zee gave Pops a look: go easy, she doesn't know.

"I'm fine, darlin'. Don't you worry about any of that. Let 'em fuss. It'll be just fine. And you can call me Pops."

Ms. Lorraine smiled shyly, said hello, and followed Pops to the living room hand in hand.

Jenita looked at Zee. "What is he talking about? See? This is exactly why I didn't want to stay here. I didn't want to put anyone out. I should have just stayed at the Marriott." She slipped quietly out the kitchen door toward the guesthouse. Zee was right behind her.

"What Pops said has nothing to do with you staying here. We all want you here."

"We? Why?"

"Jenita—"

"What?" She kept walking.

"It's raining. Come back inside."

They were already on the guesthouse porch. She fumbled with the key. "The way your dad looked at me, the way he and Ms. Lorraine looked, the way all of y'all have been looking at me, like y'all know something I don't."

"May I help you with the door?" He reached for the key.

"Not unless you tell me what's going on."

"I'll tell you later. I promise."

"Please just give me a few minutes to freshen up. I'll meet you back at the house."

She showered. Prayed. Thought.

Before she left home, Sheila, Rhonda, and Ms. Sylvia had each offered their unsolicited weekend advice. None of them had known then that Zee would fly back two days early just to see her, or that he'd kiss and hold her like he truly missed her the whole time he was gone. None of them knew she'd end up staying in the Snucks' guesthouse, cooking in Renae's kitchen, being received the way she had been, or that she would apparently be the subject of some family fuss. A conference call was exactly what she needed to slow her racing thoughts down. She had to say it out loud to someone.

As usual, they went straight in.

Sheila and Ms. Sylvia were not convinced Zee had been celibate.

"Ain't no way," Sheila said. "Eight years? Ain't no damn way."

Rhonda pushed back. "Why would he lie? Now that he knows she knows he's wealthy, fine, and single, sharing comes along with the territory. Some women would gladly share. Why would he need to lie to Neat?"

Ms. Sylvia said, "A man that fine can get ass on accident. Women fall into his lap. Or… Lord, I didn't even think about that. Is he into men?"

Sheila said, "I'm the last one to question anybody's orientation. But something's holding him back, either he can't get it up, it's too small or he has a weird fetish. That's what you want to know."

Rhonda whispered, "Oh no. The burn. What if… what if it goes further than we know?"

Sheila said, "Like Fire Marshall Bill." They cackled.

Jenita understood, honestly, why it was hard to believe. A kind, thoughtful, handsome, accomplished Black man, celibate for eight years? She'd had the same flicker of skepticism. But she also knew what they didn't. She knew about prom night. She knew about the war and what it had taken from him, not just physically. She knew that a trauma most people don't even have language for, a boy being drugged and violated, had shaped decades of his life. They didn't know any of that.

He hadn't gone into graphic detail when he told her. He hadn't told it from a place of sadness or looking for pity but more like passing along information that explained why he'd spent years in intensive therapy and why he remained in monthly sessions still. He talked about how much it had helped save his mind: the coping tools, learning to manage the PTSD, the gradual improvement in his quality of life, and how it had turned him into a vocal advocate for mental wellness among combat veterans. She hadn't shared any of that with the girls.

She saw the full picture: a boy who lost his mother to violence, who carried that grief alongside these other wounds, and who had responded by building deliberate strength, a relentless, palpable wealth of compassion and dogged protection for everything he loved. She saw him.

She also hadn't told them about the night he let her see and touch his injury. She'd seen where the scarring began and ended, just above his navel. That had made her think about his skin more broadly: the damaged-but-beautiful bronze of it, the six-pack that had softened slightly with age, his broad chest and arms that had lifted her clean over a deep puddle when she left his house in the rain without a second's hesitation. She kept those details to herself.

Ms. Jackson had told her years ago, when she first started seeing Warren: "Baby, you can tell your lil girlfriends a lot. But don't you dare tell them everything about your man."

She knew aged wisdom when she heard it.

❧

After a loud, lively, wonderful family dinner, she and Zee walked some of the paths they'd driven earlier, now that the rain had stopped. They held hands. She thanked him for not announcing to his family that they were official yet. She wanted him to meet Harmony first, and her sisters, and some of her friends. He said he could wait as long as she needed. As long as he knew she was his lady, he was over the moon.

He wanted to show her something. They took Frank's golf cart. She loved being alone with him. The world went quiet when it was just the two of them, and she felt settled and wholly herself.

He drove up a narrow asphalt path and told her they'd need to walk a short way from there. Steps had been cut into the face of a large boulder, and he had to lift her up to reach the first one.

"The only people I've ever brought here are Mike, Renae, and Frank. Pops built this for me after my mom died. He told me it was my getaway from the world, whenever I needed it."

It was a beautiful cove, overlooking layered grassy mounds and clusters of trees. Even at night, it was a picture of stillness. A covered bench and a soft solar light were the only additions, simple, and enough. She could feel something here, a satisfying spiritual presence, a space that had been held and tended over many years.

They sat up there for hours.

They texted friends and family to let them know they were together and fine, and then they talked. Deeper than before, if that was possible. They held hands and held space for each other across everything, from the heaviest secrets to the things others had called weird or too small to matter. No kissing. No embracing. Just the life exchange between them, which had become its own kind of intimacy that neither of them had ever found with anyone else.

"Why do I feel so comfortable telling you things nobody else knows? Am I dumping or talking too much?"

"If you are, so am I. But I don't see it as dumping. And it's not trauma bonding. It's sharing our lived experiences. We're building mutual understanding, a sense of safety. Giving each other testimonials about our own recoveries."

"Yes. I agree wholeheartedly. And Jenita, do you know what I've been doing?"

"What?"

"My mom and my uncle Louis could both sing. I mean sang! I grew up surrounded by every kind of music. But love songs—I could never fully receive them. Not until we sat on that pier seven weeks ago. I listen to smooth jazz and instrumentals mostly; some of that was music therapy, but a lot of it was simply that I couldn't identify with lyrics. I wanted to. So badly. What I've been doing lately is pulling up love songs—sixties, seventies, eighties, nineties—and putting your face in them."

"That is the sweetest thing anyone has ever said to me."

"From the time I wake up until I go to sleep, it's you. And speaking of sleep, I've struggled with insomnia for years. But the past few weeks, especially the nights we've fallen asleep on the phone, I've slept longer than I have in a very long time."

"Zee."

"I'm not trying to be sweet. I'm telling you the truth. I loved Crystal the way a teenage boy can love a girl during one year of high school. I did. But I have never loved a woman as a grown man. Never. You came into my life, and now love songs have something to say to me. They sing about you."

"I can't say I've never loved. I loved Warren, no question. But he took his life before that love had a chance to fully bloom. And since then, like I told you before, I don't think I ever fully bloomed either. I put my head down and went to work, caring for Harmony, building a safe life for us the best way I knew how." They sat in the quiet of that for a while.

"I cannot wait to meet Harmony. She seems like a remarkable young woman."

"She is. I am so proud of her."

"You're an incredible mother."

"Thank you. I could say the same about you as a father."

"Thank you. We've both got adults now." He smiled. "Speaking of adults, I know we're adults, but let me get you back at a respectable hour."

He had to lift her down from the lowest step, and once her arms were around his neck, she didn't let go. He held on, too. Then the rain started again, soft and sudden. Neither of them moved.

"Have you ever hugged anyone or slow danced in the rain?" she asked.

"No. I haven't."

She held him close and he pulled her in, and they swayed.

"Have you ever kissed anyone in the rain?"

"No. Will you be my first? Please."

Zee exhaled, her words moving through him like a chord. He kissed her, fully and without reservation, neither of them thinking about the time, wet hair, or their wet clothes or the fact that any member of his family could walk by or come looking.

"I want to be your only, Jenita."

CHAPTER 28

Too Much

The next day's awards ceremony was outstanding. The school gym was transformed, draped in deep reds, greens, and pops of blacks yellows—colors of remembrance and celebration—the Devereaux children and extended family all played their part in making sure the family legacy lived on for generations to come. Zee was the hub of it all. The people they employed, the entrepreneurs and realtors they mentored, were thriving because this family had invested time and money and stayed invested. High-caliber Black and brown-owned businesses lined the sponsor tables and exhibition displays, and local government officials, philanthropists, and quiet wealth in Pine City far exceeded what you'd expect from a town its size.

The thank-you speeches and the genuine gratitude gave Jenita a window into an extraordinary legacy. One awardee spoke through tears about her veterinay clinic, which employed twelve people. Another credited the Devereaux mentorship program for helping him secure the first commercial property his family had ever owned. The attention and the scale of it were astounding.

The talent show was beautifully produced by Mike and Quincy. Between acts, the band eased through soulful instrumentals, and the room moved easily between laughter, applause, and the easy sway of people who knew the music before the first note finished. She was proud of her former students. Zee seemed determined not to be visibly impressed by the production, though he clearly was. He and Pops kept their compliments minimal while everyone else went wild.

As usual, women, community leaders, and networkers competed for Zee's attention. He gave each one a brief, professional acknowledgment before introducing or steering himself back to Jenita. "My sincere apologies. I wasn't even supposed to be here this weekend."

Prep for Frank's party ran nonstop through the night. It wasn't until after three in the morning that Zee walked her back to the guesthouse. The men stayed up in shifts tending the hog, and Pops would fry fish in the morning. She and Renae had plans to have coffee and tea in the guesthouse at eight before everything jumped off. Do these people sleep?

Renae asked if she could invite Tink over, because they wanted to share something with her. Tink arrived in all-white Pocahontas pigtails, a pink linen dress with a white eyelet shrug, white toe-out slides, and a fresh pink pedicure. She looked soft and smelled lovely. She admired Jenita's perfume and outfit and thanked her for putting up with her big, wild, and zany family. Tink seemed to already sense how overwhelmed she was by all things Devereaux, and by Zee being the engine behind it all.

Renae didn't seem to feel her weariness. She launched into what she had shared with Zee in her office. Jenita was even more overwhelmed—it gripped her spirit in ways she couldn't dismiss, but she wasn't ready for it. Not like this. Renae shared the dream, and when she finished, Tink offered her interpretation, which landed almost verbatim with what Jenita had felt listening.

Fatou had come to Renae in a dream. "In the dream, me and Zee were children, dressed all in white, sitting on a beach. Pops and Tink had placed a white sheer over us. We were all facing the ocean, solemn. Pops and Tink couldn't soothe us.

"Mama said, 'What's wrong with my babies?'

"And we just cried and cried. She kissed Pops on his cheek, and he walked away. She hugged Tink; they spoke and Tink walked away wiping her tears. And when Mama came to console me and Zee, we looked at her asking why she left. I stood up and hugged her around her waist, jumping and crying, and said, 'You left me with no one to play with.' Zee laid his head at her feet, holding her around her ankles, sobbing, and said, 'You left me with no one to love.'

"Mama chuckled the way only she could. We held on tighter because we thought she was laughing at us. I said, 'Mama, why do you laugh at your children?' She said, 'I am not laughing at you, *mes beaux bébés*. I am so happy. I have seen your hurt and your pain and your tears all these years, and God let me choose a gift for you.'

"I said, 'We don't want a gift.'

"Zee said, 'We want you.'

"Mama kept laughing and said, 'But God helped me pick this beloved one, and you must promise to love it. Look! *Regarder!* There it is. Look!'

"We wiped the tears and sand from our faces. 'Look, there!' Squinting, we saw a figure coming toward us, holding two babies who had been crying, too. I jumped up and down, clapping! Zee jumped up and ran toward it with everything he had. Snucks was off to the side laughing.'"

Then Renae said, "It was you, Jenita! It was you, sissy!"

Jenita was already in tears. She knew.

Tink asked if she understood what it meant.

"I think I do. But…"

"You know what it means, probably better than I do. But what I believe is that God, Fatou, and your Nana Katie Mae brought you and Zee to one another and used Mike and Renae to make the path." She let that settle. "It doesn't force you to love one another, but it does mean you were meant to meet, however you two see fit. Renae knows you're for Zee, and Zee knows you're special. But they should never treat you like a trophy piece between them. Don't ever allow that. Frank means you well. You and he survived hard childhoods the same way, with laughter. That's a medicine. A gift. But don't you dare let the Devereaux wind snuff your flame. Keep your fire, baby. God sent you. Fatou and your Nana chose you. But don't you do one thing the Holy Ghost doesn't tell you."

Renae squeezed her and left. Tink stayed. "And who died early on you, sweetheart? Not your Nana. Was there a baby? God said it's all right. God was with you then and never let you go." She anointed Jenita and prayed over her, encouraged her to hear God for herself, and declared that if the dream had been misinterpreted, God would not allow it to live outside the walls of this house!"

Jenita wept.

The abortion surfaced. The complex, private answers to questions no one had asked out loud drained what was left of her social battery, which this weekend had been drawing down steadily. She didn't say anything. Tink kissed her forehead, patted her cheek, and left.

She needed to lie down. She slept for an hour and woke to the sound of children splashing in the pool outside the guesthouse and the smell of barbecue drifting in. She thought. *Whew. I haven't met anyone like that since Nana. It's fine for me to see, but it's something else to have someone see me about me.*

Her spiritual, emotional, and social capacity were all in the red, like a dashboard that wouldn't pass inspection. She needed to go home. She got dressed, partially packed her suitcase, and intended to leave right after dinner.

LaKisha and Tiff knocked on the door. "Ms. Hall! We're ready to eat." She came out and walked back to the house with them, asking Tiff all about the honeymoon and reminding her how beautiful a bride she'd been. Mike greeted her with the same warm hug he gave her every time she'd fed him and let him stay on her couch over weekends in college.

The Snucks' dining room table seated twelve. She sat between Zee and Mike, and at first, she felt settled. The love and the laughter and the easy ribbing; they filled her in on the inside jokes and the running stories from their shared history. It made her feel welcomed and estranged at the same time.

She had never had family experiences like this. She looked around the table at all these faces and felt she couldn't absorb or memorize enough to ever really belong. She knew she'd leave with them knowing more about her than she knew about them. There were too many people, too many personalities, too much to invite into her world. Other relatives and friends and children filled every room. Pops and Zee were their usual laid-back selves but tossed in comments about business and the market between the high-energy conversational juggling act. Zee excused himself several times for calls.

Renae kept calling her sissy. Frank's serious side, when he talked business, was surprisingly brilliant. Everything was coming through her walls, her floor, her ceiling. She felt inadequate, out of her depth, and way out of her league.

It all caused her to think. *What am I doing here? And why did I just tell that man I'd be his girlfriend?* She had said yes, and they'd turned their kissing and holding right back on. She had even let him fondle her breasts and she massaged his manhood.

He stopped them both.

"You are too precious for this to happen here. We need to leave before I do things with you, we won't make it back to Renae and Frank's."

She had committed to the man she knew right now, and he had been such a gentleman about her uncertainties and her very reasonable fears. He said he was deeply in love with her. She knew she was in love with him. But this was too much, too soon. Her thoughts were swarming.

What was I thinking? Was it a caught-up decision? Was it those Superman laser-beam eyes? Or the patience he showed me while I ate? Did I break some Black sisterhood code by saying yes? I'm too old to fall like a smitten schoolgirl. Lord knows I am as smitten as it gets. His family is too big. His money is too much.

His being so deeply and unashamedly in love with her was too soon and too good to be true. Her thoughts continued. *What if they consumed me? Drowned out who I am? Took me away from the family I do have, from my friends? What if I ended up on this hill, cut off? What about Harmony? My house? That dream. And I never told Zee about the abortion or what it caused. What will he think of me?*

Her thoughts were doing the Olympics. Outwardly she held herself together. God and Nana weren't saying anything—she couldn't hear in all this noise. Fight or flight set in, and there were too many of them to fight. She decided to tell him she'd answered too soon.

She offered to help clear the table. Frank said, "That's for anyone under eighteen. They've got it."

She excused herself and walked quickly toward the guesthouse. Zee followed.

"Why are you walking so fast?"

"I answered you too soon." They stood on the front porch. "I need to leave."

"Whoa. Wait. Where are you going?"

"Home. I need to leave."

"Why?"

"It's too much. Way too much."

"What, me? My family? What Renae said?"

"All of it. Too much, too soon, too fast."

"Don't worry about them. This is me and you."

"It's not just me and you. And I understand that about you."

"Is it too fast when it's what we both need, want, and know we're heading toward?"

"We don't know that for certain, Zee."

"I do. There's no doubt in my mind and I'm not trying to rush you. Tell me how you want to slow down. I'll do whatever it takes. I'm just not trying to hinder what has already taken too long."

"We don't know, Zee. I don't."

"I've been wanting you my whole life. I just didn't know where you were. And I think you feel the same way. You're just more afraid to admit it. Me? I'm scared as hell not to. Don't hold your breath, please."

"Holding my breath feels safe." Tears fell. "I can't depend on you to breathe for me." She sat down, frustrated.

"I'm not breathing for you. We breathe in sync. I can't go back to suffocating or waiting on some imaginary clock or calendar for permission."

"But the air up here is thin. My lungs aren't built for your fast-paced, high-altitude life, your enormous family compared to mine, your enormous businesses, the fanfare, the around-the-clock activity, the women who want your attention. Your enormous pile of money. I can't handle all of that."

"You handle me. Effortlessly. Like no one else ever has. All of me."

"But Zee, your heart is crowded and your hands are already full." Crying now. "You love your family, your work, and it's too much for me. You love them with everything. I can see it. It's so rare and so beautiful." She was throwing things into her suitcase as she talked.

His eyes watered. "I had to. I didn't have you to love. They're in my world. Jenita, you are my world. Already. I haven't had a breath or a thought that didn't include you since the moment we met. I gave my family and my businesses all my time and all the love I had because I didn't have anyone of my own to pour it into. My love for you is on a completely different level. And you wouldn't be this emotional trying to run from me if you didn't love me, too."

"I am in love with you. But you can't separate the two worlds without tearing yourself apart. I wouldn't even want you to, that's how much I care. You just met me. I'm not worth competing with all of that."

"Competing? You're in a class by yourself, Jenita. You won on day one. They already know. Ain't no competition. None." He paused. "I told you I was in love with you earlier because I thought telling you I love you would be too much. But it's the truth. I love you and I'm in love with you. And the way I love them and my work still isn't the way I love you, need you, want you. Not even close."

"It's too much, Zee. Too heavy and too lofty at the same time. I've had too many uncertainties to count and now that I finally have stability, I can't give up my safe, comfortable small world to be the girlfriend of a busy, wealthy, hometown hero with a family this size. I'm not a business acquisition. I can't just follow you home and fall in line. This big, rich, ever-socializing world is overwhelming. I need to stop it before—"

"Before what? Stop what? Love?"

"Before I can't."

"I couldn't stop it if I tried. Please give me a chance."

"I did. And it's too much. I'd have to give myself up."

"I haven't asked you to give up a single thing. If anything, I want to give you me. I want to give you the world."

"A world too big for me to live in."

"How can you say it's too big when you haven't let me show it all to you yet?"

"My point exactly. If this is too big now, I can't imagine—" She sobbed.

He cupped her face and wiped her tears with his thumbs. He thought about the first time their eyes met after Mike's wedding reception—the night he knew, without a doubt, that he wanted her to be his wife.

She closed her eyes. It was breaking her heart to see his disappointment. If she only understood how much he loved her and how completely he intended to protect her from being overwhelmed.

"What would you lose if you just gave us a chance?" He waited.

She opened her eyes slowly, resting her hands on his wrists as warm tears slid around his thumbs. "I'd lose myself, Zee."

"Please don't believe that. I love and adore you."

"You can't juggle two worlds without risking dropping one or losing yourself. Your world is well-established and full. I'm new. I love you too much already, and I love them too much, for you to live with that kind of pressure. Dropping any of it would destroy both of us."

He dropped his hands and his head. She kissed his lips. But if she didn't leave right then, she wouldn't find the courage to.

"Please don't give up on us already. Please."

"I have to. So you won't lose what you've worked so hard to build. And so I won't lose myself." She looked down and walked out, rolling her luggage behind her.

Pops, Tink, and Frank were outside. Zee gave them a look, and they turned quickly back toward the house. Frank's leg caused him to lag a step, and under his breath he said, "Damn, WD—" He finished in thought. *But she's right. There's a lot to being a Devereaux. Hang in there.*

Zee stepped around in front of her and asked quietly, "What are you so afraid of, sweetheart?"

"Everything."

CHAPTER 29

Finding Their Way

It had been almost two months since they'd seen one another. But a few days after she left, they'd begun texting again, and from there the calls came back, daily. She just hadn't been ready to see him in person. They had a few conversations that got genuinely heated, in every sense, but she felt like it was more torment than relief because she ached for his presence, his warmth, the way he held her.

She imagined him every time she played "Angel" by Anita Baker. She had taken what he'd taught her, and now whenever a good love song came on, she put his face in the lyrics. She listened to "I'm Coming Back" by Lalah Hathaway and Rachelle Ferrell on repeat while she painted, a piece she felt nudged to create with him in mind. It made her feel, like he had said, that she had loved him long before she was born, or when the old songs were new.

Her sisters and Ms. Sylvia kept at her. "Call him, Neat. You know you love that man."

She had also resumed counseling with Faith, her interfaith Black spiritual counselor and chaplain, a brilliant woman she'd first sought out for grief counseling after Warren's suicide.

Their sessions used to run bi-weekly because of the Ingrams' ongoing harassment and the guilt she'd carried from the abortion she had in the weeks after Warren died. The complications from that procedure had caused infertility. She was twenty-three years old when she was told she wouldn't be able to have any more children. In her sessions now, she was also working through her daddy issues, mother's neglect, her grandmother's physical abuse, the hazing she'd experienced during her initiation, and the realization that much of her current overwhelm had its roots in a fear of losing control.

As part of her healing, she had become more intentional about how she showed up. She served as an advisor, speaking plainly with collegiate and alumnae members about accountability and the kind of sisterhood she believed in—one that didn't require harm to prove belonging.

She prayed and maintained her relationship with God, which had saved her mind and her quality of life. The hypervigilance she'd carried for years, for herself and for Harmony, had once been necessary. Seeing how quickly she still ran from situations that posed no real threat was eye-opening. She was learning to keep trusting her spiritual sensitivity without letting fear make the decisions.

At Zee's end, Pops, Tink, and Renae ached for him.

Out on the pier fishing, Pops told him: "From what you've shared, I believe she loves you, too. Pull on your patience. Give her all the space and time she needs."

Zee prayed, kept his monthly therapy appointments, and took his feelings for Jenita with him into those sessions, working through the nuances of safely ending his celibacy, understanding that what felt to him like certainty and commitment could feel like intensity to her.

All he knew was that "Yearning for Your Love" by the Gap Band and "Don't You Know That?" by Luther Vandross said exactly what he couldn't. He was so lovesick that Frank had backed off the jokes. He knew his brother was in love for the first time. Frank had empathy he didn't advertise. He knew what it was to love one woman from the beginning, because Renae had been his from the day she used to bring him lunch at school. Zee used to tease him that Renae was the only woman crazy enough to love his crippled ass.

Frank's comeback: "At least I ain't been sick after three or four months over WD-40, and you ain't even got one stitch of pussy, with yo crispy ass."

"Yeah. But if I ever do… man, if I ever do…"

Jenita finally agreed to a fresh start, to a take-it-slow date. She was happy and excited; he was excited, strategic, and sure. He kept it simple: a movie first, then dinner. That way there'd be no pressure to fill every silence, and he wouldn't spend the whole meal staring at her.

Zee made serious and overdue changes. He delegated responsibilities that should never have been solely his to begin with, and most of the people he handed things to had been waiting and ready for exactly this. The Reaux had exceptional staff; he had simply been micromanaging them. Now they felt free to do what they'd been hired to do, and they were good at it.

He had several straightforward conversations with his family about wanting to be more serious with Jenita. Some struggled; he had been carrying them in so many ways. Others understood and were genuinely happy for him. Some of Pops' extended family had opinions about whether she was a "suitable" choice.

Pops shut it down. "Y'all came off a shrimp boat. Now you're talking?"

Renae and Frank missed Zee as their third wheel. It had always been the three of them. But Renae wanted her brother happy, and the dream still sat with her. It had to be God and Mama. She grieved the rapid blossoming of her friendship with Jenita a little, because Jenita and Zee were spending their free time together now, except when he brought her to Sunday family dinners or when they went out as couples. Jenita wanted time with Renae, too, and Renae could feel it, but she held back deliberately to give them room to build. It would be better for everyone in the long run. Pops, Tink, and Ms. Lorraine did everything they could to make Jenita feel welcome. Frank jokingly insisted she wasn't.

She buried herself in work and missed him aching. When Zee's plane landed after a string of international closings, he called immediately.

"Hello, sweetheart. I miss you."

"I miss you so much. Hey, handsome, I just walked in the door."

"How was the scholarship gala?"

"You first."

"You first."

She kicked her shoes off and laughed, the kind that comes from relief more than humor. "You are not going to believe tonight." She dropped her purse on the chair and sank onto the couch, tucking her feet beneath her.

Zee had a driver and sat in the back seat, loosening his bow tie. "I'm all ears."

"Okay. So, Madison, the student I told you about? The accounting major?"

"The one carrying her whole family on her back."

"That one. She was nominated for a full-tuition scholarship for grad school. Her mother couldn't get off work. Her boss had promised, then took it back. Madison almost didn't go."

Zee's jaw tightened. "Of course."

"I told her: 'No. This is a way out. I'll take you.' When I picked her up…" She paused. "She had on her best, Zee. It just wasn't right for the room. It was a formal gala."

He already knew where this was going. "You gave her your dress."

"I did." She smiled softly. "Changed in a bathroom stall. Gave her my necklace and earrings, put her hair up. She still had on sneakers because her feet were bigger than mine. Didn't matter. She looked beautiful."

Zee leaned his head back.

"She won," Jenita said quietly.

He exhaled. "I knew she would."

"She thanked me in her speech. Talked about dinner at my house. The art supplies. Neat Harmony. The work-study program. Told the whole room she was wearing my dress." She laughed, shaking her head. "The whole place stood up, Zee. Even the people who hadn't clapped all night."

"And her mother?"

"My girls went and got her. It worked out perfectly. They were leaving Rhonda's campaign rally." Jenita's voice went quiet for a moment. "They asked Madison's mom and me to come up onstage. I didn't want to. I had on black leggings, my red DST 1913 shirt, and my walking shoes."

"But they stood up again."

"For her. For me. For all of it." She got quiet, wondering if she'd said too much. "Your turn."

Zee smiled, full of pride for her. "That's my baby. They got it exactly right. But all I want to talk about right now is seeing you tomorrow. I can hardly wait. Thank you for inviting us."

Warmth spread through her chest. "Me, too. I can't wait to see you."

❧

The sisters wanted to check out the Devereaux men in person. Renae just wanted Black girl company. Frank wanted to tag along and play detective. Zee simply wanted to be near Jenita. She invited them all to her home.

She couldn't quite believe Zee, Renae, and Frank were sitting in her humble abode. As they all got acquainted, laughing, talking, trading stories, she took a quiet moment to be grateful for how their paths had crossed. A small group of people getting to know one another. This was her speed. This was her style.

Zee watched her settle into it and understood even more clearly how everything Devereaux had overwhelmed her. Growing up in it and having helped build it, he had stopped seeing how hard it might be for someone new to feel at home in it. Her sisters saw him looking at her like he could put her on a plate. They loved that for her.

Everyone was stuffed. Compliments about the food went around the table. They did introductions and, as expected, Frank and Sheila immediately stole the show. The laughter was continuous. Rhonda asked, "Zee, what do you see in our Neat?"

"Neat?"

"Jenita. We've called her that since middle school."

"My Nana gave me that nickname when I was little."

"Neat." He looked at her. "I love that. It's perfect for you."

"Don't get distracted," Sheila said.

He turned to Jenita. "Are you comfortable with me answering?"

"I'm good."

"You sure?"

"Quit stalling, man," Sheila said.

"Ease up, Sheila." Jenita smiled.

"To answer your question, I'll tell you what I've told Jenita many times." He took her hand. "I see everything in this woman. I know it sounds crazy, but I loved her the first time I laid eyes on her. I just didn't recognize it as love until we talked all night on the pier. She sees me inwardly the way no one ever has. She makes me feel emotionally safe. She sees what I look like, and she sees who I am inside."

"She is a breath of fresh air. She is intelligent, mature, a brilliant and critical thinker, kind, conscientious, feisty, deeply spiritual, thoughtful, generous, funny, classy, studious, talented. Fine and beautiful, cute and sexy as hell all at the same time. I don't think she'll ever fully comprehend how appealing she is to me. She is adventurous, a great listener, peaceful, considerate, appreciative, sensual, curious, spontaneous at times, honest, understanding, compassionate—"

Frank cut in. "You gave her thirty words too many. Tell us what you don't like about her."

"If there's anything I don't like right now, I'll share it with her privately."

"Well!" Rhonda said slowly, clapping. "I heard that, Mr. Devereaux."

Sheila leaned forward. "Rhonda, don't get distracted. Now, how does a most-eligible Black bachelor stay celibate for eight years? And the internet claims you have millions, but we know those numbers can be inflated."

"I don't care about his money," Jenita said.

"I do," Sheila said plainly. "But about this whole celibacy façade."

"As far as the money," Zee said, "my family has been blessed to turn tragedy into wealth. But we would have chosen poverty if it meant keeping my mother, Uncle Louis, and Mike's mother. The celibacy is not a façade. I have been celibate for eight years. I was engaged once, and it didn't work out because we both knew it was a business arrangement. Her family wanted children. I found out I couldn't give her any. We liked the idea of each other but didn't love each other. They ended it."

"And now I could not be more grateful," Frank said.

"Same," Renae echoed. "I couldn't stand her."

Zee continued. "I felt emasculated. On top of some other things I'd been through, that was the last of it for me. I had to do something. So, through prayer, traditional therapy, music therapy, which produces results similar to meditation, even a vegan stretch for a while, and celibacy, I was able to heal a whole lot of things. I'm not perfect—"

"But women must throw themselves at you constantly," Sheila said.

"Some have."

"How do you resist all those women down at Brown Sugar Beach?"

"I've been around the beach my whole life. My pops even had Renae and me get our massage therapist certifications when he saw how much spa services could earn. I grew numb to all of it, especially when a woman is trying to display everything. I had genuinely given up on love. And the kind of man I've become…love and intimacy have to go together. I wouldn't want it if the vibe ain't right. I stopped thinking about either. I didn't have any vibes with anyone during my celibacy, until I met this incredible woman."

He turned to Jenita and took both her hands. "And with all due respect, Jenita, if I am ever blessed with the opportunity to make love to you, may God have mercy on your body, because its pleasures will be mine to give. And may God have mercy on my mind and my body, because they'll belong to you."

Sheila and Rhonda erupted. "Woot! Woot!" Fanning themselves.

Renae clapped, her heart full. She had never seen her brother speak so openly about anyone to people he'd just met. Never so talkative with strangers. Not once in his life.

Frank saluted. "Get it, Zee. I taught you well, Devil Dog." He understood the weight of what Zee had just said and didn't want to undercut it.

Jenita was warm from her head to her feet and could not blame a hot flash. She placed her hand on her chest and closed her eyes because she could feel him looking at her by the way he was holding her hand and slowly rubbing the back of it.

He stood and asked quietly if he could speak with her in another room. Rhonda pulled out Jenita's chair for her, showing her approval. They left Frank and Sheila in a mock argument while Rhonda and Renae cleared the table and washed dishes, getting acquainted.

He didn't wait for permission. He kissed her, bold and certain. At that moment she knew she would never run from this man again.

"Neat." He smiled. "Perfect." She blushed. "You know what I don't like? Not being with you. I meant every word I said in there. Every word. Thank you for all of this—for introducing me to your sisters, for having us in your home…and this delicious meal. I could get used to this…to you. See you Thursday. Just the two of us."

The next day, Jenita drove home to see her parents. Something she hadn't done in years. Zee had been nudging her toward it, and she'd been nudging herself. Seeing the Devereaux family, with all their imperfections still bound together, made her wonder if there was anything salvageable in her own.

Her father, J.D. Hall, had let his religious beliefs harden into condemnation—for her pregnancy out of wedlock, and in various roundabout ways, for Warren's death. He had rubberstamped the Ingrams' accusations of entrapment and blamed her for disrupting his life, too. Her mother, Mable, never agreed with him out loud, but told Jenita privately that she had also been pregnant before her own wedding, which was the root of her grandmother's particular fury. *Hypocrites.* Jenita thought. *Just like the Ingrams.*

What moved her to go was simple: the Devereaux family had hypocrites and liars and sanctimonious people in it, too. Her sisters did. Ms. Jackson had. Ms. Sylvia. Coworkers, students, everyone's family had someone like that, and they still managed at least a cordial relationship. Sheila's father was a bishop who had disowned her over her bisexuality and condemned her from his pulpit when he heard about the club. But cancer had softened his body and his convictions, and they were working their way toward something. When people age, they either double down or soften up.

Mable had softened. J.D.'s farm-battered body was frail. Harmony had come along, too, and she was champing at the bit to tell her grandparents about Zee and the Devereaux family, pulling up social media pictures of the hotel, the wedding, everything she had access to. She told them about Mike, about how excited she was for her mother. Mable seemed quietly happy. J.D. was surprisingly talkative. There were some sticky stretches in the conversation, but it was genuinely worth the trip. Far from perfect, and far from over. But forward.

Jenita and Zee made their relationship official before their weekend trip to the Bahamas. What they both loved was how naturally their affection moved, the mutual desire to give and receive it. Touches, caresses, embraces, forehead kisses. Because sometimes men need forehead kisses, too. Sitting on his lap while rubbing his head. Her head on his chest. Cuddling on the couch wasn't a means to an end. It was the thing itself.

He picked her up Thursday and they took a long walk through the park. For the first time she heard him sing. He was being playful at first, but she could tell right away he could really sing. They stopped at a railing overlooking the Jaxton lake and he held her from behind and sang parts of "Knocks Me Off My Feet" as performed by Luther Vandross. She let her head fall back against his chest.

"I love the way you hold me, Zee. Let me turn around so I can hold you."

"Can we stay right here for a minute? Holding you holds me, too."

"Of course. It feels nice. And you sound so good."

"Do I?"

"You have an amazing voice."

"I'm just serenading you with what you're helping me rediscover. Whispering sweet nothings in your ear. I love you."

"I love you, too. And with that voice, those are sweet somethings."

He turned her gently to face him. "I don't want you to get tired of hearing it, but Lord knows I do love you. You knocked me off my feet on day one."

"I love you. Just when I think I've said it too much, you make me feel like I can't say it enough. I love you, Zee."

"Jenita. Neat—will you be my girlfriend?"

"Yes."

They held each other as if it were the first and last time. A passerby whistled. Zee asked them to take a picture. They posed. Then he looked at her and asked, "If we were alone right now, would you want me to make love to you?"

"Yes. Would you want to make love to me?"

"Yes, Lord. But I don't want our first time to be just anywhere. Where would you like to go?"

◈

That night, Zee shared a few tasteful pictures of them together on social media and changed his status to "In a Relationship," tagging her. She was enamored. He got thousands of likes as usual, comments still turned off. Jenita went quiet on social media, because, well.

She was launching a new cohort for the fall semester and couldn't take time away from work. But the Devereaux family jet turned out to be a very manageable size. With her spontaneity and his resources, they flew to the Bahamas the next day.

They had talked about being together at length. Now it was actually about to happen. She was anxious. *Will there be fireworks? Will I please him? Will it be the best either of us has had?* He wasn't worried about any of that, but he validated her feelings and assured her they would work through anything together, honestly.

He told her the truth: because of his past, he didn't want to receive oral sex—not to be hypocritical, but he would love to give it. Jenita admitted that no man had ever made her feel like she was his best partner, and she had never felt confident giving oral sex. And receiving? She could take it or leave it. She had never had an orgasm with a man.

As they entered the hotel room, he said, "At any point, tell me. You don't have to do anything you don't want to."

"You, too." She was half joking.

He wasn't. "It's been so long. I know you arouse me like no one else, but I've put so much pressure on myself to make such good love to you that my heart is racing."

They took separate showers and came into the bedroom at the same time. She wore a simple black satin thigh-length cami. He wore a black ribbed tank and black boxers. Their nervousness was unwanted company. He drew the curtains and sat at the foot of the bed and invited her to sit on his lap. They kissed until they felt more themselves. The lamps went off without a word. They pulled the duvet back and slid under the sheet.

Under the sheet they kissed and slowly took each other's clothes off. She was ashamed of her rolls and scars. He didn't want his injury to be a turn-off. Knowing neither was requiring the other to offer up their body as proof of acceptance made them both relax.

"May I taste you, Neat?"

"Yes."

He kissed and moved slowly over her, every inch—blemishes, the softness of her stomach, the natural dimples of her skin, and the faint scars time hadn't fully erased—as if they were made for his mouth and hands, as though he could see her, even in the dark, exactly as she was. Treating her breasts like he was thirsty, kissing and tasting her body like he was hungry, welcoming himself between her thighs like he was home.

She had never felt anything like it. It came to her. *If I don't have an orgasm, this alone is more care and pleasure than I've ever felt.* He kept assuring her by showing and telling her how much he loved her and her body. "You taste so good to me…these honey thighs are softer, and you taste sweeter than I ever imagined."

She couldn't speak. Her moans told him everything he needed to know. And then, suddenly, her hips rose off the bed on their own and a marvelous sensation she'd never felt as intense bathed her in a sparkling warmth from the top of her brain all the way through her trembling body, exiting through her fingertips and the tips of her toes like sunrays.

"What are you doing to me?"

"Just loving you, my baby." He continued to thoroughly enjoy himself.

He was as turned on as she was. She steadied her breath. He asked if she was okay. She could only nod, and he held her not ready to let her go.

"Would you like me to bring you a warm cloth?"

"No, I'll do it." No man had ever asked her that before.

"Let me. Please."

She watched his beautiful body cross toward the bathroom and return, bare and unhurried. He moved toward her slow and sure, broad shoulders relaxed, strength wrapped in ease. His body was defined, the kind of strength that had settled in over time rather than been chased, carrying a quiet assurance that filled the room without a word. She remembered how long it had been since she'd received a man. She let her eyes linger on him without apology, taking in the strength of him, the warmth of him, before he lay back down beside her. "I loved making you feel good. Watching you."

He wasn't in any hurry for whatever came next, but she seemed to think she should be. Having her first orgasm with a man, she assumed intimacy had to be immediately transactional. Her turn, now his. He'd said he didn't want oral, so she kissed his neck, his chest, and reached for him.

He paused. "We can take our time. Tell me how you feel."

"I have never felt so good in my life. I don't even know what just happened to me."

It made him blush. "Let's just lie here and enjoy it." He held her, kissing her temple, his hands moving slowly over her.

"I am. But you haven't had an orgasm yet."

"I wish I could describe how deeply satisfying it is just watching you." He began to touch himself. She watched.

"Shouldn't I be doing that?"

He moved the sheet back. "Please, baby."

The softness of her hand made him reach for her and pull her into a kiss. She loved how something so simple to her undid him completely. He could have let that be everything, given how long it had been since anyone had touched him.

She kept her hand on him. "Where's the condom?" He reached for the nightstand. She lay back as he put it on and she opened to him. He did his best to be gentle. She was still warm and ready, but it was uncomfortable for a moment, not painful. He gave her more care first, then slowly eased back inside. He stayed still and told her how much he loved her. "This… right here with you—it feels so good."

He took his time ending his celibacy with the only woman he had ever loved and felt wholly loved by. He kissed her and began to move carefully, steadily, asking if she was okay. She wanted all of him. She looked into his eyes as they went dewy with pleasure, stroke by stroke, until he came, his forehead buried in the curve of her neck. He rested on her softness sustaining his immense satisfaction, unhurried. The realization settled deep. *Ain't no way I ever felt this good. No damn way.*

When he rolled to his side they lay still, cuddled and quiet, sitting with what had just happened between them.

"Neat."

"Zee."

"What are you thinking?"

"You really wanna know?"

"Yes."

"For real?" She giggled.

He raised his head. "What's so funny?"

"You ever seen *Aladdin*?"

"The cartoon?"

"The song, 'A Whole New World.'"

He started laughing. "Hold up, we just made love after a combined thirteen years without. And you want to talk about a cartoon?"

"Wait." She laughed. "It wasn't just your celibacy or my abstinence. It was my first orgasm during sex. It has never been more intense… and it was with you."

She threw her arms wide and sang at full and terrible volume, "And it's a brand-neeew worrrrrrld…!"

He laughed and shook his head. "You absolutely cannot sing and you got the lyrics wrong."

"Talent is not required. You can be Peabo, I'll be Regina. Know it if you sing it and sing if you know it."

He laughed. "A brand-new world." He pulled her close. "And there's no place like home."

CHAPTER 30

Home for the Holidays

Thanksgiving was usually quiet for Jenita, but this year she brought Zee to meet her parents and family. The Devereaux family usually hosted a big Thanksgiving celebration at the hotel the weekend before, then closed The Reaux on Thanksgiving Day and the Friday after. Jenita, Harmony, and Zee would spend Thanksgiving with her family and then drive to Pine City for a Friday dinner at Tink's house.

She, Harmony, and her mother made four dozen each of Nana Katie's pecan cookies and sweet potato muffins. Jenita had updated the recipe with a butter-pecan crumble on top and set aside three dozen of each to take to Queen's Hill. For the first time in her life, she and her daughter gathered pecans together from the same tree Jenita used to pick from with her nana. She also invited her cousin Deuce, who was ostracized by the family for coming out as bisexual. He had a small local farm and brought collards and sweet potatoes he'd harvested himself. They shelled pecans and gathered eggs from the chicken coop to use in the desserts.

Zee took one sniff and knew immediately. "Oh. These are the famous cookies and muffins Mike was telling me about." He tasted one. "Delicious." The women made sure to select the prettiest ones to bring to Queen's Hill.

J.D.'s voice, once strong and overly authoritative, sounded a little fragile alongside Zee's. The two of them talked football, basketball, hunting, and fishing. J.D. invited Zee outside to walk his land. He told him about the tobacco he used to crop, and how, after the RJ Reynolds lawsuits, he'd switched to cotton and soybeans. He was too old now and too worn down to work it the way he once did. He told his stories with pride and Zee listened with real attention. Still, he found himself quietly wondering: how does a seemingly decent old man carry so much contempt for his own daughter? How did he side with the Ingrams after knowing Ms. Ingram had assaulted his pregnant child? Why had he kept himself and Mable at such a distance from Harmony all these years? They walked and talked for close to an hour before Mable called them in out of the cool air.

Zee already had some of those answers. Frank, Joe Lester, and Reggie had run an unrequested but thorough background check on Jenita and her family early on. Police records showed that the Hall family's crops had been torched by arson, a few days after Jenita filed her police report. No one was ever caught. The timing lined up with the same period the Ingrams and J.D. were pressuring her to abort Harmony and annul the marriage.

"Coincidence my ass," Reggie had said when he shared it with Zee.

Zee didn't agree with how J.D. had treated the woman he loved, and the toll it had taken on her. But he didn't condemn the old man either. J.D. was a few years older than Pops, and Lord knows Pops had made some questionable, fear-driven decisions to keep his family secure. What it did was make Zee want to love and protect her even more. He told her about the background check. She understood. Her sisters had run one on him, too, though not as thorough.

They stopped at Jenita's house on the way back to Pine City, planning to leave in the morning. Harmony loved Zee. The two times he stayed overnight he slept on the couch, and while he was in the shower, Harmony leaned over to her mother.

"Mama, Mr. Zee must really love you. If I were rich, you wouldn't catch me sleeping on our couch. Plus, y'all act like nobody know y'all have sex."

"That ain't your business, Miss Joy."

"It's obvious, though. You can't stop looking at him and he can't keep his hands off you. It's cute."

"I feel good and safe with him. Hush."

"I can tell. I'm just saying, some people would love to have that. Mommy, I don't care if y'all sleep together here. You probably do it when I'm at school anyway."

"What we do is not your business, missy. And for your information, we have never slept together in this house. Mind yourself."

The next morning, loading the car, Zee said, "I don't know if it's your couch or the peaceful vibe in your home, but I slept all night. Like a baby."

Thanksgiving with the Devereaux family was big, loud, and wonderful. Tink's house was warm and festive, and Jenita watched Harmony fall right into it, laughing, playing games, eating, dancing, singing karaoke. Between Renae's children, cousins, and friends her age, it was as though she'd been coming there for years. Mike and Tiffany's introductions helped ease everything. Is it just me who found it all too much?

She watched her not-so-little girl happy in ways she hadn't seen before, thoroughly in her element. She realized, observing her, that she had been carrying the full weight of Harmony's happiness and fulfillment on her own back for years. Her only contribution this time was literally bringing her to the table. Harmony handled the rest and handled it better than Jenita had.

The family devoured all three dozen pecan cookies and all three dozen sweet potato muffins in minutes. Jenita didn't get one. She was satisfied from the day before and relieved they were so well received, it felt like sharing a piece of her family with theirs. She settled on the front porch with Tink and Ms. Lorraine, and a few minutes later Zee walked out with a muffin and two cookies for the three of them to share. It reminded her of how Nana Katie always made sure she had her cookie or her muffin before everything disappeared.

"Thank you, Zee. You are so attentive."

"I'm supposed to be."

Tink nodded. "I know that's right."

Afterward, Zee invited them over to see how construction on his house was coming along. From time to time, he had asked for Jenita's opinion on finishes and layouts, but she hadn't seen it in person at this stage. It was breathtaking, inside and out. She could see exactly where he had taken her suggestions.

She recognized her touches in the white kitchen, the custom cabinetry, terrazzo flooring, and the huge Taj Mahal quartz waterfall island with seating for six. Desert Dusk Mohawk carpet in the great room and a floor-to-ceiling limestone fireplace. A full marble bathroom. The formal dining room had a tray ceiling with appropriate crown molding and wainscoting, a contrasting bay window, and a cozy breakfast nook. Near the front entrance: a smaller octagonal living room and a home office. In the basement: a theater room and man cave, two bedrooms with a Jack-and-Jill oversized bathroom, and a weight room with two each of every machine, a full set of black weights, mirrored walls all around, and a jacuzzi.

The heated pool, the French doors off the kitchen, and the five bedrooms and four bathrooms he had neither asked her input on nor shown her. His four-car garage and golf-cart garage held his spotless blacked-out 2011 Dodge Ram 2500 and a new 2012 Mercedes-Benz C-Class. The grounds had Bradford pear trees, well-placed evergreen shrubs, long-standing pines, and a row of browning palmetto trees along the driveway. Small solar-powered spherical water features lit the front walkway at night.

She kept her impressions to herself. Nothing in her simple life could fully account for the responsibility and maintenance this place would require.

The holiday season consumed everyone. The Reaux had back-to-back holiday parties. Sweets by Renae was running at full capacity, baking for events. Lorraine's was outfitting clients for galas. The D.E. beautification team was handling residential and commercial decorations. Zee was buried in year-end financials and ongoing meetings about what seemed to be a major sale, and wouldn't you know it, Pops and Ms. Lorraine announced they were getting married.

They kept it small: just Tink, his children and her nieces at the courthouse, and they welcomed Jenita. Pops told her that watching her and Zee together had inspired them to stop waiting. "Y'all make love contagious." Ms. Lorraine added sweetly, "Especially when I see y'all dance together." Jenita felt truly honored, because she knew what she and Zee had was real.

Zee and Renae had been teaching her Chicago-style stepping and hand dancing. She especially loved dancing with Zee to "Darlin' Darlin' Baby" by the O'Jays because he sang every word to her as they moved. He was so damn smooth it was almost unfair. When they slow-dragged, he'd sing softly along with "Forever Mine," making her practically dissolve. She wasn't nearly the dancer they were, but she loved learning and loved being close to him while she did.

While Zee and Renae danced, she could also tease Frank that she was the better dancer between them whenever they danced together. "You still ain't shit, Neat."

"Whatever. Look at you, hobbling, but at least you're aging well. Like an old Buick: overheating, throwing smoke, plenty of miles, still rolling."

Ms. Lorraine looked lovelier than Jenita had ever seen her, and Pops looked happier than she had ever seen him. They all danced at the small reception in their charming home. Jenita could only stay for the day before traveling for work, which was a reasonable excuse to step away from the controlled chaos. But she, Harmony, her sisters, and family had already been formally invited by Pops and Tink to come back for Christmas.

This would be the last year The Reaux and most D.E. businesses would close from December twenty-fourth through January thirty-first. The hotel had begun attracting guests year-round, and the Valentine's Soiree was already sold out with every room booked. But they wanted to celebrate the holiday together and mark the beginning of their long-awaited month off.

Her consulting business was gaining real traction, and she was traveling more than usual. She hadn't seen Zee in almost two weeks. She missed him, but being busy made the time move. At night their calls still ran long. She had given this particular presentation many times and knew it like the back of her hand, but she'd tailored it carefully for this audience at a Washington, D.C. conference, with a room full of professors, faculty, and alumni from HBCUs. They were engaged, asked a heavy load of questions, some signaling they were already on board and others working through legitimate concerns. She moved to the back table to register those who were ready, answer the more individual questions, and take pictures and selfies with anyone who asked.

"May I take a picture with you, Ms. Hall?"

She knew that voice. It made her feel safe on the outside and warm on the inside. A few people nearby seemed to recognize him and whispered. Without turning around, she said, "My boyfriend may not approve."

Quietly: "You are so fine. Please?"

She turned and they hugged. He gave her a quick kiss.

"I am so happy to see you, Mr. Devereaux."

"Not as happy as I am, Ms. Hall."

He wanted to do considerably more, and so did she, but they both respected professional and public spaces. She wanted to wrap herself around him completely.

Dinner was good, and they both knew what came after. He loved everything about her. She loved this man; his mind, his big and generous heart, his thoughtfulness, his quiet strength, and the way he woke her body up. Before him, she had treated intimacy as something she performed to keep a relationship together or prove her commitment. It felt acceptable. She could live without it. No fireworks, a faint whistle. Certainly, no orgasms. And now this. This was mind blowing and body bliss.

She felt that in every stroke he was giving her physical love that had been steeping for years, pouring it directly into her core. She was as thirsty for him as he was for her. She finally understood Sheila. Maybe not the specific way Sheila satisfied her appetite, but why the craving existed at all. Even their desire to simply hold one another was mutual. He had this way of affirming that he loved her whole body, including everything she tried to hide.

Whenever she sat down, she'd blouse her shirt, lean forward, or use a pillow across her lap. Whenever they cuddled fully clothed, her forearm would come up like a shield. One evening they were spooning on her couch watching a movie when he said, "Can you move it?"

"Move what?"

He tapped her forearm lightly. "This."

"My arm? Why?"

"Move it and let me show you."

"Show me what?"

"Move it and I'll show you."

She kept her hand flat but lifted her elbow. "What, Zee?"

He slid his hand underneath, rubbed her stomach, closed his eyes, and made a low, satisfied sound.

She sucked in immediately, squirmed, and claimed it tickled far more than it did.

"I'm not trying to tickle you. But if it makes you uncomfortable, I'll stop." He removed his hand and turned back to the movie.

Her stomach stayed clenched. She didn't say anything. But her thoughts went. *Who does that? What in the world? Why does he want to rub my rolls? What is he going to say next, that I should do some crunches?*

A few minutes later, she reached over and put his hand back.

He rubbed and gently massaged her softness, closed his eyes again, and said quietly, "Mmm… I don't know why you try to shield yourself from me like I ain't never seen you. I love every part of you, my baby."

"But I have rolls, and you have abs. Just wait until I get some hard abs, a two-pack, four-pack—"

"My abs don't look the way they used to either. And I love your soft curves."

He exhaled slowly and kept rubbing until his thumb was barely moving, and he drifted off. It was unbelievable to her at first, then awkward. But as she let herself get quiet and sit with what he'd said, she relaxed her stomach, accepted the warmth of it, and fell asleep, too.

CHAPTER 31

Countdown

On Christmas Day, Jenita and Harmony stayed with Tink. Her parents stayed with Pops and Ms. Lorraine. Her sisters and their families filled the Snucks' humongous basement and guesthouse. Her cousin Deuce stayed there, too, and Frank welcomed him and kept him laughing.

Offering him a drink, Frank said, "I had let that vinyl spin on the turntable because you know it ain't Christmas until you hear the Temptations sing "Silent Night". Man, please be patient with me, I'm trying to figure out all this LGBT… alphabet stuff. Which one are you? You play offense, defense, free agent, or special teams?"

Deuce laughed. "What's special teams?"

"Transgender."

"I'm not transgender. I'm the 'B', bisexual. So, by your system, do I play offense or defense?"

"See what I'm saying." Frank raised his glass. "Well, I hope all y'all win the Super Bowl. Cheers."

Deuce clinked his glass, still laughing.

Neat yelled from the other room: "Anybody but Dallas!" More laughter.

As always, everything the Devereaux family did was rooted in downhome hospitality, and their wealth just made it grander. From the decorations to the space to the food and the music. This year, for the first time, the main holiday activities would take place at Louis James Convention Hall, the closest venue to Tink's house, as if she wanted Louis's memory near.

The hall was still dressed from the bank's gala the night before: white Christmas trees and wreaths in every size, blue and silver ornaments in various textures and finishes glistening throughout. It looked like a Macy's window winter wonderland. Renae had sent the five-day itinerary weeks earlier that made Jenita tired just reading it. But Harmony was fully ready. She made sure they both had everything needed for three coordinated outfits for photos, a twenty-dollar white elephant exchange, games, prizes, line dances, dance contest, Christmas sweater contest, karaoke, breakfast buffet, chicken wing contest, bake-off, and a New Year's Eve crab boil and fish fry.

Rena added a schedule for the progressive dinners.

"Y'all know how we do, start one place, eat at another, dessert at somebody else's, and fellowship all the way through… ending up full and laughing." She had left the New Year's Eve finale off the itinerary because it was a surprise, and she hadn't told Frank because Frank could not keep anything from Pops and Zee.

Ms. Lorraine's nieces ordered matching black jeans and either red or white sweaters with festive socks for everyone. The women wore white; the men wore red. They insisted Jenita get into all the Devereaux family shots. She hesitated and then gave in. Zee had quietly been more than ready. Each family took individual photos, then group shots, all the women, all the men, all the children. Her first holiday photo with her own parents. The pets had a group shot. Frank called for everyone with a prosthesis to step together for a photo. He knew he would stand alone and then demanded the solo shot just for himself. They did.

They sang carols. Renae's itinerary ran behind schedule, as it always did, and still went off without a hitch.

On New Year's Eve, everyone bundled up and made their way down the hill, cars, golf carts, the whole family, to Brown Sugar Beach for the annual family ritual and prayer led by Tink. No phones except for Frank, Zee, Joe Lester, Reggie, Mike, and Quincy, who were handling logistics and security. Ramps had been arranged in the sand so the elderly wouldn't have to walk far in the soft sand.

Frank, Quincy, and Mike lit the bonfire. Tink moved through the circle and anointed every head with oil, speaking a unique blessing over each person. When she finished, she asked J.D., who was a deacon, to administer communion and offer a prayer to settle his Baptist soul. He sent up a good one, in Jesus' name. Jenita was proud of her daddy. Tears filled her eyes just watching him, and her mother, and her sisters and their families, all encircled around that fire. She realized it was the first time they had all been together.

Tink prayed prayers of appreciation for the ancestors. Tiff, Renae's daughters, and Harmony gave everyone a biodegradable floating lantern in memory of those they had loved and lost, and their guests were welcomed to memorialize theirs as well. Not a dry eye as Pops lit each one. It was solemn and spiritual and soulful and healing. More than eighty lanterns were released, carried gently out over the water by the wind, their glow catching the tops of the waves.

Renae read a poem she had written about Senegal, the birthplace of their mother and her family, and how it sat directly across the Atlantic from where they stood. Zee followed with a tribute of gratitude that settled over the whole gathering like a warm hand.

As the ceremony wound down, Tink gave a reminder to those who had heard it before and instructions to those who hadn't: small cinnamon-filled pouches, one for each household.

"First thing tomorrow morning, go to your front door. Stand in the doorway facing inside. Pour a little cinnamon into your right hand, speak blessings over it, pray over it and blow it into your home. Not outside your house. Let it sit for twenty-four hours, then sweep it up, add it to hot mop water, and mop every threshold that leads outside. Do it on the first of every month! It'll clean out that stagnant energy and invite prosperity, warmth, wealth, success, and positive energy into your household." She said it like it was not up for discussion.

Mable had been quietly weeping, and suddenly she broke open. Her husband and Rhonda's husband, who was a physician, went to her. Jenita kept asking if she was all right and she nodded yes. When she could speak, she told them: her grandmother and her mother, Katie Mae, had performed the same hoodoo ritual on the first of every month. Already emotional from releasing her lantern, hearing the ritual felt like being visited. They were with her.

Hugs went around the circle among people who now shared a sacred, spiritual, deeply felt bond. Jenita's mother held her the way she hadn't since elementary school. When they finally let go and Jenita turned around, Zee was down on one knee.

She had not known that he'd asked her father for her hand in marriage on Thanksgiving, or that he had told everyone he was going to propose. She wept, both hands over her face.

"Jenita Rochelle Hall, I love you and trust you with everything I am, everything I have, and everything I will ever be. I have never met anyone in my life who sees me spiritually, mentally, emotionally, and physically, the way you do. I cannot live my life happily without you. Will you do me the honor of being my wife? Will you marry me?"

Earlier that day, Jenita had been carrying two things she wasn't sure how to land. First, after all the fuss she had made about not exchanging Christmas gifts, she had gone and got him one anyway. Second, "Whew, Lord." This one might upset the whole family, except Renae, who was in on it. But even Renae was nervous, and Renae was never nervous. She was already talking a mile a minute, and Jenita noticed she had called Frank by his name instead of Snucks. It made him nervous. Frank called Jenita.

"Neat, what have you got going? You've got Snucks all wound up. Whatever that soggy brain meat of yours cooked up, you made it contagious. You got Snucks actin' loopy."

All she had time to say was, "Hush, Squeak."

Before the bonfire, she asked Zee if they could slip away to his house alone for a few minutes. He thought it was odd but didn't hesitate. "Zee, I know we agreed not to exchange gifts. But I—"

"Nah. After all that fuss? I know you did not."

"Well. Technically, "

"Oh, wait. You giving a brother some Christmas cheer? I thought we were taking a break from that for a while, but I'll never say no to you. Yes, Lord! We can go back to the hotel. Presidential suite?"

They had already stolen a sunrise that morning, a long walk followed by lying on the floor of the empty hotel lobby together, just the two of them.

She laughed nervously. "No. It's at your house."

"Nothing's in there."

Mike had placed it earlier while they were out. They pulled up and she directed him to the golf-cart garage. He raised the door and saw a gift wrapped in white fabric with a black and gold brocade bow, resting against the wall.

"Happy birthday, Merry Christmas, and Happy Housewarming, my love."

"Jenita Rochelle, you were not supposed to get me anything."

"It's not only for Christmas. Will you open it, please?"

"Only because it's from you."

When he folded back the wrapping, she took it gently from his hands before he could see the front. "I just want you to know how much I love and adore you, Zee." She turned it around.

He gasped. His eyes pooled, and he was instantly somewhere else, transported back to the day the photograph was taken. She had done most of the painting herself, but her finishing skills fell short of what she wanted to give him. She commissioned Madison to add professional touches to her oil painting of the last photograph Zee had taken with Fatou.

She had first seen it on his desk the day of Mike's wedding, badly creased, and Zee had told her he'd pulled it from Fatou's wallet after the accident. She took a picture of it after he left her to rest, following one of those quiet nudges from God and Nana that she had learned to obey without always knowing why, until later.

One of the many things she loved about Zee was the way he let himself feel everything. He didn't regulate his emotions to impress anyone. His tears, his joy, his fear, his pride, he let it all be real. She found that deeply attractive. Refined masculinity.

He held the frame to his chest. He hadn't seen that image without the creases and the singed edges from the motel fire in decades. She held him, feeling everything he felt about his mother. And after Renae's dream, she knew she needed to put Fatou on canvas with her Ibra.

He thanked her with everything he had and told her this was the sign he needed. A weight she hadn't realized she'd been carrying lifted.

Now two more things. First: the beach ritual. She laughed to herself. Lord, if they bring out a chicken foot… I hope it isn't too much for Mama's Christianity or Daddy's Baptist. Second: the finale.

When Zee got down on one knee, Jenita's thoughts flew. *Marry him.* The thought of everything she felt she'd have to give up. She loved her mature woman life and freedoms, her sanctuary home, her job, the safe little world she had built. Her mortgage was paid off. Harmony was in her sophomore year. Her consulting business was growing. She finally felt free. Zee had encouraged her to stop hiding, and she could feel herself opening up in ways she hadn't allowed in years.

But marriage, so many things rushed in to make her want to run. Giving up her home was not negotiable. It was everything she had to show for her own hard work, proof that she had not been born to struggle. And though Zee had genuinely pared back his work life, there was still a bigness to it that could swallow her freedom if she wasn't careful. She thought about the quality time they spent together, the long talks, the laughter, the music, and the way they showed up for each other professionally. Every time he came to her house, he said how calming it felt, and he'd quietly fix something she'd mentioned in passing without making it a thing.

He and Harmony had a real relationship, something that meant everything to her. He got on well with her sisters. Deuce liked him. Her parents had approved.

But I am used to my privacy. My time. My space. I love Zee. I like Zee. I want and need this man. But when I don't want to cook or get dressed or do my hair, I don't. When I want to paint all day or lie around watching TV, I can. Do I even want to factor in someone else's wants and expectations every single day?

Standing in the three-way mirror at Ms. Lorraine's for her final dress fitting was surreal. The small voices of uncertainty and fear went quiet in the face of the love she had for this selfless man who had loved her with his whole being, openly, without shame, from the very beginning. *Is this a fairytale?* Jenita thought. *Is it real? How can someone love me this way?*

Whatever the questions, there was no question she had ever answered more surely than when she said yes on New Year's Eve on Brown Sugar Beach. The joy drowned every apprehension she had. She had been afraid of things she imagined—things that never happened. She realized her own negative imagination had been the obstacle—not Zee. And through it all, he had remained patient and present.

After she said yes, she found out everyone had known. She was overjoyed, tears flowed freely. They had talked about a future together before, and the one time he had mentioned marriage directly, she'd said, "I need too much freedom. And I'm too old."

Zee had told her what Tink said when he asked her about it. "Marrying late and right is better than marrying early and wrong."

When she said yes, he could not stop smiling. Frank, who had publicly become Zee's most vocal champion throughout the whole courtship, said, "Aw shit, now we all have to get rabies shots. Her mama and daddy, too."

They counted down to 2013 with fireworks and toasted with Frank's contributions of Dom Pérignon and Zee's preferred Monticello sparkling apple cider. Just after one in the morning, they all made their way back up to the convention hall, full of love and warmth in every direction. Jenita still had one thing left to pull off, and if it didn't go well, it could deflate the whole beautiful night.

By one forty-five in the morning, she stood on the stage with the family and friends leaning in. "…And without further ado, give it up for Fatti Lou's Band." She paused to let the name land. Fatou and Louis.

The curtain opened. Mike sat behind a keyboard with a mic. Quincy stood beside him with a mic and a bass guitar. Tiff and two friends from college were on background vocals. Another keyboardist, a lead guitarist, a drummer, a saxophonist, and the AV technician, all friends, all former students. They had been secretly rehearsing and had played a few shows as a cover band since college. They knew how much Pops and Zee and the family disapproved of taking music too seriously as a career, and they had kept it to themselves.

The family's shock lasted about as long as the first notes. When they heard them sing, nobody could pretend otherwise.

By the second song, "Let's Stay Together" by Al Green, Zee was out of his chair. "That's my son! Sing, boy!" He was smiling and fist-pumping like Mike had just hit the game-winning shot in the finals at the NBA playoffs. Frank stood with his arms crossed and wept with pride quietly. Renae had already been to rehearsals, but she danced and high-fived everyone in reach and sang along as if she were hearing it for the first time.

"My babies did that!"

When Pops and Tink closed their teary eyes, they could not tell Mike from Louis. The band played a thirty-minute set, and even the elders clapped and called for an encore.

Mike invited Zee to the stage. He had heard him humming and singing the same song, off and on, since he started seeing Jenita. She had no idea it had been worked into the set.

"Dad, now that you're officially engaged, you want to come up and sing that song you're always singing about Ms. Hall?"

Zee hesitated. He sang privately, therapeutically, and it had been decades since he'd done it in public. But in his signature way and words, not giving a good got-damn what anybody thought, he got a chair, placed it in the middle of the floor in front of the stage, and had Jenita sit in it. He sang "Riding on a Cloud" by Will Downing, warm and velvety and beyond anything she could have imagined. He made it through the bridge, then handed the mic to Mike to carry it home. Zee stepped off the stage and sang the rest directly to his fiancée as they danced. "You're all my heart has been yearning for." Everyone with a partner danced.

Mr. Ibrahima Alexander Devereaux was in a boardroom with his attorneys, financial advisors, and accountants, all of whom were pressing him about a prenuptial agreement. Jenita had wanted to sign one; she didn't want anyone to think she was after his money. She didn't have great abundance, but what she had was enough, with a few extras, and she had built it herself.

The few arguments they had were mostly centered on money. Her refusing to let him buy her things. Insisting on paying for dates or splitting them. It wore on Zee sometimes. Having what he had and nobody to share it with had been its own kind of loneliness for years.

He felt God had given him this wealth for the two of them, for Mike, for Harmony.

Their biggest argument had come when she tried to reimburse him for the drywall anchors he'd bought while hanging heavy artwork at her house.

"Really, Jenita? Now you're insulting me, it wasn't even ten dollars. That actually hurt."

They went back and forth fully. "I didn't mean to hurt you. I just don't know how to receive."

"Don't you understand I'm in your life to help you learn?"

He listened to his legal team and made his decision. He would sign a prenup that protected D.E. When something was serious, he called her by both names. "Jenita Rochelle, I need you to bring an attorney and meet with me, my attorney, my financial advisors, and my CPA."

She called one of her Delta sisters, an A-list attorney, the renowned Andrea Baines, Esquire, Owner and Founder, Baines Wealth Services. LL.M. Taxation, ACTEC Fellow, to accompany her and make sure her home, her future pension, and Harmony's standing as full beneficiary of all her assets and policies remained intact. Her sisters had already told her Zee's net worth through D.E. was approximately nine million dollars. Jenita could not conceive of that amount and wanted no part of being responsible for it. She expected the meeting to move quickly. They had already agreed to sign whatever the other presented.

When everyone was seated at the boardroom table at Andrea's law firm and introductions were made, she handed Zee Jenita's prenup. Without reading a word, he flipped to the last page, signed it, and initialed every page as instructed. The notary signed and notarized. Jenita said she'd sign, but nothing in her was not going to read it. Then Zee's attorney slid a binder to Andrea. She moved her pen slowly above each line, turning pages deliberately while Jenita read alongside, not always certain of the legal language.

Andrea asked if Zee and his team could give them the room. Zee kissed Jenita's forehead and he and his team went to the lobby.

"Jenita. Did you know that Zee owns Alal International Real Estate Brokerage?"

"Yes. Why?"

Andrea's eyes widened as she kept reading. "Did you know it's not part of D.E.?"

"Yes."

"What do you know about it?"

"I know it's international, that it brokers residential and commercial real estate with a focus on people of color, independent agents, high-end and luxury properties, primarily for Black buyers and buyers of color. Why? What's wrong?"

Andrea kept reading and turning pages.

"Andrea. What?"

"Shh."

"Don't shush me."

"Sorry. Hold on."

Jenita got up and started pacing. Is he in debt?

"Jenita, come sit. You need to see this yourself."

"What? Does he owe taxes?"

"No. The nine million dollars associated with D.E. is accurate, and here is the prenup for that portion for your signature. But he finalized the sale of Alal International in November. We would not have had access to that information yet." Andrea set her pen down. "Your Mr. Ibrahima Alexander Devereaux's net worth is two hundred and eighty-seven point eight million dollars, and he does not want a prenuptial agreement. He has signed documentation acknowledging that his legal counsel strongly advised him otherwise. There is nothing else for you to sign today. What's in this binder are notarized printed copies of his portfolio, along with signature forms for joint financial accounts, not to be executed until after you are legally married."

CHAPTER 32

Love from J to Z – 2013

After Renae hosted the Senegalese Henna Time at The Reaux, a festive, culture-filled pre-wedding celebration that Renae had promised would be "way better than any regular bridal shower", Jenita sat in the morning light and turned her hands slowly, admiring the intricate metallic gold henna painted from the night before. She was still smiling about the whole unforgettable evening: the dancing, the singing, the food, all of them dressed beautifully in Senegalese attire. Her soon-to-be sister-in-love, her lifelong sisters, sorority sisters, friends, and close colleagues, all together. What happens during Henna Time stays at Henna Time.

J.D. Hall stood in the bridal dressing room, his posture as erect as a farm-worn back and arthritic knees would allow. "Neat, you look so beautiful." His voice caught. "Seeing you right now makes me know that my greatest battles have always been the ones I've had with myself. I've lost too many to count. But the ones that hurt me the most are the ones I lost taking them out on you."

He wept. "I didn't protect you. I'm sorry. I am so sorry."

"I know, Daddy." She had learned in her sessions with Faith that an unhealed parent becomes their child's first bully. Not an excuse, but an understanding that had helped her heal.

His heart held both pride and remorse, seeing his only child, his baby girl, whom he had verbally berated and rejected most of her life, looking like a Nubian queen.

She wore a traditional all-white silk Senegalese-inspired gown: form-fitted, slightly off the shoulder, with a heart-shaped neckline, floor length, studded with Swarovski crystals, and a twelve-foot custom embroidered tulle train and matching veil. White satin stilettos. Her white Nigerian gele sat beautifully over tasteful makeup that let her natural glow come through unhindered. The gele opened in the back, and her loosely spiraled locs, dusted with tiny iridescent pearls, cascaded down her back. Absolutely astonishing.

She was anxious and certain at the same time. She was marrying the love of her life, the man she had once been too afraid to dream about. She was gaining the family she never thought possible; imperfect and fully hers, already embracing her, Harmony, her sisters, Deuce, and her parents, patiently helping her find her footing in their uncommon world. Her heart fluttered when the wedding planner gave her and J.D. the five-minute notice.

The décor at Louis James Convention Hall had never been so elaborate, yet it never lost its simplicity. Zee had told her the budget was unlimited, that she should hire whoever she wanted and do whatever she felt right. His only requests: clear her schedule for the two-month honeymoon trips he planned, sparing no expense. And the wedding and reception wrapped in time to fly out by four o'clock.

"That's all I want, Neat. You for two, and four o'clock."

She had asked Zee's cousin and Ms. Lorraine's nieces, who were The Reaux's wedding and events coordinators, to guide her, because she had no point of reference for planning at this level. She shared a few of her ideas and, more importantly, the feeling she wanted the day to hold. The wedding was themed "A Journey of Love from J to Z." They had each seen the ceremony and reception spaces separately that morning, and it was beyond anything she had imagined.

The twenty-foot ceilings had been covered and pitched in alternating draped white satin and tulle that cascaded down the walls. All fresh white flowers. Hanging seventy-inch white wisteria garlands, bunched closely together and tied with invisible wire. Padded white leather chairs with metallic gold rims and gold legs for their 150 guests, who had been asked to wear white formal attire, and everyone understood the assignment. Each aisle seat was dressed in white peony blooms. An all-white floral archway overflowing with Sweet Peas, Ranunculus, Stephanotis, and Tuberose. White candelabras with brass accents and a matching white leather kneeling bench with communion elements. Regal. Simple. Elegant.

The March ceremony began at noon as the twenty-five-piece orchestra played right on time. Madison sat off to the side, facing the audience, behind a floral-camouflaged easel with a blank canvas, ready to paint wherever the moment led her. Two Black ballerinas in white leotards and ankle-length white tulle tutus, wearing braided fresh white floral headbands, danced elegantly to the orchestra playing "Overjoyed" by Stevie Wonder, sung by a gifted member of Fatti Lou's Band.

Afterward, Mable, Tink, Pops, Ms. Lorraine, and the honored guests were escorted in, walking the gold mirrored aisle runner. Faith led Zee and Frank out to stand beneath the archway.

Zee wore a traditional Senegalese wedding dashiki and pants in white with thin metallic gold trim at the collar and cuffs. All six-foot-plus groomsmen wore matching white dashikis and pants with gold trim down the center, paired with Gucci Jordaan cotton-white loafers, just like Zee's.

The bridesmaids wore their individual choice of white formal dresses, white heels, and elegant white geles. They carried white calla lily bouquets with olive branch accents wrapped in white silk. Sheila processed in as maid of honor, then Mike and Harmony, then Renae and Quincy, and Reggie escorted Rhonda. Renae's twin grandbabies, Alex and Dria, were the ring bearer and flower girl.

Zee kept dabbing the corners of his eyes with his handkerchief. Frank kept watch beside him, giving the steady "stay cool, bruh" shoulder pat of a consummate best man. The doors closed.

Then, to everyone's surprise except Zee's, Quincy stepped forward. Mike's emotions kept getting the better of him throughout rehearsals. The orchestra began to play, and Quincy sang "Never Felt This Way" by Brian McKnight with skill that silenced the room.

The doors opened and Faith raised her hands. "All rise."

There stood Jenita, glorious and smiling, on her father's arm, holding her full silk-wrapped calla lily bouquet with olive branch details.

Zee could hardly contain himself. He bent forward at the waist, hands on his knees, eyes never leaving his bride. A day he had stopped believing would come. Frank was already wiping tears from behind his sunglasses. When she and her father crossed the threshold, Zee straightened and said it clearly, for everyone to hear: "Jenita Rochelle, you are so beautiful."

He took one step forward. Then, under his breath, singing softly to himself: "You keep me from being lonely… I want to give you my everything…" Another step, down from the platform where only he, Frank, and Faith had been standing, moving toward his bride. Faith glanced at Frank with a look that said plainly: get your man.

Too late. Zee was already on the second step, one hand extended toward her, his voice breaking with tears. "You're going to marry me today, baby?" Tapping his other hand on his chest. "Me?! Oh, I love you so much, Jenita." He stepped down again. Frank moved to hold him back. Mike reached him first, placing a hand on his shoulder.

Covering Mike's hand with his own: "I love her so much, son."

"I know, Dad. I got you."

Quincy sang on masterfully as Zee mouthed the words through his tears. Extended family, colleagues, and friends had never seen this side of the stoic, reserved, business mastermind, Mr. Ibrahima Alexander Devereaux, and it made the moment that much more precious. As she came closer, through her own tears and her smile, she said softly, "Yes, love. I'm going to marry you."

Frank finally made it down, voice unsteady: "Come on, bruh."

Zee whispered, "I love you. You are so beautiful to me," walking backward up the three steps, eyes still on her.

J.D. gave her away. Zee took her hand and escorted her up to stand beneath the archway. Once they faced each other, she wiped his tears with her handkerchief. Faith was wise enough to pause and say, "Whew. Let's all take a deep breath and get our whole selves together." Gentle laughter, and they did.

She asked J.D., Mable, Pops, and Tink to come lay their hands on the couple during the prayer. She made her officiant address, and then they exchanged vows.

"Jenita Rochelle, I have loved you my entire life, before I ever laid eyes on you. When I saw your beautiful face the morning you walked into my life, I knew on day one you were special. I wanted you. Day two, I had to be with you. Day three, I told my whole family I loved you and was going to marry you and take such good care of you. Before I knew you, you were my why and my because, and we have been one long before being publicly pronounced. Your presence soothed places in me I didn't know still needed to be healed by your touch. You give my love a safe place to go. You are my emotional safe place when I need to feel weak, when I need time to regain my strength. Your spiritual essence, generous heart, brilliant mind, wit, and your beautiful soul deserve to be nourished and cherished in the ways I have been craving to give. You made sense of my pain and were not afraid to touch my physical, mental, and emotional scars. I want to wake up to you and take care of you every day. Meet your needs, give you everything you want, and fulfill every dream you've ever had. There is not a man who has ever been born who loves a woman the way I love you, my baby."

"Ibrahima Alexander, my love, I love you with my whole being. You have given and shown me a level of unselfish love, patience, care, and adoration I never knew existed. Your masculine vulnerability, your protection, your generosity and creative eagerness to love and cherish me are humbling. You have never tried to change me, tame me, or shape me into someone others might find more fitting. You support and delight in my creativity and you are always open to one of my spontaneous ideas. You saw me better than I allowed myself to see me. You see my flaws and my weirdness and love them and me anyway. You pay attention to me, every detail. You resurrected my deep, deep capacity to love. You receive all my love, as I am, as if I and my body have always belonged to you and with you. They do. I do. Loving you is easy because you are so beautiful, inside and out. I give myself to you wholly, my love. I love you."

They exchanged rings. Zee placed a two-carat pavé diamond platinum band alongside her one-carat D-IF pear-shaped platinum engagement ring.

"I do."

She placed his two-carat two-row platinum band.

"I do."

After they lit the unity candle, one of her former students sang "I Believe in You and Me" as performed by Whitney Houston and absolutely nailed it. They took communion. Faith made the pronouncement: Mr. and Mrs. Devereaux. "Mr. Devereaux, you may kiss your bride."

Zee smiled. He rubbed his hands together slowly, which drew a ripple of laughter from the room. He took a deep breath, exhaled, and lifted the hem of her veil, carefully raising it over the top of her gele while Sheila helped and took her bouquet. Jenita lowered her head to assist. But when she raised it again, she did what she had rarely done without blushing. She looked directly into his eyes. Her eyes slowly swept his body from his shoes to his face, where she paused to gaze deeply, then slowly back down.

Zee bowed his head. "Lord have mercy."

Frank said loudly, "Pray, bruh. Pray! 'Cause I can't help you with that. You're on your own now."

Laughter broke wide open.

Zee and Jenita laughed with everyone and waited to collect themselves. When she was ready, she looked at him the same way again. She cupped his face in both hands as he placed his hands on her hips and drew her in. He leaned down and they kissed, the kind that made some people cheer, made others blush, and sent a few reaching for their fans. They brought it back to classy. Then they jumped the broom.

The reception hall was drenched in white and exquisitely done. The service buffet offered an abundance of everything, and no one went wanting. Renae's protégées placed multi-tiered, multiflavored wedding cakes at stations throughout the room. Their first dance as husband and wife was a DJ mix of "For You" by Kenny Lattimore into "For You I Will" by Monica, perfect. She danced with J.D., and Zee danced with Tink. Toasts, speeches, and presentations came from parents and everyone in the wedding party.

Renae had people in tears talking about her and Zee's twinship and how blessed she was to have Jenita as the sister she'd always wanted and the friend she'd needed. Rhonda and Sheila spoke about their sisterhood, a bond more than blood, layered in decades. Frank's toast was the funniest of the night. He reenacted and exaggerated the scene when his prosthesis refused to cooperate while he was trying to keep Zee from walking down the aisle during the ceremony. "Man, that foot was spinning in circles."

Fatti Lou's Band showed out covering R&B from the seventies, eighties, and nineties, "Candy" by Cameo, "Kiss" by Prince, and the dance floor was full on every song. Then her DST sorority sisters circled her, had her sit, and sang their traditional "Sweetheart Song," sung a cappella for special occasions.

Before they left, Mike and Harmony asked for a private moment with just the four of them in Zee's office. Just when they thought the tears were done. Mike took her hands. "Ms. Hall, I mean, Mrs. Devereaux, I talked to my dad, Aunt Renae, Aunt Tink, and Harmony. If you'd allow me, may I call you Mom?"

She felt it was the best wedding gift she could have received. "Mom? Son, I would be honored." She wept.

The four of them held each other and it was a beautiful, bonding moment. Zee had known about Mike's question. What he had not known was that Harmony had had the same conversation with Jenita and Mike, and had asked if she could call him Dad.

Zee hugged her and lifted her up. "Yes, baby girl. You've been my daughter since the day I loved your mama. Forever. I love you, Harmony Joy." Tink had told him he'd have a daughter one day.

They danced and laughed and greeted every guest and took exactly one photo-bite of cake each and hugged everyone until they were thoroughly exhausted. But Zee was still determined to leave by four. They did. Reggie drove them to the private hangar where their pilot and in-flight assistants were waiting. The luggage had already been transported and a change of clothes for each of them was already on board.

❦

They had decided together, after they first started being intimate and felt they were moving too fast, to abstain, and they had held to it after he surprised her in November in Washington, D.C. Now, glancing at their rings and then at each other on the plane, the weight of that restraint was right there between them.

"So… all that restraint. All that carefulness."

He smiled, slow and knowing. "Necessary then."

"And now?"

He leaned closer, lowered his voice. "I've got you now, baby. It's on. No guardrails. No explanations, hesitations, or reservations."

She laughed, relieved. "No worrying about being too much?"

"Nah. Nothing for eight years, then we didn't even try to pace ourselves." He blushed. "Waiting four months to make sure you never felt used. Making sure that sex, no, damn good sex, wasn't our foundation."

He looked at her, remembering the first time he looked into her eyes. "I have a beautiful wife. Inside and out. Now I just want you unguarded."

She looked back at him with full intention. "Good. Because I'm done being careful."

He kissed the back of her hand the way he had that very first day, as the plane began to taxi. She felt the same warmth she had felt then.

"Fasten your seatbelt, Mrs. Devereaux, and enjoy the ride."

"Already, sweetie." She smiled and winked.

She interlaced her fingers slowly into his. No nerves. No second-guessing. Just warmth and certainty and the quiet hum of the plane beneath them. He looked at her with pure, unbridled desire. She met it with a smile that said she wasn't holding anything back either. He laid his head back, smiled, closed his eyes, and held a quick fantasy. "I cain't." The pilot's voice crackled overhead. The seatbelt light came on. They leaned in at the same time, foreheads touching, a silent agreement made between them.

CHAPTER 33

This Is Not a Game

Their first flight landed in San Juan, Puerto Rico, where Zee introduced her to their fully furnished five-bedroom, six-bathroom oceanfront home, modern inside and out, with first- and second-floor balconies and an infinity pool. Since neither of them could ever get enough of the ocean, she fell in love immediately. Their adrenaline was running so high that they couldn't sleep on the plane. The entire flight they had talked about the wedding, snacked, and kissed.

As they settled in, they didn't realize how exhausted they were until they woke up on the balcony couch. She came to after three in the morning; he was still asleep. She didn't wake him. She closed her eyes and drifted back off on his shoulder. He rubbed her hand gently until she stirred. By then, it was after four.

"Zee! We didn't make love on our wedding night."

"I know, my baby. We'll make up for it."

On her way to shower, she noticed how thoroughly he had prepared for them. Her favorite scents, toiletries, and hair products were already in her bathroom. Candles they both loved. Their favorite snacks and beverages. And a garment bag with her name on it. Inside was the most exquisite custom-made lingerie she had ever seen: a sheer antique-white floor-length gown with a heart-shaped French Leavers lace bodice, Swarovski crystal spaghetti straps, an open V-back from her shoulders to the small of her back, and tiny lace-covered buttons trailing over her fullness all the way to the floor. The matching sheer robe looked almost too delicate to put on. She could hear "Love's Holiday" by Earth, Wind & Fire drifting through the room. They had been together before, but she was jittery. *He's waiting for me. Am I ready for my husband?*

In the other bathroom, Zee stepped out of the shower and found a garment bag waiting. A tag in her handwriting:

To: My Husband.
Please wear this for me. Only this.
Let me see you, my love.

He unzipped it to find a cream-colored silk robe with matching lounge pants. No tank shirt. She knew he always wore one. This was her way of telling him she didn't want him to. *This is my wife. She sees me. All of me. Why am I trippin'?*

He had thought of everything. Weeks ago, he had arranged with the staff for rose petals and tealight candles to be laid while they were in their showers. The turned-down bed, wine chilled for her, sparkling cider for him, water, chocolates, strawberries and grapes, a professional massage table with warmed oils, and the playlist he had been perfecting since January.

She peeked her head out of the bathroom and saw what looked like hundreds of tealight candles and thousands of rose petals. She closed the door. Took a breath. Exhaled. Opened it.

He heard her. "Is that my wife, Mrs. Devereaux?"

"Yes, Mr. Devereaux. Where are you?"

"Follow my voice, the candles, and the petals."

She tiptoed along the path, watching the train of her robe around the tealights. When she came into his view, he could only shake his head slightly. The candlelight made her look like she was floating toward him, and it gave just enough light to show how beautiful she was.

"My goodness. You look angelic. Mm, mmm, mm. I thought when you walked down that aisle to me yesterday, you couldn't possibly get any more gorgeous. I was wrong. You are absolutely breathtaking, woman."

"And you, Zee, you are so handsome. So fine. So sexy to me."

He walked toward her and held out his hand. "Come here to me, my baby."

"What you gon' do, love?"

He answered in a deep tone, shifting into a Senegalese accent, then into French, words he had spoken and translated for her before, but never like this, romantic, absolutely disarming, and hella sexy. "*Je t'aime. Tu es si belle et si sexy. Je vais prendre mon temps pour te faire l'amour tendrement.*" (I love you. You are so beautiful and so sexy. I am going to enjoy taking my time making sweet love to you.)

"Come here to me, Mrs. Devereaux."

She shook her head because he was not playing fair. Standing there with his robe slightly open against his skin, the loose lounge pants gave away just enough to make her suddenly aware of him in a way that made her pause and appreciate. And he knew how much she loved his voice in every language. She was melting and feeling the warmth and heaviness between her legs already. This was far from their first time, but having waited four months, and being married now, this was a time to cherish.

Sensing her nerves alongside his own: "Let me tell you a bedtime story."

"Okay."

"Once upon a time there was a scrumptiously irresistible woman and this cool dude who was completely crazy about her. He would do anything to please her, and he's going to show her just one of the many ways he can make her and her body feel happily ever after."

She laughed. "The end?"

"No. The beginning."

"Really, Mr. Devereaux?" Still standing back, still admiring her husband.

He extended his hand. "Let me show you."

"Tell me what you're going to do."

"I can show you better than I can tell you." He stepped closer, put his arms around her waist, and slid both hands down to her hips, squeezing her into him. Then he pulled back to admire how desirable she looked, taking her hand, and let his eyes follow his fingertip as he slowly traced each of his wife's fingers, her hands, her arms, her shoulders. Then, he softly kissed her face and her neck. She breathed in his cologne, felt the softness of his full lips, the warmth of his broad slightly hairy chest, and his hardness pressed up against her.

"Is this for me?"

"Yes. Always."

With "Let Me Make Love to You" by the O'Jays playing softly behind them, she clasped her hands at the back of his neck and let her eyes move slowly and deliberately across every part of his face.

"It drives me crazy when you look at me like that."

"Like what?"

"The way your eyes slowly move across my face like you're taking inventory."

"I am. I'm memorizing it. When we kiss, I can't help but close my eyes, and I'll still be able to see exactly how fine you are while I'm basking in how good you make me feel."

"Give me that sweet mouth."

They kissed deeply for a long while, until he kissed her neck and down her shoulder, using his lips and then his teeth to ease her straps down.

"You always smell so delicious."

The straps fell, revealing more of her body. He slipped his robe and pants off. His body alone made her heart rate climb. She rubbed his shoulders, his chest, slid her hands along his arms, his torso, his back, palmed and caressed him, then she let her eyes move over him the same way they moved over his face, and for the same reasons.

"I love your whole body, Zee."

He went down on both knees, reached up, and slid her gown down over her hips, revealing her fully, and kissed her waist, taking deep, slow inhales of her skin. She rubbed his head while watching him enjoy what she equally loved receiving.

While he attended to her with his mouth and hand, his other hand slipped between her legs and drew a moan from her. He kissed and tasted her through the sheer fabric. The warmth, pressure, and anticipation left her warm and glistening with desire. This was an ideal position for him. He slid her panties down, draped her soft, honey-brown thigh over his shoulder, and gave her his full attention. The deeper he went, the weaker her other leg became.

"Let me lay you down, baby."

He lifted her as though she was featherlight, and laid her down, positioning her body at the bottom corner of the mattress, and placed a pillow under her head and another on the floor for his knees. She looked at him, a little uncertain, still entirely seductive.

"It's okay, baby. I've got you right where I want you. I hope you don't mind if I take my time."

That made her tingle from top and throb below more.

Much later, her trembling thighs lost their loose hold around him. She pressed the heels of her hands into the mattress, trying to scoot back, panting. "Sto… sto… stop, love. I can't…"

He looked up at her, tightened his grip, and eased her back toward him by her hips. "I'm not finished yet."

"Stop, baby… I cannot take any more."

He stopped immediately. He loosened his hold and kissed her inner thighs. "I'll let you catch your breath, baby."

He waited until she was calm, then gently cleaned away the evidence of pleasure, unhurried, devotional. He came up to cleanse his face, mouth, and hands, returning to rest his head on her breasts. She wrapped him in her arms as he settled in.

"You taste so damn good to me, Neat. I could stay here all night."

Within a few minutes, she was fast asleep, quietly purring. He smiled, covered her, and fell asleep feeling like the luckiest man alive.

He woke hours later to her kissing his chest, taking him in her hands, sure of what she wanted, as "Say Yes" by Floetry played. He sat up with his back against the headboard as she straddled him and guided him inside her. No condom. She whispered in his ear in time with the music. "Just rest." She let her eyes and her body talk to him in every love language. He felt like her slow winding strokes were drawing his best dreams out of his mind and his body at the same time. He called her name as pleasure overtook him.

"Oh, Jenita…"

She stayed in place until their heartbeats slowed, holding each other. He trusted her with his whole being and seeing her want him, all of him, this way was healing things in him he hadn't known were still waiting to be healed. She was free and unashamed, fully enjoying his sexual healing and her new, uninhibited freedom for the first time in her life. They both knew this was a setup for more.

He leaned her back until she was flat, the tips of her locs hanging just over the edge of the bed. She guided him, welcoming him back where he longed to be.

"I love you so much, Zee."

Taking his sweet time, he looked into her eyes and whispered along with Maxwell's "Til the Cops Come Knockin'" as he moved in a steady rhythm. He loved hearing her say his name with pleasure. He felt both weak and strong, feeling her warm, snugness.

He savored the texture of her breasts and was unraveled by every moan. She rubbed his face and kissed his chest. That lasted for several slow strokes as he absorbed each kiss, now barely able to whisper the lyrics, pleasure taking over completely, and he couldn't do both. The strokes won.

Their quiet duet of sounds became the music and the lyrics. He knew how to pace himself, when to be tender, and when to be more assertive. His strokes deepened and became more vigorous; they both felt their connection intensify, a deep spiritual presence intertwining them as they climaxed, something that was nothing short of ethereal.

This was true love in its highest physical form. Real lovemaking between a husband and his wife. Mental healing, passionate intimacy, and sexual ecstasy on a soulular level.

Their honeymoon took them on an intimate journey of immense physical pleasure and spiritual and emotional love: from Puerto Rico to Bora Bora, French Polynesia, the Maldives, Mauritius, Bali, Santorini, Greece, the Amalfi Coast and Positano, Praslin Island, Venice, and Rome and Florence, each one a honeymooner's dream, three of which were properties Zee had acquired over the years.

He had planned for her house to be the last stop on their honeymoon. It was a relief to be home, and also strange, because he would be sleeping in her bed for the first time. What made it harder was knowing that in a few days, she would be packing to move to Queen's Hill. Choosing what to take was difficult. Actually, packing it was harder. But the uninterrupted time together in her space, making love to her husband in her own bed, that was magnificent. They fed each other's sensual and sexual appetites freely. Whenever she touched his body, something settled in his mind like she had drawn the blueprints.

She was making breakfast. "I had no idea life could be this wonderful."

He came up behind her and held on. "It is. I used to be afraid to take two days off in a row. Now I want all my time with you. How am I supposed to leave you? These thighs? My goodness gracious, Your Thighness." He bowed playfully.

She returned the bow. "Trust me, I understand. I'll have the same challenge leaving you and your royal rod, or is it a staff? Either way, y'all have truly comforted me."

He went weak.

She traced his lips with her tongue, still smiling. "Especially now that sex on the beach is not just a drink. How did you get a beach house with a private beach and a covered cabana?"

"That's what I do, baby." In between kisses: "And… since I don't drink… I had to make it happen… my way."

He held her and turned serious. "I have thoroughly loved being with you, making love to you, and traveling with you. I hadn't experienced those places the way we did. It's been incredible, Mrs. Devereaux."

"Maybe we'll take another week or two. Let ourselves settle a little more. I think it's so thoughtful that you've waited for me and never spent a night in our new home."

"Absolutely." Kissing her neck. "We still have furniture and décor from our honeymoon stops to situate, and a whole house to finish furnishing together."

"I can't wait, sweetie."

"Me either."

He was ready to be with her around the clock, but he knew she needed her own time and space, and he wondered how the parts of the house he'd designed she hadn't seen would sit with her. And after all this time together, how would he adjust when she needed to retreat, or when her upcoming solo trip to Berlin, Germany came?

It was a business trip that had been in the works long before they met. He wanted to go with her but understood she was preparing to travel alone. He didn't want to be clingy. But he also never wanted to sit inside the depth of loneliness he had lived with before, the kind he hadn't fully recognized as dark until he had something to compare it to.

The movers didn't need much time. She moved slowly, as if leaving behind an old friend. But she knew she could come back whenever she wanted; she was not ready to rent it out.

They had picked out bedroom furniture together, but she hadn't seen the layout. He wanted it to be a surprise. This man was gratifying her every desire, and her resistance was fading. As he had done at each honeymoon stop, he had carried her over the threshold. He did the same here, then blindfolded her and led her down the hallway toward the bedroom.

As she reached to remove the blindfold, "Welcome home, Mrs. Devereaux."

Harmony's room and bathroom, and the guest bedroom and bathroom were not far from the dining room. Then there was their wing.

Their bedroom was grand: a tray ceiling, ultra-soft beige wool Saxony carpet, double-sided fireplace, wet bar with mini fridge, wine cooler and upper and lower cabinets, a bay window with cushioned seating, and enormous his-and-hers customized closets with full dressing rooms on opposite sides of the room.

"Zee, these closets are bigger than my whole bedroom."

He had designed a loft getaway just for her, with skylights and every paint and craft supply she loved. "Oh, my goodness, all of this for me?"

"Of course. Come on, Mrs. Devereaux, there's more." He continued the tour: a theater and music room. On the other side of the bedroom were individual water closets and dual sinks with ample counter space and custom storage, each accessible from their respective closets. Shared between them was a sepia porcelain tile wet room, featuring an oversized floating tub for two and a shower with twelve heads. French doors offered direct access to the heated pool.

"Push this button."

She did. The ceiling retracted.

"Zee… all of this?"

"There's more." He led her along a concrete path to a 1,100-square-foot guesthouse with a porch and a swing, decorated in a style that felt unmistakably like her own home.

"Our daughter, our son, and your sisters had a hand in that."

Her tears flowed like tropical rain until she had a slight headache from it. "Thank you, love. You thought of everything."

He held her with full seriousness. "Nah, my baby. I just thought of you."

Two months later, three days into her Germany trip, Jenita was homesick. She had never been that far from Harmony, and the distance from Zee was heavier than she had expected. Marriage had deepened everything, the love, the desire, the longing. He had spoiled her completely and unapologetically: emotionally, intimately, physically, and whenever she allowed it, materially. Being away from him made her realize how thoroughly she had grown into their rhythm.

Harmony, meanwhile, was exactly where she needed to be, spending her first Brown Sugar Beach summer with new cousins and Aunt Renae, sun-kissed and fully at home in a way that made Jenita ache and smile at the same time.

Zee missed her badly and kept asking if she wanted him to fly out. She wanted him to. Badly. But he had just returned to work he loved and excelled at, and she refused to interrupt the steadiness he had worked so hard to rebuild. She would come home.

CHAPTER 34

His and Hers – 2017

Time, as it does, kept moving. Four years passed. A lot changed, though none of it felt abrupt while they were living it.

Enjoying being married to the love of her life, the geographical move gradually reshaped their days. Harmony graduated, spread her wings, traveled abroad, and then surprised them all by getting engaged the year before. Mike and Tiff made them grandparents twice, an unexpected joy that further grounded Jenita. Loss came, too. Her father passed, and they moved her mother to Queen's Hill, close enough to care for her while keeping the farmland. Deuce took over, tending it and growing soybeans, collards, and sweet potatoes, supplying D.E. Enterprises and keeping the land alive, productive, and tethered to new, positive family memories. She also licensed Nana Katie Mae's sweet potato muffins and pecan cookies recipes to Sweets by Renae.

The guesthouse was perfect for Mable, and she and Tink immediately hit it off. Jenita left WSSU, grew her company, and was preparing for another Neat Harmony, LLC business trip. After Zee started a real estate school and a new brokerage focused on affordable housing, she earned her residential and commercial real estate licenses and progressively found her groove as a Devereaux. At her pace. Her way. He taught her to handle a weapon and taught her well.

Looking back, Jenita would later understand that those four years hadn't divided her life into before and after. They had layered it, love upon love, grief and growth alongside gratitude and change.

As she got ready for the monthly birthday dinner, her forty-sixth, with Renae, her sisters, and a few of their close friends, she thought about that mountain of changes. She had woken up to her husband, taken a sunrise stroll with him, played frisbee on the beach, swam in their pool, and showered. Zee's playlist had included "You're My Latest, My Greatest Inspiration" by Teddy Pendergrass and "If This World Were Mine" by Luther Vandross and Cheryl Lynn as they enjoyed another morning of loving, lunch, and a nap. She still couldn't believe how dramatically her life had changed.

She had no idea she could ever love a man the way she loved Zee, and his love for her was completely unbridled. Sometimes she still wondered how her life had blossomed into this. *Who needs to dream when life is this good awake?*

She also grappled with not wanting him to think she was oversexualized. Did he know he had turned her all the way out, up, down, sideways, vertical, horizontal? He did. It was entirely his fault. He had filled her body to the brim with pleasure until she erupted in uncontrollable euphoria every single time. Clitoral orgasms from his mouth, vaginal orgasms when he was inside her, that was just their normal now. She wasn't sure he fully understood how wonderful he made her feel. He did.

He felt the same. Because whenever he kissed or held her or tasted her body or was deep inside her, it felt like paradise. He felt seen, appreciated, loved, and whole. He was all man in her presence and completely satisfied when he pleased her.

I had no idea that healed pain could make the best love.

He never wanted her to feel like he was trying to use her body to make up for years of celibacy or anything else. She didn't. He was overjoyed by how she welcomed him with an open heart, open mind, and open arms.

The love he had for his wife exceeded anything he had ever imagined. He instinctively knew when she needed him to hold her from behind, when to kiss her neck as she rested her head on his chest, when to give her space, when to just listen, and when to show up with exclusive tickets to wherever she wanted to go.

She could feel when to surprise him at work, when to sit on his lap, when to sit together on the pier or on a blanket at the ocean's edge, quietly eating peanut butter and jelly sandwiches and flying kites. When to pray together. When to turn a walk on the beach into a race she knew she'd lose. Or she might be home when he came through the door and, instead of greeting him, launched a spontaneous game of hide and seek.

When he felt he'd been wanting to cuddle too much or she was having a hot flash, he would turn away in bed so she could cool down. The moment she did, she would scoot right back or crawl all over him. He loved it. She knew when to send him a new playlist or sweep him away for an aimless drive or a short flight.

In the middle of a workday, he'd think, *She had me roller skating and skinny dipping on the same night.* He felt young. They used their massage table just to relax each other's bodies sometimes, not always as a prelude to anything, though occasionally it was because the lovemaking that followed felt like it might be their last time on earth. They were still working out the rhythm of his need for non-sexual touch and cuddle time and her need for space and spontaneity. She hadn't realized how much her life had lacked physical warmth. He hadn't realized how much his life had lacked bliss.

He was endlessly patient and taught her everything he knew about finances, real estate and the hospitality industry without ever making her feel small. Using her warmth, she introduced him to the value of balance, how to align fun, his creative gifts, and spontaneity to recover parts of himself that trauma and grief had silenced. Their willingness to learn from and receive each other made their bond not just emotional or physical but intellectual and deeply spiritual.

No matter how much he did to show her how much he loved her, and it was a seller's market in every sense, there was still something in her that would not let go of her house. She didn't have the confirmation she needed. He never seemed bothered by it, even though they both could see she had over-renovated it, as if she were a guilty mother making up to a child she had neglected. But she finally decided to rent it, and that meant cleaning out the odds and ends she'd left behind and collecting a few keepsakes. Begrudgingly, she was making her last trip.

Zee's patience was wearing thin because what was supposed to be a quick pickup had turned into a full day of her combing through every little thing. He passed the time on his phone, checked property management updates, sent a few business emails, and caught up with Frank and Reggie about a ball game.

He walked into the bedroom to move things along. She pouted. "I know it's been forever. I'm done. I'm really going to miss my lil ole house." She turned to tuck an old bracelet back into her small pink wooden jewelry box, the kind that plays music when you open it, with a tiny ballerina on a spring inside. He stepped behind her and rubbed both shoulders, resting his chin against the side of her neck.

"Neat, where did you get that?" He stepped back.

"This is my very first jewelry box. A Christmas gift from Nana. I will never throw it away."

"Not the jewelry box. The bracelet." His eyes widened. She could see concern move across his face. "This?" She held it up. "I've had it since I was a little girl."

"No. Where did you get it? Where exactly did you get that?" He seemed shaken in a way she had never seen.

"Zee, I just told you. I've had it since I was a child. What's wrong?"

He pressed his palm against his forehead and dragged it back to his hairline. Just staring at the broken bracelet in her hand like he'd seen a ghost.

"Where did you get it before you put it in the jewelry box?"

"Oh. I found it on the beach when I was little. I honestly can't remember how old I was."

"Which beach?"

"You know what, Brown Sugar Beach. It was the last time my sweet Nana Katie Mae went with us to the beach. She said it looked expensive, but the gems were so big that it was probably costume jewelry, and the clasp was already broken. I kept it for sentimental reasons. It reminds me of her."

He said very little on the drive home. She thought he was frustrated because she had taken so long. *Did I wear out the last of his patience?* He had never given her the silent treatment. Is this where the story changes? Did he think it came from another man? But Zee ain't never been like that. Was it some kind of PTSD episode? She had never seen anything close to that in him.

All he said was, "I'll tell you when we get home."

They put on "Just Between Us" by Norman Brown and let it ride.

He pulled into their garage. "Don't move. Please do not move." He bolted from the car before she could respond. For the first time ever, he hadn't opened her door. He just ran. She sat in the garage, fearful and confused, not knowing what to make of any of it. He came running back.

"Look."

He opened his hand. In his palm was an identical bracelet, in pristine condition.

She gasped and dug into her bag for the jewelry box. "Where did you get that?"

"It was my mother's. She had two."

They both stood staring at the two bracelets. She swallowed hard. Zee was frozen.

"This has to be an incredible coincidence."

"No. No coincidence. These are my mother's bracelets."

"They must have made more than one, Zee."

"If they did, they got it from a jeweler in Senegal."

Now she was frozen, too.

"My mother had two bracelets her mother passed down to her, made for my great-grandmother, who was royalty. They were two of the very few things she brought from Senegal. She never took them off. She lost one on the beach and everyone helped her look for hours. We never found it. She was devastated. For years afterward she would walk the beach still looking."

They walked into their home in silence. She sat in her oversized lounge chair reminiscing. He sat beside her, still baffled. "Zee, I think I saw your mother when I was a little girl. When I was digging in the sand and making sandcastles, I found the bracelet. Later, when we were eating lunch under the big pavilion, I remember seeing a dark-skinned, shapely woman playing with some children who were too far away for me to see clearly. All I can remember thinking was that I had never seen an older woman seem to have so much pure joy playing with children."

"My God. That was Mama. She played frisbee and red light, green light with us all the time. That was me and Renae and probably Frank."

CHAPTER 35

What Now?

Before her next trip to Germany, she wasn't feeling well but kept it to herself because she didn't want him to worry. She had been tired and getting headaches for a few weeks before she left, not worsening but not improving. Now in Germany, without the comfort of her husband or her home, she told herself she was being a spoiled brat and needed to tough it out. This was Neat Harmony, LLC's most lucrative partnership yet, a subcontract with a continuing education firm, consulting international companies on integrating the arts and art appreciation into traditional workspaces. Zee worked nights when he could, so his schedule aligned with her calls.

Five days in, she saw a doctor in Germany. They attributed it to jet lag or international stress and told her to stay hydrated and keep taking Tylenol. And as they tend to say to every Black woman over forty who carries extra weight: lose some. She and Zee had picked up a few good-loving pounds between them. But she knew better, because she almost never got sick and almost never had headaches.

On day nine, she fulfilled her contract obligations and decided not to stay the remaining four days with the rest of the team. She ran into trouble trying to change the airline ticket the contractor had provided.

Ten minutes after she told Zee she was stuck, he had her first-class one-way ticket booked. She was exhausted and had a mild headache when he picked her up from the airport. They talked about a few real estate deals he'd been working on, and she loved listening to him talk about his work, always tickled by the contrast between the man he was with her and the man those across the negotiation table never suspected to be anyone's teddy bear.

When they got home, he had cooked for them, but she had eaten on the plane. He could see right away that she was running on empty.

"My baby is tired."

"Not too tired to make love to you. I can run us a bubble bath while you put the food away."

"I'll set up the massage table."

They bathed together, played, showered, and then he massaged every part of her body with warm oil. There was never a shortage of affection between them. And when they came together, their intimacy was intense, never casual, intentional and concentrated. He always made it his business to make sure she came first, and, as often as he could, last—because the way she received him, fully and without holding back, was part of what satisfied him, too. She was convinced her headache went away. That night she slept for twelve hours and might have slept longer had he not woken her for lunch.

The headaches came back. She was sleeping ten to twelve hours a day for a week, and they couldn't blame jet lag anymore. Zee begged her to see a doctor. Still holding onto an old pre-marriage habit of handling things herself, she made an appointment with her doctor in Jaxton, who couldn't see her for two weeks.

❧

Renae still couldn't get over it. "I cannot believe my sissy found Mama's bracelet. You were always right here with us, and Mama was with you the whole time! This is a miracle. I'm putting this on Facebook. This story should be on the news." She had wept when they told her, and shortly after had the bracelet repaired and presented it to Renae at a Sunday dinner. "If y'all aren't meant to be together, nobody is."

But this particular Sunday dinner, Renae came running to their car with her arms wide open before they even had the doors open. "We missed y'all something terrible!" Frank came out behind her. "I missed my brother." He hugged Zee, then hugged and kissed Jenita on the cheek. "I'm still mad at Neat for stealing that bracelet from Mama. You got my food?"

"I missed one of y'all. It's right here."

"Ooh wee! Fried liver and onions with gravy and rutabagas. I got the rice in the house. You know I love you, sis." He meant every word. He had told her some time ago that his only memory of his grandma Brinkley was her picking him up once and taking him to her house, where she made exactly that. Jenita made it for him from time to time, and Frank felt extra loved every single time she did.

They had been on their fifth anniversary hiatus and then she'd gone to Germany, so this was their first Sunday dinner in a while. They arrived unusually late and were both yawning. In the living room with about eight of the men, Frank looked at Zee. "Bruh, what is wrong with you? You draggin'."

Zee tipped his chin toward the kitchen doorway, where Jenita was standing.

Pops chuckled. "Don't blame my sweet Neat. It ain't her. You're just mannish and you come by it honestly."

"I am, Pops, but it is Neat. She is lovin' a brother down, and Lord knows I love every minute of it."

Frank turned the TV down. "WD. Come here."

"What, Squeak?"

"First of all, your mama living here now makes her fair game. Right? And "B.", Zee in here lying on you."

Laughing: "One, you better leave my mama alone. And B, my husband wouldn't lie on me."

"He did."

"Okay." She turned to walk away.

"You got her trained, Zee. She doesn't even want to hear what the lie is." The men laughed. "Neat! Come back for a second." Now he had the women's attention too and they followed her back in.

"I asked Zee why he's so tired and he said you're working him out, is that true?"

She raised and lowered her eyebrows once, smiled slowly, and nodded repeatedly. The room erupted.

Zee stood. "See? But let the record show, I count it a blessing. My blessing indeed." He looked her up and down. "Keep up with your rabies shots, bruh. Take her mama with you when you go. She's been twitchin'."

Even Mable laughed.

Frank moved on to something else, and the women drifted back out. Pops leaned toward Zee and said quietly, "I know you, son. What else is on your mind? I can tell."

"I need to find out why my baby keeps getting these headaches. For the past two weeks she's been sleeping ten, eleven, twelve hours a day. She was fine when we were in Dubai, but she's been tired and headachy since right before she went to Germany."

Frank, privately concerned but covering it: "Oh, man, she starting with the headaches? She's probably just finally learning to hold out. I tried to hold out on Snucks but I ain't good at it."

"Headaches, yes. Holding out, not even a little. Plus, after she… I…we…well, Dubai. I will never be the same. Lord have mercy. I am a blessed man."

That night her head hurt again, and Zee said, "I called the doctor here and they can see you tomorrow. I'll leave it up to you to confirm, but I'm begging you, please go. You can still keep your appointment with your Jaxton doctor, too." She agreed. Zee went with her.

The doctor ran a full CBC, urine samples, and an MRI, and told her that if anything flagged, they would be in touch within a few days. She also finally had her medical records transferred. Wednesday, she got a call to come in. They hadn't given results over the phone, and nothing had shown up yet in her electronic health record. She was worried. Zee was, too.

They walked into the doctor's office hand in hand. This was the Devereaux family's Black family physician, and the medical center housed several specialists. They sat in his office waiting. They had prayed. Tink had prayed. They hadn't told anyone else except her mother and Pops.

"Zee. Mrs. Devereaux."

"You can call me Jenita."

"Jenita. It's good to see you again. I remember what an astonishingly gorgeous bride you were, and you haven't changed a bit."

"Thank you."

"Are you trying to hit on my wife, Doc?"

"You know I would if I weren't... well... asexual. So, there's that." He laughed. They laughed. He explained that he had some results back but had consulted a specialist who would be better equipped to walk them through everything, she was running behind due to an emergency surgery. They could wait in his office or come back. They were too uneasy to wait, so they walked outside and got ice cream.

They were quiet and Zee kept pulling her close, assuring her of his love. "No matter what, we're going to be all right, my baby."

She wasn't entirely sure, feeling in her bones that something significant was about to impact her new unbelievable, good life. God and Nana Katie were telling her only to be at peace.

It was the longest forty-five minutes. When they returned, both physicians were sitting in the lobby waiting for them. That made it worse. "Good to see you again, Zee," the specialist said, smiling.

"You, too."

They all walked to the office. Jenita exhaled. "Whatever it is, just tell me now." She sat. Zee stood.

"All right. You're pregnant."

"Pregnant? Me?"

"Yes."

"Pregnant. No. I'm forty-seven years old. I can't, because I can't. Plus, I'm in perimenopause."

"Yes, you can. Because you are. You're also extremely anemic."

"Wait, she's pregnant? That is not possible."

"Not possible!" Jenita echoed.

"Your urine and bloodwork tell us otherwise."

"I can't be pregnant. I cannot get pregnant."

Zee leaned forward. "She can't be pregnant, because I can't get her pregnant! I mean *you* told me I was sterile, what, twelve, thirteen years ago now?"

"Well."

"Well, hell. That is what you said!"

"I'm pregnant? I'm forty-seven."

"Yes, you're about eleven weeks pregnant."

Zee sat down. "How is she pregnant if she can't get pregnant, and how did I get her pregnant and can't get her pregnant, and I'm damn near fifty?"

Both physicians laughed.

"Y'all got jokes. Because you're the only ones laughing. My wife is not laughing. I'm not laughing."

"No jokes, Mr. Devereaux. This is nothing short of a miracle."

Jenita stared at the tile floor. The OB-GYN and fertility specialist walked them through it carefully. Jenita's records confirmed severe damage from the botched procedure after Warren died, which had caused her infertility. Zee's diagnosis: due to his Gulf War exposure to toxic chemicals, he had not only an extremely low sperm count but a ninety-nine percent rate of morphologically malformed sperm, multiple structural defects linked to chemical exposure. Both of them had known their own diagnosis for years. Neither had imagined this.

"Are you telling me I got my wife pregnant?" He got out of his chair. "Neat, we're pregnant!" His worry and confusion and the flash of irritation at them for laughing dissolved completely into pure elation. "We're pregnant!" The ultrasound confirmed it a few minutes later. She lay stunned, scared, and incredibly, fully happy.

Almost four months later, Zee came back to the bedroom after showering. "I'm heading to the meeting with the developers and investors to go over the bids on the fifty-home starter community. I moved it to the hotel to, hopefully, sweeten them up a little."

"Go ahead, love. You don't have to be with me twenty-four seven. We can't live scared."

"I know, baby." He rubbed her belly gently, the way he had rubbed it for years as they fell asleep. She would put his hand there if he didn't. They called it his sleeping pill.

"No wonder it was feeling round. I mean I have rolls, but now this…"

"This is beautiful. Me and my baby made a baby on our fifth anniversary. I know that's when it happened. And I'm glad the infusions and vitamins have you feeling better. But they pissed me off when they asked to swab my cheek for DNA to confirm paternity."

"That's standard in our situation, sweetie. But when they said eleven weeks, I counted back and knew it was Dubai."

"I should've known what was going down when we first got in that room. You pulled me close by my belt loops. Lord have mercy."

"It's your fault for having us in that good baby-making position. Twice. Wait, if you call me 'my baby,' what are you going to call this baby?"

"This is our baby, my baby."

She laughed. "Go ahead to work, sweetie."

"I'll try to be back by one. Rest. Please." He rubbed her belly again. "You hungry?"

"No."

"You've still got to eat. I can make you something before I go."

"I can make you something before you go."

"I'll grab something at the hotel. All I want you to do is take it easy."

"I will. I have a taste for blue crabs."

"That's your and Frank's thing. Want to go to Cooper's? Or I can pick some up. He and Renae have been wanting to come over for a swim anyway, the sun is blaring down too hard on their pool."

"That would be good. I miss our family pool days."

"Please tell me you're not thinking about swimming."

"No. But I can splash Frank from the edge. I thought you were going to barbecue this time."

"I can do both, grill and get crabs for you and Frank." He got dressed in a tailored taupe suit, crisp white shirt, a brown ombre bow tie, and brown Ferragamo loafers.

She got up from the bed. "My man is too fine and smells too good for me not to walk him to the door." She walked him to the garage, and he kissed her deeply, held her, kissed her baby bump, and left. She ate a few saltine crackers and sipped on cold ginger ale because our baby did not approve of real food before noon. She laid her hand on her belly. Hey, our baby. Mommy loves you so much already.

She and Zee had waited three weeks to share the news. From the beginning, the doctors had told them the pregnancy was extremely high risk and to prepare for the possibility of miscarriage, birth defects, or developmental challenges. Though it had caught them completely off guard, they were committed to love their miracle baby God blessed them to make no matter the outcome.

Harmony and Mike cheered and playfully argued over who the baby would look like and who it would be closest to. Pops, Tink, and especially Renae were beside themselves. Frank was already making all kinds of Godfather plans. Her mother, Ms. Lorraine, the entire Devereaux family, her sisters and their families, friends and employees, everyone was over the moon about their miracle.

She stopped traveling and worked from home several days a week, which gave her real time with her mom, Renae, Tink, and Frank. Sheila and Rhonda came to visit the day after she called them. Sheila came in with hugs all around. "Lord knows, if I didn't love my carefree life so much, I'd be jealous. Well, hello there, Sarah! Hey, Abraham, and hats off to whoever raised you to be a husband and not a headache. You must be giving our sister like she deserves. Now, if I ever go senile and want to get married, I need you to find out if one of your Senegalese relatives is available."

Rhonda gave them a tabletop oval plate on a stand: "Happy Spouse, Happy House." "Renae and I have already discussed it; we will both be Godmothers. I love y'all so much. Please don't let Sheila and Frank call this child Baby D. They've already discussed it. And Lynn is a perfect middle name, after me."

After her crackers and ginger ale that morning, she found out Renae had an event at the hotel. But Frank's barbershop was closed on Mondays. He called to check on her, and she told him she had a taste for blue crabs. Zee called later and said he'd be closer to four. She and Frank decided he'd pick her up and they'd go to Cooper's together and eat all the crabs they wanted in peace, without Renae and Zee complaining about the work involved. Blue crabs were the one thing she and Frank ate at exactly the same pace. They'd miss their spouses' deep belly laughs, nearly wheezing, at the joking and bantering between her and Frank, though, the two of them could carry on an entire conversation in Pig Latin whenever Zee and Renae switched to what Frank called "cursive."

After they ate, Frank needed gas. She took the opportunity to get them ice cream. At a stoplight, Jenita said her back hurt badly. She looked down and saw blood. She said it calmly.

"Frank. Take me to the hospital."

"Oh shit, Neat." He leaned on his horn immediately and ran the light.

She was doubled over but not screaming. "It hurts so bad, Frank."

He called Zee. Zee and Renae jumped in his truck, but they were deep in beach traffic. Renae called her doctor.

"Neat… Neat…" He reached back and pulled her shoulder. She was unconscious.

"Neat! Wake up! Wake up, Jenita!" He was driving as fast as he could, blowing the horn, rolling through every intersection. Still at least ten minutes from the hospital. She was bleeding worse.

Frank prayed frantically, "Lord, please don't let nothing happen to my sister or this baby, or I will never forgive myself. I can't let Zee down again. Lord, please!"

"Jenita! Come on, Neat!!"

Zee's voice came through the speaker. "Frank! Why isn't she saying anything?"

"She passed out, man. I'm trying to get her back."

"Drive, man. Drive!"

Zee kept calling her name, talking to her through the phone. She didn't respond.

Frank pulled up to the emergency entrance, jumped out, and hobbled around to her door as fast as he could. He got her out and cradled her against him and carried her inside. Nurses met him with a gurney. He was crying, rubbing from his hairline backward, only then fully feeling how much he loved his sister, and how much she had changed everything.

She was his friend. His joking partner. His spades partner. His bad-singing duo. His crabs partner. His dance partner when Renae and Zee left them in the dust on the floor. And most of all she had made Zee so happy it changed who Zee was. Changed Mike. Changed Renae. Changed his own life. One person had done all of that.

Jenita required emergency surgery. Laylah Marie Devereaux, same middle name as Tink's, was born at two pounds, five ounces. Frank had saved their lives. Had she been home alone that day, they both would have died.

She spent days in the ICU, her body fighting for what her life had become. Little Laylah had Jenita's dimple, Zee's eyes, and Aunt Renae's complexion. "Isn't She Lovely" by Stevie Wonder was the only fitting song in the world. Made from love.

Tink had told Zee he would have a daughter.

She received the best of care and was the absolute sweetest preemie in the NICU for several months before going home to the most loving and affectionate parents, who beamed with joy that did not dim. A whole family and a host of friends with open hearts, open arms, and every intention of pouring love into her.

Frank had Godfather T-shirts made with Laylah's newborn photo on the front and took off work more times than he admitted, always arriving first and holding her longest.

"Let's set the record straight, Snucks and Zee and Neat: she is my Baby D. Mine, dammit. I delivered her. Y'all go get your own. I'm the pappy." They all laughed.

Fatou's influence and Ms. Jackson's influence live on, from the premise of loving and treating people well and always finding a way to help somebody else when you can.

One of the ways Zee and Jenita celebrated their heritage, their love, and their legacy, in gratitude for the miracle and life of little Laylah Marie, was building a nonprofit foundation and free clinic: MiHaLa.

They named the foundation using the first two letters of each of their children's names. The MiHaLa Clinic's mission was to assist middle-class families with mental health support and advocacy, concentrating on music and art therapies, as well as fertility education and financial support for Black families and families of color pursuing fertility treatments, reproductive healthcare, and adoptions.

Using the arts, they funded their efforts by hosting music concerts, plays, art auctions featuring works by collegiate artisans, and dance recitals and competitions at Brown Sugar Beach.

Life has its ups and downs and ways of reminding us: it's not about what you go through. It's about how you get through it. Better together. A village. Community. Because like Nana Katie Mae said, "Just 'cause they call it Brown Sugar Beach don't mean it's sugar or always sweet. Now you know for yourself, don't ya, baby?"

BROWN SUGAR BEACH PLAYLIST

An Invitation to Listen

Music lives in this story.

Every song listed here appears within these pages—woven into moments, memories, and emotion. Together, they carry the rhythm of love, longing, joy, healing, and everything in between.

Listen as you read, revisit them after the last page, or let them meet you wherever you are.

Listen as you read, revisit them after the last page, or let them become part of your own story.

Scan the QR code or visit:

https://www.iamtracymac.com/tracymac-books

A Sensory Soundtrack

1. "God Is Standing By" Walter Hawkins
2. "At Last" by Etta James
3. "Don't Stop 'Til You Get Enough" Michael Jackson
4. "What's Going On" by Marvin Gaye
5. "Choose Ye" by The Winans
6. "I Am Here" by Commissioned
7. "Imagine Me" Kirk Franklin

8. “Better Days Ahead” by Norman Brown
9. “Until Sunrise” by George Duke
10. “Before I Let Go” Maze ft Frankie Beverly
11. “All I Need Is Love” by Tim Bowman
12. “You Are My Lady” by Freddie Jackson
13. “If Only For One Night” by Luther Vandross
14. “Beauty” by Dru Hill
15. “Love Ballad” L.T.D.
16. “Beautiful Surprise” by India Aire
17. “Alright” by Ledisi
18. “Angel” by Anita Baker
19. “I’m Coming Back” Lalah Hathaway & Rachelle Ferrell
20. “Yearning For Your Love” by The Gap Band
21. “Don’t You Know That?” by Luther Vandross
22. “Knocks Me Off My Feet” by Luther Vandross
23. “A Whole New World” by Regina Belle and Peabo Bryson
24. “Darlin’ Darlin’ Baby” by The O’Jays
25. “Forever Mine” by the O’Jays
26. “Silent Night” by The Temptations
27. “Let’s Stay Together” by Al Green
28. “Riding On A Cloud” by Will Downing
29. “Overjoyed” by Stevie Wonder
30. “Never Felt This Way” by Brian McKnight
31. “I Believe In You And Me by Whitney Houston
32. “For You” by Kenny Lattimore
33. “For You I Will” by Monica
34. “Candy” by Cameo
35. “Kiss” by Prince
36. “Love’s Holiday” by Earth, Wind & Fire
37. “Let Me Make Love To You” by the O’Jays
38. “Say Yes” by Floetry
39. “Til The Cops Come Knockin’” by Maxwell

40. "You're My Latest, My Greatest Inspiration" by Teddy Pendergrass
41. "If This World Were Mine" by Luther Vandross and Chery Lynn
42. "Just Between Us" by Norman Brown
43. "Isn't She Lovely" by Stevie Wonder

ACKNOWLEDGMENTS

Writing may be a solitary act, but no book is ever created alone. I am deeply grateful for the many people who supported, encouraged, and inspired me along the way.

To my husband, Owen McNeil—my partner, my safe place, and my quiet strength for more than three decades—thank you for being the one behind the scenes more often than anyone will ever know: my unpaid back office, my graphic designer when deadlines press in, my sounding board when ideas are still forming, and my constant encouragement when the path forward feels uncertain. You have believed in every turn I've taken and every book I have written, sometimes before I believed in it myself.

But beyond all the practical ways you show up for me, you are my best friend.

The love we share is the reason I understand romance the way I do. Because of you, I know the beauty of being desired and cherished in the same breath. I know the tenderness of a love that deepens with time, the quiet intimacy that lives between laughter and long conversations, and the sacred fire that keeps passion alive in a long marriage.

What we have is real.

Our life together—more than three decades of friendship, commitment, patience, joy, and enduring attraction—has shaped the way I write about love. If readers ever feel truth in the romance on these pages, it is because I have lived it with you.

And if I had the chance to do this life all over again, I would still choose you.

To our daughter, Jayda McNeil, MyWarmCake—the perfect blend of both of us and beautifully her own woman—your wisdom, work ethic, and sense of humor are second to none. Watching you grow into who you are now preparing to complete your Doctor of Physical Therapy degree from Winston-Salem State University has been one of the many great joys of my life. My legacy, your future is bright and the healer you are is necessary.

You will always be my baby. I love you forever. I like you for always. May God continue to bless and keep you and may the God in you to continue to rise.

To my parents, Walter E. Jones, Sr., Bishop Emeritus, and Thomasine Rawls Jones, Pastor Emeritus—thank you for loving me in ways that allowed me to grow into my own beliefs. Even as my theological views evolved, you never condemned my questions or my journey. In this season of life, as the tables have turned and I now care for you from a distance, our relationship has deepened into something even more beautiful friendship.

To my family, friends, and friends who have become "framily," and to the readers who supported my previous books and helped them become bestsellers—thank you for trusting my voice. Your encouragement gave me the confidence to continue writing and to explore new creative territory.

I am also grateful to those who have trusted me to serve in leadership roles as a counselor, coach, chaplain, and pastor, and to the many people who simply call me sister and friend. Your presence in my life continues to shape who I am.

A heartfelt thank you to Jessica Tilles of TWA Solutions, who took a chance on me as a new author thirteen years ago. I am grateful to Trice Hickman for making that introduction back then. Jessica has proofread, edited, and typeset every one of my books. With the exception of the graphics for *Brown Sugar Beach* and *Thought Systems*, she has also designed the typography and layout for all my covers.

With more than 26 years in the publishing industry, Jessica brings both expertise and honesty to her work. She does not wear gloves when giving feedback, and that kind of truth is a gift to any writer who wants their work to be better. She has also been generous with her knowledge of the publishing process, helping me grow not only as a writer but as an independent publisher.

In many ways, she helped take the improvisations I carried quietly for years and transposed them into sheet music others can now read.

Somewhere in the midst of all that professionalism is a fun-loving dog mom who manages to make the entire process feel lighter. Thank you for helping bring my books into the world.

My sincere thanks to my beta readers—Karen Woodfolk, Cece Daniel-Williams, and Tomeka Ruffin-Delaney—for reading early versions of this story and offering thoughtful feedback. I am also grateful to the anonymous beta readers who reviewed passages submitted without my name attached. Your honest reactions helped shape this book in meaningful ways.

A special thank you to Trice Hickman, an award-winning, bestselling author I deeply admire and a cherished friend since our days at Havelock High School and as roommates at Winston-Salem State University. Trice has encouraged every book I've written and quite literally held my hand through the process of publishing my first self-published book more than a decade ago. Your belief in my voice has meant more than you know.

To my Senegalese sister-friend Ndicke Seck (Nikki), thank you for welcoming me into your culture since the day we met in Raleigh in 2006. Over the years, you have shared your traditions, foods, language, professionally serviced my locs (Amina), and your beautiful sense of community with me. Your influence helped inspire the Senegalese matriarch in this story, and I'm grateful for your help with the French and Wolof translations included in the book. And yes, Henna Time found its way into these pages because of you.

I would like to express sincere appreciation to Delta Sigma Theta Sorority, Inc., my FavorR.E.D. 30:1 line sisters and my special sisters—

who have become family—and the members of my Knightdale–Wake Forest Alumnae Chapter in the Sensational South Atlantic Region, as we continue onward together in sisterhood, scholarship, service, and social action. Among Delta women, I have always found the encouragement and freedom to love God in Christ Consciousness, be whole, accomplished in purpose, rooted in service, and unafraid of the fullness of our womanhood—individually and collectively, unapologetically.

My gratitude also extends to Peace Place LLC d/b/a TracyMac Publishing, the creative home that allows my stories and voice to reach readers through independent publishing.

Finally, while this is a work of fiction, some of the cultural inspiration in these pages reflects real traditions, observations, and lived experiences over many years. I remain grateful to those who trusted me with pieces of their heritage and stories. Had it not been for my own relationship with God, my spiritual, self-discovery, self-recovery, and professional and therapeutic journeys, this book would not be possible.

I'm grateful.

And I love y'all for real,

TracyMac

About the Author

TracyMac is a three-time bestselling and award-winning author, interfaith leader, spiritual counselor, and certified coach, mental health advocate and mediation professional whose work centers healing, wholeness, and the lived experiences of Black women and communities of color.

Her writing is informed by decades of professional coaching, spiritual counseling, teaching and training, mental health advocacy, and theological study, as well as a deep engagement with the complexities of love, loss, faith, and restoration.

After publishing multiple national bestselling nonfiction works in the areas of purpose, spirituality, and interfaith healing, TracyMac makes her fiction debut with *Brown Sugar Beach*, a soulful love story rooted in memory, emotional maturity, sensuality, and sacred connection.

Her storytelling honors Black love in its fullness—romantic, sexual, spiritual, and whole—without urgency or apology.

TracyMac writes for readers who understand that healing is layered, pleasure is purposeful, and that love can deepen, evolve, and be renewed long after life's challenges reshape us. Born in Portsmouth, Virginia, she now lives in North Carolina with her family.

Other Books by TracyMac

Nonfiction

Available in paperback, eBook, and audiobook

The Book of Purpose: The YOU Testament

Available in paperback and eBook

Relationships: Nothing But the Truth

Thought Systems

Come Sit With Me

If this story stayed with you…
if you saw yourself in these pages,
or felt something shift, soften, or settle within you—stay a little longer.

Brown Sugar Beach is more than a place in this book.
It's a space we carry.
A place for reflection, connection, and truth-telling wrapped in love.

I'd love to hear what this story meant to you.

If you'd like to remain in this space with me:

Share your favorite moment or quote on social media using #BrownSugarBeach
Tell someone who would feel at home in this story
Leave a review—your words help this book find its way to others

And if you'd like to stay connected:
Visit: iamtracymac.com
Instagram: @iamtracymac
Facebook: TracyMac

There's more to come.
And there's always a place for you here.
— TracyMac ❤

FOR BOOK CLUBS & REFLECTION

1. *Brown Sugar Beac*h explores how love shapes us over time. How did the relationships in this story—romantic, familial, and communal—shape the main characters' understanding of love?

2. The timing of connection plays a significant role in this story. How did life experiences prepare the characters for one another?

3. How did generational influences—parents, extended family, and community—impact the characters' choices and emotional lives?

4. Many relationships in the story unfold quietly or off the page. How did these moments contribute to your understanding of the characters' growth?

5. What does "readiness" for love look like in this story? How do the characters' past experiences shape their ability to recognize and receive love when it arrives?

6. The setting of Pine City and Brown Sugar Beach serves as more than a backdrop. How does place shape identity, memory, and connection in the novel?

7. Which moment or relationship resonated with you most—and why?

www.ingramcontent.com/pod-product-compliance
Lightning Source LLC
LaVergne TN
LVHW041106080826
845145LV00007B/1707

* 9 7 8 0 9 8 9 1 0 1 3 6 3 *